THE GREAT FORGETTING

THE GREAT FORGETTING JAMES RENNER

SARAH CRICHTON BOOKS
FARRAR, STRAUS AND GIROUX
NEW YORK

Sarah Crichton Books
Farrar, Straus and Giroux
18 West 18th Street, New York 10011

Library of Congress Cataloging-in-Publication Data
Renner, James, 1978–
    The great forgetting / James Renner. — First edition.
        p.   cm.
    "Sarah Crichton Books."
    ISBN 978-0-374-29879-1 (hardcover) — ISBN 978-0-374-71420-8 (e-book)
    I. Title.

PS3618.E5769 G74 2015
813'.6—dc23

                                                          2015010247

Designed by Abby Kagan

Our books may be purchased in bulk for promotional, educational, or business use.
Please contact your local bookseller or the Macmillan Corporate and Premium
Sales Department at 1-800-221-7945, extension 5442, or by e-mail at
MacmillanSpecialMarkets@macmillan.com.

www.fsgbooks.com
www.twitter.com/fsgbooks • www.facebook.com/fsgbooks

1   3   5   7   9   10   8   6   4   2

FOR JO

THE GREAT FORGETTING

EPILOGUE

The scoutmaster paced back and forth in front of the morgue, a cigarette in one hand and a black plastic garbage bag in the other. He was a tall man in layers of flannel, skin stretched from the sun and hard living. He looked up as the coroner's sedan turned into the gravel lot behind the low brick building, and then flicked what remained of his Pall Mall onto the rocks.

"Christ, Mason, I called you half an hour ago," he said to the potbellied man who pried himself from the car.

"Sorry," muttered the coroner. "Let's go inside, Reggie."

Before 9/11, Earl Mason's gig as coroner of Somerset County, Pennsylvania, had been relatively predictable. Someone died too young, he'd send the body up to Johnston so doctors could cut it open and find out why. The others, he'd pretty up and place inside a casket in his funeral home on North Street, in Shanksville.

And then Flight 93 crashed into the ground out near the old strip mine in Stonycreek, killing forty passengers and four hijackers.

Mason was forced into the spotlight, not the most comfortable place to be for a paunchy man with a slight lisp. He became the face of Somerset County, the person reporters called first. Everyone wanted details about the crash site, details only a coroner could provide. They wanted him to talk about what happens to the human body when it collides with the earth at something close to the speed of sound.

He learned quickly how his words might be spun toward an agenda, a realization that became the seed of countless nightmares. He once told CNN, "There were no human remains for me to identify." What he had meant was that the force of the impact had vaporized the bodies as well as the plane itself. But the conspiracy nuts had latched onto his poor choice of words, used it to support some cockeyed theory that the plane was empty when it crashed. Point of fact: there *were* human remains to identify. Before the sun had set on September 11, 2001—fourteen years in the past, now—Mason himself had found a single Converse shoe near the crater in Stonycreek. Inside the shoe was a severed foot. A hunter named Burgess had discovered a suitcase full of belt buckles four miles from the impact site, undamaged except for a light staining of blood on the destination card.

Mason was the curator of what remained of Flight 93, of the things the passengers left behind. The stress caused him to overeat and he was pushing three hundred pounds. And so when Reggie Porter called to tell him that one of his scouts had found a dismembered arm while picking up litter around the perimeter of the Flight 93 memorial, he was in no real hurry to drive to the office.

Mason and the scoutmaster entered the lobby through a set of automatic doors, then turned left into a room full of stainless steel tables and cabinets. The stench of formaldehyde made Reggie cough into the sleeve of his flannel coat.

"Let's see what we've got," said Mason, taking the trash bag from Reggie and upending it above the exsanguination table. A thick, hairy arm tumbled out. It had been severed above the elbow, its fingers curled in a tight fist.

Reggie grimaced at the remains. "A Tenderfoot found it a few feet into the woods, downhill from the memorial. Stepped in to take a piss. Said it was just laying there."

"It's a joke," said Mason. "He's playing a joke on you."

"I don't think so," said Reggie.

"This couldn't have come from Flight 93. This appendage shows no sign of decomposition. Also, I don't think it's human."

"What?"

"Look here." Mason rolled the arm over with the tip of a pen and pointed. The position of its thumb was lower than it should be. It looked sort of like a primate's hand, like a chimpanzee hand. The skin was wrinkled and worn and padded.

"Where did Bobby Clutter get a monkey's paw?"

"Yes, well, that is the twenty-five-thousand-dollar question." Mason snapped on a pair of latex gloves and pulled back on the index finger, slowly. "Hmm," he said.

"What?"

"There's something in its hand."

The coroner walked to a cabinet and returned with a metal probe, a pair of tweezers, and a scalpel. Mason used the scalpel to cut through its thumb and a black ooze bubbled from the open wound.

"Jesus," said the scoutmaster.

Mason maneuvered the probe under the clenched fingers and reached in with the tweezers. With a tug, he pried loose a man's watch. It was expensive—the timepiece of some upper-management VP.

"There's writing on the back," said Mason. "It's engraved."

"What's it say?"

Mason squinted. "It says, 'RIP, Tony Sanders. 1978 to 2012.'"

"Then you're right, it couldn't possibly be from the crash."

For a moment Mason didn't answer. He was trying very hard not to register the fear and puzzlement that was threatening to squeeze the air from his lungs. "Of course not," he managed to say.

"So where'd it come from?"

Mason shrugged. "Not Flight 93," he said. Then, with effort, he set the watch back on the table and escorted the scoutmaster out of the building. "Thanks for bringing this in, Reggie. Best not to talk about it any more than you already have. I don't need reporters knocking on my door. And there's some logical explanation, I'm sure." His mouth had gone dry and his head was throbbing with the beginning of a migraine.

The coroner thanked the scoutmaster again and waved, once, before turning back inside. Alone, Mason jogged quickly to the examination room.

I'm remembering wrong, he told himself.

But he knew better. He'd had plenty of time to memorize their names. He heard them in his dreams.

He walked briskly to a shelf and pulled out a large black binder. He set it next to the simian hand and flipped it open. It was Flight 93's passenger manifest. His finger swept down the list of names. There. *Tony Sanders.*

He looked over to the watch resting on the table as if he expected it to explode. It didn't. His eyes fell on the half-opened hand.

The monkey's paw, empty now, revealed another secret.

Tattooed into the wrinkled skin of its palm was a bright red swastika.

PART ONE

TIME ENOUGH AT LAST

Any state, any entity, any ideology that fails to recognize the worth, the dignity, the rights of man, that state is obsolete.

—ROD SERLING

STOPOVER IN A QUIET TOWN

1 Later, Jack had time to wonder about how it all began. He understood how it ended. It ended in betrayal, destruction, death. But how did it begin? Could he follow the thread of his story back to a single moment in time where he might have saved everyone and everything? He could. He could. And he was surprised to find that this moment was rather mundane.

The day classes let out for summer, Jack returned to his apartment with a cardboard box of History Channel DVDs and found a blinking red light on his answering machine. His suite was on the sixth floor of a six-story tenement on Lakeshore and the elevator was on the fritz. Again. Out of breath, he set the box on the dining room table, aware, suddenly, of the emptiness here. This was not a home.

There was nothing on the walls. No photographs or paintings. It even smelled empty—that generic foodstuff aroma, ghosts of a thousand Stouffer's frozen dinners. The blinking red light demanded his attention. He pushed the button. It was his sister, Jean.

BEEP. "Jack. The Captain thinks I'm her again. He's back in Vietnam. He's getting closer. Thought you should know." *BEEP.*

Fuck.

"The Captain." That was their father, a retired Continental Airlines pilot. During the war he had flown cargo in and out of South Vietnam and had apparently taken up with a Saigon prostitute named Qi while living there. When he got really bad, the Captain called his daughter "Key," as in "*Qi.*" He would yell at her: "No more Uncle Sams, Qi! Not for you." Once, he had backhanded Jean so hard he'd given her a black eye. Dementia. Alzheimer's maybe.

Jack didn't want to go back to Franklin Mills.

But he did.

Mostly, though, he didn't.

Jean wasn't calling to ask him to come home. She wanted to keep him in the loop was all. The Captain was coming in on final approach and it was likely to get bumpy before the end.

He didn't want to go back. Franklin Mills was full of traps. Jack traps. Because Samantha was there, too. *Sam.* But the only warmth in the entire apartment was a purple loofah a woman named Danielle had left behind three years ago.

Jack tossed some clothes into a bag. Ten minutes later he was in his rusting Saturn, driving south on 77, out of Cleveland, toward a town on the edge of a deep lake, a town with a single traffic light. A town full of secrets.

2 By the time he got there his father was sleeping again. The old man dozed in the hospital bed Jean had set up in the living room, where they used to watch monster movie marathons. Labored breaths ruffled the Captain's bushy white mustache back and forth like dune grass.

"He rearranged the fridge today," Jean whispered. "Said he wanted to help clean. What he did was he condensed all the half-empty jars to make room. He put the jelly in with the pickles and the ketchup in the pepper jar." She laughed quietly. "He's getting worse."

Jack led his sister onto the back porch, stepping lightly through the sliding glass door and quietly closing it behind them. Through the budding boughs of the oaks behind the house they could see the glassy black surface of Claytor Lake, a private swimming hole that had shuttered in 1984. All that remained was a rickety lifeguard stand that would surely tip over in the next summer storm. The breeze had a cool bite, like it was early April instead of the last day of May, but Jack didn't mind.

Jean lit a Winston Light, their mother's brand. She looked a lot like their mother: that straight hair the color of wet sand, those thin eyebrows and little mouth.

Virginia Felter should be here, taking care of the Captain. She had been capable enough, a rawboned lady who drove a bus for John F. Kennedy Consolidated. When she was still alive, Virginia was often found in the bus garage behind the high school smoking Winstons and talking shit with the mechanics. But four years ago, just before the Captain started in with his "transient ischemic attacks," Virginia suffered a massive coronary while hosing bugs out of number 8's grille. Dr. Palmstrum reckoned she was dead before she hit the ground.

And so the Captain was his children's burden. Mostly Jean's. Jack sent money. The Captain's pension helped some. And there was Continental stock. Still, watching over the Captain was a full-time job. Somehow Jean also managed to look after her six-year-old daughter, Paige.

"Mind if I stay on a bit?" he asked. "I could help you with the Captain."

"Of course," said Jean, exhaling ribbons of smoke that twisted over their heads like thin spirits. "Your room's all made up."

"I could watch Paige if you want to get out to a movie or something. You seeing anyone?"

Jean laughed and looked at her brother sideways.

"Hells no," she said. "Not with the Captain the way he is. It's slim pickin's around here. Might like to get together with Anna and catch a movie in Kent." Anna was her sponsor. She flicked the cigarette into the yard. Then she said, "What do you think of Nostalgia?"

Jack's breath caught in his chest. He'd seen the storefront of the new antiques place on his way through town. He smiled meekly and shook his head.

"Sam's there every day," said Jean. Her voice suggested a dare.

"Last thing she said to me was that she never wanted to see me again."

"That was before Tony disappeared," said Jean.

"Well, if she saw me, we'd have to talk about him."

"Get it out and over with."

"Nah," he said. He looked back toward Claytor Lake and shook his head.

"Anyway," said Jean, shrugging her shoulders and shivering a little.

"The Captain," prompted Jack. "If he gets worse, will he get violent?"

"He's on new meds for that."

"If he does, though, we'll have to take him up to St. Mary's."

"Not yet."

"What else do the doctors say?"

"That it ain't Alzheimer's. Something like it, though. They're still calling it dementia. Anything they don't understand is 'dementia.' Got him on antibiotics. He has low-grade pneumonia from aspirating food. We have to mash everything."

"How long?"

"Shit, Jack. A year? Maybe more."

"Make him right or make it quick," he whispered.

"Amen."

"Qi!" The Captain's voice, powerful and demanding, carried through the thick glass of the sliding door. "Qi! Dung noi gi voi nguoi linh do, goddamn it!"

"I don't know what the hell he's saying when he's like this," said Jean. "Why'd he have to go and learn Vietnamese?"

3 The Captain was sitting up, a knitted blanket covering his legs, shouting at them in that clipped Asian mountainspeak. He huffed angrily when he saw Jack. "Who the hell are you?" he asked. "Qi. Who the hell is this? Khong phai vay, Qi! Khong phai vay."

Jean stroked his father's arm. "Shh. Dad?" she tried. "Dad?" But his gaze remained fixed on Jack. "Captain Felter?" He looked up at his daughter. "Captain Felter, this is your son, Jack. You remember Jack."

The Captain squinted. Recognition washed over his face in a visible wave. "Johnny!" he said. "Hey, ya, buddy! Hey! Yeah. How you been?" His voice was dry, like an eight-track that had been played too much.

"Good," he lied. Jean nodded and then set off for the basement to fold clothes and give them a moment. Jack sat in the recliner, a ratty, worn tartan thing, frayed armrest showing the wood beneath. It had been his father's throne during forty-eight-hour turnarounds. It's where the Captain had sat when they played chess.

"Defense, Johnny. Don't worry about getting to my king yet. Anticipate my next move. Try to think what I'm thinking. Play your opponent."

"How are you, Pop?" he asked.

"Right as rain, my man."

"I'm going to stick around a while. Crash in my old room for a bit if you don't mind."

His father nodded, smiled. For a few seconds, the Captain continued to admire his son, but then his eyes began to dart about the room. The bookshelves were full of compendiums of America's wars: picture books of bloody battles, hunting magazines and *National Geographics*. Facing them was a tube TV and converter hooked to a dish. Fox News was on, muted (*Thank God for small favors*, thought Jack). On the wall behind the television were framed photographs: the Captain, his arms around two men in gray fatigues under wet jungle canopy; Jack, age four, high in a fir tree; Jean at twenty-one; Virginia, thinner than Jack had ever seen her, feeding the Captain a piece of cake from her hands inside a VFW hall.

"Isn't it amazing?" the Captain whispered.

"What?"

"It looks just like our old house. How did they find all the same stuff? It all looks the same! Right down to that Winnie-the-Pooh cookie jar your mother bought at Busch Gardens in 1982."

Jack braced himself.

"Where do you think you are, Dad?"

"I don't know, man. But, listen, I walked outside earlier today and this isn't Park Avenue."

The Captain was born on Park Avenue in nearby Rootstown and had lived there until age nine. "You think you live on Park Avenue?" asked Jack.

The Captain laughed. "Well, uh, yes, Johnny, I do. That's where home is. This isn't home. They just want us to think it is." A pause. "Also, there's a woman here looks just like your sister."

"Dad, that *is* Jean."

"No, Jean was here yesterday. That's a different woman."

Jack flinched when he felt a hand on his shoulder. Jean squeezed, gently. "Just go with it," she whispered. "Don't argue. He'll just get confused and stop talking if you do. If he wants to live in the past, let him."

"So why are you home so early?" the Captain asked him. "Don't you have baseball practice? Coach Young is starting you at short-stop Tuesday."

"Canceled."

"Oh, okay." He licked his lips and stared at his daughter, embarrassed that he didn't know the strange woman's name.

"Some ginger ale?" asked Jean.

"Please."

After Jean walked away, he caught Jack's attention and pointed to the cabinet below the nearest bookcase. "Get it out," he demanded.

"I don't know, Pop."

"Don't be such a vagina. Let's play chess."

For the next hour and a half, they did. Jack played four games against his father. By the end, he wasn't holding back. He used conservative openings and strong defenses, but the Captain won every game. Whatever was eating away at his memories, it had not yet consumed the files where he kept chess strategy.

"You still only see *your* pieces," the Captain sighed as he dropped the rooks back in the Parker Brothers box. "Chess is about anticipating your opponent's agenda. You have to play both sides."

4 She wore a furry yellow-and-black costume and shook with excitement, the fat girl with the colorless hair. "*Uzzzzzzzz,*" said Paige, her eyes closed as she conjured her best bumblebee impression. She reminded Jack of that girl from the Blind Melon video.

Paige balanced on a red plastic stool so that Jean could make alterations to her costume—her first-grade class was staging an end-of-school "Backyard Zoo" pageant. Jean bent over, pins sticking out of her mouth as she tried to secure the stinger. "Hold still, sweetie," she kept saying.

"I could sting you, Uncle Jack, but then I'd have to die," Paige said, suddenly serious.

"Why would you die?" he asked.

"See this stinger," she said, wiggling her backside, pulling it out of her mother's hands. "It's full of barbs. If I sting you, it sticks and then rips off my butt and my belly goes spilling out the hole."

"Paige! Jesus," said Jean.

"It's a fact," she said. "Also, I'm a *queen* bee. I'd be a worker bee but they musta fed me royal jelly."

In the dining room Jack was helping the Captain with a bowl of chicken dumpling soup that had passed through the blender. It was a hot mess of meat and dough and broth. The Captain watched a nine-inch portable TV propped up on the table. Above the Fox News scrawl, helicopter footage showed a charred black crater burning silently a mile from downtown Ferguson. A drone strike had killed a dozen domestic terrorists. Free Will Baptists. They'd packed a U-Haul with explosives and were planning on taking down the St. Louis arch.

"I'm glad you're here, Butch," the Captain said, patting Jack's hand. "Glad you're home."

Butch was his father's brother. But Butch had never come home. He had died inside Tan Son Nhut Air Base during the Tet Offensive.

"You're welcome," said Jack.

"*Uzzzzzz*," said Paige. He concentrated on her voice and fed the Captain another spoonful of soup.

5   There was only one bar in Franklin Mills, down by the traffic light at the center of town. The Driftwood was a dimly lit worka-day pub with a paint-chipped juke and one pool table, a ten-minute drive from the house. Along the way Jack scanned the shadowed country roads, drawing down memories like a different sort of draft.

There was the redbrick cheese store where a bully named Chris once lived. One night when they were fourteen, he and Tony rode their Huffy Pro Thunder two-speeds out here at three in the morning and lit a nest of firecrackers under Chris's bedroom window. A large, hairy-chested man in white briefs had come crashing out of the front door, swinging an antique scythe. *I git you motherfuckers!* he screamed.

There was the spot where he'd hit a patch of black ice on his way to pick up Sam one morning, sending his Subaru into a spin that had deposited him in the wrong lane moments behind a semi bound for Youngstown.

And there, slipping out of the darkness: a giant stone church attached to a squat brick building—St. Joe's. Jack went to school there until seventh grade. It was where the local Boy Scout troop met on Tuesday nights. It was where he met Tony.

He fell in love with Tony before he fell in love with Sam. And it happened the same way it did with women: all at once.

In 1992, Troop 558 met inside the pole barn behind the church. It was a den of boys and a museum dedicated to their wayward adventures. On the back wall hung framed photographs of Boy Scouts in khaki uniforms at Camp Manatoc (in the winter) and Camp Algonkin (in the summertime). In the center was a panoramic: a contingent of older scouts grouped on a plateau at Philmont. On another wall hung wooden shingles in tidy rows, arranged by patrol unit. On each shingle was the name of a boy. An American flag was tied to a wobbly pole in the corner by the space heater. Wide shelves displayed awesome relics, like an Indian chief's peacock-feather headdress and a pair of wooden Bigfoot feet that could be tied around your shoes. There was also a stuffed and mounted bird that looked sort of like a dodo, provenance unknown. In winter, the two space heaters made it so hot inside that it felt like you were wrapped in a woolen blanket. It was winter when Jack noticed Tony sitting below the dodo, reading a textbook.

Tony was an eighth-grader at John F. Kennedy public. He was a skinny kid with poky knees and a sharp jawline. He wore wire glasses and his hair was spiky, a strange yellow-orange from cheap spray lightener. Jack unfolded a wooden chair and dragged it over to him.

"Christ," said Jack. "Is that for one of your classes?"

Tony adjusted his specs and bit at a nail. "It's my mom's. She's taking a class at Kent. Nights. It's psychology."

"You wanna be a shrink?"

"No. I'm going to own a bunch of batting cages. Make some real money. I'm going to drive a bimmer. That's a BMW. My first car's going to be a BMW. Bet me."

"I believe you."

Tony looked up then. "I've seen you before. We were at Claytor Lake one summer before it closed. Your mother knows my mother."

"I don't remember."

"Yeah, you were playing with the Rizzi twins on the barrels."

Jack nodded. "So what's in the book?"

Tony closed the text. On the cover was a bright green aspen leaf sectioned into a jigsaw puzzle. "There's some freaky shit in here. Like scary, freaky stuff."

"Like what?"

"Stuff about memory. Like you can't trust anything you remember. For instance, there's this experiment they did with a bunch of college students? On video, they showed this crime take place. Guy steals some stuff out of a woman's bedroom. Then they hand everyone a test, ask questions about the crime. What they remembered. Except the way they worded the questions made them remember it different. One question was, 'How many earrings did the burglar take?' All the students had different answers. But here's the scary part."

"What?"

"The burglar never took any earrings. He took necklaces and panties and stuff. But no earrings. The questions made them remember it different. Even after they showed the students the video again, some of them still believed they had seen the burglar take the earrings. They were convinced the teacher had switched tapes."

"Weird."

"I know. It makes you wonder."

"Wonder what?"

"Well, if anything we remember is real. We. Us. Our parents. Their parents. I mean, if memory can be screwed up just by asking questions a certain way, how can we be sure anything we remember is true?"

"You lost me."

Tony looked off, over Jack's shoulder. "Sometimes I get the feeling none of this is right."

"None of what is right?"

He leaned in closer to Jack and whispered, "Haven't you ever noticed how old Berlin Reservoir seems to be?"

"What?"

"Berlin Reservoir. All those stone walls. It looks ancient. But it was supposedly built in the fifties. Doesn't everything seem so much older than it's supposed to be?"

"I don't know."

Tony shrugged. "It's always creeped me out, that reservoir. Whatever. The thing is, memory is about trust. We have to trust that what we remember is fact. And we have to trust what other people remember for things we never saw. Like when Berlin Reservoir was built. It's creepy when you think about it."

It was creepy when you thought about it, Jack realized. That night he thought about it a lot. It was a disturbing and thrilling realization, that our grasp of the truth is dependent on the honesty of older generations, on the companies who write history books. To Jack, it felt like the first Big Idea, the first adult thought he'd ever had. He felt a gratitude for Tony. For sharing such a grown-up thought and thinking he was worthy of such sharing.

From that night on they spoke of Big Ideas before every scout meeting. They exchanged numbers—back then all of Franklin Mills had the same prefix, so you had to remember only four—and talked about their Big Ideas on the phone. It was a different friendship. This wasn't kid stuff. This wasn't about getting together and playing baseball. This was important. And Tony had found him worthy. And for that, yes, he loved him right away.

6 The juke was playing "Gimme Three Steps" when Jack walked into the Driftwood, Skynyrd thrumming from tinny speakers that made the band sound older than they were. The cagey air smelled of stale popcorn and yeast, the beginnings of a party that promised to go nowhere. At the back, a lanky guy in a frayed Indians cap leaned over the pool table. A younger man stood by him, arm propped on a cue. Next to the bar was a row of lacquered booths nudged out of alignment. A middle-aged couple sat on the same side of a table, nursing bottles of Red Stripe. A gargantuan fellow in bib overalls perched on a stool at the bar, watching a flatscreen. Jack took a seat at the other end and set his wallet on the counter. A young woman slid out of the kitchen and ambled over. She had dark hair pulled back in a tight ponytail. Under her left eye was a wide scar and she did nothing to hide it.

"Hiya," she said.

"Dortmunder?" he asked.

"Tall?"

He nodded and handed her his credit card. He felt a little shiver in his chest, his body anticipating the hoppy beer. It had been a long drought. Hard to drink when you have 180 students to keep tabs on. Had been for him, anyway. Some teachers all they could do was drink to get through a day.

The young woman returned with his beer. Jack sipped it and watched the television across from him, which showed images of the smoking crater outside St. Louis.

"Where the fuck are you, Leroy? I'm at the rookery, numbnuts. I'm not going to fight these whelps alone!"

The loud voice startled Jack. For a second he thought the large man at the bar was speaking to him. But the man was staring at the other TV. It showed a computer-generated hillside and a character in Viking armor waiting outside tall wooden doors set into a mountainside. The man playing the video game looked strikingly similar to his on-screen avatar, down to the curly red beard that reached to his chest. He wore a Bluetooth and held a gray controller in his hand.

When another character (this one a spindly wizard) appeared on-screen, the man sighed with relief. "I see you. I don't care what you had in the microwave. You gotta tell me when you walk away." Suddenly the Viking character rushed inside the cave, where he and Leroy were quickly consumed by a swarm of flying baby dragons. "Fuckers!" the man shouted at the screen. He pulled out his Bluetooth and tossed it onto the bar. "Maiden!" he called. "More mead!"

The lady with the scar returned and poured the man a Miller Lite. "Nils. Don't shout. Okay?"

"Sorry."

"And I'm not your fuckin' maid."

"Maiden."

"Whatever."

Now that he got a good look, Jack recognized this man. *It's Nils like thrills,*" he used to say when they were kids. "Hey, Nils," he said.

The Viking looked over. "Jack Felter! What in the actual fuck?" Nils—full name Nils May—smiled. Nils's old man owned an excavating business that operated out of a tin garage off the highway. Drinking wells, mostly. The large man slid off his seat and skipped down to Jack, wrapping him in a bear hug. He smelled of brisket. "I haven't seen you since the reunion, man! Northfield Park. We bet on some ponies. You got the trifecta, son of a bitch. How the fuck are you?"

"Good," he said, climbing out of the squeeze. "Back for a bit. Helping with my dad."

"I heard. Alzheimer's?"

"Something like that."

"My mother had MS. That's some tough shit, man." Nils sat next to Jack. "I come down here on Wednesday nights to play *Warcraft*. Tell my wife I'm playing poker. She hates, *hates WOW*. Calls it *War*crack. Shelly lets me hook it up here if I order a few drinks. Gotta spend at least ten dollars, though. Yeah. Working down at Georgio's. The pizza place? Delivering. Good money." Nils nodded and sipped his beer, waiting for Jack to say something.

"I always, I don't know why, but I always wanted to open a pizza shop," Jack said. He thought he could get real good at making pizza, make it so each pie came out same as all the others—same sauce, same texture, same meat-to-cheese ratio. No surprises.

"Maybe that's why you're here," said Nils.

Jack laughed. It was the first time he'd smiled since coming home. Nils was a good guy.

"Hey," Nils started, "you heard about Tony Sanders, right?"

And the smile was gone. "Yeah," he said.

"What happened there do you think?"

Jack didn't say anything. He looked to the moose head on the wall between the TVs, antlers dressed in purple Mardi Gras beads. There were no moose around here. Not anymore.

"Just . . ." Nils waved his hands in the air like a magician. "Poof! Ta-da! Gone. Vanished without a trace."

"They were about to arrest him for kiting checks out at that hospital," said Jack. "He didn't want to go to prison. Probably in a cabin in Kentucky somewhere waiting for the end of the world."

"I don't know, man. I heard he had some problems right before it happened. Shelly said he come in here once wearing a helmet made out of a spaghetti colander."

This was new information to Jack, who had followed the story about the missing doctor on the *Akron Beacon Journal*'s website with a detached curiosity. "Hadn't heard that."

"He was acting weird," said Nils.

"I knew him better than just about anybody. He *was* weird. But never suicidal." That was a lie. But Nils didn't need to know otherwise.

They sat in silence, finishing their beers and pretending to watch the news. Then Nils put a dollar under his empty glass, stood, and began to gather his gadgets, which he put in a manpurse slung low over one shoulder.

"Whatever happened, it's shitty. I guess I shouldn't be blabbing about it. It's just so . . . bizarre. I know you two were close back in the day. Used to watch you two pal around at camp. Didn't mean nothing."

"No worries, Nils. Long time ago."

The redheaded giant slapped him on the shoulder a couple of times and then walked away, back to a wife who did not understand his longing for alien worlds.

Jack ordered another tall one and watched the crater burn. A crew of firemen were spraying the edge with jets of water, as if that could solve anything.

"Hello, Jack." A familiar voice, that husky, low rattle he used to love. "A little birdie told me you were back in town."

7   Samantha took the stool Nils had warmed and regarded Jack with a hesitant smile.

Her hair was not quite red and not quite brown. Copper, she called it, though that wasn't quite right. Cinnamon? Rust? It was uniquely Sam, like so many things. It was cut differently. Bangs. And straight. Not layered, like before. It made her look older. Time had marched on in his absence—a rude sonofabitch. He remembered her with chubby childish cheeks that made her eyes small. Those cheeks were gone now, and her eyes were wider. She wore a thin plaid shirt opened to the third houndstooth button, her neck and nose awash in a galaxy of spring freckles. He used to count them as he lay beside her, naked, while she dozed away an afternoon. Once, he had gotten as far as 141.

"You look *old*," she said, that half smile twisting up.

"Yeah," he said, touching the silver hairs at his temples. "It's the kids."

She knew he taught history to high schoolers the same way she knew he was here. "Jean called me."

"I figured."

Shelly marched out to ask if Sam wanted a beer. "No thanks. I just stopped in for a second."

"I don't know what to say," said Jack when they were alone again.

"I know."

"I'm sorry."

"For what?"

"I'm sorry Tony ran away, left you behind to deal with all his shit."

She looked at him closely. "Oh," she said. "You really think he ran away."

"Why . . . what do you think?"

"Tony killed himself, Jack. I watched him go crazy. It was quick. At the beginning of June, he was fine. By the first of July, he was out of his mind. I think he drowned himself in Claytor Lake. Filled his pockets with rocks and walked into the water like Virginia Woolf."

"What?"

"He was fighting depression, maybe schizophrenia. If you really think about it, all the symptoms were there, all the way back to when we were kids. Remember that night out at the lake?"

Jack flinched.

"Of course you do. The day before he disappeared, he went back there. I know he was there because he tracked sand all through the kitchen when he came home."

Jack looked around, but the couple in the booth behind them were oblivious to their conversation. "Didn't you tell anybody?"

"Not then," she said. "Life insurance won't pay out on suicide. I thought if he stayed missing long enough, I could just declare him dead. But then the cops found out about the money he was stealing from the hospital and it looked like he was running. I tried to get a judge to issue a death certificate just last month, but the prosecutor filed a motion to block it, because of their open investigation. It's fucked. I know I sound like a heartless bitch for just caring about the money . . ."

"Sam . . . ," he started.

"But he shut me out completely in the end. It was hell. And, well, fuck him for doing it, you know? Leaving me like that. So selfish." She sighed, shaking her head. "Your visit couldn't have come at a better time, you know?"

"What do you mean?"

"I need some help. Do you feel like helping me, Jack?"

He didn't, actually. But Virginia, for all her faults, had raised him better. "What do you need?"

Sam was instantly relieved. She looked younger again. More like the girl he'd left behind.

"I need you to find Tony's bones and pull them up out of that lake."

8 Someone was tickling his feet.

In the darkness Jack forgot where he was, that he'd come home to Franklin Mills and was sleeping in the bedroom where he'd slept as a child. He was quite startled for a second, sure some pervert burglar was caressing his toes. He shot up against the frame.

Paige jumped and scream-giggled with delight. Her shadow was framed by soft light from the hall. Her hair was done up in pigtails that stood out from her head at ten and two. "Mommy told me to

wake you up, Uncle Jack! Up, up! It's a great day for up!" She
bounded down the hall, and a moment later he heard her galloping
down the stairs.

He remembered, now, leaving a note for Jean to wake him. Sam
had asked Jack to meet her at her shop. He had agreed, though he
told himself he had no real intention of helping her pull the remains
of her dead husband out of Claytor Lake—he didn't even know if
such a thing was possible. It was too deep. Too dangerous. And it
couldn't be drained because the miners had blown a hole into the
aquifer back in '52.

Jack showered and dressed in jeans and a Miami U sweatshirt.
He came down, sat next to his niece at the kitchen table, and devoured a bowl of Honeycombs. The house reeked of high-octane
coffee. Jack hated the smell—it reminded him of Sister Mary Agnus's
dragon breath. But if coffee and cigarettes were what it took to keep
his sister clean, he'd keep his mouth shut. The Captain reclined in his
bed in the living room, watching *Fox & Friends*.

Jack often wondered how two die-hard conservatives had produced such liberal children. His father had never cared for his
chosen profession ("Public schools are how the socialists indoctrinate
the masses"), but the Captain forgot his son was a teacher as soon
as the dementia set in. Jack wondered if there wasn't some subconscious part of his father directing the destruction of his memories,
an algorithm to his forgetting. A happy foreman of the mind. Non-
union, of course.

"The bus!" screamed Paige, jumping up so fast she knocked a bit
of milk out of Jack's bowl. She grabbed her backpack off a hook by
the shoe rack, gave her mother a wave, and was halfway down the
drive before the door settled behind her. Jack watched the yellow
bus come to a stop. It said *John F. Kennedy Local Schools* on the side.
Jean could not afford to send Paige to St. Joe's.

"You better be off," said Jean, looking at him in a curious way he
didn't care for.

"I'm not getting involved," he told her. "I'm just going to hear
what she has to say."

"Who are you?" the Captain asked from the other room.

I hardly know, at present, he thought. "I'm Jack," he said. "I'm your son."

"No, you're not. Jack was here yesterday."

9 He drove the familiar route into town and it felt a little like stepping back through time.

The summer after Jack's sophomore year, Sam moved to Franklin Mills from Warren, a factory town near the Pennsylvania border. One summer afternoon, Jean found her sunning on the shore of Claytor Lake—which was officially closed by then but overrun by neighborhood kids who claimed it as their own private beach from June to September. Sam and Jean were on their way to eighth grade.

Jack didn't think much of her at first.

*For one thing, Sam was too young to be on his radar. He still thought of his sister as a little girl, and, by extension, all her friends must be little girls. For another, Sam was annoying. Around noon, she and Jean would take a break from swimming and walk to the house for lunch. Most days, he was inside with Tony playing Nintendo—*Duck Hunt, Master Blaster—*and the girls would sit on the couch behind them with their sandwiches, enveloped in a cloud of sun and coconut, and Sam would start in on her whispering. Sam was always whispering to his sister. Like she couldn't be bothered to talk in Jack's company. And after the whispers came the giggles. Or worse—the high-pitched screams. She was flat-chested and wore long rock-and-roll T-shirts (*Journey, KISS*) over her bikinis. Also, Jack was in love with Jessica Farley that summer. She was a young woman, a* blonde, *in his own grade. Sure, Jessica had never spoken to him, but he had a plan for when they would see each other again in the fall—he had written a list of conversation starters cut into a square and laminated that he kept in his wallet, at the ready. For many reasons, Jack did not see Sam. Not until the week of the county fair.*

It was mid-August and Franklin Mills was suffocating. It was the kind of heat wave that pushes down the branches of the trees and turns blacktop into a bubbling mess. A stubborn high-pressure system had settled over north-east Ohio like a giant dome. Dick Goddard, the godfather of Cleveland mete-orology, called it a once-in-a-lifetime event. Scientists at NASA's Lewis Research Center said it was like a mini version of the red spot on Jupiter. It was ninety-six degrees in the shade when the Captain returned from Arizona on turnaround and the Felters packed the Suburban for the journey to the county fair—a cooler of soda and beer, sunblock and mosquito repellent, blankets for the ride home. Jack got to bring Tony. Jean brought Sam.

They split up when they arrived at the fairgrounds, a bluegrass field cov-ered with long white tents. Clickety steel rides sparkled aggressively in the hot sun. Virginia had promised to volunteer at the St. Joe's sausage sandwich stand and the Captain wanted a good seat for the demolition derby. The girls set off for the 4-H barn and Jack and Tony headed for the carny games, loaded down with singles the Captain had pulled from a pocket.

"There's tricks to beating some of these games," Tony said, leading the way. Tony always walked with his hands in his pockets, leaning forward like he was fighting the wind. Jack tried to keep up, snaking through the crowd of people in Dale Earnhardt tees and cut-off jean shorts. "There," he said, pointing to a rugged man in a red-and-white-striped top hat standing beside a mechanical scale.

"You can beat guess-your-weight?" asked Jack.

"It's never just guess-your-weight. It's guess-your-age, guess-your-birthday, too."

The carny was talking to a plump young woman with a pretty face. Even Jack could tell she was pushing two hundred. Why she had asked the man to guess her weight instead of her age or birthday would forever remain a mystery.

The carny scribbled something on a piece of paper, handed the slip to the woman with an air of condescension, then leaned back on his display of prizes.

The woman sniffed. "The hell you say," she spat.

The carny shrugged. "Step on the scale," he invited. "Prove me wrong."

For a moment, she considered it. "You have it rigged high."

"The scale is as true as a St. Joe's girl on her wedding day," he said.

"Give me back my money," she demanded.

"All sales are final. Pick age next time. You have a young face."

She opened her mouth to say something, then restrained herself. Her friends patted her on the back and then escorted her toward the funnel cake booth.

"I'll take that bet," said Tony. "And I'll take that when we're done." He pointed to a slingshot tucked in the upper corner of the prize wall. It didn't look street legal.

"That's an upper-level prize," said the carny. "I have to guess wrong on your age, weight, and birthday for an upper-level prize. How about a frosted Foghat mirror?"

Tony pulled out a wad of cash. "I have ten dollars. It's three dollars a guess, right? How about we put the whole ten on just one guess, my birthday, and if I win I get the slingshot?"

The carny looked around. The stream of the crowd continued down the main drag. Nobody was looking their way. The carny pocketed the greenbacks and pulled out his notepad. When he wrote this time his hand was precise with its penmanship.

Jack had a sinking feeling in his stomach. They were dealing with a professional and he had pegged Tony as a mark. And maybe he was. And now he would have to front his friend enough money to make it through the rest of the day. Still, the odds were technically in Tony's favor—the carny had to come within two months of his correct birthday, after all. But there must be some advantage he didn't see. Some secret carny mind-reading hoodoo.

"What's your birthday?"

Tony smiled. "October twenty-seventh."

The carny wadded up the piece of paper and chucked it at them. "You fuckin' cheat," he said.

Jack reached down and grabbed the paper, held it tight.

"The slingshot," said Tony, pointing.

"Take your money back," the carny said, pulling the singles out of his apron pocket.

"No," said Tony. His voice had never sounded so adult. "The slingshot. Or double my money. Unless you want to take it up with the fair chief."

Jack doubted there was such a thing as a "fair chief," but the carny got the drift. He dug back into his apron and came out with twenty dollars. "Here," he said. "Now scram. Get the fuck away from me."

Tony pushed the bills into his jeans and grabbed Jack's arm, "C'mon," he said, pulling them toward the rides. As they walked, Jack opened the crumpled paper. It was hard to read. Just three letters. Jack thought it might be "Jan" for "January."

"He made it hard to read on purpose," Tony explained. "That way, he can say it means January, June, or July. Since he gets a two-month handicap, he'll always win unless your birthday is in October."

"How did you know that?"

"My old man has a book about how to beat carny games," Tony said, nonchalantly. "If you know the tricks you can really clean up when they come to town. My dad used to take me to fairs all over Ohio. We'd come back with a trunkload of merch."

Tony treated Jack to a roll of tickets and they spent the next hour riding not-quite-up-to-code death traps. At the end of the main drag was the Caterpillar.

The Caterpillar was a long train of white pyramidal pods, each enclosed under Plexiglas. The train rolled around a giant loop, carrying its passengers upside down, over and over, before reversing direction and going around the other way. The gimmick was that the pods were arranged in pairs, facing each other, and when the Caterpillar climbed the loop, the car in front of you collided against your own, bringing you to within a few inches of another person's shocked face.

"Ah, man," said Tony, pointing out their windshield at Jean and Sam in the pod across from them. Jean flicked him off. Sam, seated directly across from Jack, whispered something funny in his sister's ear.

The car hitched forward, pulling them up the loop. Jean and Sam's pod was traveling backward. Then the force of gravity brought Sam's car crashing against Jack's. It was a thunderous clap. It was the sound of the pods colliding. It was the sound of Jack's future altering course, the sound of his destiny snapping like an elastic band drawn past its breaking point.

Sam's face was inches away from his own, and for the first time he looked into her eyes. Dark as volcanic rock. They pulled at him like mini black holes. And he saw her: her billion freckles, her copper hair, the gap between her two front teeth, the way her hot-pink T-shirt fell off one shoulder. He noticed a thousand little things in that second of time: the way her hair was *so sun-bleached near her scalp that it was hard to tell where it grew from her forehead; her thin little eyebrows; her cracked lower lip. She stared back at him, daring. He had never looked into a girl's eyes for so long. She smiled and mouthed a single word, "Hi."*

They looked at each other, thin smiles playing at their mouths, until the ride ended. When it was over, Jean pulled Sam toward the 4-H tent. Jack watched Sam go. Some distance away, nearly lost in the mob of people, she turned to find him looking after her.

The back of the Suburban was set up with sleeping bags for their journey home when the fair closed at eleven that night. Before they were on the highway, Jean and Tony had nodded off. Jack's hand found Sam's. She stroked his fingers. He reached over and gently touched her arm. They held each other the whole way back, his face in her long hair that smelled of the sun and the earth and the hot Ohio air.

10   Nostalgia was at the corner of State Route 14 and Tallmadge, across from the Driftwood, an emporium full of repurposed antiques. Sam was a picker before picking was a thing. When they were dating she used to drag Jack all over Ohio searching for dilapidated barns full of treasures in forgotten corners of the state, places with names like Knockemstiff and Mingo Junction. She'd dress in overalls and pull her hair back in a ponytail. She could talk a farmer out of a handwoven Amish rocker for thirty dollars. He'd seen her do it. They never knew what hit them.

In college Sam learned how to refinish her finds and flip them on Craigslist. Enough for beer money. Made a name for herself in Ravenna. After Tony disappeared, she cashed in their savings and bought the corner of the new plaza and placed a sandwich board outside, made herself too busy to think about what was happening.

Jack stepped inside Nostalgia at five to eight, the cowbell above the door clinking softly. The place was a cluttered, cozy mess: half-open drawers full of wood stamps, shelves of Underwood typewriters, cabinets full of jade figurines, a rolltop desk stacked with paperback books, Grossvater beer logos. The air was dusty and smelled of industrial binding glue.

"Back here!" she hollered from another room behind the big-button cash register. He walked through the polka-dot sheet that served as a door. Beyond was her workshop. Sam crouched beside a chifforobe, sanding a stubborn corner. She dropped the scour, wiped her hands on her bibs, then pulled off a pair of plastic safety goggles. "What d'ya think?"

"It's you," he said.

"I meant to say so last night, but I was real sorry to hear about the Captain," said Sam, leaning against the dresser.

"Thanks."

"He did a big favor for me right before he had his first stroke."

Jack felt a hitch in his chest. The thought of his father doing anything for Sam made him feel ugly inside.

"This place is great," he said at last. "Really great. Perfect for you. Is it going well?"

"No," she said. "That's why I need your help. Why we need to find Tony's body."

"I don't understand."

"Most weeks I don't see a dime from Nostalgia. I can barely pay the utilities. There's nothing left over. Tony's life insurance will pay out seven hundred thousand. And that will settle things."

"But you said it was suicide. They wouldn't pay on a suicide, right?"

Sam waved the thought away. "My lawyer says that if we found the body, they'd never be able to determine it was suicide," she said. "Not after all this time. They'd have to call it an accidental drowning."

Jack watched her wipe away the tear that leaked from the corner of her left eye and let her pretend it was dust. There was an emotional center under that steel. He'd seen it once or twice. This was survival mode, her armor against the world, her default state. "So just go to the cops," he said. "Tell them you think he took a swim or something that night. Never came back. They'll be able to search the bottom."

"Uh-uh," she said, shaking her head. "I tried that. This fucking detective tells me they have proof Tony drew money from one of his accounts *after* he disappeared. They're not going to waste their time."

"Well, if they have evidence he's alive . . ."

"It was *me*," said Sam. "I withdrew that money. It was five hundred bucks. I did it every other week until they froze it. Tony told me to. It was for bills. I didn't know it was a business account. How was I supposed to know? All that kiting check stuff? He wasn't kiting checks. I was withdrawing money from the hospital's petty cash. I didn't know that's what I was doing. But ignorance isn't a defense, right? It was me. It was all *me*. I tell the police, and now I'm on the hook for it."

Jack rubbed the bridge of his nose and tried to collect his thoughts. "What set Tony off?" he asked after a moment.

"He was working out at Haven," she said. "Up on Fisher? He got this new patient he was all excited about. Then he got sick real quick. Paranoid. He started boiling water before he would drink it. He said the fluoride in the water was making us crazy. The day he went out to Claytor Lake, Tony told me there were jet planes outside spraying chemicals into the air."

Sam walked to a squat hundred-year-old cherrywood drafting table. She reached into a drawer and withdrew a plastic Target shopping bag stuffed with papers and handed it to Jack.

"This is everything I found in his desk," she said. "It's all crazy talk. Read it. You get a pretty good sense of where his mind was in the end. Maybe he was just sane enough to realize he might hurt me if he got any worse. I think he was worried he might be like his father."

Jack sighed.

"I know you're the last person I should be asking for help," she said. "But I don't have anybody else."

I should have listened to my mother, he almost said. Virginia had warned him that Sam was damaged goods. *A barracuda*, she'd called her, like that Heart song.

Instead, he nodded. "Let me see what I can do," he said. "No promises."

11 Jack returned home just before noon. There was a sick feeling in his stomach, a tug of unease paired with a sense of urgency. What he finally decided was that he felt manipulated, pushed in a direction toward some unseen end. Manipulated by whom? By what? By the unnamed disease that stole his father's memories, corrupting a bond he'd taken for granted? By Sam, who could still pull his strings?

The question was as old as history itself: *Why are these things happening to me?*

At least Jean had always been true. Always with him, honest.

If anyone had reason to complain, it was her. She'd gotten tangled up with a member of Sam's family, too. And had barely survived. She had the Captain to deal with now. And yet she seemed to enjoy the defeating work of keeping their father alive. Jack felt guilty for being so selfish.

"You okay?" asked Jean as he walked to where she waited for him on the porch.

Jack reached out and pulled his sister to him, tightly. "I love you," he said, his energy draining out of his body, from his mouth to her shoulder, in a long, aching sigh. "I don't know how you stay. You're so much stronger than me."

TWO

PERCHANCE TO DREAM

1 The dead man's notes were meticulous. While the Captain listened to Sean Hannity and Jean napped on the sofa, Jack spread the files over the driftwood table in the dining room and read the thin, familiar script of his old friend's hand. The papers held a hint of his cologne, a leathery smell that transferred by touch onto Jack's skin, ghostlike.

Patient is 13 y o. In isolation since being committed 3 wks ago. Exhibits symptoms supportive of diagnosis of paranoid schizophrenia. Believes he is being held at Haven against his will by agents of the government. Refuses medication. Refuses water that is not boiled. Violent tendencies. See attached.

Jack found the report, typed in block letters under Haven letterhead, signed by one Dr. Samir Patel.

Incident Report

June 5, 2012

On intake, I did witness juvenile patient C. attack Jill Greathouse, on-duty nurse. Juvenile boy was admitted by mother at 10 p.m. this evening. C. was in state of dissociative fugue. Could not provide simple answers such as current date. Said it was July 2123. Claimed his father was part of a conspiracy against the American public. Note: C's father died in an automobile accident earlier this year; may have been trigger for patient's break from reality. As Nurse Greathouse called orderlies to sedate the boy, C. did attack her. The incident was severe. Juvenile stabbed at Nurse Greathouse with a pencil. He fell on top of her and pushed the pencil into her ear, causing rupture of her eardrum. All the while, juvenile was shouting: "Can't you hear it? Can't you people hear it?" Juvenile sedated and secured in isolation unit.

Jack formed a mental picture of Tony in a white jacket over a blue shirt and tie, sitting at a desk across from this teenage boy. Jack knew that Tony had always been playacting. He'd figured out the tricks to psychology the same way he'd discovered the tricks behind carny games or, let's be truthful, the tricks to pretending to be a friend: by reading books and practicing in front of a mirror. He had worn the white jacket, Jack was sure of this. He wore it because his patients expected to see their doctor in a white jacket. It was part of the role. As he read on, he recognized the allure this young patient must have held for Tony. There was so much they had in common.

Day 5: Teleconference with Cole's mother. She says Cole's father killed in car accident in Manhattan in 2011. Cole was with him and survived. Signs of schizophrenia surfaced shortly thereafter. Family moved in with relatives in Oberlin to get Cole out of city, provide healing atmosphere.

Later in session Cole posed this question: Where are all the people from the 1920s? Showed me pictures of people packed into

Times Square after the end of World War I. Wants to know where
all those people went. I explained they are old or already dead. I
asked where he thinks the people are. Responds: "They were all
killed." By who? Nazis.

I asked: "Are you afraid of Nazis?" Answer: "No." Asked what
he is afraid of. Cole: "The Hounds of the Catskills." Would not
elaborate. Dogs? Hounds of Baskervilles? Will check.

Cole believes father collected Nazi artifacts for disposal in
NATIONAL PARKS.

Jack stopped. Tony had capitalized "NATIONAL PARKS." It
called back a memory of the day they'd first talked at the Boy Scout
meeting. What had he said about the state park down the road?
Berlin Reservoir. Doesn't it look ancient?
Jack shuddered.

Day 6: Cole refuses to explain his delusions until I also boil my
own water. I cannot feed into his psychosis. To do so would give his
paranoia a stronger hold. We sit in silence for forty-five minutes.

Day 7: Not a word today.

Day 8: No progress.

Day 9: I promise Cole I will boil water. I am bored of the silent
treatment. What did he mean about national parks?

Day 10: Begin session, Cole says I am lying about boiling water.
Refuses to talk. How did he know?

Day 11: I have begun boiling water in an attempt to move this
therapy along. Maybe I can meet him halfway. No further progress
today.

Day 12: Cole says I have begun to remember. Can see it in my
face. Says watch out for the hounds. What hounds?

Day 13: Cole wants to play a game. It's called the "7 Impossibilities." There are 7 strange truths he wants me to accept. 1st: I must
believe that Cole has a photographic memory. He claims he can no
longer forget anything.

Day 14: I show Cole a series of numbers. Pi. He recites pi to

250 characters. Mother made no mention of photographic memory on intake. Is this a symptom?

Day 15: Impossibility 2: Water is contaminated by government with brainwashing chemicals. Will research.

Jack looked across the table at the remaining folders. Each was labeled with an orange tab. "1: Photographic Memory" contained a photocopy of the pi sequence along with articles on photographic memory and links to autism. What Jack found inside "2: Fluoride" was unsettling.

These reports were not clipped articles from peer-reviewed magazines, no *Psychology Today* or *Gestalt Critique*. These were posts from a fringe website forum printed on a home computer. One was titled "Don't Drink the Kool-Aid: How the Government Keeps the Peace by Brainwashing Americans." It was full of grammatical errors. Tony had corrected the text in red pen and written excited notes in the margins. Things like: *Of course!* and *Motherfucker* and *Boil Sam's water*.

By day 21, Tony's handwriting was stretched and messy, his grammar and spelling muddled and erratic.

Emergency broadcast test on radio today. It came on in the car, on my way to werk. I can hear them in my brain, taking out mine memories. Cole says he can help and I do rememember better now. But we forgot an entire day this time. Cole says entrance is in state parks. Will begim looking.

Then, one final entry: *Day 26: Claytor Lake. I will leave Sam behind. Safer that way. I dont want to hear the voices anymore.*

Cole had brought back the very worst of Tony. Their madness was recursive. How terrible that must have been for Tony, feeling his mental defenses crumble, feeling his mind come undone, a building energy, an amp pointed at a microphone, primed to explode.

Escaping into the cool waters of Claytor Lake must have been a kind embrace. Jack felt sorry for his old friend. Even though, on some level, he still hated him and always would.

2   "Hey, Johnny?" The Captain stared at his son curiously from the hospital bed in the living room.

"What's up, Pop? Need something to drink?"

The Captain shook his head and motioned for him to come. Jack walked over and took a seat next to his sister, who was napping on the sofa. She stirred lightly.

"What are you doing here, Johnny?" his father whispered. His eyes were fixed on Jack, focused. His father's eyes had become grayish lately. But they shone now with such a brilliant golden hue.

"I'm helping Jean with some things," said Jack.

"Don't you have classes?"

"School year's over."

"Okay. That's thing one. Now about thing two: How long have I been in this bed?"

Jean sat up and put a hand on Jack's shoulder. "Dad? You feeling all right?" she asked groggily.

"I feel great," he said.

Jean sighed. She stood, walked to her father. She pushed his white bangs from his eyes and rubbed his neck. "You're having a good day, apparently. The first in a very long while."

"Well," he sighed. "It's good to be back, if only for a bit."

"Can I get you anything?" asked Jean.

After a moment, the Captain held up two fingers. "The good stuff above the fridge."

"Daddy! You can't drink on your meds."

"Jean, the last thing I remember, it was fall 2014. The look of those trees outside makes me think it's, what? April?"

"It's June first, Dad," said Jack.

"Christ. Make it a double. I think we're past worrying about my liver."

Jean kissed him on the cheek and then went to the kitchen and poured him a tumbler of Red Label.

As soon as she was out of earshot, the Captain turned back to his son. "Why am I still in this house?" he said. "Why didn't you guys put me in St. Mary's? I don't want your sister changing my diapers."

"She wants you here," he said.

"Talk her out of it," he said flatly. He grabbed Jack's wrist and tugged him closer. "Mark," he said. "What happened to Mark?"

Jack's mind flashed to that day in the Walmart parking lot, three years ago, the day the Captain had called him down from Lakewood for Jean's intervention. He'd done his very best to forget Mark Brooks and what he'd done. But, remembering it now, Jack couldn't help but smile. It had felt so good to punch him in the face.

"Mark moved back to Warren," said Jack. "Don't worry. Jean's fine. Still sober. And Mark's never even been back to see Paige. He doesn't even call."

For a second, the Captain looked at Jack as if he was pulling his leg. Then he laughed lightly. "Good," he said. "Good."

Jean returned with the Scotch. The Captain gripped it tight. He closed his eyes and sniffed at the brim of the glass. "To the past," he said. "Let us forget the bad parts first." He tipped it to his lips and drank it like water. Then he winked at Jean and handed her the empty. "Thanks, kiddo," he said. "You good?"

"I'm good, Daddy."

"Paige good?"

"She's great."

"Good." He closed his eyes for a few seconds. When he opened them again, they were already a little more gray. "I think I'll have a hot bath," he said. "And when I'm done, let's get Chinese. And some pizza."

3 While the Captain soaked, a dry Montecristo smoldering in a chipped ashtray the color of an avocado beside the tub, Jack went outside and walked the narrow path through the trees behind the house. The nippy wind held an incongruous coolness for early June.

His little feet had worn down this path. And Jean's. Their friends. A thousand trips to the lake and back, towels slung over shoulders. It had been years since he'd walked it, and still here it was, holding

back the heather and ferns, the blackberry bushes. The last time he'd
been to the lake was the night Tony's father was arrested.

Much of the trucked-in sand beach had eroded away. The northern edge was hard clay peppered with mulberry pods that crunched
delightfully underfoot. Jack sat at the lip of the lake and thought
about the problem at hand.

He was inclined to help Sam figure out a way to pull up Tony's
body. This wasn't because he felt he owed it to his old friend, but he
knew Sam well enough to know that if he couldn't help her, she would
ask Jean. And Jean would find a way to do it, because Jean was a
sucker for people in need. And if Jean couldn't find an easy solution,
she would throw money at it. Money she didn't have.

How deep was the bottom? Nobody knew. You couldn't hold
your breath and dive down to find it. He'd tried. They all had.

Shadows cast by tall oaks danced on the lake's surface like some
shifting Rorschach test.

*"So all they can see are the shadows, right?" Tony said as they hiked along
the deer trail that led around Minnehaha Falls, frozen now because it was
winter at Camp Manatoc. "They're prisoners or something. Somebody tied
them to chairs so they can't move. So they can only look forward at this cave
wall. And then someone turns on a light behind them and so all they see, all
their life, is shadows on the wall of the cave."*

*"Okay," said Jack, trying to keep up. The trail was steep and the footing
precarious, the path slick with fallen leaves.*

*"The question is, do you save these people if you have the chance?" asked
Tony. "I mean, think about it. These people think reality is just these shadows on the wall. If you could set them free, their minds would have no concept
of our three-dimensional world. You show them a flower, they wouldn't know
what the hell it is. You'd have to show them the shadow of a flower for it to
have any meaning. If you showed them the trees and the sky, they'd freak the
shit out. They'd be terrified. Isn't it better to just keep them chained up?"*

*Jack thought it over. It was another one of Tony's nightmarish Twilight
Zoney brain-stumpers. "I'd still rescue them, set them free," he said, finally,
sniffing away the cold.*

"Why?"

"I think because I couldn't live with myself if I didn't try to help them."

"Yeah. I guess. Me, too."

"It's creepy, though."

"Guy named Plato came up with that crap like three thousand years ago or something."

"Cool."

Somewhere nearby, a crispy twig cracked loudly.

"Who's there?" called Tony.

A fat head poked out from behind a white pine. The boy had a mess of tangly red hair. "Hey, guys," said Nils.

"Were you following us?" asked Tony.

The fat ginger trundled out from his hiding place and joined them on the path. He was huffing from the exercise. But he was smiling. A big, wonderful kid smile. "You're going out to the Indian mounds on the edge of camp, right? Can I come?"

Tony looked to Jack, who shrugged.

"Okay, but you have to carry our canteens," said Tony. He handed a metal army-surplus canteen to Nils, who slung it around his shoulder dutifully. A trio now, they walked together through the empty forest and spoke of scary things.

That night Jack pulled his sleeping bag close to Tony's on the floor of Concord Lodge. Close enough so that he could feel his friend's breath on his face, and like that he drifted off to sleep.

Jack's breath caught in his throat. He was surprised to find he missed his friend.

He picked himself up off the hard clay and dusted off his jeans.

He couldn't get Tony's bones out of the lake.

But he knew who could.

4 Sam was there when Jack got back. She was in the kitchen, talking to his sister, a glass of red wine in her hand. She still wore her work bibs, splattered with white paint.

"I heard the Captain's back," Sam said to Jack as he walked through the door. "I had to come over and say hi."

He nodded and looked to Jean. "What did Dr. Palmstrum say?" Palmstrum had been their family doctor for a quarter of a century, a wizard of a man who worked out of a ranch home in Ravenna.

"Says it's probably not good. He's seen this happen before and it's always near the end. Like the mind's last rally. It could be a sign of another stroke, actually."

"Great," Jack mumbled. "Where's he at?"

"Getting dressed," said Jean.

He nodded and then helped himself to a bottle of Yuengling from the fridge. He shot a hot glare at his sister that Sam couldn't see. She rolled her eyes at him.

"What were you doing out at the lake?" asked Sam.

"I have an idea. Want to see if it pans out before I talk about it."

"I knew you'd figure something out."

"Might not pan out."

"Oh, holy hell!" shouted the Captain, ambling down the stairs, eyes on the woman with the copper hair. His face was one big, wrinkly smile. "Sam Sanders. Get your little ass over here and give us a hug."

She moved to his side and gave him a soft squeeze. "It's back to Sam Brooks," she said.

"What the fuck did Tony do? I go away a while and everyone thinks they have a free pass to be assholes?"

"Daddy, Tony's been gone three years now," said Jean.

The Captain's face drained of color. He looked at Sam for confirmation.

"He walked into the lake," said Sam. "He committed suicide, Walter." *Walter.* Sam was the only one who'd ever been allowed to call the Captain by his given name.

The Captain pulled Sam close again and kissed the top of her head. "What a pisser. What a fucking pisser. That's just . . . terrible, Sammy. I'm so sorry. And my stupid mind is all muddy and you've probably told me all this before."

"It's been long enough that I don't think about it all the time," Sam offered.

"I should pay my respects before the lights go dim again. He up in St. Joe's?"

"No plot, Dad," said Jack. "His body's still at the bottom of the lake."

"Jack has an idea, though," said Sam.

The Captain looked over to his son, alarmed. "No, buddy. No. I don't want you going down there."

"I'm not," he said. "Don't worry about it. Can we just fucking please talk about something else? It's so goddamn depressing."

"Let's order food," said Jean.

"Now you're talking," the Captain said. Only Jack saw his face as everyone else turned toward the dining room. And so only Jack saw the look of fear in the old man's eyes. Stark, overwhelming fear. And then it was gone.

5 The closest Chinese restaurant was Chen's Green Dragon in Kent, a forty-minute round trip. The Captain wanted something called yum cha. "Just ask for dim sum, dummy," he barked. Paige, who had just been deposited by the school bus, requested "those crab cheesy hot pockets," and Sam was in for an order of chicken and snow peas.

"I'll pick it up," said Jack, grabbing his wallet.

"I'll go with you," said Sam.

Before he could protest she flitted out the door. He looked up at Jean.

"Life's short," she said.

He nodded, but it wasn't true. Life is long. Longer than we allow ourselves to remember. "Is he going to be all right until we get back?"

"You mean, am I gonna go bug-eyed again while you're gone?" said the Captain. "I feel fine. Don't be such a wet towel. So sensitive. You know, you used to cry during *Scooby-Doo* sometimes?

I mean, who cries at *Scooby-Doo?* Jee-zuss. I thought you'd turn out gay. I really did. I'm not going to die while you're out getting Chinese. I refuse to, because the thought of you crying at my funeral makes me generally too embarrassed for you to allow my body to shut down."

"Okay then."

"I feel better than I have in months. Maybe I'm coming out of this thing."

Jack crossed over to where the Captain sat in front of the TV. He kissed his father on the cheek.

"Fuckin' fairy," the Captain whispered, but he smiled.

"Nice to have you back, Pop."

Sam was sitting in his Saturn looking at her teeth in the mirror when he climbed behind the wheel. He turned on the radio and 98.5 was halfway through "Crazy on You."

"Oh, yes," said Sam.

They listened to classic rock for some time without speaking. It was just warm enough that they could crack their windows a bit to let in the air. The aroma of cut grass quickly filled the car. They looked back at houses where friends once lived, fallen into disrepair, draped with ivy. He felt himself blush as they passed the oil well drive where she'd given him his first blow job.

"Do you remember how hot it was that summer?" she asked. "Do you think it'll ever be that hot again?"

"I don't remember," he said.

"Yes, you do."

He smiled.

"You got a girl back in Lakewood?"

He looked at her sideways and then turned off SR 14.

"Just making conversation, Jack."

"You're never just making conversation, Sam." He sighed. "No, I don't have a girlfriend."

"Ever?"

"No, not . . . what do you think? Not, not ever. A couple. One was pretty serious."

"What happened?"

"She moved away."

"And you stayed?"

"That's right."

"If you don't want to talk, we won't talk."

"You always have a motive."

"I'm not that person anymore. I grew up."

"So you keep telling me."

6 Later they sat at the dining room table gorging themselves on cheap Chinese, waiting for the pizza to arrive.

"This is not yum cha," the Captain said, mushing a greasy dumpling around his mouth. "But it's fuckin' good."

"Daddy," scolded Jean, canting her head toward Paige, who rocked in a chair as she picked apart a crab rangoon. She had changed into her nightclothes: pastel-green footie pajamas.

"Does this feel like a blip, or something more?" Jack asked his father. "Does it feel like you're getting better?"

The Captain thought about it while he chewed his food. "I don't know. You know what it feels like? It feels like hash. Like the hashish I smoked in Saigon." He caught his daughter's disapproving eye and waved it off. "Back then the hash wasn't mixed with anything except more hash. No angel dust, heroin, meth, none of that shit."

"Dad!"

"Sorry. Anyway, I had this beautiful kiseru, this long mother-truckin' pipe, right? A work of art. Kept it at my place in the city. Put a little Yellow Brick Road in there and you're over the rainbow. With the hash in 'Nam, you got these few minutes of clarity. Total clarity. The kind that only comes in those big moments. Like, all right, there was this astronaut, Edgar Mitchell. Never heard of him?"

"Apollo 14," said Jack.

"That's right," said the Captain. "Apollo 14. Moonshot. 1971. Anyway, Mitchell, in space, he has this profound moment of clarity in which he realizes that we are all connected. All of us. To each other. To the planet. To the universe. It changed his life."

Sam stopped eating. She was staring at the Captain with concern. *Had Tony's paranoid delusions sounded something like this toward the end?* Jack wondered.

"That's what it feels like. Like waking up. Will it last?" The Captain shrugged.

Lights flashed against the kitchen walls. A truck was pulling into their drive, a rusty green S-10 with a Georgio's magnetic sign stuck to the roof. The vehicle listed to the side as the large Viking stepped out. Nils waved at them and then reached back in for the pizza and soda. Jack stepped outside to meet him. Through the picture window they could see everyone seated around the table. Nils smiled at the Captain. "He looks okay," he said.

"He's having a good day." Jack took the food and handed Nils a twenty. Then, instead of going in, he set the pizza on a stack of firewood by the door. "Wait a second," he said. "Your dad. He still run that excavating business?"

"Yep. Septic tanks, mostly. City sewer still hasn't made it past SR 14. He replaced that tin shack with a pole barn two years ago. Got a small crew. He'd like me to help, but . . ." He looked down at his girth and smiled. "Hard labor doesn't agree with me."

"Does he have any cranes? Cranes you can drive?"

"He's got a Link-Belt Speeder. It's slow, but it moves. Rents it out to contractors for lifting trusses. Why? Having problems with your tank?"

"I was thinking about getting a crane out to Claytor Lake." He pointed through the trees. "I . . . I think Tony's down there."

"Uh . . ." Nils's eyes grew wide. "Holy shit," he said. "For reals?"

"Yes."

"Shit, man. Yeah. Yeah, we could do it. You'd need a spotter, of course. Someone down in the water to place the hook and net. Yeah, that's what you'd want to do, I think. There's this guy out of Kent State. He helped us pull out a backhoe that fell into Lake Milton. 'Course that was only fifty feet of water. But he could do it if anyone could."

"How much?"

"Got to clear it with the property owner, a'course. Not even sure who that would be. The lake went into foreclosure in '84 after the beach shut down. Someone'll have to pay the scuba guy from Kent State. Couple hundred bucks?"

7 The Captain thought he'd have time to tell Jack why he shouldn't go searching the bottom of Claytor Lake. He thought they'd have some time alone once everyone went to bed. Time enough to explain everything that needed explaining before Jack truly fucked them all. But as soon as Jack stepped outside, the Captain felt his clarity dim like someone had placed a sheet of muslin over a lamp.

No, he thought. *No, no, no. Not yet. Five more minutes.*

He pretended nothing was wrong and kept eating. Smaller bites, though, in case his mind blew out like a candle and he forgot how to swallow. He willed himself to remain focused. He read the ingredients on a soy sauce packet to busy his brain.

"I'm going to take a trip to Giant Eagle later this afternoon," said Virginia, sitting across the table from him. Her hair was pulled back in a chignon, highlighted by strands of coarse gray hair. She was feeding Jean, who drummed her fat little arms against her high chair between bites of rice cereal. "Do you want me to pick up anything?"

"Some Yuengling," he said.

"Daddy, we're out of Yuengling," said Jean, beside him, thirty-one years old again. "And you've had whiskey. How about some milk?"

He was slipping. Worse, he was slipping and not noticing the transitions from here to *there.*

His chair leaned forward as they banked the jumbo jet toward Queens. "La Guardia, this is Continental 161 on approach," First Officer Bill O'Shannon said into his headset. "Watch out for the towers, Walt."

It was their little joke. The Twin Towers of the World Trade Center were impossible to miss, rising from the banking district like religious monoliths. Targets against the sky. An accident waiting to happen.

"Roger," he said.

"Who's Roger?" asked Sam, looking at him with a touch of concern.

"Never mind. Could you find me something to write with? Some pen and paper?"

"I'll get it, Daddy," said Jean.

Through the tall windows he saw Jack talking excitedly with Nils on the porch. He knew what they were discussing. Jack thought he was doing something good.

He felt a knot in Virginia's shoulder as he worked the sunscreen across her back. The sky was bright. A cool breeze but hot in the sun. They sat on the shore of Claytor Lake, which was brimming with kids. Running kids. Splashing kids. Kids with Popsicles. The concession stand sold them for fifty cents apiece. Popsicles, not the kids. Jack, age three, was forming an airplane made of sand by their feet.

"Lower," she said.

"Here, Dad," Jean said, tapping the sheet of paper she'd placed in front of him.

The Captain took the pen in his hand.

Jack, he wrote, *get rid of the box under my bed.*

8   Jack said goodbye to Nils and brought the pizza inside. He could tell by their silence what had happened while he was gone. Even Paige was quiet. The Captain stared intently at a piece of paper in front of him. He looked up at Jack and smiled a vacant smile.

"Ah, Dad," he said. "Where'd you go?"

The Captain held the paper out to him like a present. Jack took it and looked at the short message.

He sighed. "I can't read Vietnamese."

"O dau Qi?" the Captain asked.

9   *"Where is Qi?" Walter asked the bartender from the Tennessee. They were running down Tu Do. Everyone was in a panic. It was falling. The city. The country. Capitalism. From an open window he could hear Bing*

Crosby singing "White Christmas," an odd juxtaposition to this chaos—the song was code, their cue to get the fuck out of Saigon. The Hueys were leaving the DAO this very moment. He would go. But first he needed to find Qi.

Duong, the bartender, didn't answer. Didn't even slow down. He was making for Tan Son Nhut as if he had a chance of leaving with the other refugees. Walter ran the other way, a stitch digging into his side. He should have come back sooner, but he'd been pulled into Operation Babylift, flying children out in C-5s bound for Oakland.

Qi!

He'd met her three years ago, in 1972. This fourteen-year-old, dressed in a flowered silk blouse over dark trousers, walked up to him inside the Tennessee, sidled up next to him, and whispered, "Hour for three, GI?" She was a pretty thing. Thin lips, high cheeks, dark, hungry eyes. But her face was still pudgy with baby fat. Younger than the girl, Virginia, who'd taken his virginity back home. Walter shook his head, reluctant to be rid of her.

Qi sat next to him anyway and Duong served her bac si de, a strong rice whiskey.

"Clarka Kent," she whispered.

"Huh?"

"You Superman, GI."

"Okay," he said.

And then Evan Sowell wandered in, looking for God knows what, probably looking for this very thing. Evan was a fine mechanic. But he was also a creepy sonofabitch. Evan's skin was this mottled gray and his face was covered in patchy hair and pimples. Twenty pounds underweight, ribs pushing out of his skin like there was a dark mojo eating him up from the inside out. He wore that same black leather jacket, even on the hottest days. Everyone on base knew Evan preferred young whores. "It's not illegal here," he liked to say.

Evan homed in on Qi right away. He walked up to her, a man on a mission, slipping between Walter and the girl, leaning over the bar to hand Duong fifty piastres. "I'll buy the lady's drink," he said, eyes already glowing from some cheap hashish.

Duong said something to Qi then, and she turned to Evan and nodded.

"Hot damn," he said.

Why he'd done what he did next, Walter could never really say. But before Evan could take Qi away, he set a crisp fifty-dollar American bill on Duong's bar. It was money he'd planned to send home—his mother would put half in the bank for him, the other half in her pantry. If pressed, he might have said he'd done it because he couldn't add another bad memory to his mind that day. It was already overfull. But maybe he just wanted to see what would happen next.

"What is this, Walter?" Duong asked. His English was sharp when money was on the table.

"Ransom," he said. "For the girl. She's not working for a while."

"What?" Evan asked in a childlike whine.

Qi, not grasping what was transpiring, spoke fearful Vietnamese to the bartender. He whispered something back to her. She looked to Walter, confused.

"No more Uncle Sams," he said. "Not for you."

"Hey, goddamn it," Evan protested. "What are you doing?"

"Take a hike, soldier."

Until the end of that endless war, Walter did his best to look after Qi. She was, he reckoned, his responsibility from that moment on. He secured a one-bedroom efficiency above a grocery for eight dollars a month. He let her stay there and gave her money for food and clothes on the promise that she would stop hooking and go back to school. Her parents, he learned, had burned to death during the Battle of Hue, and she was alone. He visited often, coaching her in English while she taught him simple Vietnamese. He called her "Qi," which meant "turtle." She called him "Clarka," as in Clark Kent. Sometimes he would spoon her on the bed in their little room, the sounds of mopeds and the market drifting through the screenless window, and they would nap together. That was all the intimacy they shared.

He meant to get her out of this hell.

And it was finally time.

Qi wasn't at the elementary school where she tutored children now, so he ran toward their apartment in the western section of Saigon as Irving Berlin sang to the soldiers a song of retreat.

A block away, the air around him sizzled with the high-pitched doom-wail of an artillery shell. It happened too quickly for him to drop. The shell collided with the side of a concrete bungalow, a barbershop that catered to GIs. The shock wave kicked Walter in the chest like a steel-toed boot, sending him against the side of an appliance store. His ears rang loudly. He could no longer feel the smaller two digits on his right hand. They would remain numb for the rest of his life (a secret he kept from Continental Airlines physicians).

It was another minute and a half before he reached the stairs to Qi's loft. Ten seconds more to make it up the stairs. The door was open. His legs protested. He did not want to step inside. He already felt what waited.

There was blood everywhere and in the center of it all stood Evan Sowell. He was naked and he leaned over Qi's body, which was folded backward over the bed. In his hands was a large killing knife, a Ka-Bar that Evan had stolen off a dead Marine. The man's back was to the door and he was still hacking away, distractedly, as Walter stepped into the room.

They had a term for this in Vietnam, men who killed women they raped. Double veterans, they called them.

Walter tiptoed across the room, and when he was close enough he wrapped his right arm around Evan's neck and squeezed. Evan dropped the knife to the floor. He tried to pry Walter's arm away. But it was too big. It was a python. A tangle of muscle, earned in country.

"Shhh," he whispered.

Evan tilted his head and looked up at him. He was trying to say something, his mouth working like a goldfish.

Then Evan's face changed, became something else, someone else . . .

Jack, oh God, it's Jack!

But then it was Evan again and Walter was glad he was hurting. He didn't care to give Evan the last word.

10 Jack was asleep when the Captain peered in through the open door of the bedroom, his body silhouetted by the light of the moon that fell through the window at the end of the hall. Jack didn't wake until his father's arm was around his neck, squeezing the life out of him.

Jack's first thought was that he had somehow managed to get himself tangled up in his sheets. Then his eyes flew open and he saw the shape of his father over him. He knew, immediately, this was the end.

Please, he pleaded. *Not like this.*

"Kill you," the Captain whispered, spittle dripping from his mouth onto Jack's forehead.

His arms were pinned by the Captain's legs. Feebleminded or not, the Captain was a big sonofabitch and there was nothing doing. Jack tried to elicit a gargle from his mouth, a raspy cry for help, anything, but his throat was pinched tight. It felt like his father was one foot-pound of pressure away from snapping his neck. That would come next and at least there would be no more pain.

No. Not now. Not here. Not like this, he pleaded. To whom? He didn't know. But he sent the message out from his mind, into the ether, a Mayday to the universe. He saw sparkles of light in his periphery as his brain consumed the last of his body's oxygen. Sparkles like fireflies, brief constellations.

Suddenly the room was full of screaming. Screaming as he'd never heard before. A high-pitched caterwaul that bit into his ears and momentarily drowned out the pain of his strangulation. He saw her as through tinted glass: Paige at the door in pastel jammies, mouth open as if she were singing.

As a gray veil descended, he saw Jean fly through the door. She pushed Paige out of the way, never touching the ground, her nightgown trailing after her like an apparition's end. She snatched the lamp from the nightstand and brought it over her head in a tight arc aimed for the Captain's head.

11 "Jack? Jack, can you hear me?"

A bright light was shining in his eyes and for a moment he thought he was dead. Then the light pivoted and he saw the harsh woman in the orange windbreaker leaning over him, penlight in her fingers. Red and yellow strobes played at the window. He heard excited voices downstairs, Jean yelling orders: "St. Mary's! Just get him the fuck out of here!" Paige was crying.

He tried to sit up but couldn't. He tried to speak and was rewarded with fire in his throat. It felt like he'd gargled Everclear.

"Don't try to move," the woman said. "Don't try to speak. Just blink once for 'yes.' Understand?"

He blinked.

"Good. Jack, I want you to try moving your fingers for me."

He pretended to play the piano.

The woman breathed a sigh of relief. "Good. Now, your toes."

He did those, too.

"Excellent."

He heard someone running up the steps and then Jean was at his side. "Is he paralyzed?" she asked.

"He'll be fine."

Jean buried her face in his shoulder and sobbed.

"Jack," the EMT said in a measured tone, "your head is in a brace. I don't think your neck is broken, but we're going to keep you secure until we get to the hospital. In a second my partner will be here with the gurney and we'll take you downstairs."

Jack blinked again.

"I thought he killed you," Jean said.

A moment later the gurney arrived. They lifted him onto it, strapped him down, and wheeled him through the house, out the back, and through the open doors of a waiting ambulance. In another minute they were rocketing down SR 14 toward Robinson Memorial Hospital. Somewhere ahead another ambulance carried the Captain, bound for St. Mary's, an assisted-living home where, Jack suspected, his father would spend his remaining days.

THREE

ELEGY

1   When Jack awoke in the hospital the next morning, there were flowers on the windowsill, daisies from Sam. He watched the TV hanging in the corner for a while and willed himself not to think about why he was there. Halfway through a documentary on Joseph Mengele, Dr. Palmstrum arrived and rolled across the room on a wheeled stool. The man was ancient, with a long, horsey face, white hair pinned back with some gel that smelled like antiseptic. He sucked a Werther's and regarded his patient.

"My dad had Alzheimer's before they called it Alzheimer's," said Palmstrum. "I ever tell you that?"

Jack swallowed and grimaced at the immediate pain. "No," he whispered.

"Sometimes he thought he was in a trench in Montfaucon. Nothing you could do to talk him out of it. If you came up behind him when he was like that he would toss you to the ground and smack you around a bit. Gave my mother a black eye. That's when we put him away. A'course back then it was the mental ward." He sat on the stool with his arms crossed in his lap. Finally, he said something from a part of Jack's childhood that he could no longer place. "Where is fancy bred? In the heart or in the head?"

Jack smiled faintly.

"We know so very little about the human mind," said Palmstrum. "Everything we are, wrapped up in three pounds of gray matter between our ears. Storage for the memories we create. Memories make us who we are, and when you take even one away, it it changes us forever."

Jack nodded.

"Give us a look."

Jack opened the top of his gown. He'd checked it out in the bathroom mirror already: a necklace of bruises, purply around the edges. Palmstrum touched the back of his neck with fingers of loose, warm skin.

"You feel that?"

Jack nodded.

The doctor kneaded his skin a little, probing the vertebrae.

"He almost killed you. I guess you don't need me to tell you that."

Jack's mind would not allow him to think of his father just yet, so he focused on the easy questions. "When . . . ?"

"You can leave today. No reason to keep you. I'll write you a script for the pain."

"Thanks."

"I'm no headshrinker, Johnny. I never needed one. A nip of the shine always worked for me. But there's no shame in it. Now's as good a time as any."

He shook his head.

"All right." Palmstrum scribbled on a pad of paper. "How's your sister?"

Jack gave him the thumbs-up.

"You win some, you lose some. It's always a surprise which side of the fence people end up on." He patted Jack on the head as if he were eternally four. "Take care, young man."

2   Jean came by later that afternoon and took him home. She'd gotten rid of the Captain's hospital bed and the living room felt too big. The bedroom lamp had been replaced. The only reminder of the attack was a black scuff mark on the kitchen tile where the gurney wheel had locked up. Jean had even lit scented candles to rid the house of that sweet molasses smell of the infirm.

Time ticked on and allowed Jack to begin to forget.

On Sunday he went with Jean and Paige into Ravenna for groceries. Later that day he taught his platinum-haired niece the basics of chess, showing her the movements of each piece on an empty board until she understood the rules.

"I like the horses," she said.

"Why?"

"Because they're sneaky. They can come up behind you and snatch you up!"

On Monday he walked Paige to the bus. It was her last week of school before the summer break. He waved to Mrs. Beahl, the bus driver, one of Virginia's old canasta partners.

"Welcome back," she said.

He smiled.

Wednesday night he babysat so Jean could drive in to Kent to catch a screening of *Jurassic World* with her sponsor, Anna. Jack made bologna boats in the oven, slabs of greasy meat with cheese that rolled into crispy-gooey canoes when baked. Paige ate five. They watched *The Hobbit*. Paige was fascinated by Rivendell because some of the elves had hair like hers. "Can we go there, please?" she asked. "Can we visit the elves?" She fell asleep leaning against him on the couch.

He wondered what his kid would have looked like if he'd married Sam.

He found a biography on Truman in the bookcase behind the couch and spent hours reading, napping when his eyes got tired.

Mostly he and his sister didn't talk. They didn't talk about the Captain. Or Sam. Or Tony's bones. That unfinished story seemed less important now. Sam, for her part, kept a distance.

Jack would have been content to drift through the summer this way, appreciating the little things and growing a belly. But then he went to see Paige's end-of-school play inside John F. Kennedy High School's cafetorium and, well, his story changed.

3 "*Uzzzzz*," Paige said from the backseat. She was in the bumblebee suit again. She wore antennae made of pipe cleaners atop her white hair. "Hey, Uncle Jack, didja know that it's impossible for a bee to fly but they do it anyway?"

"I didn't know that," he said softly from the passenger seat.

"It's a fact."

"You know what she looks like in that costume," he whispered to Jean.

"What?"

"Remember the hybrid human-bug at the end of *The Fly*? The original with Vincent Price? With all that white hair, she looks just like that thing. Like the fly with the human head that got caught in the spider's web."

"Ew," said Jean. She looked back at Paige in the rearview mirror. "Jack, that's creepy."

"Help me! Help me!" he cried in falsetto.

"Stop it." But she laughed as they turned into the parking lot.

He was hit with a wave of nostalgia when he stepped inside. It was the smell, that pervasive stink of government-grade floor cleaner and sweat, of books and pencil shavings. It was also the sound, the way every voice echoed off metal lockers and traveled the length of the building.

The cafetorium was a block of a room with a narrow stage set into one wall, space enough for two hundred foldout chairs and a row of bleachers in the back. The concrete walls were painted maroon and beige, emblazoned with the incongruous symbol of Kennedy pride: a marauding pirate clenching a scabbard in his teeth.

Paige walked off with a boy stuffed into a costume that was either a small horse or a large pig. Sam was holding seats for them near the front. Jack checked his watch. There were still fifteen minutes before the play and he wasn't up for idle chatter with his ex-girlfriend, so he took a walk.

Jack's senior class picture still hung outside the library next to the awkward photographs of the other members of the National Honor Society. His young face was pointed, his ears radar dishes stuck to his head. Tony's picture was up there, too. He was the handsome one.

"He's out there, somewhere," said a familiar voice.

Jack turned to find Tom Harris, a tall, bespectacled fellow who had once been his history teacher. He'd been a mentor to Tony, his favorite for a time. In his hand was a mug of coffee, some exotic blend he brought from home that smelled of cinnamon and dry leaves.

"Hi, Mr. Harris," said Jack.

"It's Tom now, John."

He smiled.

"Good lord. What happened to your neck?"

He had practiced for this. "Went for a swim up in Put-in-Bay," he said. "My friend has this boat. Jumped off the side but didn't see the lifesaver hanging there. Got tangled up in the rope. Lucky the guy had a knife to cut me loose."

"Looks awful."

"Doesn't hurt." A lie. He brought the subject back to Tony. "I heard he was acting strange right before it happened."

Harris looked grave. Jack sensed some internal debate. "There's something I probably should have told the police," said Harris finally.

"About Tony?"

He nodded. "A week before it happened he came to visit me. I could tell something was bothering him. He'd lost a lot of weight. And he was edgy. He came into my classroom and we talked for a bit after school."

"About what?"

"About disappearing. And how to do it. I thought it was all hypothetical, of course. Tony said he had a patient who wanted to disappear, start a new life somewhere. He was trying to convince this person that it couldn't be done. That it was too hard to just walk away and not have the police find you. He knew I was a current-events nut, that I read five papers a day. He asked me if I'd heard of a story about someone trying to do such a thing in the last decade. I told him that I knew of two.

"The first was a prosecutor from Cleveland who disappeared under strange circumstances in western P.A. He parked his car near a bridge. When they found his laptop and hard drive in the river, they figured he'd committed suicide. But then people started seeing him in Texas. The second was a former policeman who wanted to leave his family and live in a cabin in the West Virginian hills. He faked his death to escape his wife and the taxman."

"How'd the cop do it?"

"Drove out to Edgewater Park and put his shoes, wallet, and clothes on the shore. It looked like he'd walked into the lake and drowned. But then three years later he fell off a ladder while cleaning his cabin's gutters and ended up in the hospital. Some doctor figured it all out."

Jack felt his blood cool, icy shards running through his heart. "Why didn't you tell Sam?"

Harris looked back to the picture of Tony hanging on the wall. "All I can think is that he had a hell of a reason to leave. Without knowing what that reason is, maybe I'm putting his life in danger by telling anyone. Maybe it has something to do with Haven, where he worked. Back in the day, couple of those Youngstown Mafia guys got pinched for laundering money through nursing homes. You just don't know."

Jack chewed on this as he returned to the cafetorium. There was only one way to know for sure. By the time Paige came dancing out from the wings, her stinger swinging behind her, he'd made up his mind. Sam needed resolution. So did he. It was time to see how Tony's story played out.

4   Jack pulled into Georgio's a little after ten o'clock that night. A swath of garish yellow light fell upon the gravel lot through a screen door. Gypsy moths danced about like fairies at a feast. The peppery aroma of fried chicken delighted the night. Inside, Nils was closing out a register. He looked up at Jack as he entered. The door crashed loudly behind him.

"How you holding up?" asked Nils.

"You mean since my father tried to kill me?"

"Franklin Mills is a small town, Jack."

"I'm fine."

Nils looked at his neck. Jack let him. "You want to take some time with the thing we talked about? Probably not a good idea to stir up more trouble, huh?"

"Fuck that," said Jack. "If we can find Tony's body, I can get back to Lakewood with a clear conscience. That's all I want. When I get back to the city I'm going to stock the fridge with Dortmunder and spend the rest of the summer drunk."

"Fuckin' A."

"Yeah, fuckin' A."

"So when do you want me to get the Link-Belt out to the lake?"

"I guess all I need to do is find this scuba guy from Kent State and then get the okay from the property owner . . ."

Nils was shaking his head. "Got it all handled," he said. "I called the scuba guy. My old man had his number. He's asking four hundred dollars. It's a deal. I think he just wants to see the bottom for himself. The property is owned by Glenn Riggenbaugher, the minister from First Church? He bought it at auction. Had plans to turn it into a retreat or some shit, but then he got the diabetus. Anyway, he lives in Florida now. I found him, too. He'd very much like for Tony to have a proper burial."

"Nils, that's perfect. Why did you do all that?"

The Viking shrugged. "Scouts' motto, right? Be prepared."

"All right, then. When can we do this?"

"How's 'bout Sunday, day after tomorrow?"

"Sunday it is," said Jack. "Sunday we see if Tony really is at the bottom of Claytor Lake."

5   By the time Jack, Jean, and Paige walked the path to Claytor Lake at 8:00 a.m. Sunday morning, there were already twenty people milling about the shoreline. Jack recognized Gail and Ted Moore, neighbors from four doors down. They had brought lawn chairs and a cooler full of sandwiches and Cheerwine. Hank Aemmer, the mailman, skimmed rocks beside the tilting lifeguard stand. Shelly, the bartender from the Driftwood, pointed out places she used to sunbathe to her war vet boyfriend. Some cars were parked along the shoulder of Porter Road, the potholed street that ran behind the lake.

"Is this morbid?" Jean whispered.

Jack shook his head. "It would be if they hadn't all known Tony."

Sam was not there. She was hiding in Nostalgia, avoiding the scene for as long as her resolve held.

The crane arrived at 8:30, rumbling like low thunder. The Link-Belt Speeder appeared around the bend of Porter Road where the access drive to Claytor Lake was located, and the crowd let out a whoop and a round of applause. It was a clinkety-clanking behemoth of a crane painted McIntosh red, a metal snout jutting from the front. Nils's father, a red-haired stringbean of a fellow, waved to Jack as he maneuvered the machine to a part of the shore that had eroded to clay. Nils followed in his pick-'em-up truck, its bed full of tackle.

By nine o'clock the crowd had grown to forty-seven souls and the beach looked much as it had during long-ago summers, full of middle-class God-fearing folk lazing on blankets, watching the lake. Mr. Harris arrived with two thermoses full of his imported coffee, which he poured into Styrofoam cups and placed on a card table for everyone.

A short while later a station wagon pulled in and parked near the crane. It was the Kent State professor, a man named Dr. Bednarik, who taught sociology. Jack walked over and put an envelope of cash in the man's hands.

"How deep is it, really?" the professor asked.

"Nobody remembers. Maybe as much as a hundred and fifty feet to the bottom."

The professor smiled. "I can do about two hundred without trouble. Don't look so worried."

"Is this safe?"

Dr. Bednarik heaved the tank over his shoulders and laughed. "Probably not," he said. "But it's a lot of fun."

Five minutes later the professor waded into the water.

"I don't think I can do this," said Jean. "All this suspense. I'm going to take Paige home." She took her daughter's hand and pulled her away.

"Is Uncle Tony in the lake?" the girl asked.

"Maybe, sweetie."

"But I want to watch."

"I don't think that's a good idea. Sorry, hon."

The professor's head slipped under the water.

6   Sam arrived at a quarter to ten. "Anything?" she asked. Her eyes were puffy, her hair pulled back in a short ponytail.

"Nothing yet."

"One of the detectives is here," she said. "The guy with the crew cut."

Jack found him in the crowd, a wide man in uniform. He stared back, lips like a hyphen painted on his face. "Maybe I should have told him what we were doing."

"Why? They haven't done shit for three years."

The crowd murmured. Mr. Harris was pointing at the lake. Dr. Bednarik had surfaced and was swimming over. There was something in his left hand, a piece of metal that reflected the sunlight. When he was close enough to rest an elbow on the ledge of the quarry, he waved Jack over. Sam followed.

"Who's this?" asked the professor.

"Tony's wife."

He looked at her with a sincere sadness.

"I found your husband," he said. "I'm so sorry." He held the object out to her. She bent down to take it from him.

It was a silver watch with a large analog portal. The hands were frozen at 10:03. She flipped it over. On the back was *Tony Sanders.*

"I had it engraved when he got into med school," she said.

"It was still on his wrist," said Bednarik.

"Thank you." She touched Jack's arm. "I'm going home," she said. "Thank you, Jack. For doing this. Thanks." She walked quickly down the access road. The crowd watched her go. Then Gail and Ted Moore started packing up their snacks.

The professor sighed. "So shines a good deed in a weary world," he mumbled.

"Can we bring him up?" asked Jack.

"Well," Bednarik began, "the body is caught on the open window of an old Renault, but I think I can get it unsnagged. If I can pull the net around the remains, I think it'll come up in one piece."

The Speeder sputtered to life, its voice like a combine shucking corn. Nils's old man pulled at the levers inside the cab and the crane swung over the black lake. He lowered the netted hook into the water. Bednarik took it and descended.

Twenty minutes later the crane lifted the nude body from the lake, tendrils of inky water running off its extremities. It was wrapped in white netting, arms and legs hanging through holes. The skin had darkened to leather from the cold and muck at the bottom, and from a distance it resembled a life-size wooden marionette, a grotesque.

The people still sitting around the lake picked up their things and left the way they'd come.

Jack walked to where Nils was guiding the body to the ground. It was hard to see Tony's features in the corpse. It was all warped and stretched and there were holes in the skin. Jack wondered if the jagged rock walls of the quarry had done that on the way down. His large penis was smashed flat like jerky.

The buzz-cut detective joined him.

Jack extended a hand. "Jack Felter," he said.

The cop shook it. "Captain Marlon Hoover."

"So do we call the coroner? Or what happens from here?"

"It's your show, boss," said Marlon.

"Uh," said Nils. The large man stepped back from the body and bumped into Jack. "Uh, guys, his teeth just fell out."

Jack looked to the body, which Nils had unwrapped from the netting. The corpse's dentures sat askew in its decomposed jaw.

"What the . . . ," Jack began.

Marlon reached down and pulled out the false teeth. What was left of the gums was charred and diseased.

No, thought Jack. He turned to the professor, who was climbing onto the far shore. "Hey," he shouted. "Did you search the entire floor?"

"I did a sweep. It's not that big at the bottom, really. It slopes into a small square. A couple cars. Lots of street signs. Garbage and stuff. Why?"

"No room for other bodies?"

"What? How many do you want?"

Jack turned back to the body with the dawning realization that he was his own disaster.

"That's not Tony, is it?" asked Nils.

"No. No, it's not," said Jack.

"Who is it?"

"It's Mark Brooks," said Marlon. "Samantha's brother." He leaned down and put a fat finger in one of the wide gashes across the dead man's chest. "And, unless I'm mistaken, this man was murdered."

"Uh," said Nils. "So where the fuck is Tony?"

PART TWO

WHERE IS EVERYBODY?

This highway leads to the shadowy tip of reality:
you're on a through route to the land of the
different, the bizarre, the unexplainable.

—ROD SERLING

ONE

THE LONELY

1 Jean stood at the picture window and watched Jack drive off to find Sam. It was his job now to tell Sam it wasn't her husband in the lake but her brother. Jean lit another cigarette. It was her own fault. She knew that. Why in the hell did she go with Mark when she knew he was deep for trouble? Of course, she knew that answer, too.

When the DJ cued up Billy Joel's "Just the Way You Are," Jean walked outside, onto a wide veranda that overlooked the gardens of Emerson Country Club. Her bridesmaid's dress, a garish teal, swished loudly around her bare feet. It was night, and the sweeping rows of aspen trees were dark borders against the moonlit grass. Inside, Tony held Sam close on the dance floor.

Mark leaned on the rock wall, waiting, a bottle of Miller Lite in one hand. His hair was long, black, tucked behind his ears. How old was he? Twenty-nine? His dimples appeared as he smiled a welcome and waved her over.

"I'm Mark," he said. "Sam's brother. You're Jean, right?"

She'd had a couple of glasses of wine by then and was feeling daring, so she said, "We've met."

*Alarm washed over his face but vanished before it took hold. "We have?"
he asked. "I'm sure I would have remembered that."*

*She laughed and placed a cigarette between her red lips. He fished out a
lighter for her. She pulled deep and let the hot smoke singe her lungs. "I was
thirteen," said Jean. "I spent the night at your dad's house, with Sam. You
were on leave from the navy, I think. Your hair was buzzed."*

Mark laughed nervously. "I don't remember. Long time ago."

*"Not so long," she said. "You looked in on us when we were chang-
ing out of our bathing suits, remember? Sam caught you sneaking a peek
through the heat register that connected your rooms. You did that a lot,
didn't you?"*

*He didn't say anything for a long time. He only looked at her, reading her,
trying to understand if he was in some kind of trouble. Finally, he exhaled,
shook his head, and looked out over the golf course.*

"Memory is a funny thing," he said. "Hard to tell what really happened."

*Jean stepped close to him. Once, when they were little, her parents had
taken her and Jack to a petting zoo in Cleveland. There was a tank with a
hissing cockroach. Jack was four years older than her, but he was too afraid to
pick up the bug. Jean didn't hesitate. She liked the rush. Always had.*

"I was curious, back then," she said. "I let you watch."

*Mark grunted and took a pull on his beer. He nodded. Seemed to decide
something. He turned to her. "Still curious?" he asked.*

"Not about you. You don't have anything I need."

*He looked in her eyes. His irises were as dark as his sister's, open voids.
"You like to party?" he asked.*

She didn't say anything, only crushed the cigarette on the wall.

*He reached into his jacket pocket and brought out a small square enve-
lope, no bigger than a postage stamp. He looked back at the glass doors to
make sure they were alone, then emptied a bit of powder into his palm and
held it out to her.*

"Coke?" she asked.

He shook his head. "Better."

Had she even hesitated? She couldn't remember anymore.

2   Sam wasn't at her house, the Cape Cod she'd shared with Tony out on Giddings. And she wasn't answering her cell. So Jack sat in the wicker chair on her front porch and waited for her to return.

While he waited, he contemplated their next move. A team of investigators from the coroner's office were parked around Claytor Lake now. Cops were combing the shoreline. Eventually that mouth-breathing detective would come around with some tough questions. There was a body now, a murder. And plenty of motive to go around. Even Jack had thought about killing Mark Brooks.

Jack's mistake was stopping at the Walmart in Ravenna on the way into Franklin Mills. But he wanted to pick up a card and candy or something for Jean. He didn't want to show up at the hospital empty handed. His father had called him an hour ago, asked him to come down, quick. They'd both known about Jean's habit. She promised she'd stopped with the meth shit when Paige was born. But the Captain had found Jean passed out on the back porch that morning, after a three-day bender. Mark had sweet-talked Jean into snorting some of his new cook. "It's her last shot," his father had said. "We need you."

Jack was still with Danielle at that time. This was eighteen months into their deal and she was living at his place in Lakewood. In hindsight, she had seemed distant for a while, and it was probably not that day that really did them in but the thousand small things leading up to it. He remembered how she'd pulled her blond hair into a harsh ponytail that morning and how that had annoyed him for some reason. Yes, they were probably just about done with each other anyway.

They had parked and Jack was walking toward the store when he saw Mark coming out, wheeling a loaded shopping cart toward his El Camino. Jack crossed the lot, balling his fists as he went. When he got close, he could see into the cart. There were bags full of acetone, bottles of Drano, and boxes of stick flares. Mark looked up when Jack was still a step away.

"Hey, man," he started, and then Jack's right fist connected with his face. Mark was not a big man, not anymore. The muscle he'd built in the navy

had wasted away and he was maybe 120 pounds soaking wet. His whole
body buckled and he collapsed to the ground.

"Jack!" shouted Danielle.

"Hey, what the fuck, man?" said Mark, wiping the blood away from his
nose, painting his cheeks red.

"Stay the fuck away from my sister," he said. "And Sam, too. Go back
to Warren, asshole."

Mark looked at him a moment and then smiled. "Sam never loved you.
You know that, right? She never loved anybody. And all you got was my
sloppy seconds."

Jack's vision blurred and he lunged forward. Danielle caught his arm. In his
anger, he pulled out of her grasp and, in so doing, she fell back against a car
door. That snapped Jack out of his rage. He helped Danielle up and put an arm
around her. But that was the moment it was over. He could feel it.

"I'm sorry," he said, walking her back to his car.

Tony had answers, wherever he was. Someone had placed his watch
around Mark's wrist, after all. Had that been some kind of attempt
at misdirection? Did Tony really think anyone would mistake
Mark's body for his? They needed to find him. And there was only
one person who might know where Tony was. And that person was
a minor in a psychiatric ward—not the easiest source to question.

Sam returned a few minutes after six. She walked to Jack clutching a brown paper bag. He hugged her. It made him feel nauseated.

"It's all over the radio," she said. She pulled back to look at him.
"My brother is dead. Good. *Good*," she said. "So Tony killed him
and ran away. Great. But why did he leave me? Why did he leave
me here?"

"I don't know."

"You do! You do! You knew he was a snake. You knew he was a
selfish prick. You warned me, Jack, and I didn't listen."

"It's not your fault."

"Goddamn it! It is!" She pushed him. Out of frustration. Out of
self-loathing. Anger. All those things.

"Stop," he said. He held her arms still at her sides.

She leaned into him. Her lips pushed against his, opening his mouth. Her tongue found his. He could taste the menthol cigarette she'd snuck in the car.

He pulled away. "Stop. Please stop." He pulled her down so that they were sitting on her front steps.

"I'm sorry," she said. "That was . . ."

"What's in the bag?"

She handed it to him. It was a brown paper sack, the kind you put kids' lunches in. He opened it. Inside was Tony's watch.

"I didn't know what to do after I left. I didn't want to come home. All I could think to do was do something with the watch. A memento. It was for you. It's for you, I mean. Unless it's evidence or something now."

He turned the watch over in his hand. She had taken it to her shop and engraved more detail around the original dedication. *RIP, Tony Sanders. 1978–2012*, it read now. He thought about it for a moment and then slipped it into his pocket. He wasn't about to give it to the police until he learned more about Tony. For now, it was better he held on to it.

3 It took Jack several days to talk his way into Haven. He had to relay his request for visitation through the director to the boy's mother, who had returned to New York years ago. Luckily, the mother remembered Tony fondly. The doctor and her son had shared a special bond. A meeting was arranged for Monday morning. Jack arrived at a quarter to nine, pulling through the main gate on Fisher Hill and up a winding drive to a grand Colonial mansion that looked like something from a John Irving novel.

A smartly dressed woman with the auspicious name of Kimberly Quick escorted Jack to a tiled common room full of comfy couches. A wall of windows looked out on a small pond edged with cattails. Cole sat at a table, bobbing his head to a tune on his iPod. His hair was jet-black, still mussed from sleeping. He was sixteen, a wiry boy with bloodshot eyes that blinked almost constantly, tic-ish. He was dressed in jeans and a vintage Nintendo controller T-shirt.

"He's a good kid," Quick whispered as they approached. "But he has a temper. Also, he doesn't sound crazy. Not at first. Try to remember that he's a schizophrenic. If you need any help, just holler." She left them alone to talk.

Jack took a seat across from the boy, who pulled out his earbuds and regarded him with mild amusement.

"My name is Jack Felter," he said. "I'm a friend of Dr. Sanders."

"I know who you are," the boy said. "He told me you'd come. I just didn't think it would take three goddamn years."

TWO

YOUNG MAN'S FANCY

1 "Tony told you I'd come here?"

Cole nodded. "It was the last thing he said to me. He said that eventually you'd come visit me and when you did I should tell you where he went." The boy's voice was hesitantly deep, the way young men talk when they're afraid their voice might slip back into a childhood soprano at the slightest provocation.

"You know where Tony is?"

Cole nodded.

"Where is he?"

"It's not that simple."

"What do you mean?"

Cole looked out the window, at the cloud shadows moving over the surface of the pond. "You ever heard of Plato's 'Allegory of the Cave'?"

Jack shivered. "Yes," he said. "Tony explained it to me."

"It's sort of like that. You're in the cave and I have to get you out before you can find your friend. I think that's why he left me behind."

"Why don't you tell me where he is and we'll see how it goes?"

Cole laughed. "This is going to be very difficult."

"What?"

"Teaching you. You're much more stubborn than Dr. Sanders, I can tell."

"Cole. Please. Where is he?"

"Your friend is on a large island, roughly the size of the state of Ohio, that sits in the ocean a hundred miles northwest of Dutch Harbor, the main port of Amaknak Island, Alaska."

It was, he supposed, the last thing he had expected to hear. "What?"

"Haven't you ever seen *Deadliest Catch*? Dutch Harbor is the place they're always unloading the crab."

"I know the show. My dad watches it." He rubbed at his neck, where a pinkish bruise reminded him that nothing could be taken for granted. "But why would Tony want to go all the way out there?"

Cole smiled. "To save the world," he said. He seemed so earnest.

"If I called out to Dutch Harbor. To the newspaper. Or the police. If I called the Dutch Harbor police, Cole, and I asked them about a huge island somewhere north of them in the Bering Sea, what would they tell me?"

"They'd tell you it didn't exist. But that's because they can't see it."

"But Tony can see it."

"Yes."

"And you can see it."

"Yes."

"But nobody else?"

Cole thought about this a moment. "I suppose some people might be able to see it."

Jack shook his head.

"Dr. Sanders called it 'inattentional blindness,'" said Cole. "I guess our minds have trouble seeing things we don't expect to see. There was this study he told me about. Some Harvard psychological study. Group of scientists showed two hundred students a videotape of a basketball game. During the game, a woman in a gorilla suit walked across the basketball court. Afterward they asked the students if they noticed anything strange. Almost half of them did not—or could not—see the gorilla. Because it was so weird, their minds ignored it. Their minds edited it out."

It was another idea from that psych textbook Tony had carried around. When they were kids, Tony had told Jack about how, when Columbus discovered America, the Indians on shore couldn't see his ships. The natives didn't use sailboats, so they had no frame of reference to draw from. It was too weird. For three days, while the *Santa Maria* was parked in the water, all the Indians could see was a "shimmer" on the water. *Inattentional blindness.*

"If nobody can see this island, how do *you* know about it?" Jack asked the boy.

"My dad told me."

"What's the island called?"

Cole shook his head. "Can't tell you that. Not yet."

"Why?"

"Because," he said, glancing out at the pond again. "I can't trust you. You're still under their influence."

Jack had misused the word "paranoia" all his life. It was not a light thing. Paranoia is not thinking your coworker might be angling for your job or that your professor is subjectively lowering your grade because he doesn't like you. Paranoia is sickness. Disease. Trying to pull any sense from what Cole was saying was like listening to someone who spoke English but who had hijacked certain words and stuffed them with new meaning. Like someone from the United States trying to have a conversation with a man in Ireland when they were both drunk.

"Help me understand," said Jack.

"First things first," said Cole. "Before we speak again, you have to start boiling your water."

2   Paige was eating Pringles, watching TV, and Jean was sipping coffee at the table when Jack came downstairs the next morning.

"Have you seen my watch?" he asked.

"You have a watch? Who wears watches anymore?"

"Tony's watch. Sam gave it to me. I had it yesterday. But I can't remember where I put it."

"Where'd ya go last night, Uncle Jack?" the girl asked between mouthfuls.

"Out with Aunt Sam. She was feeling sad, so I took her to a movie."

"Is she your girlfriend?"

"Nope. Just a friend."

"Did you kiss her?"

"No."

"You wanted to kiss her, I bet."

"I don't think so."

"You think she's pretty."

"Sure."

"Then you wanted to kiss her."

"You think so?"

Paige nodded emphatically. "Like Tauriel wanted to kiss that dwarf, Kili. She pretends she doesn't. But she does."

"Oh, honey, that's not exactly *Hobbit* canon . . ."

"Mommy said you used to kiss Sam in school."

He gave Jean a sharp look. "We kissed a lot of people in school," he said.

"There's this one boy. Dusty Miller. He kissed me on the playground. Then he punched me in the stomach and ran away."

"Stay away from Dusty."

The girl shrugged. "He wasn't a bad kisser," she explained, tossing her bangs aside insouciantly. "But he smelled like whole milk. I don't think he brushes his teeth."

"Paige," said Jean, hiding her smile with coffee mug. "Why don't you play outside or something?"

"'Kay," she said. She took the Pringles can with her.

"Watch that one," he said.

Jean gave his suit a once-over. "Back to Haven today?" she asked.

"Yep. And tomorrow, probably. It's like trying to solve a riddle talking to that boy."

"We have to talk about the Captain soon," she said, holding his eyes with her own. "Executor stuff. Living will . . ."

"Later."

"Soon, Jack."

He blinked. "Okay."

3 On the way to Haven, a ten-minute drive that took him past John F. Kennedy High School, its sports fields silent for June, the radio began to buzz like an old dial-up modem. One second Jethro Tull was singing about a homeless man named Aqualung and the next the car's speakers blared the sound of an ancient computer booting up and slipping into the white-noise crash of connectivity.

"This has been a test of the Emergency Alert System," a robotic voice informed him. "Had this been an actual emergency . . ."

Jack clicked off the radio. He felt ill at ease suddenly. Nauseated. He hated those EAS broadcasts. Always had. They were harbingers. Every time he'd heard that noise as a kid, he'd looked to the horizon for funnel clouds. Or worse: the telltale white flash of a nuclear blast.

He checked himself in the rearview mirror. What a job he'd done with the razor this morning! It looked like he hadn't shaved at all.

4 "You're a teacher?" asked Cole. "What do you teach?" They were in the common room, again, looking out at the cattails.

"I teach history."

Cole's eyes widened. Then he laughed loudly.

"What's funny?"

"Nothing," said Cole. "That's perfect."

Suddenly, Jack remembered where he'd left the watch. He'd

placed it on the windowsill beside his bed as he was undressing. He could see it resting there in his mind.

"What?" asked Cole.

"Nothing."

"C'mon. What?"

"It's stupid," said Jack. "I just remembered where I left my watch."

The boy nodded but didn't say anything more. His eyelids seemed to want to close.

"Can you tell me more about your conversations with Tony? Dr. Sanders, I mean? Do you know how he got out of Franklin Mills without his car?"

"No. I can't do that. Sorry, man."

"Why not?"

"You won't boil your water."

"I did. I started last night."

Cole smiled a thin smile but didn't look him in the eyes. "Jack, you don't know enough about what's going on to be able to lie to me. You don't even know what day it is."

"It's Tuesday. June sixteenth."

Cole shook his head.

"What day do you think it is?" asked Jack.

"It's Wednesday."

"Cole, I'm sure it's Tuesday."

"I know you're sure it's Tuesday. That's the problem." The boy was getting agitated. He blinked like a soldier tapping Morse code. "It's the fluoride. They put it in the water to make you suggestible. Then they plant ideas in your mind through radio waves. Ideas like what day they want it be. Tell me, Jack, did you hear an emergency broadcast on the radio this morning?"

For a second he was too weirded out to answer. Then logic set in. Cole must have been listening to the radio in his room before their interview. He was hijacking that little fact for his delusion, using it to pull Jack in.

"That's how they plant their ideas in your brain, like what day it is," said Cole. The boy's body pitched forward, as if sleep were try-ing to take him, but Cole brought his head up again.

"Are you all right?"

"No," he said. "It's okay, Jack. Maybe it's better for you to live in your cave. I wish I could sometimes. I really do."

The boy's eyes closed.

"Cole?"

Jack reached across the table and nudged the boy's shoulder with his hand. He opened his eyes a bit.

"Why are you so tired?" asked Jack.

Cole smiled but his eyes didn't. "It's probably the bottle of pills I swallowed."

"What?"

"I swiped a bottle from Quick's cabinet before they reset the calendar and planted the idea in your head that it was still Tuesday." Cole's eyes closed and the boy's head fell against the table.

"Nurse!" Jack screamed. "Nurse! Hey! Hey, goddamn it! Some-body! Somebody!"

The nurses came. Within moments they had the boy on a gur-ney and were running down the corridor toward the clinic. Jack was ushered quickly out of the building.

5 Jack rang the doorbell three times before realizing it didn't work. He knocked loudly on the porthole with his fist and then Sam was at the door. She was dressed in a Johnny Maziel jersey that reached below her knees.

"What's wrong?" she asked.

"This town is bullshit," he said. "Is it always like this? Or is it me? Am I some kind of curse?"

"What happened?"

He shook his head. "I'm just tired, Sam. I'm tired of all the sad-ness. And I'm tired of hating you."

She squinted her eyes and lifted a hand to block the sunlight playing through the giant oak in her front yard. "You don't hate me," she said.

"That's not true," said Jack, but he couldn't help smiling.

"You're not cursed, Jack. You just trust people too much. You were always kind of stupid that way. Now did you come here to feel sorry for yourself or did you come to kiss me?"

"I would like to kiss you."

"Okay, then."

He stepped inside and closed the door with the heel of his shoe. Sam twisted up to him on her tiptoes. Kissing her was like kissing a memory.

6   She slept beside him, her downy arm raked over his chest, but Jack did not sleep.

It was early afternoon. The sun through the half-open window gave her bedroom a honey light and a breeze rolled the curtains in a way that mimicked their breathing. The only noise was the hum of early cicadas in the trees surrounding the house and the occasional car crackling gravel on Giddings. Sam snored softy.

Jack couldn't sleep. Tony was all over this room: in that framed photograph from their honeymoon (arms around her in front of some Boston lobster shack), in the slender sports jackets hanging neatly in the closet, in the stack of yellow-spined *National Geographics* gathering dust on the nightstand . . .

"Mister Jack?" It was Virginia, home from bus garage. It was the afternoon of the first day of his junior year of high school and Jack was in the living room playing Zelda, trying not to think about Sam. Sam was all he could think about anymore. She was his consuming secret. He found himself lost during the day, imagining their rushed moments together, the nights they would sneak away and meet up on the shore of Claytor Lake. He flinched at the sound of his mother's voice. When Virginia called him "Mister Jack," it meant he was in for one of her legendary tirades, one likely to end with a call to the Captain and a promise of three smacks with his belt when he returned.

Jack should have expected this. When school was in and Virginia was at the bus garage with twenty men who loved gossip more than a quilting club, the rumor mill was lightning quick.

He set the controller down. She still had her keys in her hand. "In the car," she said through clenched teeth. Then, to Jean, watching from the couch: "We'll be back soon. Get some supper going."

He sat in the passenger seat of her Ford Escort and braced himself. She reached into her purse, resting in the space between the seats, and fished out a Winston Light. Her hands trembled as she lit the cigarette. She pulled deep and exhaled out the window and then was a little better. She started the car and they drove down Tallmadge, away from the center of town. He had a feeling there was no destination but privacy.

"I don't know what you were thinking, Johnny."

"What do you mean?"

She shook her head but did not look at him. "You're not smart enough to be able to lie to me, yet," she said. She took another long drag. "If Sam's brother, or her father, if either of them had found out first, they might have killed you. I really think they might have. Do you know how that makes me feel?"

He couldn't look at her. So he looked out the window and counted the trees.

"Her brother, Mark, is dangerous," she said. "The school was notified when Sam's family moved here from Warren. A cop come down from the city to brief the guidance counselor. Family shipped Mark off to the military instead of a psych ward. And that probably makes him even more dangerous."

"I don't understand."

Virginia sighed. "We live out here so that you don't have to know things like this," she said. "You'll hear it at school eventually. No getting around it. Surprised Jean doesn't know yet. Hell. Maybe she does. I don't know her as well as I used to."

They passed over Berlin Lake, the muddy water stretching out from under the bridge on either side, stagnant water so hot the fish were dying. Beyond was North Benton and still she did not turn off. It was like she was distancing them from the news itself. Or trying to. The way Einstein had wanted to drive away from the clock tower so that it was never noon. As she spoke, Jack *focused his attention on an aspen leaf that had gotten stuck under one of the windshield wipers.*

"Mark was raping Sam, Johnny. They caught him at school with her behind the bleachers. And if it was happening there, out in the open, you can imagine what was going on in their home."

"No," he said.

"Mark was still a minor by a few months. Family got a lawyer, kept Mark out of jail. When it was over, they moved away and the father forced Mark into the navy. Their mother died in the middle of it all. Wrapped her car around a tree. They called it an accident."

"Pull over."

Virginia skidded the Escort onto the shoulder and came to a quick stop. Jack threw the door wide, leaned out, and puked into the grass. The bile stung his throat and cleared his head. He spit a few times until the nausea subsided, then pulled the door closed.

"How did it happen?" she asked. "You and Samantha."

"I don't know," he said. "It just happened. The fair."

"Johnny. You can't see her again."

"I heard you."

"She's bad news. If she's not crazy already, she will be. You can't escape those memories. She's not safe, Johnny. She's a little barracuda. Understand?"

He did. But he didn't want to. He shook his head.

"She's also in the eighth grade," Virginia continued. "You're a junior now, kiddo. This is all kinds of trouble."

"Okay."

"She'll ruin your future." Virginia flicked the spent cigarette out the window and then pulled the car back onto the road and turned back toward home.

But Jack knew he couldn't stay away. Every time he closed his eyes he saw Sam. He could feel the pressure of her lips on his own, the way her upper lip was always chapped and cracked.

That night at Claytor Lake he found a note from her folded into the nook of a chestnut tree that gave them shade.

I know you know. Please stop. It's okay. I don't even care.

That night the heat wave broke. A wave of cool air blasted the house at 3:00 a.m., knocking slate shingles off the eaves. Morning brought rain, and it didn't let up for three days. Ten homes along the Cuyahoga were swept into the river, gobbled up and spit out as timber into Lake Erie. The world, after, felt new.

Jack kept the note with him and thought about what to do. A week later, he taped it to his bus window with his own message written in black marker on the back. Her bus faced his in the parking lot when school let out. A simple message, but profound: I love you.

Such public displays are never overlooked in school. They become one of those stories told in the lunchroom for years. A junior proclaiming his love for a lowly eighth-grader? That's good stuff.

As his bus pulled away that day he saw her smile. Smile and nod and mouth one word: "Okay."

When Sam awoke, the sun was low on the horizon. She pulled herself up enough to rest her head on Jack's chest. Her right hand drew words on his skin that he could not read.

"Stay," she said.

"Okay, then."

7 Cole's mother, Imogen, was a fit aristocrat with bright gray hair that ended harshly at her shoulders, as if it had been snipped off in one go by a pair of giant shears. She was the creative VP for a midtown advertising firm. She had written the slogan for Rivertin, the drug her son had overdosed on: *Return! Revive! Rivertin! Forever better.*

By the time Imogen flew to Akron the doctors had pumped Cole's stomach. The boy lived. Another five minutes was all it would have taken. She was angry. At everyone, it seemed, but Jack.

He came at her request to a meeting with Haven's director, Dr. Jimi Frazier, two days after Cole's attempted suicide. The director's office was high-ceilinged and lit by soft lamps. There was a gurgling pebble fountain in the corner and an array of diplomas and pictures on the wall behind his mahogany desk. Imogen sat across from Frazier, next to Jack, in a cushioned chair, legs crossed at the ankles, eyebrows furrowed.

"Do you know what it's like to entrust the well-being of your only child to someone, Dr. Frazier?" she asked.

Frazier was stoic, unreadable. "I have grown kids in the world, Imogen," he said. "I know what it's like to fear for them."

"This place is supposed to be safe."

"Yes."

"It's supposed to be a goddamn *haven*, Jimi."

"Yes."

"So how did this happen?"

"Your son is clever. One of the most intelligent young men we've ever treated. If he wishes to kill himself he will find a way. Here or elsewhere. What we have to do is treat that impulse. Cole has to *want* to live." He looked from her to Jack. "We were making progress until Mr. Felter intervened."

"Are you blaming me for this?" asked Jack.

"Before he disappeared, Dr. Sanders filled Cole's mind with false hope," Frazier said to Imogen. "He promised Cole that his friend Jack would have all the answers. When Jack didn't provide them, that three-year-old delusion came crashing down."

"That isn't how it played out," said Jack.

Imogen lifted a hand to quiet them. "Here's what I see. I see that it took your staff over a year to get my son to communicate again after Dr. Sanders left. And I see that it took Jack all of thirty seconds. For whatever reason, my son is responding to him. I know he's not a doctor. But he *is* a teacher. He knows something about kids. I want Jack to find out why my son tried to kill himself—"

"Wait," Jack started, "I couldn't—"

"And in the process, Jack might be able to get some answers about Dr. Sanders's whereabouts. And that, I believe, would help the both of you. Aren't you looking for him, too?"

Frazier leaned back in his seat and rubbed his bald head.

"Cole really does want to see you again," said Imogen. "You're the only one he's asked for."

"I'm not a shrink," said Jack.

"He doesn't need a shrink. He needs someone he can trust.

He's trying to tell us something. We need someone to figure out what it is. I can't do it. I can't talk to him like that. I look at him, all I see is his father."

8   Imogen walked Jack to his car. The day was bright, sunlight reflecting off the whitewash of the Haven home. She placed a hand on his arm.

"Jack," she said, her voice wavering. "Have they told you about Cole's compulsion to pull people into his delusions?"

"Yes," he said.

She batted away a stray strand of hair and seemed to consider her next words. Finally she said, "Let him."

"What?"

"Let him draw you in. I think the only way we find out what's going on with my son and what happened to your friend is for someone to really see what's cooking inside his brain. And you seem healthy enough for it."

If you only knew, lady, he thought. *If you only knew how I got these marks on my neck.*

When he didn't say anything, she continued. "I think his other doctors were too quick to dismiss everything Cole told them."

"Like what?"

"Cole believes his father was a secret government agent who collected Nazi artifacts."

Jack shrugged. "You think, what? There's something to it? Was your husband working for the government?"

"If you'd asked me a year ago I would have said, unequivocally, no. He was a day trader. No way. He couldn't hide something like that from me. I mean, it sounds crazy, right?"

"It does."

"About a year ago I moved out of our home on Long Island and into an apartment in the city. During the move, I found some things my husband had hidden from me."

Imogen reached into her pocket and came out with something in her hand. She passed it to Jack. The object felt cool wrapped inside his fist.

He opened his hand. It was George Washington. "A quarter?" he asked. It was dated 1957.

"Turn it over."

On the reverse, where a bald eagle should have been, was a swastika. In place of *E pluribus unum* were the words *Arbeit macht frei*.

"What the hell is this?" he asked.

"I have no idea, Jack. But I found it tucked into the pocket of my dead husband's favorite suit."

THREE

COME WANDER WITH ME

1 Cole smiled. "You look good, Jack," he said. "Less suggestible."

The boy sat on his bed in his room at Haven. He was dressed in pale pajamas. There were deep dark circles below his eyes and thick black wires trailed from under his shirt to a heart monitor beside the bed. The white machine beeped softly in the corner.

Cole's bedroom resembled a boarding school unit. The walls were painted a bright, textured blue. There were posters everywhere Broadway shows, mostly, with a one-sheet for *Wicked* by the window. A wide desk from IKEA was covered in magazines—*Wired, Entertainment Weekly*—its shelves stuffed with dog-eared paperbacks about government conspiracies. A wide-screen TV hung from the ceiling, connected to three different gaming systems, including a vintage Nintendo 64.

Jack sat in a leather recliner beside the bed. It was Monday, eleven days after Imogen had showed him that incongruous quarter, a week since he'd begun to boil his own drinking water, a habit both Jean and Sam monitored with growing concern.

"You met my mother, I guess."

"Yes," said Jack. "She's . . . persistent."

Cole laughed. "She gets what she wants."

"What was your father like?"

"Not yet," said Cole.

"Then what do you want to talk about?"

"Gradients."

"Gradients?"

"Do you know what a gradient is?"

"Like when a road goes up a hill?"

"Sort of. But I mean gradients for the *mind*. It's a common psychological tool. It's actually a big part of Scientology."

"Are you a Scientologist?"

"I'm not crazy, Jack. But I read about them. Scientologists have this thing called 'auditing,' where you relive the traumatic events of your life over and over and over. What they're really doing is molesting memory. Raping your brain. But we can use some of their methods. I'm going to teach you to safeguard your memories, the memories the government wants to take away. To do that, we'll use a gradient."

Jack nodded to let Cole know he was listening. His fingers tingled. It was hard to listen to the boy's voice. He sounded so confident.

"A gradient," Cole continued, "is a system of baby steps toward something bigger. Little truths that prepare you for some ultimate understanding. In Scientology, right, those kooks believe that seventy-five million years ago this alien Xenu flew to Earth in a DC-8 jumbo jet with his enemies' souls in the cargo hold. If you told someone that story when you introduced them to Scientology, they'd think you were batshit crazy. So what they do instead is use a gradient of smaller ideas to slowly prepare a person for this big mind-fuck at the end. When you first join Scientology you learn simple stuff like how L. Ron Hubbard was the shit and how to purify your body and crap."

Jack nodded.

"Or," said Cole, "think of it like this. You don't teach a kindergartener calculus, right? If you gave them a triangle and told them to give you the angle of each corner, they'd chuck a block at your head or something. You teach a kid addition and subtraction first. Then multiplication. Division. Algebra. Trig. Then calculus. That's a gradient. Storytellers do this all the time to gain the reader's trust. Intro the characters. Intro the mystery. Intro the setting. Then: bam! You gotta ease them into it. If Stephen King had started *It* by saying, 'Hey, there's this alien from another planet that looks like a spider but pretends to be a clown that lives in the sewer and feeds on the fears of children,' you'd probably not pick it up because fuck that crazy shit."

"Okay," said Jack. "So what's the gradient for this story?"

"I came up with it myself," said Cole, his eyes wide and excited, like a kid about to teach a friend the rules of baseball for the first time. "It's a seven-step gradient. By the end, you should be able to understand what's going on. And if you wanted to, you might even be able to see that island I told you about. I call the gradient 'the Seven Impossibilities.'"

"You played this with Tony."

Cole rolled his eyes. "It's not a game, Jack. But, yes. I did."

And it's what drove him crazy, Jack thought. "How does it go?"

"I explain to you seven truths, each progressively harder to accept than the one before. You don't have to believe them. At least I don't think you do. You just have to accept the *possibility* that what I tell you is real. That it *could* be real."

"What are they?"

"One at a time, Jack. That's how it goes."

"All right."

"The first one is relatively easy to accept. Impossibility One: I cannot forget anything."

"I've seen Tony's notes on this. He gave you a piece of paper with a sequence of numbers. Pi, right?"

Cole looked offended. "No cheating, Jack. Don't read Dr. Sanders's notes. If you still have them, put them aside until we're done. It won't do you any good to skip ahead. The gradient won't work if you know what's coming."

"Sorry," he said.

"Yes, it was pi to two hundred fifty digits."

"So you have a photographic memory?"

"Kind of. I didn't always have it. It's a result of the accident."

"Accident?"

"In 2011, I was . . . in a car accident in Manhattan. I was in a coma for three weeks. Doctors put a metal plate in my head." Cole took a round fridge magnet from the stand behind his bed and, with a flourish, flicked it over his left ear in a gentle arc. It changed direction midair and clunked to his skull with a sickening *thunk* that made Jack cringe.

"Cool trick," he said.

Cole pried the magnet off his head and set it back on the side table. "When I woke up after the accident, I couldn't forget anything anymore. I still remember the way the hospital room smelled and the names of every nurse and doctor who came in to probe and poke at me."

"Must get old quick."

Cole nodded. "In a way it's like all those moments are playing out at the same time as this one. Forgetting allows us to separate time. The more distant a memory, the more faded it is. I don't have that. Waking up in the hospital after that accident feels like this morning to me. Actually, it feels like right now."

"Is that what . . ." He stopped himself.

Cole smiled. "Is that what made me crazy? No. The thing is, I'm not crazy. The rest of the world is. And, yes, I know how crazy that sounds."

Jack felt himself beginning to like the boy. He had spoken about the big ideas of the universe only with Tony. *And this is how it begins,* he realized. *This is how Cole sets his claws in you.*

"Test me," said Cole.

Jack held up his hands. "I concede. You have a photographic memory. No problem."

The boy shook his head. "You have to participate."

"I don't know how to test photographic memory. I'm a history teacher, Cole, not a psychologist."

"The best tests are visual. Photographs. Do you have any pictures in your wallet that are highly detailed?"

He did, in fact. Generally he was not a superstitious man, but Jack carried a totem of sorts. Had carried it since he was sixteen. It felt like signing a contract, pulling the picture out of his warped black leather wallet and handing it to the boy, a boy who was the same age as Jack was in the photo. A counselor at Camp Algonkin had taken the picture during summer camp in 1995. It was a picture of Jack and Tony in full Class A uniform standing in front of the log cabin dining hall.

Cole looked at it and laughed. "Nice ears. And that's Dr. Sanders, right?" After three seconds he handed the photograph back. "Quiz me."

"What's in my hands?"

"A rope tied in a bowline. Was that for a merit badge?"

"No. It was how you got in to dinner. You had to tie knots to get in to eat. They had a guy checking knots at the door."

"Ah."

"What's in Tony's hands?"

"Nothing. Did he cheat, Jack? You passed your rope through the windows so he could get in, didn't you?"

"I did."

Cole nodded. "I got to know a lot about Dr. Sanders's character. Not all of it was good."

"What . . . uh . . . what's on the cabin, next to the doors?"

"The Boy Scout emblem, the fleur-de-lis, the lily, a death flower."

"Do you say anything that isn't cryptic?" Jack asked. But he was smiling. "What's . . ."

"Let me speed things up," said Cole. "There is a young boy with brown hair in line behind you who is wearing mismatched socks. One green, one beige. Behind him is a Life Scout named Nils May or Mason or something—his mother has written his name on the waistband of his pants and I can't quite read it. The flag on Tony's sleeve has been sewed on upside down. And the picture was taken at precisely five-twenty-eight p.m., on Friday, July twenty-eighth, 1995."

Jack looked at the photograph carefully. "How the hell do you know that? I don't even remember when it was taken."

"There's a calendar on the wall inside. You can see it through the second window on your right. Class A uniforms mean end-of-the-week dinner; I was a scout, too, Jack. That's a Christmas tree hanging upside down from the rafters. I assume it's the traditional Christmas-in-July theme week. Ergo . . ."

"And the time?"

"I have no idea about the time. That part I made up."

"Nice."

Cole shrugged.

"Okay. I believe you."

"Good. So tomorrow we can talk about Impossibility Number Two: how the government uses fluoride to brainwash society."

He was letting the boy control everything: their environment, their progress. Not wise. But what choice did he have? *I'm tethered to reality*, Jack told himself. *I can chase this a little further. I'll find my way back.*

As he stood he thought of the question that had troubled him since the day Cole had OD'd. "Last week, you said we'd forgotten a day. That it was really Wednesday and not Tuesday, remember? You thought that we were reliving Tuesday for a second time."

"I remember."

"If we had already lived that day before, if we had repeated it somehow, what did we talk about the first time around? What did we talk about on the day I can't remember?"

"You told me about that day at the fair," said Cole. "The time Tony conned the man in the striped top hat."

2   Later that day, Sam found Jack in her kitchen nook, hunched over her outdated Dell desktop. He had the spare key. He slept here now. Theirs was a fast regression. Until a time came when one of them bothered to notice, she thought.

"What's doing?" Sam asked, planting a kiss on the side of his mouth.

Jack smiled, but she could tell he was distracted. "Research," he said. "This kid. Cole."

"Is this the crazy stuff?"

"Fluoride mind control? Yeah, it's out there."

"This is what broke Tony," she said, pointing at the screen. "He started boiling his water just like you're doing. And then he'd sit at the computer for hours. He used to sit right there."

"Tony was predisposed," said Jack. "Don't worry. I don't believe in this junk. But if I can get Cole to open up, maybe we can figure out how Tony left town. Maybe even find out *where* he is."

"And then what?"

"Then we find out why he killed your brother and how much trouble he's in."

"I meant what happens with us if you find him?"

"Oh," he said. "You want closure, right? I know I do. I need closure."

She stoked his hair. "Silly boy. There's no such thing as closure," she said. "I'm going to run a bath. I'm going to soak and smoke some pot. Come up with me."

"Soon as I'm done. Promise."

"It's Samantha, right?"

"Sam," she said. She was sitting in a squat room that was nothing but walls of glass separating the middle school guidance office from the rest of the administration wing. She watched Mrs. Brown, her science teacher, copy papers on a mimeograph machine twenty feet away. Across from Sam was Ms. Rissert, all hips under a purple mumu. She wore black cat-eye glasses that were all the rage.

"Is everything all right, dear?"

And here was the ledge she was supposed to step off. What Jack had convinced her to do. Where does this take me? she wondered.

Sam tried to start the waterworks but found no tears. Maybe every person has only so many.

"Hon, I know about your . . . situation. I know why you moved to Franklin Mills. I am so sorry. Unfortunately it's something I see a lot. A lot. Hard thing for families to work through. Is that what's troubling you?"

"That my brother makes me give him hand jobs?"

Ms. Rissert blushed and let go a nervous laugh. "Ah. Uh. Well. My. Yes. He's gone, right? In the navy? That's the arrangement, right?"

"He's home on leave."

She wrote something on a notepad. "He should have separate lodging. No good." She looked up at the girl, the eighth-grader. "Has your brother done anything . . . untoward?"

"Untoward? I don't know what that means. But he didn't make me give him any hand jobs."

Ms. Rissert sighed.

"He made me use my feet this time."

Ms. Rissert shook her head. "I'm going to do something about this. He should not be in the house. I'll have to talk with your father, of course."

"Okay," said Sam. "You should do that. Also, when you speak to my father, please ask him to stop making me take showers with him. He says he's trying to conserve water, but I don't know what that has to do with the hard-on he rubs on my ass when we're in there."

Sam watched Mrs. Brown fighting the mimeograph machine. Pink ink dripped down her flabby forearm. Sam drummed her fingers on the chair and then gave a challenging look to her guidance counselor. "So, what happens now?"

"Well, Samantha," said Ms. Rissert, "a lot happens now. But when it's over, you're going to be safe."

It was a long time before she saw Jack again.

Sam's first set of foster parents, to whom she was introduced that very night, lived in Boardman and had three sons. Sam wondered how the court matched kids with prospective guardians. There was no inherent intelligence behind the system. She pictured an upside-down top hat filled with the names of all the abandoned kids. Foster parents must come in and draw names at random. Within the space of a week Sam had given the oldest boy, a sixteen-year-old named Tad, a blow job and taught the youngest, a ten-year-old named Calvin, how to roll a joint. In hindsight, she had probably sabotaged that one on purpose to see if she could.

The second set of fosters was a tubby woman and her tubby husband, an accountant from Youngstown. They had no children. The man watched Sam shower through the bathroom window. Sam caught him the third night, and by the next day she was in the home of Stan and Melissa Polk.

The Polks had two kids: a daughter, Sarah, a year older than Sam, and Ben, age four. They lived in a duplex in Ravenna not far from the high school. They gave Sam her own room. The first night Sam pilfered a couple of Morleys from Melissa's purse. She tried to get Sarah to smoke with her on the back porch. No doing. Sarah wouldn't touch it. The girl just watched. After a few puffs Sam got bored and pitched the cigarettes into the bushes. The second night she left the bathroom door open a crack while she showered, to see if Stan was a creeper. But when she stepped out, the door was closed. On the third night Sam snuck out of her bedroom window with a change of clothes in her backpack and set off toward town. She was running away. Running to no-where. Just running to run. She was at the corner under a humming halogen light when someone said her name. It was Stan Polk. He stood behind her, hands in his pockets. "Where you off to?" "Arizona," she said. "Arizona's pretty far. You'll need money for the bus." He handed her seventy dollars, folded neatly. Her hands looked so wrinkled and orange in the light. Look how old those hands looked. No one else could possibly understand how old she felt, how old and low. No one could survive feeling this way. She started to cry. "Not your fault," said Stan. "You just forgot how to trust people. In the morn-ing, if you still want to go, I'll drive you to the Greyhound station in Akron. I'll pack you twenty sandwiches. Peanut butter and jelly." Sam walked back home with him. She was still there three months later when Jack pulled into the driveway in his first car, that rusty black Volkswagen Rabbit. It was Sam's birthday. She was fourteen.

Sam was still alone when the tub water turned tepid, the joint noth-ing but ash in the tumbler on the floor. Jack never made it upstairs that night.

3 The next day, Cole was off the heart monitor. Jack found the boy inside his room, standing on a chair, looking out the window at Fisher Road, arms swinging as if he were conducting a pit orchestra. The boy wore earbuds hooked to an iPod on his belt.

Jack knocked loudly on the doorframe. Cole tugged the earbuds out and tossed the iPod onto his desk. "Hello," he said, looking at Jack and then at the folder in his hands. "You brought notes."

"I did some research," Jack explained. "I told you, I'm in this."

Cole sat in the chair beside his desk and motioned for Jack to sit in the recliner. The boy was sweaty, out of breath from his conducting. He wiped at his forehead with the bottom of his shirt, revealing a pink, hairless belly.

"I'm a research geek," said Jack. "It's the by-product of loving history. There's a ton of research in college. You either love it or you drop out."

"Tony hated it."

"He would."

"So, did you find anything interesting?"

Jack leaned forward in the recliner. "I'll tell you what interests me," he began. "This is forced medication of the American public. No argument there. Fluoride is medication in our drinking water. I never really thought about it like that. But the benefits are clear." He paged through his notes. "Adding fluoride to our water supply costs about ninety-four cents per person per year, and studies have shown a forty percent reduction in cavities since fluoridation became official policy, in 1951. That saves everyone from paying higher insurance premiums. When I was in middle school we used to gargle with a fluoride rinse every Wednesday because so many of us only have wells out here. They brought Dixie cups filled with the stuff to our classrooms. Never had a cavity."

Cole nodded. "What did you make of fluoride's link to the Nazis?"

"A lot of people think there's some connection. But there's nothing really to back it up."

"The first time fluoride was put in drinking water was inside Nazi concentration camps," said Cole. "It made the prisoners more docile."

"I mean, I saw that. But I couldn't find a single supporting document."

Cole pulled a black binder from the shelf above his desk and opened it to a page marked with a pink tab. "This is a letter from a research chemist named Charles Perkins to the Lee Foundation for Nutritional Research, dated October second, 1954: 'Repeated doses of *infinitesimal* amounts of fluoride will in time reduce an individual's power to resist domination, by slowly poisoning and narcotizing a certain area of the brain, thus making him subversive to the will of those who wish to govern him.'"

"But . . ."

Cole held up a finger. "He goes on to say, 'I was told of this entire scheme by a German chemist who was also prominent in the Nazi movement at the time.'"

"I saw that, Cole, but I could find no evidence that Perkins really existed."

The boy looked back to his folder. "How about this? It's a quote from Dr. E. H. Bronner, Albert Einstein's nephew: 'Fluoridation of our community water systems could well become their most subtle weapon for our sure physical and mental deterioration.'"

"I found that, too," said Jack. "Like I said, I'm a research geek. I looked into it. The only documents linking this guy, Bronner, to Einstein appear to be hoaxes. Bronner was not even a real doctor. His biggest claim to fame was a cure-all soap made from olive oil and hemp."

"Is that right?"

"Yes."

Cole stared at Jack for a while, unreadable. Then he smiled. Jack had the overwhelming sense that whatever he was doing, even as he was discrediting some of the boy's theories, he was doing exactly what Cole wanted him to do. The boy was manipulating him. And he wasn't even trying to hide it.

"Do you know what fluoride *is*?" Cole asked.

Jack nodded. "That part is a little . . . disconcerting. It's a by-product of fertilizer manufacturing."

"It's hazardous waste," said Cole. "And the sources on this issue are a little more credible. *Time* magazine, 2005: 'Ingested in high doses, fluoride is indisputably toxic; it was once commonly used in rat poison.'"

"Yeah. That's not good."

"In 2000, a congressional subcommittee discovered that fluoride had never been subjected to toxicological testing by the FDA."

"Is that true?" asked Jack.

"It is. It was never tested because the FDA knows it's dangerous. Hydrogen fluoride is considered hazardous waste by the EPA. It's regulated. You can't bury the stuff as easily as you can put it in our water. And not just our water, Jack. In regions where they don't yet have fluoridated water, they put it in their *salt*."

Salt was, Jack knew, a time-tested source of benevolent forced medication; iodized salt, after all, was created to reduce cases of mental retardation in rural communities.

"Have you looked closely at your tube of toothpaste lately?" Cole asked.

Jack laughed. "Can't say I have."

"Next time you're in your bathroom, check it out. There's a warning label on there, the kind they put on packs of cigarettes. It says if a kid swallows more than a pea-size drop, you're supposed to call poison control."

"I didn't know that."

"Most people don't. If they did, they'd have to ask why, if your kids can't swallow a little fluoride, why are we putting it in their *drinking* water? Why are we bathing in it?"

"Okay, it's creepy. I don't know about Nazi scientists being behind it, but it does make me wonder."

"Did you look into how it all started?" asked Cole.

Jack referred to his notes, flipping to the beginning. "Guy named H. Trendley Dean is credited for first fluoridating drinking water.

He conducted an experiment in 1945, put fluoride in the water system in Grand Rapids, Michigan. It was so successful it caught on with the rest of the country by the early sixties."

"How much did you learn about Dean?"

"Let's see . . . um . . . he was the first director of the National Institute of Dental Research, in 1948."

"What did he do before moving to Grand Rapids?"

"He was the director of epidemiological studies for the United States Army."

"Care to guess where Dean was stationed during the war?"

Jack blinked. "Germany?"

"That's right. That's exactly right."

"So you think our own government is putting fluoride in our water because we learned from the Nazis that it makes us easier to control?"

"Something like that," said Cole. "But let's not worry about the whys just yet. These Impossibilities I want you to think about are the hows. This is *how* the government is executing the biggest con in history. Once you see how their machine is set up, you'll be able to see what they're up to. Don't worry. We'll get there."

"So what's next?" asked Jack.

"Chemtrails."

"Chemtrails? What are chemtrails?"

"Those lines in the sky," said Cole. "You see them every day. Exhaust from jet planes. Dangerous chemicals raining down on us. Mind-control drugs mixed in with jet fuel."

"Looks like I have some light reading."

Cole laughed. "Want to play *Mario Kart* before you go?"

"Are you kidding?" said Jack. "I never lose."

4   Just outside Franklin Mills, Tallmadge Road becomes SR 14, a two-lane highway that weaves through allotments and over mud-colored lakes before intersecting with SR 88 in Ravenna. Jean took a right onto 88 and drove toward Mantua, a sleepy town on the top

of a hill. She drove through the brick-fronted downtown, a scene from a cheap Western, and on through a neighborhood of wide lawns and antebellum houses draped with bunting for the Fourth of July. Down a side street, beyond a train car that had been converted into an apothecary, Jean pulled into the parking lot of a low brick building: St. Mary's, home to sixty patients suffering from various forms of dementia, primarily Alzheimer's.

Jean wished she could erase her own memories. She welcomed any disease that might eat away at the neural connections inside her that housed remembrances of Mark Brooks. He'd introduced her to meth and that had been like heaven for a while. She craved that corruption even now. Could feel that pull, that tug toward welcome oblivion.

God grant me the serenity . . .

Jean didn't remember the night Paige was conceived. Had it been consensual? Mark never explained it. Jean pretended that she remembered, and never asked. As much as she had reason to be repulsed by him, all reason exhausted itself after a snort of his stuff. That drug. That poison. Well. There was a reason it was an epidemic in Franklin Mills. It woke you up to the beauty of being. It lifted you out of the squalor. It made you want to live and live and live. Jean knew they had sex sometimes, in the exaltation, when everything was on fire. But Mark couldn't keep it up for long. A small price. Let him do his thing. She had been lost. And in the end it brought salvation of a kind, didn't it? Paige kept her anchored. Paige brought her back.

And now, Jack. Having Jack back was good. She owed it to him to find out exactly what the Captain knew about Mark's murder. Because he had to know something. The Captain had been with both Mark and Tony the day Tony had disappeared. She wiped away the tears with the back of her sleeve and got out of the car.

The lobby was modern and clean, all heavy carpet and high-backed chairs, end tables full of magazines. The wings were dimly lit. The halls smelled of sweat and shit and a damp hotness masked by Lysol. She found the Captain in room 16.

"Mr. Felter?" said the orderly who had accompanied Jean, a large black man with vacant eyes.

The Captain sat in a pleather recliner, facing a watercolor painting of cattails and lily pads that hung on the wall. He didn't respond.

"Your father is not well," said the orderly.

"We'll be fine," said Jean.

The orderly walked back down the hall after a load of linen.

Jean went to her father and was startled by what she found. The Captain had wasted away in the two weeks since she'd had him committed. He was a skeleton wearing a skin suit. How much weight had he lost? Could it be twenty pounds already? That seemed impossible. But she could see the tracks of his ribs under his white cotton shirt, the radar dish of his hips against his corduroy slacks. His arms were limp sausages upon the armrests. The Captain's eyes were gray and unfocused. He was adrift in his broken memories.

"Dad?" she said. "Captain Felter?"

His right iris tugged south, then floated back.

"Captain Felter," she said again, sternly.

He looked at her, through her. His mouth opened; a rivulet of drool cascaded over his bottom lip and fell onto his shirt.

This man was so strong, she thought. *He used to carry me on his shoulders. He lifted rocks out of the ground for our fireplace.*

"Tell me about Mark," she said.

The Captain licked his lips.

"Captain, what happened to Mark Brooks? Did Tony kill him, Dad? Or was it you?"

His mouth opened and closed like a fish fighting for air. And it seemed like something was coming out, some kind of sound. He was trying to say something.

Jean leaned closer. She brought her ear almost to his lips and listened.

"What box, Dad?" she asked. "What do you mean?"

He opened his mouth again and what came out this time was much louder and more defined: "Where is she, Duong? Where is Qi?"

Jean put a hand on his arm and it silenced him. His eyes returned to the painting on the wall. He said nothing more. She could bear to sit with him only another five minutes. Then she left.

5 Jack brought a gift for the boy the next morning, something he'd found in a box of Tony's old things. "I got something for you," he said, tossing a gray cartridge at Cole, who snagged it in midair.

"*GoldenEye?*"

"The best multiplayer shooter ever created. You might be able to beat me in Mushroomville, but I clean house with grenade launchers in the Temple."

"Cool." The boy smiled, clearly touched. It had been a while since he'd been given a gift by anyone other than his mother, Jack could tell. Video games, to be more specific, were the kind of presents that came from fathers.

Jack took a seat and folded his hands over his notebook. "So, chemtrails."

"Chemtrails," said Cole, setting the cartridge down. "What did you find?"

"Enough for another *X-Files* movie," said Jack.

"I wish this was fiction."

"A conspiracy to mix mind-altering drugs into jet fuel? It's pretty fringe stuff. Not much in the way of credible sourcing, either. And nobody can agree on motive. I mean, some think the government is trying to combat global warming by putting chemicals into the air to deflect sunlight. Others say they're making it rain vaccines so that sick people don't drive up the cost of health care. You think, what? The feds are mixing fluoride with the fuel?"

"Fluoride or something else that makes us suggestible."

"What do you have to back it up?"

"What about the simple fact that there is something going on?" said Cole. "You talk to old people, know what they say? They say jet trails used to dissipate. They called them *contrails* back then. That's short for condensation trail. Contrails form when jet fuel creates water vapor behind an aircraft. Only now the trails don't disappear. So their chemical makeup must be different."

"How are we supposed to know our parents aren't remembering wrong?" he posed.

Cole smiled. "Good point, Jack. Good point. But you're getting ahead of yourself. What about this? In 2001, a United States congressman introduced a law to ban chemtrails. Now if chemtrails don't exist, why did he have to ban them?"

"First of all, that congressman was Dennis Kucinich, the guy who says he saw a UFO at Shirley MacLaine's house."

"But what about—"

Jack held up a hand. "I'll give you this much," he said. "It's not without precedent. Some governments *have* sprayed deadly chemicals on cities in the past. Britain's Ministry of Defense experimented on civilians after World War Two." He opened his notebook and withdrew an article he had printed at Sam's house. Cole read along while Jack paraphrased.

"According to an article published in *The Observer* in April 2002, the MOD used airplanes to disperse large amounts of zinc cadmium sulfide over residential neighborhoods in an experiment that lasted from 1955 to 1963. They wanted to know how biological weapons would spread if the Soviets ever bombed them. It was an epidemiological study, like the fluoride experiments in America. Of course, we now know that cadmium causes lung cancer."

Cole scribbled notes in the margins of the printout.

"It gets worse," said Jack. "From 1961 to 1968, the MOD sprayed an aerosolized form of *E. coli* above an English village from a ship off the Dorset coast, exposing a million people to the bacteria. To this day, people in Dorset suffer higher rates of birth defects and miscarriages."

He paused and Cole looked at him with an expression Jack thought might be relief. "If they could spray *E. coli* from a ship," said Cole, "they could rig something to spray from a jet. And if the U.K. is doing it, don't you think we are, too?"

"In fact," said Jack, "the CIA has admitted to using civilians as guinea pigs for chemical and psychological warfare experiments in the past. In the sixties and seventies they dropped acid in the drinks of strangers in bars to test the effects of LSD. From 1959 to 1962, the CIA funded a 'stress' experiment using live, unwitting subjects at Harvard, under the direction of Dr. Henry Murray. To test levels of psychological stress, Murray and his group isolated certain students and then belittled and berated them until they thought they were worthless. They broke those poor kids. One particular subject, dubbed 'Lawful,' did not take well to the test and began writing threatening letters and then a rambling manifesto. You probably know Lawful's other nickname better, the Unabomber. The CIA created Ted Kaczynski." Jack set his notebook down. "But secret chemicals mixed in with commercial jet fuel? Too many people would have to know."

"So maybe what you do is you get them to forget," said Cole.

"What do you mean?"

The boy shook his head.

"So what's next?" asked Jack.

"Impossibility Number Three is something I can actually prove," said Cole. "I can show you."

"Something here at Haven?"

"No. But close by."

"Wait. You want me to drive you somewhere?"

"I wish," said Cole. He pulled something out of his pocket. It looked like a modified Bluetooth. He tossed it to Jack.

"What's this?"

"It's a Looxcie," the boy said. "I ordered it off Amazon. It's a camera. You put it around your ear. Streams live video to a secure URL I can access on my laptop. I'll give you directions over the phone. Cool, huh?"

Jack considered this, weighing the risk. "All right," he said. "But I want you to show me *exactly* what Tony saw. I want to go where he went."

"Deal."

They shook hands. The boy's was clammy and Jack wondered, again, if Cole was trying to pass delusion to him like some communicable sickness, like something an epidemiologist might study.

"Grenade launchers in the Temple, then?" asked Cole.

"Let's roll," said Jack.

6 Later, Jack sat on Sam's porch sipping a Diet Coke, watching jets paint a crisscross grid over the sky. It was beautiful, in a way. Humanity's mark on the heavens. Cole was right; the contrails, chemtrails, or whatever, didn't dissipate. It was like they'd been drawn in permanent marker.

He wasn't crazy. He'd seen crazy. He knew crazy.

Jack wasn't crazy.

I'm not crazy.

No, he wasn't.

Sam joined him on the porch. By then the chemtrails were tinged a warm rose as the sun played with the tops of the trees.

"Whatcha lookin' at?"

"Nothing," he lied. "Just thinking."

"I thought I smelled some old engine trying to turn out here."

"Funny."

She sat next to him and twisted the hairs at the back of his head with her fingers.

He smiled. "Everything you do makes me feel nineteen again."

She rested her head on his shoulder.

"Where'd you go today?" he asked.

"Into town. Started the paperwork."

"Paperwork for what?"

"Divorce, Jack. If Tony's still alive, I have to make it official."

Above the horizon the first star appeared, a dim beacon on the red. Its light was millions of years old and only just arriving.

"I like it here," he said.

"Franklin Mills?"

"Here, with you."

She tugged his earlobe. "You can be a real cheeseball. But I love you, too. Now come inside and take off my clothes."

7 "Ready," said Jack as he started his car the next morning. He sipped from a small thermos and studied his reflection in the rear-view mirror. He looked like a cheap cyborg. The Looxcie was hooked around his right ear and his Bluetooth was attached to his left. Back at Haven, Cole could see what Jack was seeing, streaming live on his computer, and they could speak to each other using the Bluetooth. The future really was now.

"Ready," said Cole.

Jack pulled out of Sam's driveway and onto Giddings, steering the Saturn toward Tallmadge.

"Looks good," said Cole. "Head for the highway."

"What am I looking for?" asked Jack.

"TacMars. Ever heard of TacMars?"

"Is that something astronomical?"

"TacMars. As in Tactical Markings. TacMars are directional markers placed out in the open, on road signs. Directions to secret government bases." He spoke calmly, earnestly, and for all his preparation, Jack found himself wanting to believe.

He turned right onto Tallmadge, passing Mr. Bunts's squab farm. "How did you learn about these TacMars?" he asked.

"My father worked for a government agency," said Cole. "They called themselves 'the Collectors' or 'the Twelve Angry Men,' because there were only a dozen of them for the whole world and they were all men, I think. Don't know if they were always angry. Man, Dad had a temper sometimes, though. Anyway, that's what they called themselves. He worked in the financial district, like he told my mother. But he didn't trade stocks. Technically, he worked for the NSA, but nobody at the NSA would have known who he was. Where his office was, was the thirteenth story of a skyscraper. These Collectors hunted down certain artifacts. If these artifacts fell into the wrong hands, they could reveal the Big Mystery—the mystery that made Tony run away."

Cole paused for a moment while a nurse came in to give him his morning meds. Jack could hear her in the background. Through the open window he could smell the blooming lilac and dandelion. Spring had finally come to Franklin Mills, just a week before summer.

"Sometimes my father would take me with him," Cole continued when the nurse was gone. "Once, we drove all the way to Buffalo to pick up an artifact. We kept to back roads in this weird car he drove for work, this shiny brownish thing that hummed like a vacuum cleaner. A man who lived in a double-wide trailer in the mountains had it. It was a plaque. Looked like something you'd win for being employee of the month somewhere. Except the engraved date said 2031. My dad bought it off this guy. Collecting was only half his job, really. What he had to do then was deposit the artifact. There are drop-off points hidden all over the United States—the world, in fact. And to find these facilities you have to follow the TacMars."

"Okay."

"The code is relatively simple. Once you understand it, you'll see TacMars everywhere. Here's one coming up now, Jack. Look."

Up ahead, Jack saw a brown sign directing traffic to the baseball fields behind Nostalgia. GILMOUR PARK, it read. BASEBALL, HIKING TRAIL, PUBLIC RESTROOMS. There were three white arrows pointing to the right.

"Three arrows is the key. Three arrows on a sign always means 'Collector Facility, this way.' It's always three arrows. Get it? If you see a sign with one or two arrows, that's just a normal sign. If there are three, that's a TacMar."

"Your dad told you this?"

"He showed me. There's another one!" On the shoulder just before the on-ramp to I-76 was a small green sign. It had three arrows pointing northwest toward the highway: KENT, AKRON, CLEVELAND, it read. A fourth arrow pointed up, toward RAVENNA.

"The extra 'up' arrow means 'airlift,'" said Cole. "If the Collectors ever got in trouble, that's where they could get airlifted back to headquarters."

"All right."

"All right I believe you or all right, what?"

"I mean . . . the Ohio Department of Transportation is in on the conspiracy, too?"

"Hey, don't be a jerk."

"Just trying to understand your theory."

"ODOT just puts the signs up. The agency designs them."

"Okay."

"I told you I'd show you."

"Arrows on road signs aren't enough to sell me on secret government drop points," said Jack. "But it's a cool idea."

"No," said Cole. "I mean, I'll show you. I'm taking you to one of the drop-off points. You can go in and see for yourself."

8   About an hour later Jack found himself cruising a dirt road in that desolate, overgrown region of Ohio near the Pennsylvania border. He thought their destination might be Pymatuning State Park. Jack could smell the lake through the open windows. Pymatuning was an enormous man-made reservoir that had drowned seventeen thousand acres of prime farmland a century ago. Cole directed Jack down a two-lane road that wound through the village of Jamestown, where a Tastee Freez was being overrun by Little Leaguers. "Are we getting close?" he asked.

"Have you seen any TacMars?"

"I'm not sure."

"Look!"

A maroon sign appeared on the right. PYMATUNING STATE PARK, it read. DAM. SPILLWAY. RESTROOMS. Three arrows pointed to the right. A forth arrow, this one tilted, pointed northeast.

"What's with the tilted arrow?"

"That's code for 'drop point.' You know, where they could get rid of the artifacts."

"So . . ."

"Just follow the signs."

Jamestown gave way to rural countryside, quiltwork patches of corn and alfalfa. Old Victorians in stages of disrepair leaned easterly on single-acre lawns. Jack passed a tackle shop that doubled as a grocery, then followed the TacMars onto a dirt road. The lake appeared through the trees on his left, a wide expanse of deep brown that sparkled in the sun. It was full of boaters. Fishermen cast lines from shore, white contractor buckets full of sunfish at their feet.

"Before white men, this was Mound Builder territory," Cole whispered in his ear. "The Indians built giant rock mounds here to honor dead warriors. But it's all hidden underwater now."

"Are there angry Indian ghosts here, too?"

"There's no such thing as ghosts, Jack."

Around a corner, the dam appeared. It was a quarter mile long, lined by slabs of granite that sloped to the water. The lee side was a sharp hill that cut to a creek fed by the reservoir's steady release of water. Jutting from the dam was an odd medieval-looking cottage made of stone. It seemed out of place, ancient. It had a single wooden door and windows barred against the world. A cast-iron weather vane twisted in the breeze above its slate roof. It sat above the water, and the bridge connecting it to the dam looked like the kind a troll might live under. THE GATE HOUSE, a sign said.

"The Gate House is one of the ways into the Underground," said Cole. "Everything we need is in the Underground. My dad only really went there to deposit the stuff he collected. He took me inside. I'll show you."

What happens when I go inside the Gate House and all that's in there is a bunch of stinky lawn mowers? Jack wondered. What might the boy do when confronted with the evidence of his own insanity? Of course, that wasn't what he was most afraid of. What he was most afraid of was opening the Gate House door and finding a staircase leading into the darkness, into some capital-*U* Underground where incongruous Nazi artifacts were being stored for purposes unknown.

He turned the car into a gravel lot across from the Gate House. He got out and looked at the old rock building.

"What if it's locked?" asked Jack.

"I know the combination."

Jack was about to cross the road when the Gate House door opened and a figure dressed in a charcoal suit and a Panama hat stepped out. The man was too far away and the sky too overcast for Jack to make out further details.

Cole screamed in his ear and Jack jumped at the sound. "A Hound!" he shouted. "Holy shit, a Hound!"

"What is a Hound?" asked Jack.

"It will kill you. It will kill you if it sees you. Run!"

Jack didn't run. But he did turn around, away from the Gate House, and walked down the other side of the dam to a line of trees below the parking lot.

"What do you want me to do, Cole?"

"Get into the woods," he said. "Hide behind a tree. Be quiet."

"Why?"

"I don't care if you believe me or not," Cole whispered. "Please just humor me for the next few minutes. If you don't, that thing will kill you."

Jack sighed and stepped into the woods, onto a carpet of fern and skunkweed. When he was a hundred feet in, he turned around. The man in the Panama hat was standing between the gravel lot and the forest now. He was holding some tool, twisting it together in his hands. Part of it looked like a small radar dish.

"Fuck," whispered Cole. "In a second the Hound is going to be able to hear your thoughts. You have to empty your mind."

"This is nuts."

"Clear your mind of any thought about us. If it hears you thinking, it will come down here and kill you."

"I don't believe in this, Cole. I—"

"Do I sound like I'm making this up?"

No. He didn't. If this boy was crazy, his insanity was complete and total. Jack felt the first pangs of real fear, though he couldn't tell if he was actually afraid of the man in the Panama hat or if he was simply afraid that he'd allowed the boy to get too far into his head.

"How do I clear my mind?" asked Jack.

"A wolf, a goat, and a head of lettuce sit on the shore of a lake," said Cole. "There is an island in the lake and a boat to take you there. If left alone, the goat will eat the lettuce and the wolf will eat the goat. How do you get the wolf, the goat, and the lettuce onto the island safely?"

For a moment what Cole had said was such a non sequitur Jack thought the boy's mind had finally broken. Then he understood. It was a logic puzzle, a way to keep his mind from forming any thought except for the solution.

"Come on, Jack."

"Give it to me again."

Cole did.

Jack pictured the problem. In his mind he saw a wolf, a goat, and a head of lettuce sitting on the side of Pymatuning Lake, a rowboat resting on the sandy shore. He pictured himself pulling the goat on board, rowing it to the island, letting it out to munch on the scrub grass, then returning for the lettuce. But when he dropped the lettuce off to return for the wolf, the goat ate it. He tried again, this time returning for the wolf, only to have the wolf devour the goat on the island. He'd never been good at these brainteasers.

Finally, Jack gave up and peered around the tree. "He's gone," he said.

"Good."

"Who do you think it was?"

"A Hound," said Cole. "The Hounds are the security force for the Collectors. They're not human. Not entirely. They were created by that Nazi scientist Mengele."

"Wait. Josef Mengele?"

"Right."

"What do you mean, 'created'?"

"I don't know the details. I just know they're called the Hounds. That's what my dad called them. He was a fan of Sherlock Holmes, and since those things' headquarters are in the Catskills, he called them the Hounds of the Catskills, after the book *The Hound of the Baskervilles*. He told me that in the book, people were being killed by a giant beast on the moor that they thought was a devil dog but it actually turned out to be an escaped orangutan. Funny thing is, he remembered it wrong."

"Yeah?"

"Yeah. The orangutan wasn't from *The Hound of the Baskervilles*. He got the story mixed up with 'The Murders in the Rue Morgue,' the Edgar Allan Poe story that *inspired* Sherlock Holmes. Anyway, he called them the Hounds."

"You're asking me to believe too much," said Jack. "It's too much all at once."

"Everything will fit together soon," said Cole. "I promise. Just have a little faith in the story I'm trying to tell you."

"Back to the Gate House, then?"

"Not with that thing out there," said Cole. "There might be more. Jack, it's like they knew you were coming."

9   Sam knew just by looking at him that Jack had lost control of the situation with the kid. His face was pale in the diffused lamp light of Nostalgia, his eyes shifty and bloodshot from too much thinking. It was a look Sam knew well. It was the same way Tony had looked the day he came home with sand on his shoes, the day he disappeared.

"I couldn't stay in your house," said Jack, leaning against a framed Uncle Wiggily board game from the twenties. "It felt strange to be there by myself."

Sam was behind the register, reading a crinkled copy of *The Long Tomorrow* she'd found hidden in the bottom of a box of tattered paperbacks. Gordon Lightfoot played softly from the overhead speakers.

"You okay?" she asked.

"I'm fine," he said, too quickly. Then he shook his head. "It's just, I thought we were close to something today. Like maybe I was close to a clue about where Tony took off to. But it didn't work out."

"What did you two do all day?"

"We talked about stuff like secret military codes on highway signs. Tonight he has me looking into something called HAARP."

"Harp?"

"H-A-A-R-P."

"What is it?"

Jack shrugged. His cell phone rang, a shrill chirping from his pants. He looked at the display, said, "One minute, Sam," and walked out of the shop to take the call.

As Sam watched him go she was suddenly aware that she was in love with him again. Their love was not such a passionate thing. This was old love. Stronger, almost indifferent, like old magic. And with it came a quick forgetting of the span of years that had separated them, a conscious back-turning from the bad decisions that had kept them apart. And wasn't there was something magical in that?

There are days in everyone's life they would forget if they could. Days for do-overs. Days full of enough bad decisions to distract the course of a life forever.

For Sam and Jack and Tony, that day was the same day: September 11, 1999.

It was Virginia who called. When it was bad news it was always Virginia.

It was a Saturday morning. Sam lay on Jack, her head resting on his naked chest. They were sharing a twin bed in his dorm at Miami U. She had driven out to see him the night before and they'd stayed up past three watching cheesy horror movies and fucking. Fast-food bags and condom wrappers were strewn about the floor and the room smelled of delicious funk.

Jack reached behind his head and snatched the phone from its cradle. "'Lo?" he said.

"Johnny? It's Mom."

He heard the panic in her voice. His first thought was that his father had died in a plane crash en route to La Guardia.

"What happened?" he asked. The tone of his voice alarmed Sam and she looked up at him, waiting.

"Huhhh," Virginia sighed. "It's Tony. Tony's mother. She's in the hospital. In a coma. I think she's going to die, Johnny."

"His father?"

"He beat her head in with a radio. Then he called the police and told them what he'd done. The cops found him on the porch, still holding the radio, rocking back and forth, repeating one word: forget, forget, forget."

"Where's Tony?"

"Nobody knows. He hasn't called you?"

"No."

"You better get home."

They left Sam's car at school and raced back to Franklin Mills in Jack's rickety Rabbit, its muffler kicking against the carriage. By the time Jack got there the Captain was back with some new information: doctors at Robinson Memorial were saying Tony's mother would likely survive but there would be significant brain damage. Tony's father, meanwhile, was confined in a straitjacket in the county jail. "His mind just broke," the Captain said. Virginia sat with Jean at the kitchen table, their eyes puffy.

"I'm going to look for him," said Jack, pulling Sam by the hand toward the door.

"I've been all over Franklin Mills," the Captain said. "He ain't here, man."

"I can find him."

For the next five hours, until the sun was a memory on the westerly clouds, Jack and Sam drove over the quiet roads of Portage County. They tried everywhere they'd ever been: the movie theater, the arcade in Kent, the nudie bar in Rootstown, the bowling alley. But no one had seen him or his ridiculous BMW.

A quarter moon peeked through the treetops by the time they returned to SR 14. Instead of pulling into his family's driveway, Jack continued on to Porter, hooked a right, and drove up the access road to Claytor Lake. There, hidden in the waist-high goldenrod, was Tony's car.

"You don't think he killed himself?" whispered Sam.

Jack shook his head. In fact, that's exactly what he thought.

In the moonlight Jack could make out the dark liquid glass of the water's surface and the hard edge of the earth around it. They searched the shadows *of the shoreline. There, a silhouette against the stars. Tony stood atop a sand-stone boulder on the ridge to their left.*

"Whatcha doing, Tony?" he asked.

Tony shrugged. His face was slack, devoid of emotion. There was less than an inch between his feet and the drop-off.

Jack leaned against the boulder, beside an Iroquois petroglyph that resembled an aspen leaf. He watched his friend sway slowly, like he could hear music they could not.

"I told everybody. I told them he was sick. Nobody believed me."

"I know, man. I know."

"I've been standing here all day. I don't want this memory, any memory from this day. It's too much. Don't want it. I should kill myself, I think. But I can't. I'm too scared. I'm a coward."

"The hell you are."

Tony shook his head. "I don't know what happens next. I don't have a family anymore. Not really."

"You have us, Tony," said Sam.

He looked up and held her gaze.

"Come down," said Jack.

"It feels like giving up if I come down now."

"So jump," said Jack. "The water's nice and cool. Jump and I'll come in after you."

"Good fucking idea," said Tony. He stepped off the boulder and fell ten feet to the water below. Jack was a second behind. He swam underwater to his friend and grabbed him by the shoulders, hugging him closely as they rose to the surface.

"I can't feel my legs," Tony said.

"It's okay," said Jack. "I got you."

Jack started laughing. It was a hysterical laugh, full of relief instead of joy. He laughed so hard he struggled to breathe as he pulled Tony to the shallow end. Sam was in the water, too. She'd had time to strip down to her cheap cotton underwear. The water was icy but refreshing. The three of them rested in the shallows, bouncing against the sandy ledge.

Jack hugged his friend.

"Get off before you give me an accidental boner," said Tony.

Jack backed away and Sam swam to Tony and hugged him. Then she laughed. "Not a moment too soon," she said.

Sam looked at Jack. She was seventeen now. A young woman who'd kicked off her fears in the years since the county fair and that scorching August when they were kids. There was a question in her eyes, and they were so close in so many ways she didn't need to voice it. Jack nodded, smiled, and drifted on his back toward the beach. Sam turned to Tony and slipped her legs around him. She leaned forward and brushed her chest against his.

"What are you doing?" he whispered.

"Making you feel better," she said. She took his right hand and placed it on her left breast. Then she moved up his body and placed her mouth on his. His lips were softer than Jack's. Almost feminine. He broke away to look for Jack, but he was stepping out of the water already, giving them privacy. "It's okay," Sam assured him.

In a moment Tony was tossing his clothes away. And then he was inside her, she was around him, and when he came, he bit her lip and she moaned softly.

They took Tony back to Jack's dorm at Miami U and later that night the three of them climbed under the flannel blankets of the narrow bed. Tony kissed Sam as Jack spooned up to her from behind. They made love like that, each in turn. And when they were finished they slept through the morning.

It became routine. Every week when Sam drove out to visit Jack, Tony rode with her. They'd watch TV, drink beer, and inevitably end up naked in bed together. Jack was never suspicious of their time back in Franklin Mills. He trusted them. But who did Tony have anymore other than Sam?

Jack didn't understand when Tony arrived alone one weekend.

"I didn't mean to, Jack. I didn't. It just happened," Tony told him.

They were in love. Sam was moving in. There was a ring. Not an engagement ring, but a ring. This was happening.

"We don't want to lose you," said Tony.

Jack had pointed at his dorm room door and that was the last time he'd seen his old friend.

A few minutes later, Jack came back inside Nostalgia. He looked frazzled, manic.

"Who was that?"

"Cole," he said. "I have some more work to do. Meet you back at your place?"

"Home," she said, kissing him. "I'll meet you at home 'round eight."

Jack smiled. "See you at home."

10 "I wouldn't call if it wasn't important," said Cole. "That Hound followed you back to Franklin Mills."

Jack paced back and forth in the gravel lot outside Nostalgia, his phone pressed to his ear. "What are you talking about?"

"I saw it drive by Haven in one of those weird cars. It parked outside, looked at my window. I could see its funny hat."

"Cole, that man I saw at the park was some surveyor or something. He was mapping the lake or taking a water sample. That's what he was doing with that GPS or whatever it was in his hands."

"I think we need to step up your learning curve," said Cole. "We can finish the gradient tomorrow, if you're up to it."

"I am," he said. *More than ready to be done with it*, he thought.

"Then look into the Sixth Impossibility tonight, too."

"Okay."

"Here it is. Our current calendar is not accurate. This is not the year we think it is. That's the Sixth Impossibility. Our chronology has been altered."

"And what about the Seventh?"

"We'll get to the Seventh together," he said. "Tomorrow."

THE WHOLE TRUTH

They ended where they began, in the common room of Haven at a table by the window overlooking the pond. Cole was playing checkers with a thin black man when Jack arrived. A transistor radio propped against the window played an old Nirvana song.

> As a friend
> As an old enemy

"Time's up, Russell," said Cole.

"I gotchoo anyway," the man said, pushing pieces into a box and winking at Jack. When he got up to leave the man rapped his knuckles on the table three times, scratched the back of his head, then knocked three more times and nodded. "Got the devil in me," he told Jack.

"Can you keep him in there?"

"Keep him in there with threes. Thirty-three steps to my room.

Three sheets on my bed. Got to be threes, man. Threes keep him in. Don't you worry. I got it unner control."

"Thanks," said Jack.

The man saluted him and then walked away, counting his steps.

"That man's crazy," said Cole.

Jack sat down.

Cole looked out the window. On the other side of the lake a man stood against the shore with a fishing rod, his outline gray against a cobalt sky.

"What did you learn about HAARP?" asked Cole.

Jack opened his notebook. "High Frequency Active Auroral Research Program. Located in Gakona, Alaska," he said. "Found some pictures online. Pretty cool setup. A giant field of radar antennas in the middle of the Yukon wilderness. Looks like the bad guy's base in some James Bond movie. Construction began in 1993, funded by the air force, navy, and the University of Alaska. The official purpose of HAARP is to study the top layer of Earth's atmosphere. The ionosphere is kind of a natural force field of charged particles that surrounds the planet. We need the ionosphere to bounce long-distance radio signals over the horizon. Or did, before we had satellites. The government's current interest in the ionosphere has to do with detecting nuclear missiles launched from Russia."

"And . . ."

Jack grinned. "And HAARP has become the nexus of nearly all conspiracy theories. The project gets blamed for earthquakes, plane crashes, freak weather phenomena, everything from Gulf War Syndrome to that blackout we had in Cleveland a few years back." Jack held up a finger. "And yet, and yet . . . as with all good conspiracies, there is a kernel of truth."

"Such as?"

"HAARP uses technology based on the patents of a physicist from Columbia University named Bernard Eastlund. Now, Eastlund was all about weather manipulation. Made no bones about it. He wanted to kill tornadoes using microwave beams. And Eastlund had a theory about how to beam energy into the atmosphere so that it can be harvested at another location. Essentially he wanted to turn the ionosphere into a giant battery. No need for long pipelines to pull crude out of Alaska. You could convert the fuel to energy, send it into the ionosphere, and pull it down in New York City. But Eastlund's device could also be used to knock out an entire country's communication system. It could be turned into a weapon."

Cole nodded. "Essentially, HAARP is a giant radio transmitter," he said. "Perhaps the most powerful transmitter in the world. And yet nobody seems too interested in what message they might be transmitting."

Jack held up a hand. "It's not radio broadcasts like we think of them, not drive-time radio on WMMS."

"But it's the same equipment."

"Is it?"

"Yes, and if they wanted to broadcast WMMS to the entire Western Hemisphere, they could."

"But you don't think they're broadcasting *Rover's Morning Glory*, do you?"

Cole shook his head.

"What do you think they're broadcasting? What message is HAARP transmitting?"

"A very simple message," he said. "Forget, forget, forget."

Those words frightened Jack. Frightened him so much that he couldn't think of anything else for a moment. Where had he heard that before? He tried, but he could not remember.

After another second, he asked the question: "Forget what?"

"Forget what year it is."

"What year do you think it is?"

"I'm not entirely sure. I don't think anyone is anymore. But it's probably 2123. Give or take a couple years."

"What?"

"That's the Sixth Impossibility. I'm talking about the idea of an altered historical timeline, Jack. As a history teacher you have to know that such a thing is possible."

"I know a little about the notion of 'phantom time,'" said Jack, thinking back to his senior year at Miami U. After he lost Sam, he buried himself in classwork. He escaped into his mind, researching everything from the birth of Christianity to the postwar United States. He'd discovered the idea of phantom time that spring and had written his thesis on the emerging theory. "In 1991," Jack explained, "a German art historian named Heribert Illig presented evidence suggesting the Dark Ages, specifically the years 614 to 911 A.D., never occurred. Illig believed someone had inflated our modern calendar, that the calendar makers skipped over those years. He called this missing three hundred years 'phantom time.' There are scholars who believe that Pope Sylvester the Second may have altered our calendar by as much as six hundred years just so that he could be pope for the turn of the first millennium. A famous Russian mathematician, Anatoly Fomenko, claims the ancient Roman Empire existed only seven hundred years ago."

"Yes," said Cole. "Yes, yes, yes."

"However," Jack continued, "the more you look into these theories, the more flimsy they become. We have plenty of evidence that the ancient Romans were, in fact, ancient. But, okay, yes, history is constantly being rewritten and edited. Russian history books refer to Stalin as 'the most successful' leader ever. We do it, too. Our history books sometimes skip over the Civil War because they're printed in the South. You want to be careful, though. We're stepping into the realm of revisionism. Alternative history is the cornerstone of the neo-Nazi movement. They deny the Holocaust ever happened."

Cole watched him silently from across the table.

"But could someone turn our calendar back like they were resetting their watch to daylight saving time? Make us believe it's 2015 instead of 2123 or whatever? No. Not possible," said Jack. "What would you do with all the stuff that was made during those forgotten years? All that evidence?"

"You collect it," said Cole. "And you bury it. The only thing easier than rewriting history is *deleting* history."

Cole pushed a crumpled picture across the table to Jack. It was a

black-and-white newspaper photograph. A city. Cleveland, he saw—
there was the Terminal Tower in the background. Downtown, Public
Square. The photograph was full of people, packed to the corners of
the frame. People dressed in dark suits and hats, people hanging off
the backs of streetcars. He'd never seen so many people in one place
in all his life.

"When was this taken?" asked Jack.

"In 1929," said Cole. "You tell me, Jack. Where did all those
people go?"

He shrugged. "It's Cleveland. They moved away like everyone
else."

"I have pictures like this, pictures from before World War Two, in
New York, Chicago, Cincinnati, every major city in the country. The
United States was *full* of people back then. *Brimming* with people. So
where did they all go?"

Jack sighed. "Cole, why don't you just tell me what you think
happened? Can you give me the big picture now? Because, frankly,
I don't see how it all fits together. Fluoride, chemtrails, TacMars.
What does all that have to do with these pictures? Help me out."

Cole's eyes scanned the room. Two middle-aged women with
tired faces sat on a couch and stared at a TV on wheels, watching
Dr. Phil. Otherwise, they were alone.

"My dad didn't tell me everything, but he told me enough," Cole
whispered. "So here it is. World War Two was much bigger than
we were told. It went on through the fifties, escalating to all-out
nuclear war. A billion people died before the Allies finally defeated
the Axis in 1964. But before this victory, a most horrific and unfor-
gettable thing happened. A nearly complete genocide. And the blood
was on our hands."

Jack blinked. And listened.

Cole cleared his throat and continued. "When it was all over, we
wanted to forget what we let happen. That's what this is all about.
Forgetting. We built HAARP to transmit a code that fucks with our
minds and makes us forget. We put fluoride in our water and chemicals in the sky to make our minds more suggestive to this broadcast.

We filled our heads with an alternate version of history, a history where we never allowed this genocide to occur. It took us a hundred years to build the infrastructure to make this deception possible. Then we flipped the switch and suddenly everyone thought it was 1964 again. A hundred years, gone. Poof! Never happened."

Jack's mind buzzed. As crazy as it sounded, he could see it. He could understand the intention. That frightened him the most. If someone could create a forgetting machine, wouldn't our leaders be stupid enough to use it? Of course they would.

Cole went on. "But there had to be a handful of people who could remember the real history, right? In order to keep the machine running and to get rid of the evidence of that forgotten century. That's the Twelve Angry Men, the Collectors. They were given the Hounds as a security detail, mindless soldiers."

Cole was more like Tony than Jack had feared. His old friend had undoubtedly stepped inside this delusion enthusiastically, shirking off stone-cold reality with some relief. Jack knew now that Tony would have gone anywhere that Cole told him to go, done anything the boy suggested he do, because, in a world that didn't understand them, they spoke the same language.

And then he remembered.

Forget, forget, forget.

That had been what the voices inside Tony's father's head had told him. "Where did you tell Tony to go?" he asked.

"The only place that's safe for people who know about the Great Forgetting. The island. He used the Underground to get there."

"Pymatuning? The Gate House?"

"It's the closest way down."

Finally, a place to start.

"You look like you've figured something out," said Cole, with a smile.

"Yes. I think so," said Jack. "Thanks for sharing your story. I know it couldn't have been easy for you."

The boy laughed. "Ah, condescension! I shouldn't have expected anything more."

"I'm not trying to be condescending."

"It's all right. It's a crazy story, I know."

"It's too much to take on faith," Jack said. He was anxious to leave, anxious to start the real search for his old friend. "But I believe you believe it. I believe your father believed it, too. I don't think you're intentionally lying to me." He stood up and went to shake the boy's hand.

"Sit, Jack," Cole said with some force.

"I really have to go. There's a lot . . ."

"I'm not quite done. Give me one more minute."

Jack sat back in the chair with not a little trepidation.

"I know it's too much to take on faith," said Cole, turning the volume on the transistor radio up a bit. "Don't you think I know that?" He swept the dial to 100.7 FM, WMMS. *Rover's Morning Glory* was on; Rover's nasal baritone was egging on a female contestant who'd come on his dating segment.

"I wouldn't expect you to just trust me, so I'm going to show you."

"Show me what?"

The look on Cole's face alarmed Jack. It looked like pity. Like he pitied him for some reason. What on earth was the kid about to do? Jack readied himself for a quick escape. What if Cole had a knife?

"In a moment, you're going to be presented with a choice," said Cole. "You can either accept the story I've just told you is true, which is crazy, right? Fucking crazytown. Or you must choose to believe that you have suffered a mental breakdown. Not really a nice choice, I admit. But we're running out of time and you have to be pushed one way or another. I saw a Hound yesterday. It's not safe here."

"I'm going to go."

"If you leave now you'll never see Tony again. If you give me one more minute we'll find him together."

Jack paused. Waited.

"Give me your cell phone."

"This is fucking crazy."

"What could I possibly do with your cell phone that would change your mind? Or have you already started to doubt yourself?"

Jack slammed his cell phone on the table. Cole snatched it up in an instant.

"The forgetting machine monitors all electronic communication," he said. "It listens for certain key words in conversations. In the event anyone accidentally discovers the truth, the system is programmed to automatically reset a day and wipe everyone's memory. I know how to trigger it." He dialed a number before Jack could say anything, as if there was anything to say.

"Mom?" said Cole a moment later. "Mom, it's me. No, this is Jack's phone. No. Listen, I have something to tell you. I learned something today. I learned that history has been pushed back a hundred years. The government rewrote people's memories and reset the calendar. It was called the Great Forgetting. Okay, bye."

Jack could imagine Imogen sitting in her office in New York, eyes wide with shock, sure her son was having a psychotic break two states away. It was cruel.

Rover's voice continued uninterrupted on the radio. He was ranting about the traffic on I-77 now.

"What day is it?" Cole asked Jack as he handed the cell phone back.

"It's Friday."

"You sure about that?"

Jack flipped open his cell phone and pointed at the display. "Friday, June twenty-sixth," he said. "See?"

Cole nodded.

"I can't believe you did that to your mother," said Jack. He had no idea what he would say to Imogen when she called back. Wasn't he somehow responsible for this kid's well-being at the moment? Jack looked around for Dr. Quick.

"She'll forget I even called her. She always does."

Jack started for the double door that led to the dormitory. There was a window there that looked into a nurse's station. He'd be able to get someone's attention there. Halfway to the window, Rover's voice cut off. The sound of a computer modem switched on.

No, he thought. *No. A coincidence. A terrible coincidence.*

"This is a test of the Emergency Alert System . . . ," the robotic voice said.

"Jack!" Cole shouted. "Jack, come back!"

Jack's tongue felt numb inside his mouth, a strange piece of meat. The room swayed in his vertigo. He stumbled back to the table and sat across from Cole again.

"This is a coincidence," he said.

"No," said Cole. "I'm sorry. It's not."

A few seconds later the EAS signal cut off and Rover returned without missing a beat in his rant.

"It was just a test of the Emergency Alert System," said Jack. "You knew it was programmed for now. Somehow you knew, didn't you?"

Cole shook his head, that damned look of pity on his face. And then Duji's voice, the voice of Rover's spunky female cohost, came on with a check of the day's current events. "Good morning," she said. "This is the shizzy for Thursday, June twenty-fifth, 2015 . . ."

It's a joke, he thought. He flipped open his cell phone. It read *Thursday, June 25.*

"You reprogrammed it," he said.

"The radio, too?"

Jack ran to the nurse's station. "Don't do that, Jack! Not a good idea!"

A young woman in rainbow scrubs sat at a computer beyond the Plexiglas window. He leaned down to the gap at the bottom and said, "Excuse me, could you tell me the date? What day it is?"

She looked at the display of her own phone. "It's Thursday, June twenty-fifth," she said. "Geesh. It feels like this week will never end, right?"

He didn't say anything. Instead, he returned to Cole.

"This isn't happening," he said.

"That's one choice," the boy said. "You could be crazy. You could be crazy if you want. Or you can accept that I'm telling the truth."

Either I'm crazy or the world is, he thought. *And isn't that what every patient in this building thinks?*

"How?" he asked. "How can it be happening? You can't just hit the reset button and wipe everyone's memory of the last twenty-four hours. I mean, all the little things . . . some people would be scheduled to work on Fridays but not Thursdays. They'd find themselves at work when they should be at home. How would they explain that stuff?"

"The signal that goes out from HAARP is an algorithm," said Cole, "an elegant code designed to motivate each person's mind to rewrite their own memories. If your memories of that day are inconsequential, your brain just erases it. Like an old episode of *Seinfeld* on your TiVo, you never know it's gone. But if you find yourself suddenly at work when you shouldn't be, your mind will construct a memory of you switching shifts with a coworker or something. We are naturally wired to make sense of changes in our environment. The algorithm sets the parameters, but it's your own mind that makes the adjustments. It's really kind of cool."

"And paper calendars and physical evidence and stuff like that? Stuff you can't reprogram."

"We see only what we expect to see," said Cole. "You can hold a desk calendar up to that nurse's face and all she'll see is Thursday written on it."

Jack thought back to that psych experiment Tony told him about, the one where the gorilla walked through the basketball game and no one noticed. Inattentional blindness, he'd called it.

"But then why do *we* remember?" he asked. "You and I."

"That's the Seventh Impossibility," said Cole. "Whatever happened in that accident didn't just make it so that I couldn't forget anything, but either the trauma or this metal plate"—he knocked on the titanium behind his left ear—"made me into a kind of dampener for the signal. Like those things you can buy online that cancel out cell phone signals in movie theaters? As long as the person around me isn't drinking a lot of fluoride, they won't forget, either. Just being around me causes people to remember all kinds of things. Not just this signal. But, like, if you misplaced your car keys, if you hang out with me, you'll remember where you put them. Stupid stuff like that."

Jack recalled one of their first meetings. He had searched the house before coming to Haven, looking for Tony's damn watch, only to remember where he'd left it when he was with Cole. Was that part of this or was it just his mind making sense of a coincidence?

"This is crazy," he said again.

"Yes. It is. But you're not. Are you?"

He could feel his mind organizing the facts, trying to come up with a better narrative than Cole's. "You hypnotized me," he said.

"I knew it would take you longer than Tony to accept this," said Cole. "But now you're just being stubborn."

"This can't be true."

"You can say it a thousand times and it won't change. You think I want this to be true? You think I don't know how crazy this sounds? Look around, man. I'm in a mental ward. This sounds so crazy they locked me away. You think I don't want to be back in Manhattan, having breakfast at Balthazar and spending the day on a fucking schooner getting hand jobs?" Cole was getting agitated. Little bubbles of spit gathered at the corners of his mouth. The nurse looked over and made a note on a clipboard. He lowered his voice. "The only reason I let them keep me here—for three goddamn years—was because Tony told me before he left that you would come looking for him and that you would find me and that when you did you would get me out of here."

"Get you out of here?"

"You have to take me to the island. We have to go together."

"What? I'm not going to Alaska. I can't. And I'm definitely not taking you. That's called kidnapping."

"You can't just go home, Jack. How can you just go home after this?"

"Look. I don't know what's going on," he heard himself say. "Obviously, something has happened. Yes. I admit that. But I'm a long way from believing the government deleted a hundred years of human history. I don't know what the next step is, but I'm damn sure it's not taking you on a cross-country adventure."

"So, what then?"

"Give me some time to track down Tony. I think maybe I can now. We need to find him to explain the murder he committed."

"Whoa. He killed someone?"

"It looks that way."

"Who?"

"Sam's brother. He may have used the body in a weird attempt to trick everyone into thinking he was really dead."

"Jesus," said Cole. He seemed less confident all of sudden. "Did this guy, Sam's brother, did he need a little killing?"

"That's not the point."

"Tony must have had a reason." The boy was quiet for a moment. Then he shook his head. "You won't find him. It's a waste of time. If he made it to the Gate House, he made it to the island. If you go looking for him alone and they reset again, you'll forget everything we've talked about today. If I'm not near you when that broadcast goes out, I can't keep your memories safe."

"I won't take you with me," said Jack. "Not without more proof."

"What more proof do you need?"

"How do I know this last Impossibility isn't some clever trick to get me to bust you out here?"

Cole didn't say anything. He looked hurt.

"I mean, you're a 'dampener'? Really? Bundle that up in all the other stuff and why wouldn't I believe it? But it's unprovable. I mean, how could someone possibly prove you . . ."

Jack stopped talking. A dangerous idea was forming. There *was* a way he could prove if Cole's strange power existed and whether he really needed the kid to keep his memories safe.

"All right," he said, finally. "I'll get you out of here. For a day.

And if you're telling the truth we'll decide, together, what to do next. But if you're lying, I'm driving you back here and going after Tony alone."

"Where are we going?" asked Cole.

"I'm taking you to meet my father."

PART THREE

THE FUGITIVE

If in any quest for magic, in any search for sorcery,
witchery, legerdemain, first check the human spirit.

—ROD SERLING

ONE

PERSON OR PERSONS UNKNOWN

1 "You wanted to see me?" asked Kimberly Quick. She had just finished morning rounds and appeared a bit frazzled, her blouse spotted with butterscotch pudding. She maintained a certain stern beauty, though, like a young lieutenant on first watch.

"I'd like to take Cole on a day trip tomorrow," said Jack, walking with her.

Quick stopped for a moment. "You want to take him outside?"

"I think it would do him some good to get out again," said Jack. "Not far. There's a gaming convention in Akron this weekend. Corn on the Con. Lots of nerdy stuff. I think he'd dig it."

"I'd have to ask his mother."

"Of course."

"And he'd require constant supervision. He can be violent."

"I won't turn my back on him."

She loosened, smiled. "It would do him good. Some other kids his age. Let me see what I can do."

2   It had been a month since he'd had a good workout. In Lakewood, Jack ran four days a week. He preferred the last hour of the day, so he could watch the light slip off the planet and feel the cool wind cut off Lake Erie. He'd arrive back at his apartment an hour later with the streetlights on, soaked in briny sweat, his mind clear.

Jack wanted a clear mind, hoped such a thing was still possible. And so when he returned to Sam's empty house on the day Cole told him about the Great Forgetting, he rummaged through Tony's clothes until he found some sweats, then set off down Giddings not knowing how far he intended to run.

It was the end of June and the air was warm and fragrant with cow dung. His feet slapped the soft blacktop and his eyes ate up the quiet grandeur of the country. Beyond Sam's house a field of soy stretched below a farmstead, a rotting Amish-built thing, tired and weatherworn. Heifers in a pasture encouraged his adventure with eager grunting.

The roads of Franklin Mills were single-lane affairs with no edge lines. He had forgotten how much fun it was to jog down the middle of a road. No need to worry about crosswalks or commuters speeding to work. If a car did come, he'd hear it a quarter mile away, tires peeling the pavement, the sound of Saran wrap pulled off a chilled ceramic dish.

Jack decided on a long circuit down Alliance to Calvin, onto Porter, and back toward Giddings. A half mile from Sam's place, he spotted the weird car parked on the side of the road.

The car was the color of fresh leather, somewhere between red and brown, and shaped like something out a 1950s sci-fi movie: sleek, angular, more like a jet than a car. Its windows were tinted beyond the legal limit, outlined in chrome that sparkled the sun in a way that suggested illusion, *glamour*. The vehicle was pointed at him, resting on the shoulder. The driver's-side window was rolled down. A man in a charcoal suit and a Panama hat sat behind the wheel, watching him.

When Jack was within earshot, the man waved for him to stop.

Heart racing so fast he could feel it in his temples, Jack stood across from the car and waited to see if this . . .

Hound

. . . man meant him harm. There were no witnesses out here.

The man pushed back the brim of his hat. For a second Jack thought he was looking at the victim of some industrial accident, someone who had suffered third-degree burns to his face. But then he saw that the deep creases in this man's skin were merely well-worn wrinkles. There was, however, something definitely wrong with the man's nose. It was too short, too flat. A birth defect of some kind. The man's ears stuck out below his hat and his eyes were oddly small and too close together.

"Howdy," said the man in the Panama hat. His voice was shrill, as if it were being forced through a thin pipe.

Jack nodded.

"I'm afraid I'm lost," the man said. "Must have taken a wrong turn back in Albuquerque." The man laughed at himself. "Could you help me get back to the main road?"

"You mean SR 14?"

"Oh, I don't know, partner. Whichever will get me back to Akron, I guess."

"You'll want 14 to the expressway," said Jack. He pointed back the way the car had traveled. "Three roads up and to the right."

The man in the Panama hat reached into the darkness of the passenger seat and for a moment Jack thought he was going for a gun (*or maybe one of those satellite dishes so he can listen to my thoughts*). But then the man pulled out a comically large map, the kind that folds into an accordion you can never quite put back together again. The man's fingers were long and narrow, the backs of his hands covered in a mat of coarse, dark hair.

"Would you please point out the designated route? I'm afraid I'm not very good at directions."

"I really have to be going," Jack heard himself say.

"Well. You're a busy man, I'm sure. Lots of people to talk to."

"Just back the way you came. Three streets. Take care." Jack started jogging back toward Sam's house.

"Toodles," he heard the man in the Panama hat say as he fled.

When he turned around, the strange car was gone.

3   Walking into Nostalgia later that afternoon felt like reading a story for the second time. Sam had queued up Gordon Lightfoot on the iPod dock. She was even in the same position as she was the day before, leaning behind the register, reading that book. Like the rest of the world, Sam didn't know that she was reliving Thursday all over again.

"Empty house," said Jack, testing it, feeling numb, feeling crazy. He felt sick. Hollow. He didn't want to play this game. His mind filled with the vertigo of that feeling you can say only in French. That *déjà vu.*

"Hey, buddy, you okay?" she asked.

He sat down and pushed the crazies out of his mind the best he could. "Sorry," he said. "I'm kind of in my head today."

"You want a beer? I got some in a cooler."

He nodded and she disappeared behind the curtain. He could hear her rummaging in the icebox back there.

"Are you going to start making hats out of aluminum foil?" she yelled.

"No." But, he wondered, if Cole asked him to, would he? If one of those creepy men in the Panama hats was standing outside this shop and he had to make a hat out of aluminum foil and wear it on his head to keep the thing from reading his mind, would he even hesitate?

"Earth to Jack." She set the beer down in front of him.

It was unfair that this was happening now, when they were finally together again. "Should I really be trying to find Tony?" he asked finally.

Sam tucked a stray strand of hair behind her left ear and sighed.

"The divorce, Jack. Mark's murder? All these things are chasing us. I feel like I'm drowning in it. If you can find him, we can move on." After a second, she added, "And he should answer for what he did, goddamn it."

"If I bring him back, they'll arrest him. For the ten grand that disappeared from Haven at least. And maybe Mark's murder."

"Probably. But he won't stay long. They'll have to send him to a mental hospital. And living out the rest of his life in a psych ward sure beats living in whatever homeless shelter he's hiding in now, right?"

"Yeah."

"You really think you can find him?"

"I think I'm very close."

"Good," she said. "But if it comes down to a choice . . . like, if it's between you going crazy, too, or us never finding Tony again, it's okay that we never find him."

Too late, he thought, but he reached out and touched her hand.

4   The next morning, which, as much as he could figure, was the second Friday of that week, Jack drove to Haven to pick up the boy.

Cole was waiting under the portico with Dr. Quick. He had a denim backpack slung over his shoulder and he was dressed in new khakis and a polo. He looked out of place this far from any city, a prep school kid lighting out for the territories. Imogen loved the idea of her son venturing out of the hospital, she'd told Jack on the phone. She had absolutely no memory of the bizarre conversation she'd had with Cole the day before.

"Three o'clock?" said Quick, leaning into the passenger window after Cole climbed in.

Jack nodded. "Earlier, maybe," he said.

She waved as they pulled away. Cole reached over and turned off the radio.

"Worried about a test of the Emergency Alert System?" asked Jack.

He shook his head. "Nah. Besides, the EAS works whether you have your radio tuned to a station or not. Radio waves go through the air, you know. There's no escaping it. I just don't like Nickelback."

"What's in the bag?"

"Clothes. Hair gel. Toothbrush. Flashlight. Some other shit."

"Why? We're just going to Mantua and back."

Cole smiled and looked out the window.

"Do you know something I don't?" asked Jack.

"We're not coming back."

"You want to bet?"

"Sure."

"Five bucks."

"Make it twenty."

Jack shook the kid's hand.

5   Jack was anxious and sweaty by the time he parked in the visitors' lot at St. Mary's Assisted Living Home in Mantua. Since the attack, he'd done well to push the memory of that night out of his mind. The Captain had always been a tough man to love. Gruff. A man who told you he loved you by how hard he squeezed your shoulder. On some level Jack knew that he should not blame his father for trying to kill him. But he wasn't sure he could forgive him, either.

"Your sister was here a few days ago," the nurse said as Jack signed in. Of course Jean had been here. She was quick to forgive those who needed her.

"Are you his grandson?"

"No," said Cole. "Just a friend."

"Well, I'm sure he appreciates the company. It'd be really nice if Qi could visit, too. He's always asking for her."

"Doubtful," said Jack, and left it at that.

They walked a long hall to a room among a dozen others. A red square was pinned to the back of the door below the name

W. Felter—a code for nurses that the patient inside could be violent, a TacMar for the infirm. Jack shivered. Cole must have sensed something, because the boy actually put a friendly hand on his arm. He opened the door.

The Captain sat in a recliner facing the wall, where shadows from the window danced about in ever-changing patterns. He was perched forward, drool collecting in a dark circle on his corduroys. The room was stifling hot, but his father was dressed in a long-sleeved flannel shirt buttoned to the top. Gray stubble like steel wool around his blond mustache. His arms, once thick as anacondas, were dead milk snakes. Cole stepped in after Jack and closed the door.

At the sound of the latch catching, the Captain bobbed his head in their direction. The boy stepped forward and kneeled beside the old man. Cole stared with fascination and reached out, as if he were about to touch Walter's mouth, but pulled his hand back at the last moment. The Captain did not move.

"Alzheimer's?" asked Cole.

"No. But dementia of some kind."

"Jack, I don't know if whatever I have works like this. I can make a person remember things if the memories still exist, but I don't know what dementia does to the mind. Doesn't Alzheimer's destroy the cells that store our memories?"

"Then there's no way to prove what you told me. That I need you to safeguard my memories."

"After what happened the other day, you're going to doubt anything I said?"

"I think something is going on," said Jack. "That your father knew something the rest of us don't. But am I sure all of the pieces fit together the way you say? No. And I'm still just looking for Tony here, remember? I get the feeling you want me to do something more."

"I want you to save the world."

Jack rolled his eyes.

"The box . . ."

Jack turned at the sound of his father's voice. The Captain was staring back, eyes suddenly lucid and afraid.

"Jack!" said the Captain. "Jesus, Jack. The box under my bed. You have to get it out of the house!"

Jack jumped as the cell phone in his pants pocket vibrated against his leg like a trapped bumblebee. It was Jean. He ignored it. "Do you know where you are?" he asked his father.

The Captain looked around. "I dunno. Is this St. Mary's? Yes? Good. That's fine. But you have to get the box, Jack. Right now."

The cell phone went off again. Jean again. He flipped it open. "What?" he barked at her.

"Jack, where are you?" She was in tears.

"I'm with the Captain. What is it? Is it Paige?"

"No. Jack, get out of there."

"Why?"

"The police are here. They went through Dad's war stuff. There was a knife in a box under his bed. It matches the knife that killed Mark."

"What?"

"That detective left about a minute ago. He thinks you did it. I think he's coming to St. Mary's for you right now."

Jack didn't say anything. He found he couldn't form a single coherent thought.

Jean's voice came back. "Did you have anything to do with it, Jack?"

"What? No. Of course I didn't."

"What about the Captain?"

Jack held the receiver to his chest and, in a harsh whisper, asked, "Dad, did you kill Mark Brooks?"

"Of course I did!" the Captain yelled.

"Jean, I have to go," he said.

"Get out of there!"

He hung up. Cole, he saw, had pushed himself against the door, trying to become invisible in the midst of such turmoil.

Here he was again, faced with another impossible choice: let the detective arrest them or flee. His life, that life of teaching, that quiet, simple, sometimes wonderful life was over.

The boy really was special. That much he knew. The Captain was back. Cole had brought him back. He could see that now. Did it not stand to reason that Cole was right about everything else? Was it finally safe to believe?

"Fuck!" Jack shouted. "Fuck!"

"What do you want to do?" asked Cole.

"We run," he said. "And we take him with us."

TWO

ESCAPE CLAUSE

1 At exactly 9:00 a.m. Paige ran into the living room, where Jean was sorting through family photographs, and exclaimed, "Holy shit, holy shit!"

"Paige!" Jean yelled. "Jesus! Don't fuckin' swear!"

"There are a hundred police in our driveway."

Jean ran to the picture window. The drive was full of cop cars. A dozen, at least, snaking onto SR 14 and back along the berm to the Moores' place, lights flashing. She watched, a protective hand on her daughter's head, as twenty men with guns scrambled out of their vehicles and rushed toward her front door.

"Mom," whispered Paige. "What did you *do*?"

Jean forced herself to move. She walked to the door and opened it as the lead cop, a fat man with a rough crew cut, stepped onto her porch, a batch of folded blue papers in his hand. Jean remembered this one: Captain Marlon Hoover. He was the detective who'd come around asking questions after Tony disappeared.

"What the hell is going on?" she asked.

"We're here to search the house, Jean. Step aside."

"You got a warrant or something?"

He handed her the papers and nudged her to the side with his shoulder. She pulled Paige out of the way, stepping onto the porch as two more cops barreled in. A female officer Jean didn't recognize stood beside her, hands on her belt. The rest of the cops scurried in, one by one, like a swarm of cockroaches.

"Mom? What's happening," asked Paige. She looked like she might cry.

"It's okay," said Jean, kneeling to her eye level. She wanted to cry, too. But she swallowed her frustration and fear and tried on a smile for her girl. "They just made a mistake. Don't worry."

"We're not bad guys," Paige said to the female cop standing beside her. The woman looked away.

Jean watched police officers tip over books and flip through the picture albums for contraband. Sheriff's deputies opened cabinets and checked under rugs. After a few minutes, Marlon stepped outside.

"Where is he?"

"Who?"

"Jack, goddamn it. Don't get smart with me."

"Why do you want Jack?" Her eyes were starting to leak. Her fingers shook as she dug into her back pocket and fished out a Winston Light.

"Don't smoke in my face," he barked.

"This is my house, so fuck you." She lit the cigarette and sucked the smoke into her waiting lungs. Paige squeezed her hand in a protective way.

"Where is he?" Marlon asked again.

"Why do you care?"

"Cut the crap. He and your old man killed that little girl's father. Don't you give a shit?"

Jean choked, puffs of white smoke shooting out her nose like a choo-choo train. "You're fucking crazy. Jack wouldn't kill a fly."

"Bullshit, Jean. I've got two witnesses saw him assault Mark while you were detoxing out at Haven. I've got video. If Jack didn't kill him, who did?"

"Tony ran away, didn't he?" she said. "You think he disappeared the same time Mark did and it's just a big fucking coincidence?"

"So tell me this. Why was Jack at Pymatuning last week? A ranger spotted him lurking around the reservoir. Know what else we found up there? Mark's car. It was abandoned at the reservoir three years ago. So if Jack didn't have a hand in the murder, explain that one to me."

Jean laughed in his face. "You're crazy!"

He snatched her wrist in his thick right hand and squeezed. "Say it again. Call me crazy again, you dumb bitch!"

"Marlon," the female cop said.

"We got something!" A young detective appeared in the door-way. "We got something."

Marlon released Jean and dashed upstairs. She followed right behind, scooping up Paige as she went. The Captain's room was at the end of the hall, untouched for at least six months, ever since he'd been confined to the hospital bed downstairs. It was dusty and the room still held his musk. Forty framed photographs of Jean's mother rested on the top of a low wooden dresser. A detective kneeled beside the bed, hands on a black cardboard box he'd pulled from underneath.

"Give it," said Marlon.

The detective handed it over. Marlon lifted the lid. Inside was the Captain's old uniform, neatly folded, along with twenty piastres, a postcard from Nha Trang, and a marine's Ka-Bar.

"Booya," said Marlon. "Bag everything. Bag the box, too." He moved for the door, and as he did Jean backed against the wall. "Your fault," he told her, a fat finger in her face. "If you hadn't shacked up with that meth head, nobody would be here today."

2   "Where're we going?" asked Cole, his hands gripping the dash-board tightly as Jack flew down country roads.

"I don't know," he said. "East."

"Don't speed, goddamn it," the Captain yelled from the back. "You'll get us pulled over. Jesus God, you drive like a woman. Actually, your mother was a better driver. You drive like a gook. You know what, pull over and I'll drive. I can barely move my legs and I know I'd drive better than you."

"Dad! Be quiet!"

Life alters course like this, Jack thought, not slowly but all at once, in herky-jerky jumps. His mother's sudden death. Tony's betrayal. Those things had changed him overnight. Giant detours of his personal timeline. Here was another one.

How would today change the course of his life? Who would he become? A fugitive? A conspiracy nut? One of those fanatics you heard about on the news sometimes, the ones who get shot to death driving through some roadblock in D.C.?

He was a kidnapper. He'd kidnapped a seventeen-year-old boy. He'd kidnapped his father from hospice. The staff didn't know the Captain was missing yet. But they would. Soon enough, they would.

Finding Tony was the least of his worries now. Except, wherever Tony was hiding was logically the best place for them to lie low, too. If they could find it.

"We need to get someplace with lots of people," said Jack. "Somewhere we can hide in plain sight but not be seen. I need time to think."

"Oh, for fuck's sake, I'll just tell them I did it!" the Captain shouted. "I'm already halfway to my final reward."

"At least two people saw me deck Mark at the Walmart the day you killed him, Pop. How do I explain that? Bad timing? Shit. How did it happen?"

"He tied to kill me and Tony when we went out to the trailer to get him to leave town. It was him or us."

"Without Tony to back you up, they'll say you're covering for me."

"It's not like your prints are on the knife."

"They could be, though," said Jack. "You think I didn't go

through all your old war stuff when I was a kid? I used to take the knife out into the woods and play Vietnam."

"That's fucked up."

"Well, why the hell do you even have it? Why did you keep it all these years?"

"Qi," he said simply.

"All this trouble for a hooker."

"Watch your mouth. You have no idea what you're talking about."

"Get on the interstate," Cole interjected. "Make for Canada, then we can head west for Alaska."

Jack laughed. "The police will be looking for this car. Forget Canada—we won't make it to Pennsylvania."

"Lee Harvey," the Captain said.

"What?" For a minute, Jack thought his father was regressing, reliving the broadcast of Kennedy's assassination or something.

"Oswald hid in a theater. He needed somewhere to hide in plain sight."

"Yeah," he sighed. "That's good, Dad. Alliance, then." The dollar theater in Alliance was an inspired idea for many reasons. For one, it was just beyond the border of Portage County, outside the jurisdiction of Franklin Mills PD. For another, it was attached to a mall, which would be crawling with blue-collar families stocking up on smoke bombs and sparklers for Fourth of July barbecues. Sure enough, the parking lot was nearly full when they arrived twenty minutes later.

"Here," the Captain said as they helped him out of the car. He slipped a dime into Jack's hand.

"What's this for?"

"Switch out your plates."

Jack started to protest but quickly saw the logic in this move. He set about the task using the dime to loosen the screws on the plates of a Dodge Caravan parked nearby. In five minutes, it was done. They walked into the mall, acutely aware of the security cameras hanging from the concrete eaves. Jack bought tickets for *Avengers: Age of Ultron* and pushed his father along.

"Popcorn?" the Captain said.

"No. What are you thinking? We're not here to have a good time."

"I'm hungry, goddamn it. It feels like I haven't eaten in a week."

Jack handed Cole a twenty and told him to grab a soda, too.

"If they have Jordan almonds . . . ," the Captain called out, but then Jack wrapped his arm around his father's shoulders and made for cinema 7.

They sat in the back. A couple dozen patrons—teenagers, mostly—came in before the previews. As the theater dimmed, Cole returned, carrying popcorn, soda, Jordan almonds, and Milk Duds, and took a seat in front of them. He might have been having the best day of his life.

Jack helped the Captain to some soda and checked a handful of popcorn for stray kernels that might get lodged in his food pipe, and then placed the remainder onto a large napkin in his old man's lap.

"That little snot forgot the butter," the Captain whispered.

Jack closed his eyes against the loud, unrelenting violence on-screen and tried to think. The most logical thing to do would be to turn himself in, let the courts ferret out the truth. Surely he couldn't really be convicted of murder, right? Not when all he did was punch the guy in the face. If the choice was that simple, that's just what he would have done. But what about Cole, the unexpected miracle sitting beside him? He'd restored the Captain's mind. Cole was affecting the people around him like some kind of living Wi-Fi signal. In the face of such a thing, Jack's own fate seemed a little less important.

Miracles, he knew from studying the Crusades, were dangerous things. Miracles inspired action. Miracles changed the world. Nothing could be taken for granted anymore. Nothing could be taken as fact. Not when a man's mind could be healed simply by sitting next to a boy with a titanium plate in his skull.

There were no known parameters for this new reality. There was no instruction manual to the Great Forgetting. How, exactly, did it work? Who controlled the mechanism? Did Cole have these answers?

He didn't think so. The kid knew a lot. But his father surely hadn't told him everything.

Jack needed to understand the stakes. Tony could afford to disappear into Wonderland without asking questions. All Tony cared about was himself. Jack had responsibilities and he needed to know if this misadventure was worth setting those responsibilities aside. If it was worth being a fugitive.

There might be a way to learn more about the Great Forgetting, Jack realized. But that meant continuing east. They would need a new vehicle. Something inconspicuous. A used car would buy them a day or two, but eventually the FBI would snag the transfer from the DMV. He couldn't take Sam's car. Jean's, either, for that matter. It took him a second more before he found the answer and a plan began to take shape. Risky, yes. It meant returning to Franklin Mills. But Franklin Mills was not a small village. It was full of empty roads. It might be possible to slip in and out if they were quick about it.

Slowly, Jack became aware of the sound of his father's ragged, whispered gasps. His first thought was that the Captain was choking on his popcorn. But then he saw that his father was crying. Tears cascaded down the old man's cheeks. He had never seen his father cry and it frightened him. He put a hand on the Captain's back.

"Dad?"

"Ah, Johnny," he said. "I remember now. I remember how I ended up in the home. I . . . I can't even apologize for it, it's so bad."

"Wasn't you."

"Yes it was."

"Wasn't you, Dad."

"But Jack, it was *my* hands."

3   When *Avengers* ended, Cole helped Jack walk the Captain into a screening of *Jurassic World*. The Captain explained how this wasn't even really stealing. "Back in my day, squirt, a quarter got you in the door and you could stay as long as you wanted. The admission is for the *theater*, not the movie. People forgot that." Cole sat with them, since it seemed like they'd had time to talk through family stuff. After *Jurassic World*, they snuck into *Tomorrowland*, and when that was over, it was dark outside and they were hungry again.

They drove to a Wendy's and ate inside the car. The air grew stale and salty with their meaty breath.

"Tell me about this island," Jack asked, halfway through his buffalo chicken sandwich.

"It's a place where all the people who chose to remember went to live. The people who were against the Great Forgetting. My dad said there weren't many. A few thousand. They didn't want to forget like everybody else. So they were given Mu, the island, and told to never come off again."

"Wait. Your island, it's the lost continent of Mu?"

"You couldn't have heard of it."

"I have," said Jack. "Mu is mentioned frequently in early historical writing. It's an old story. Supposedly Mu was this small continent in the middle of the Pacific Ocean. There was this archaeologist, Augustus Le Plongeon, an expert on Mayan culture. Most of what we know about the Mayans can be attributed to his expeditions to South America in the late nineteenth century. He was sure that the Mayans had come from this island of Mu. Not only that, but Le Plongeon said ancient Egypt was founded by inhabitants of Mu after a mass exodus from the island six thousand years ago. Le Plongeon claimed Mu was where humanity began."

"Well, you'll get to see it, Jack. How about that?"

"Why is it so important we go there?"

Cole combed his fingers through his hair. He liked Jack, he did. He reminded him of his favorite teacher at Pencey. But they should be three hundred miles from here by now. They were wasting time. "Because," said Cole, "the people on Mu don't know that someone has hacked into the machine we used for the Great Forgetting."

"What are you talking about?"

"Around the time I was checked into Haven, someone began resetting the calendar again. A day here, a month there. Deleted. Gone. It always happened after national tragedies. The bombings in

Decatur. Sarin gas in the D.C. subway. Everything was reset by the EAS broadcasts and the attacks were deleted from memory, forgotten. Someone has been altering the history of current events. The people on Mu need to know someone is playing with the old equipment. The machine was only supposed to be used once. Used once and then maintained until all the artifacts were collected. Tony went there to tell them. To get them to help him take down HAARP maybe. Stop whoever is resetting the calendar all the time."

"Who is it? Who's hitting the reset button?"

"I don't know," said Cole. "It's fucking scary when you think about it. I mean, what's their motivation? What's their agenda?"

"This is what I'm getting at," said Jack. "We don't really know what's going on, so how could we know we're even on the right side? Before I go running into some situation on Mu, if such a place exists, I want to know what we're dealing with. I want to know what the hell this is all about. Your dad must have known."

"I'm sure he did," said Cole. *And that's why he's dead*, he thought.

"And the other Collectors know, too."

"Yes. Probably. Sure."

"And you can take me to their office?"

"Bad idea," said Cole. "There's Hounds there, too, man, not just Collectors."

"But the Collectors have to come in and out like everyone else."

Cole sighed. "You want to go to Manhattan," he said. "Walk right into their headquarters?"

"I want to kidnap one of the Twelve Angry Men."

For a moment nobody said anything. Then the Captain leaned forward, the leather seat snapping loudly beneath him. "Can someone please explain to me what the Christ is going on?" he said. "For a while I thought you guys were talking about some *Star Trek* episode or some nerd bullshit. What the fuck is the Great Forgetting?"

As Jack began the delicate process of explaining everything, Cole curled up in the passenger seat, his head humming with a blood-sugar doziness. Sometimes the boy felt like he was a hundred years old when he considered everything that had happened to him since the day he'd learned what his father really did for a living. That memory felt so old, Manhattan so far away, like it had happened in some book he'd read in grammar school.

It was supposed to be a nice surprise.

Instead of staying the last night at Pencey before Christmas break, Cole had folded his clothes into his Nike duffel bag and taken the 11:00 a.m. train into the city. He'd gotten the idea to show up at his father's office. Then they could go to that theater in Battery Park and have lunch at Suspenders. They could talk about what books they were reading and where they would go on vacation.

When Cole arrived at Penn Station he hopped the C to Church Street, stepping into the brutal cold whipping through the skyscraper canyons just before three-thirty. Dressed in jeans and a Pencey sweatshirt, Cole hurried to his father's office.

New York in winter always left Cole feeling uneasy. The city was too sterile, all those wonderful and brutal summer smells lost in the chill air. And every sound sounded strange, metallic. A voice could carry for blocks if the wind was right. It felt like a dying metropolis, like a great capital about to fall, its citizens fleeing to better places, forgetting to take him along.

A hurricane of hot air ruffled his long bangs as he pushed through the revolving glass doors of the skyscraper where his father worked. The grand lobby was granite-tiled and reflected the bright sun that fell through thin cathedral windows. He followed a bronze path toward a polished directory beside a bank of elevators. There were so many floors that you had to take three elevators to reach the top. His dad worked for a company called Nu-Day Trading, that company with the aspen leaf logo. He searched the directory, over a hundred businesses listed alphabetically, but there was no "Nu-Day Trading." It was possible Nu-Day was one of those "subsidiaries," a company within a larger company, like those nesting dolls Cole's nanny, Tish, had given his mother.

Cole parked himself on a bench by a wall of windows and considered what to do next. They didn't allow cell phones at Pencey, so he had no means to call his father and didn't know his office number anyway. He supposed he could use a pay phone to call Tish. She would have his father's work number.

But that would ruin the surprise. As he thought over this conundrum, he spotted his father's hat over a stream of people making for the elevators. His dad wore one of those old reporter's hats in the winter, a gray one that looked like something from a Turner Classic Movies movie. Cole scrambled after him, folding himself into the lift. There were at least twenty people packed into their car. The elevator rose smoothly. They were in the one that terminated at the forty-fourth floor.

Peeking over the shoulder of a bearded man who smelled like burned chicken, Cole spied his father up front, by the buttons, the brim of his hat tilted down as he read over a quarter-fold newspaper. Cole slipped into the opposite corner. He hoped his dad would squeeze out somewhere and he could follow, unseen. It was a great hunt and he would follow his quarry to its den before springing the surprise! He watched the lights slowly dim on the great board of buttons and noted, with some curiosity, that there was no button for the thirteenth floor. Just an empty space on the stainless steel there.

People—some people, anyway—said he looked like his father, and Cole thought that was just fine. His dad had this chiseled look, like one of those big goddamn faces from a spaghetti western. The kind of face they don't make anymore.

There were still seven other people in the elevator when they reached the forty-fourth floor. When the doors opened, everyone stepped off. Everyone except for his father. Cole froze at the back of the elevator. Something in the hardness of his father's shoulders told him this had not been a welcome surprise. He was suddenly afraid. The doors closed.

His father pushed the red button that held the elevator in place. Then he turned his head and looked at his son. "What are you doing here, Cole?" he asked.

"It was a surprise," he whispered.

His father's eyes moved, scanning the elevator, thinking. He looked to the camera in the corner of the car, then back at the boy. He stepped closer to his son. "I have something to do," he whispered. "It's going to take some time. You can wait in my office, but you can't make a sound. Okay? Not a peep. Then we can go."

Cole nodded.

His father grimaced as if he'd tasted something sour and then turned back to the panel of buttons. He pulled the STOP knob and Cole watched as he

reached into his pocket and brought out a small round object. It was a button! The thirteen button. His father placed it in the empty space where it
belonged and then he pushed it. The button lit up from within.

"What . . . ," he started to ask.

"Shh," his father said. "Pretend you didn't see that. I'll explain later."

The elevator shuddered and then began to drift down again. It stopped at
the thirteenth floor, and when the doors opened Cole's father collected the
button and disappeared it back in his pocket. Then he put a hand on his
son's back and ushered him out of the elevator.

The thirteenth floor was dark. The overheads were turned off and the
only light was the copper sun through the narrow windows along the perimeter. Rows of empty cubicles, chairs stacked on top of desks, wrapped in plastic. Long forests of servers along the back wall.

"Over here," his father said, pushing Cole to the right, down a short hall
and into an office that looked uptown at the Chrysler Building. The decor
was sparse, but he could tell it was his father's—there was a picture of his
mother on the windowsill. Cole threw his duffel bag on the leather couch
against the back wall.

"I'm sorry I didn't call," he said.

His father brought a finger to his lips. "No more talking. Sit quietly. No
games. Don't use the phone. Read something. I mean it. Not a sound."

"What is this place?" Cole asked.

"Give me twenty minutes," he said. Then his father was leaving. He
locked the door from the inside on his way out.

For the first twenty minutes, Cole paced around the room, which was not
really that large. He picked over the knickknacks on the bookshelves. For a
while, he regarded a strange postcard from a city he'd never heard of. Cahokia.
Wherever that was. On one of the bookshelves he found a misprinted novel.
The Hound of the Baskervilles by Edgar Allan Poe. He'd heard once that
mislabeled books were collectors' items.

After an hour, he went in search of his father.

When he opened the door, he heard voices, muffled, coming from the
other end of the floor, beyond the expanse of empty cubicles. He walked that
way, quieting his footfalls. Beyond a kitchenette, he came upon a carpeted
passage. Cole felt uneasy, like he was trespassing.

Around a corner he found a bright glass room. On the other side of the glass was a large desk. A bald, dark-skinned man in a Hawaiian shirt sat there, looking like death. Standing behind him was a man in a charcoal suit and a Panama hat, and beside this man was Cole's father, who had taken off his fedora and hung it on a hook on the wall. His father had something in his hands. It looked like a small radar dish attached to a TV remote. Wires snaked from this device and attached to electrodes on his father's forehead.

"You're a long way from Mu, amigo," said the man in the Panama hat, his voice an octave too high and rough, like his windpipe had been stepped on. "Why are you in New York?"

The man in the Hawaiian shirt was crying. "I don't know what you're talking about!" he said. "You have the wrong man. I don't know anything about this 'Moo.'"

His father pointed the dish at the man in the chair. He adjusted a dial, then looked up at the man in the Panama hat. "He's lying," his father said. Cole had never heard him sound so stern. "He's thinking about the beaches on Mu. And those birds that live there. He's been to the island."

The man in the Hawaiian shirt sobbed loudly. Then the man in the Panama hat slapped him right in this mouth. Smack! The man screamed. Cole cringed and pushed up against a wall in the shadowed hallway.

"What are you doing in New York?" the man in the Panama hat shouted.

"I'm sorry!" the man in the chair yelped. "I just wanted to see the city again. A vacation. That's all!"

Cole's father shook his head. "Lying," he said. "He's thinking about wires and a pipe. He's thinking about a car bomb. But he couldn't get the fertilizer."

"Don't! Do not . . . don't make me forget. Please! I have a family."

"Zaharie Shah, you have been found guilty of treason and sentenced to personality modification," said his father.

"Please," the man cried. "Don't change my memories! Don't make me a pedophile. Don't make me a bad man. I was only trying to do what was right."

"Stop crying," Cole's father said. "All we want are your memories of Mu. You can still be a pilot. We'll put you someplace nice."

The man in the Panama hat stepped into an alcove in the corner. It sounded like he was pouring a glass of water. In fact, that's exactly what he was doing. Cole saw it now. A tall glass of water. He set it in front of the man in the funny shirt.

"Drink," said the man in the Panama hat.

With shaking hands, the man in the chair took the glass and brought it to his lips. The worst seemed to be over, because his father relaxed and leaned against the wall. When he did, his hands swiveled in such a way that the little radar dish pointed down the hall, where Cole cowered, thinking, Dad, what the fuck? What the fuck is this? Who are you? I don't know you. Who are you?

His father's eyes snapped to him. He looked through the glass right at his son, then pretended to focus on the man in the chair, who was, by now, half-way through his glass of water. "Scopes," his father said to the man in the Panama hat, "I have to step outside."

Cole's father pulled the electrodes off his forehead, set the instrument on the desk, grabbed his hat, and stepped out of the glass room.

Cole thought about running. He knew he was in trouble. But he was frozen to the floor; his feet refused to budge.

His father snatched him by the collar and dragged him around a corner. "Cole," he whispered. "Goddamn it. I told you to stay put."

And he couldn't help it. He was in the seventh grade now, and far enough into Pencey's military regimen that he had backbone, real backbone, but he couldn't help it. The tears came. His chest heaved in hitches.

But his father was not mad. He pulled Cole's head against his suit jacket. Cole could smell his cologne, leather and clove. "Shh," he said. "Shh. Hey. Not your fault. Not your fault." His father pushed him toward the elevator.

Cole sniffed away the tears and watched his father dig into a pocket and come out with a rectangular fob that he stuck into a catch on the wall. The elevator doors opened and they stepped inside. The doors closed and the elevator started down.

His father scratched his forehead where the electrodes had left little red sucker marks. He was thinking. Thinking hard. "Man oh man, buddy."

"What . . . was that?" Cole asked.

"Shh. Not here. Let's get across the street."

Putting a hand on Cole's back, his father led him through the lobby, out the revolving doors, and across the windy street to the hotel on the other side, a plush red-carpeted hideaway for visiting venture capitalists. With a nod to the doorman, his father ushered Cole inside and then to the left, down a hall to a men's room. His father checked beneath the stalls for feet and, finding none, returned to the door and turned the latch. He leaned against the sink and brought his hands to his mouth.

"I'm sorry," said Cole.

His father shook his head. "I should have sent you out. I was trying to hurry. My fault. It's my fault."

Cole stared at him, not sure what to say.

"Shit, kid. Where do I begin?" He reached into his suit pocket and brought out a toothpick, which he placed in his mouth. It had been this way since he'd given up smoking.

"You read my mind in there, didn't you?"

His teased the toothpick to the other side of his mouth. "Cole, even your mother doesn't know what I do. It's safer that way."

"What do you do?"

"Well, I'm thinking of telling you. The truth. I got no one to talk to about it. No one. And that does things to a man. Having a big part of him he can't share with anyone, you know?"

Cole nodded, but he wasn't sure he did know.

"But listen, kiddo. And I'm dead serious. You cannot tell what I'm about to tell you to anyone. A grown-up secret, right? You've got your kid secrets where some friend tells you what girl he likes and that's a secret you can tell to a couple other friends because it's not such a big-deal secret, okay? But this is a serious secret. There are times you can't even think about this secret, that's how secret it is. Understand?"

"Yes," said Cole.

"Cole, everything in your history books is a lie."

Jack's old man didn't need the seven-point gradient to accept the general idea of the Great Forgetting. Such revelations can be accepted quickly when there is a significant degree of trust between the story-teller and his audience, when it's, say, between a father and son.

"You understand what this means?" said the Captain. "Everyone in Congress, the Supreme Court, the president. It's a puppet government. The only person with any power is whoever's resetting people's memories. If you ask me, it's a Democrat. Only a liberal would have the gall to rewrite history and pretend he's doing everyone a favor."

Just before they crossed into Franklin Mills, Jack made a brief call, speaking in whispers. "You think they're tracking our cell phones?" he asked Cole when he finished.

"Maybe not the police, but the Hounds could be," he said. "Get rid of it."

Jack tossed the phone outside and Cole turned to watch it shatter on the highway like a small red bomb.

"So where are we going?" he asked.

"Claytor Lake," said Jack.

4 Jack killed the lights before he turned onto the access road off Porter. He maneuvered the Saturn up the drive by leaning his head out the window and using moonlight to see his way through the goldenrod. He angled the car beside a rusty green truck. Jack was pleased to see a large tent and some rudimentary camping equipment in the back secured by bungee cords. The air outside was spicy with that muddy water smell. A large figure stepped from the truck and the vehicle pitched to the side and back again.

"Nils," said Jack. "Thanks for coming."

The Viking shook his head. "Man, you're all over the news. Lou Maglio was just on. Said it was going to be the biggest manhunt in Ohio history," he said. "They think you took the kid and your father hostage."

"And they think I murdered Mark."

"Uh-huh. You and the Captain. But I know you didn't. Why would you ask me to bring his body up? Doesn't make sense. Besides, about everyone in town had motive to kill that sonofabitch. You know he tried selling meth to my wife?"

"Guy was dangerous," the Captain said shortly. "More than you know."

"Yeah, I seen what he did to Jean. Glad to see her come through. Anyway, you didn't come here to chat. You best skedaddle. They got a cruiser parked in front of your house, right through them trees." Nils tossed Jack the keys.

"How you getting home?" asked Jack.

"Suppose I could use some exercise," said Nils. "I'll help you with the car, if you're ready."

Jack grabbed Cole's backpack and the change from the cup holder. Nils helped get the Captain in the cab of the truck and then they returned to the Saturn. Cole took the passenger side, Nils the back bumper. Jack reached in, clicked it to neutral, and leaned against the doorframe. "On three," he said.

A minute later the car slipped into the water and gently pitched over the edge of the drop-off. They watched the back wheels point toward the stars and bob there for a moment as bubbles simmered around its sides. Then the car sank beneath the dark surface of Claytor Lake, drifting to the bottom, where it joined the silent junkyard on the floor, home to crawfish and giant carp.

Jack shook Nils's hand. "Don't tell Sam about this," he said.

"No."

Cole took the bitch seat as Jack had one last look at his family's house through the trees. The light was on in the living room. Jean was probably sitting by the phone, waiting for him to call. He wanted to walk over there and say something to reassure her. But even if he could, even if there wasn't a cruiser and two patrolmen watching from the road, he wouldn't know what to say.

He adjusted the mirrors and turned the key. The truck's engine sounded like a sick bear. When they rolled back onto Porter, Jack hit the lights and made toward the interstate. They'd have to find a place to stay for the night. Might be best to hit an ATM, too, before they froze his accounts.

How far will we get? he wondered. New York City seemed so far away. And Alaska? Traveling all the way to Alaska would be utterly insane. The longer they ran, the more people they'd have following them. In a day or two, the FBI, the marshals, the police, everyone would be hunting them. And if they arrested him before he could prove that something much more important was going on, they would lock him up and never let him out and then no one would know. Revealing the Great Forgetting, if it was true, that's all that mattered now. It was bigger than all their troubles. Wasn't it? The only thing Jack knew for sure was that he didn't want to lose his memories. And he didn't want to see his father regress into that drooling old man watching shadows in the hospice. No way. He'd gotten his father back and he wasn't going to give him up again.

New York was their best chance. A Collector could walk them through it. The stakes. Who was behind the new forgettings. Then, if he could get a reporter involved, a Mike Wallace or whoever could do that sort of thing, maybe that would be enough. Maybe they could help him find Tony. And then Tony could tell the police that he'd had nothing to do with Mark's murder. Maybe he could get the Captain someplace safe. Maybe. Maybe. Maybe.

5   "Where is he?" growled Marlon Hoover. The detective sat in a chair across from the woman with the cinnamon hair, in a ten-by-fifteen-foot concrete block of a room they used for interviews. When she didn't answer, he continued. "*Miz* Brooks, you have to see by now that Jack fooled you like he fooled everybody else."

"He didn't kill my brother. Why would he kill my brother?"

"Maybe 'cause of what Mark done to you when you two were kids. I read your juvie file. They placed you with fosters when the school found out. Your husband was stealing money from the hospital. He knew we were coming for him. He needed to fake his own death, start over, so he goes to his old friend Jack. They need a body to put in that lake, to try to fool us, make us think it was Tony if we ever went looking. And Jack, he knows someone he'd like to kill, doesn't he? Yes. Yes he does. And here's the bonus: with Tony and Mark gone, he gets you all to himself."

"That's ridiculous."

"I knew Tony wasn't dead. Cowards like him ain't got the stones for suicide. He's been out there, living the good life. Probably shacked up with some girl who isn't half as damaged as his wife."

"You come up with that yourself?"

"Mark was stabbed with a marine Ka-Bar, the same sort of knife we found at the Felter house. Jack killed him. And his old man helped before he went full retard."

She looked to the corner of the room where someone had placed an ant trap; it looked like a discarded hockey puck, dead ants lying around it like specks of black paint.

"Why did Jack drive to Pymatuning last week?"

"I told you, you dumb motherfucker, I don't know."

"Watch your language, missy!"

"I know my rights," she said. "You can't keep me here. Not if I ask for a lawyer."

"This ain't the city, Miz Brooks. This ain't no county seat, even. This is Franklin Mills. You're in here with me. No recordings. No one else in the room. If I say you didn't ask for a lawyer, you didn't ask for no goddamn lawyer."

Sam stood and tried to leave, but the door was locked. It was a pointless attempt at escape, but her petulance infuriated Marlon. He came out of his chair like a lion uncaged and pulled her from the door. She reacted, shoving him back with all her strength. He backhanded her, hard. "Oh, you bitch!" he said between clenched teeth.

She stared at him, a hand on her cheek where it was red from his hand. There was something in this man's eyes she'd only ever seen in her father's, a barely managed fury like a face burned by acid, beneath a thin mask. This detective was another dangerous man.

"Get gone, *Miz* Brooks," he said, unlocking the door with a key attached to his belt. "And think hard about whose side you want to be on. How will history judge you when all this is over?"

"I'll sue you," she whispered as she walked by.

"Doubtful," he said.

6   They rested for the night in Bellefonte, a ways off I-80, north of State College, inside a centuries-old structure called the Bush House Hotel. Jack paid cash, avoiding eye contact with the Pakistani man behind the counter. Cole walked the Captain to their room. They were quickly becoming friends—the Captain had entertained Cole with some of his best war stories during their drive: the one about fishing with grenades in Laos; the one about the guy who'd slept in pajamas in the jungle trenches; the one about the forty-foot-long python that darted across the road in front of their convoy. The Captain had always been best with other people's kids.

"One bed, you cheap bastard?"

"Money's tight," said Jack. "I don't know when we'll be able to get more."

"Well, I ain't sleeping with you. You steal the goddamn covers. You always did that. Wrap yourself in a cocoon like nobody else needs them. And I can't sleep with the boy because he might be gay."

"I'll sleep on the floor," said Jack. "Just try and get some sleep. We leave early. I want to be in the city by noon."

"This is the worst fucking road trip."

They watched the news— Jack found a Steubenville station after some flipping. His flight from justice had not yet caught the interest of reporters outside Portage County. *Give it a few more hours*, he thought. He hoped for some national crisis, a presidential scandal, anything to distract the media until he figured out exactly what he was doing. Stuff like that happened every day. Why shouldn't it do some good for once?

As if reading his mind, the Captain stirred in the bed. "What's the next move, Johnny? Have you thought that far ahead?"

"After New York? I don't know," he said.

"Start planning ahead. Don't wait to react or you'll end up playing defense. That's life. A game. Like chess."

"I know."

"No you don't."

His mind was an overloaded circuit, threatening to short. Jack felt fatigue pulling at his mind, whispering to him, promising to wash away his anxiety. But he kept imagining the door crashing in and a SWAT team rushing at them, pulling his father off the bed. Or worse. What if the door crashed in and on the other side was a team of those wrinkly-faced men in Panama hats? The Hounds? He saw a shadow under the door, someone standing in front of their room. He braced himself. But the shadow moved on.

"You asleep?" the Captain asked.

"No."

"What about the gay kid?"

Jack looked over at Cole, who was curled up in the wide chair. "I think he's out."

"Good. You want to hear it?"

"What?"

"You know what."

"Okay."

The Captain cleared his throat. Talking still took some effort for him. Jack pictured his vocal cords as two frayed rubber bands stretched too far. He wished his father would just go to sleep. He didn't really need to hear this. It wouldn't change anything.

"I gave him a chance, Johnny," he said. "We both did. Tony and me. That morning . . . Your sister was a mess. We got her into rehab at Haven, as you know, made sure Paige was safe with Anna, and then, after you came to the hospital, Tony and I went out to Mark's place to tell him to leave town. He was in his trailer, picking through the junk in the living room for a couple of two-liter soda bottles. He'd just got back from Walmart with supplies and was going to do some of those what do you call 'em . . . shake and bakes?"

"Yes, I think so."

"He'd passed some point, you know? Some point that he could never have come back from, not even if he'd gone clean. There was this smell about him. Like rot. Body rot. Athlete's foot, kind of. Sort of. Except worse. You could smell it eating him. Controlling him like some worm, because that's what drugs are, I guess.

"'Leave,' I told him. 'Get out of Franklin Mills. Stay away from my daughter and stay away from Sam and don't you ever come back.' And he looks at me, you know, sizing me up like he's a lion and I'm a gazelle or whatever. He looks at Tony and you can see he's working it over in his mind and he's thinking he's got an old man and a skinny fancy boy and maybe he can take us. It was murder in his eyes. Seen it before. Know what that look is. I thought there was a chance he was right and that we were outmatched. Who knows what those drugs do to a man's strength, is what I was thinking.

"And then he goes, then he goes"—the Captain was laughing a little, the way a man will when he recalls something tragically funny, the way he got when talking about his buddy Halftrack, the guy who'd got drunk on rice wine one night in 'Nam and, searching for a bottle opener, dug into his jacket and pulled out a grenade pin— "he goes . . . *THPPPPPPPPPFT!*" The Captain put his hand to his mouth and blew a wet raspberry. "Mark farted. Ah, God, it was terrible. Like all he'd eaten in a month was Taco Bell and meth. And Jack, we couldn't help it. We couldn't. Tony turned to me and we started laughing. Laughing at him. Oh, he was pissed! But you could tell, too, that he was embarrassed, that there was this trace of a man somewhere in there who was embarrassed but not strong enough to control his body anymore. And I guess if I'm sorry, I'm sorry for that little spark of something still inside him. Anyway, he got mad and he got stupid. Instead of jumping across the coffee table at me, he jogged around it and that gave me enough time to pull the knife.

"I brought it thinking maybe I'd scare him. Never in a million years did I think I'd actually use it. But there it was. He came at me and I reacted. I reacted because I hadn't thought through the situation, I hadn't thought through the game. And the knife came out and thank God it did because he really could have killed us both if he'd gotten up to speed. Knife went in, high in the chest because he's a stocky motherfucker, and I knew I'd pierced his heart. I'd made a choice and couldn't back away from it now. So I made sure it was done. Stabbed him seven times, deep as I could. One of his lungs popped and hissed like a kid's balloon.

"Tony took me home after that. 'I'll take care of it,' he said. He went back and torched the trailer. An hour later, I see Tony's car pull into that drive from Porter that goes out to Claytor Lake. I knew what he was doing, but I didn't understand why. Why dump Mark's body in the lake if he was going to burn the trailer down? Should have left the body to burn, too."

"What you did was justified, Dad," said Jack. "Self-defense."

"Maybe. But we did it in his home. Without an invitation, if you know what I mean. But I realized something that day. I realized that Tony was a clever SOB. He has his own agenda. His own game to play. That's why he put the body in the lake. In case Sam needed a body to be convinced. Like maybe she'd send a diver down to verify his death, huh? Shithead never figured you'd find a way to bring it up. Tony was setting the pieces for his escape that day. Methodical. Can't trust a man like that, Jack. You remember that."

"He's just searching for his own things."

The room was quiet for a bit. Jack started to think the Captain had finally fallen asleep. But then he stirred again.

"We'll never be able to tell the world what's happening, you know that, don't you?"

"I don't know anything right now, Pop."

"Everyone wants to forget. It's human nature. Never met a man who wouldn't want to forget the worst thing he'd ever done. How powerful is that urge, huh, if it's everybody in the world?"

Eventually sleep found him. It took its damn time, though.

7   Haven. It sat against the sky in an arrogant fashion, denying through its unchanging façade that it was complicit in the theft of the men who loved her. She hated this place, its airy corridors, its sterile make-your-nose-itch smells, its simple *being*. Sam thought she

might burn it down if it meant learning more about what happened to Tony and Jack.

"I'm Tony Sanders's wife," she told the security guard at the front desk. "Could you please find someone who knew my husband?"

The guard disappeared through a set of double doors and was gone for a long while, leaving Sam to read the awards of recognition on the walls above the gurgling electric waterfall. Tony's name was on some of them. *In recognition for years of service*, read one from the local Freemason society.

"Mrs. Sanders?"

A woman stood in the entryway to the common room. She was a tiny thing in a lovely blue dress, her hair dark and short, eyes no bigger than dimes.

"I'm Kimberly Quick," she said, motioning Sam inside. "I worked with Tony for some time."

They walked into a high-ceilinged room where a dozen wards played table tennis in front of a large window. A skinny black man counted out by threes in the corner.

"We met once, at one of Frazier's fund-raisers," Quick said.

"I don't remember."

"It was a long time ago."

Sam followed her into the dormitories. Immediately to the right was Quick's office. She shut the door behind them and they sat in chairs in front of her desk.

"I thought about driving out to your place after Tony disappeared. To bring a casserole or something. But I didn't know what was appropriate."

"Tell me about Cole Monroe," said Sam. It was direct, and she tried to gild it with a casual tone, but it still sounded accusatory.

"I can't discuss patients with you," said Quick, glancing toward the door.

"This isn't about patient confidentiality," said Sam. "I need to find them. Before anyone gets hurt. Tell me what you know about where they went."

Quick folded her hands in her lap. Then she stood, stepped to the door, locked it, and walked to a minifridge in the corner. She reached in and brought out two bottled iced teas, handing one to Sam. She sat on the lip of her desk, gathering her thoughts.

"Samantha, did you ever hear Tony talk about a place called Mu?"

8   An overturned semi full of snack cakes kept them out of the city until late that afternoon. For three hours I-80 was a snarling carbon generator three lanes wide. By the time the city came into view over a sweep of green hills it was after four and Jack realized they would have to hole up for another night.

Jack took the Holland Tunnel and ditched the car at a pricey garage off Twelfth Street. It took some convincing to get the Captain into a cab ("You know how often they clean those seats? About as often as you cleaned the fish tank when you were a kid"), but eventually they got him in and directed the driver to a Marriott Execu-Stay in the financial district. Jack paid the clerk in cash for two days, plus 20 percent. Cole collapsed in the bed, but the Captain nudged him off with a rolled-up brochure. Jack skipped through news channels on TV. CNN had it near the second bump. Seeing his face, that rushed DMV photograph, made him blush. He was so overcome with dry terror that he couldn't immediately process what the anchor was saying and he had to rewind the DVR to catch it.

"A manhunt is under way this evening for high school history teacher Jack Felter. According to law enforcement, Felter is the focus of a murder investigation in the small town of Franklin Mills, Ohio. Felter may be traveling with his elderly father and an underage male companion."

The screen switched to a shot of the Franklin Mills town hall, where Jack had attended middle school dances. That detective with the chop-top stood on the steps and addressed a few reporters. "Mr. Felter is wanted for questioning in the death of local resident Mark Brooks and the abduction of a teenage boy." Cole's class photo from Pencey, three years old, flashed on-screen. "We ask anyone who may have seen Felter or this boy to call the FBI immediately at the number listed below. Please do not attempt to apprehend Felter on your own. He may be armed and dangerous."

9   There was this funny show on the Food Network Sam used to watch, *How to Boil Water*, which taught you to cook even if you didn't know where to start. In reality, Sam was amazed by how difficult it was to boil water. The problem was she needed a lot. Jack had only ever made enough for himself, day by day. Sam wanted gallons. She was going to set out to find Jack and she didn't know how long she'd be on the road. And if they'd boiled their water, she was going to boil hers.

She'd learned once, in some rudimentary physics class in high school, how long it took water to boil and how, when you increased the volume of water, that time increased exponentially. Something to do with calories of energy. It was too much time. She could feel her window of opportunity closing, threatening to separate her from Jack forever.

In the end, she settled on four two-gallon pots on separate burners, cranked to high. Eight gallons didn't seem like enough, but it would have to do.

While they cooked, Sam rummaged in the basement for Tony's Boy Scout backpack, a metal-framed contraption with space for a rolled sleeping bag on top. She scooped out the dead silverfish and filled the sack with a few items she thought might come in handy if, as Dr. Quick had suggested, Cole really was leading Jack to Alaska in search of a lost continent. She raided the Twinings tea tin behind the flour, where she kept the money that was supposed to go toward a new roof. A little over seven hundred dollars.

When the water began to bubble she clicked off the burners and placed each pot next to an AC vent and waited for them to cool. An hour for eight lousy gallons of water.

By the time the car was packed, it was dark and a half-moon was low on the edge of the world. The spring peepers were terribly loud that night. She wanted nothing more than to sit on her porch with Jack, listening to the frogs in the woods make love by starlight. She wanted to tell him that she was three days late and a little afraid.

One more stop.

The Driftwood was dead. Even the juke was silent. Shelly was washing pint glasses in the sink.

Sam knocked on the bar with a bronze key held tight in one hand. Shelly came over wiping her hands on her jeans. "How're you holdin' up?"

"Mmm," said Sam with a shrug. She handed Shelly the key. "Going out of town for a bit. Can you collect the mail at Nostalgia while I'm gone? Keep an eye on the place? Thermostat's wonky. Needs to be turned down at night."

Shelly nodded. "You coming back?"

"Of course," she said.

"Hiya, Sam," said a familiar voice.

She turned to find Nils May slumped in a booth, back to the wall, his smelly sneakers resting on the vinyl seat cushion. He held a pint of Guinness against his gut. Sam walked to him. He looked like he hadn't slept in a while.

"Debbie turn you out?" she asked, meaning it as a joke, but she could tell she'd hit the nail on the head by the way the Viking's eyes got all watery.

"She'll get over it," he said. "But she's meaner'n a coon in a cage when she wants to be. Goddamn, Sam. I didn't even do nothin' this time. Not that wasn't right, anyhow."

"Give her some time." She patted his hand, like petting a mastiff. "I gotta jet."

"Where you going?"

"To find Jack. Try to, anyway."

Nils scooted to the end of the booth, set down his beer. He shook his head. "I don't think that's such a good idea. Not with the FBI after them. Did you see them swarming around the town hall this morning? Couple of 'em come in here about an hour ago, looking for food. Poor bastards."

"I'm done waiting."

"But where you going to look?"

"The detective said something about Pymatuning. I'll start there."

"What if Jack doesn't want to be found right now? I mean, maybe he thinks you're safer here."

"I don't give a flying fuck what Jack thinks. And what if Jack is the one who needs help?"

Nils started to say something, then shut his mouth. His cheeks flushed, but he clamped his jaw tight.

"What's wrong with you?" she asked.

"Nothin'."

"Out with it."

He sighed.

"Nils May," she said, "you know something about this? You got that look on your face like you do when you call your wife and tell her you're still making pizzas when you're in here chugging wheat beer with your buddy Berman. I'm no dummy."

He put a finger to his lips, peering around to see if Shelly was eavesdropping. But she'd gone around to the kitchen.

"Fuckin' what?" said Sam.

"I seen Jack last night," he whispered. "Gave him my truck. That's why Debbie's so miffed."

Sam folded herself into the seat across from him. "I want to know everything you know. *Everything.*"

10   After she put Paige to bed, Jean walked to the toolshed, where the Captain kept his rowboat. It was dark and there was no electricity out here, but Jean had a flashlight. She opened the door and stepped inside. The air was stale and heavy with the scent of petrified grass clippings. The cops had searched here, but not well. They would have never thought to look inside her dad's rusty screwdriver anyhow.

She found it hanging on the plywood wall where she'd left it. It was one of those screwdrivers you can unscrew, the kind with all the extra Phillips heads in the hollow body. Except, there were no extra Phillips heads in this one. Inside this screwdriver was a plastic baggie filled with green meth.

Jean took it inside. She set it on the kitchen table. She sat and stared at it. Her whole body shook. Craving. This would take away her pain.

When Paige was three, she'd nearly choked to death on a crayon. Jean was tweaking at the time, so focused on peeling away the old wallpaper in the kitchen, bit by bit, so she could put up a new border, that she'd forgotten, just for a moment, that Paige was sitting on the floor, drawing with crayons. She felt a hand on her leg and looked down from the stepladder.

Paige stared up at her with a purple face. Her mouth was open but no sound was coming out. From where she stood above her, Jean could see the end of a pale blue crayon lodged in her daughter's windpipe.

Jean jumped down and snatched up the little girl. She pounded Paige on the back. But that didn't work. And so she tried to reach in for it. But she reached in too fast and pushed the crayon deeper. Jean screamed. But then Paige's color came back. She was breathing. She'd swallowed it.

Jean sank to the floor and gripped the girl tightly in her arms and cried. When Paige fell asleep for her morning nap, Jean made herself snort a spoon of the stuff Mark had left behind and then she lay down on the porch and waited for the Captain to find her. He needed to see her at her worst so she could never lie her way out of it again.

Jean wiped away a tear. That was a memory she could not afford to forget, even if this stuff promised relief. She walked the baggie all the way to Claytor Lake and then emptied its contents into the water.

There were other ways to survive.

11 "There's dangerous men out there, Sam," said Nils, jogging out the big oak door of the Driftwood after her. "People worse'n your dad and brother. You can't go alone."

"I can take care of myself," she said, climbing into her car.

Nils kicked some gravel, then climbed into the passenger seat. "You never even been to Pymatuning. It's empty country. Kind of place serial killers hide out. All they got is serial killers and fishermen and you can't tell those kind apart."

"What are you doing?"

"I'm coming with you, I guess. Debbie's angry enough. Don't matter if she's a little madder, right? Can't sleep at home tonight anyway."

Sam leaned over and kissed the Viking on his hairy cheek.

"That'd make her terribly mad," he said.

In a moment, they were heading east at sixty-five miles an hour. Neither Nils nor Sam noticed the cruiser pull away from the bar and follow at a prudent distance.

THREE

A PENNY FOR YOUR THOUGHTS

1   The plan, if that's what you called a vague idea and wishes, was this: hang out by the elevators and wait for someone to come down from the thirteenth floor.

Jack wanted to leave Cole and the Captain at the hotel, but the old man wasn't having it. "Your mother, she had this habit of always asking me some stupid question during the best part of a movie," he'd said. "Right when the action was picking up, she'd say some shit like, 'I'm going to the store tomorrow, should I grab some prosciutto for homemades?' No. Fuck that. You drag me all the way to New York, I'm going to see the action. Besides, I'm better in a pinch than you. You wouldn't know what to do if things go south. You're not a fighter. It's my fault for letting you drop out of wrestling in fifth grade."

There was a wooden bench in the elevator alcove. Jack and the Captain waited there while Cole paced the wide, open lobby. The Captain read the *Times* while Jack watched the archaic dials

above the doors, waiting for one to park in the empty space between twelve and fourteen.

"We're a blurb on page seven. Not even a picture," the Captain
said. Jack was unsure if he heard relief or disappointment in his
father's voice. Probably a little of both.

By eleven, Jack was beginning to rethink their plan. Maybe they
should try the stairs. His eyelids kept closing. Forcing them open
again, Jack noticed elevator two had stopped in that special, empty
space.

How long had it been there? He suddenly couldn't feel his body.
Everything felt too cold. The arrow drifted down.

"Here we go," he said to the Captain, who was leaning against
the granite wall with his eyes closed. The old man popped up, fully
alert. His father had learned to catch z's when he could, in the bush.

Cole caught their movement and scurried over from his perch by
one of the tall, narrow windows. "Which elevator?"

"Number two."

The Captain shook his head and tried not to laugh. "You two
flakes really break my heart. Can you look any more conspicuous?
You, tie your shoe or something," he said to Cole. "You, pretend
you're walking me out," he said to Jack as he limped toward the revolving doors, feigning a bad back. Cole kneeled and untied his
shoe, then worked on tying it again, slowly.

The doors opened and a woman stepped out, heels clicking on
the granite. She was roughly thirty-five, with shoulder-length hair
that curled in dark ringlets. Gray suit, white tights. She carried a
venti Starbucks and a briefcase with a Nu-Day logo on the side. Her
face was stern, focused, but gentle somehow, as if she were thinking
about a proposal she'd given that morning that had gone better than
expected.

She pulled ahead of them at the revolving doors. Outside, Jack
stepped forward as she made to cross the street. He pushed a five-
dollar flashlight into the small of the woman's back. He tried to speak,
but something caught in his throat and, instead, he coughed. She

pulled away from him, mistaking his nudge for a bump by another rude pedestrian, but then Jack grabbed her arm with his free hand and pushed the flashlight into her spine.

"Turn right and keep walking," he said into her ear. "Understand?" The woman nodded and gripped her coffee tighter.

He was nearly overwhelmed by a sense of stinging guilt. He thought of the nuns at St. Joe's. If they could see him now. But he hadn't asked to be here. He hadn't asked for any of this.

"I'm not gonna rape you," he said.

She walked where he directed her. He made to look like they were a couple, walking back to their room. Another minute and they were in the hotel elevator. When the doors shut, the woman looked to Cole and then the Captain. "What the hell do you want?" she asked them in a whisper.

Jack slipped the flashlight back into his pocket. "I want you to tell us everything you know about the Great Forgetting."

2   Pymatuning was bigger than Sam had expected, a colossal man-made lake meandering around glacier-cut gullies. She and Nils came into the park near Black Jack Swamp, a parcel of dead trees sticking out of a smelly lagoon. They combed through parking lots by the marina, checking the dirt drives of summer cottages for Nils's truck. By the time they reached the southern tip of the lake it was getting on past eight and they were forced to suspend the search to have breakfast at a greasy spoon in Jamestown. Sam was on her second cup of coffee when the park ranger walked through the door and took a seat at the counter next to a man in bibbed overalls.

"Morning, Hadley," said the man in the overalls.

The ranger smiled back.

"You hear I reeled in a snapper off the Snodgrass deck yesterday?"

"Don't eat the turtles, man," the ranger said.

"Ain't never had turtle soup?"

"I kept a pet turtle as a kid."

"I had a fish tank. I still eat fish."

"Fish is different."

Bib Overalls shrugged. "Some action up at the Gate House this morning," he said.

This piqued the ranger's interest, Sam noticed. "What did you see?" he asked.

"Couple a men come walking out at dawn, dressed to the nines. Gray suits. Ugly mothertruckers."

"Ugly, how?"

"I don't know. Just generally ugly. You think it's really the NSA that owns it?"

"That's the story, morning glory," the ranger quipped.

"What do you think they're doing out there?"

"It's above my pay grade. But it's been busy, I'll tell you what."

"That so?"

The ranger nodded. "Saw some weirdo cruising the place last week. Guy from Franklin Mills everybody's after now. You seen him on the news?"

"The guy what took the boy and his old man? Get the fuck out."

A piece of over-medium egg stuck in Sam's throat. She coughed it away and shot Nils a look.

"Yup," said the ranger. "Got a call from a detective yesterday, telling me to keep an eye out in case they return."

"Turn on the teevee, Linda!" Bib Overalls shouted. "Let's see if they got this fella yet."

The waitress came around the counter and used a broom handle to switch on the small television suspended over the grill. Sam cringed, expecting to see Jack's DMV picture on the news again. Except what they got was a picture of a large fire at sea, shot from some great height above the waves. The nose of a giant ship sank into the ocean as they watched.

"Crank it up!" said Hadley.

Linda got the broom and knocked it against a button a couple of times. A woman's urgent voice spoke in a hushed tone: ". . . you're seeing is the Deepwater Horizon oil rig, a floating station located in the Gulf of Mexico, forty miles off the Louisiana coast. According to Coast Guard officials, a transmission was intercepted from the cruise ship *Nautilus* at seven o'clock this morning. The message was relayed by a man with a thick accent who identified himself as Mohamed Atta, an Egyptian national. He claimed affiliation with an Islamic extremist group known as al-Qaeda. Shortly after the broadcast, the *Nautilus* veered off course and crashed into Deepwater Horizon. It is not yet known if the explosion was caused by ignited oil on the rig or if there were explosives on the cruise ship. Since the impact, there has been no contact with crew members or passengers. About five minutes ago, the *Nautilus* sank beneath the waves. Estimates put the death toll at nearly three thousand souls. In this clip, captured by New Orleans affiliate WLTV, you can see people leaping from the *Nautilus* moments before it is pulled underwater. A warning to viewers, the footage you are about to see is graphic and may be extremely disturbing to children."

Sam watched in awe with the rest of the diner patrons as the images played out. Waves churned up the sides of the sinking ship as passengers crawled across the forward railing. She could tell that one was a child. Maybe eight years old. One by one, they jumped before the waves crested. But they could not escape the great currents that gripped the *Nautilus*, the unforgiving fingers of Davy Jones tugging it to the briny deep. The camera held the spot until the whirlpool collapsed into itself and the ocean settled.

"We're being attacked!" shouted Overalls. "This is it, amigo. I told you. I told you we never should have pulled out of Iraq. We should have taken Saddam out while we could."

"She didn't say nothin' about Saddam," said the ranger.

"He's behind it. You watch."

Over and over, the footage repeated. Three thousand people eaten by the vortex, as if they had been swallowed up into some other dimension. There was also footage of President Obama being pushed into Marine One by Secret Service agents, the helicopter waiting in some high school football field.

"I can't watch this," said Sam.

The waitress was glued to the set and didn't appear interested in handing out checks. Nils put a twenty on the table and then they left.

An attack like that changes everything, Sam thought. And yet it didn't change anything for them. She still had to find Jack.

3 The elevator doors opened and Jack pointed the woman to their room. Once inside, he directed her to a paisley occasional across from the bed. Cole locked the door behind them.

"I'm not a bad guy," said Jack.

"Just a little abduction now and then?" the woman said with a bitter smile.

"We're not going to hurt you. As soon as you explain everything about the Great Forgetting, we'll let you go."

"I'm a day trader. I work for Nu-Day. I don't know anything about a Great Forgetting. Who were you hoping to kidnap?"

No, thought Jack. *No, no.*

"What were you doing on the thirteenth floor then?"

"Thirteen? I don't know what you're taking about. There is no thirteenth floor." Her eyes widened a little. "The elevator stopped for second on the way down. It's been doing that. A short or something. They warned us about number two earlier in the week. Davis sent a memo."

This can't all be a mistake, Jack pleaded to himself. He looked at Cole. *Oh, Christ. Oh, holy hell.*

"She's lying," the kid said simply. "Did you think she'd just admit to everything?"

"Cole," said Jack. "Shut up a minute."

"Cole?" the woman said. "Wait. Oh, my God. *Cole.* What are you doing here?"

"You don't know me," the boy said.

But the woman seemed sincere. "Cole, honey. I worked with your father. I almost didn't recognize you. You grew up!" She turned back to Jack. "His father. It was terrible. Car accident. Right out front. He died. The boy was shook up, I remember. Taken to a hospital. I heard he was in a psychiatric facility."

The Captain sunk into the bed.

"No!" Cole shouted. "She's lying. You're lying!"

"No, sweetie. I'm sorry." She looked at Jack, pleading with her large brown eyes. "Whatever he's told you, it isn't true. I don't know how he got the both of you so worked up. Worked up enough to kidnap a woman in broad daylight. But this kid is sick. He needs help. I know that much. We all pitched in to help the mother some. Davis passed around a collection hat. I gave her two hundred dollars."

Cole was seething. The kid stepped into the bathroom. Jack figured he needed to throw up or something, that his nerves had gotten the better of him. But then he returned with a glass of water. He set it calmly on the end table next to the woman.

"Drink it," he said.

She laughed. "I don't think so," she said. "You put something in it."

Jack understood. There was fluoride in the water here, as in every other city in the country. Only the Collectors really knew it was a poison capable of bending the mind.

"Watch me," said Jack. He picked up the glass, emptied it into the sink, then moved so the woman could see him fill it from the spigot. He returned it to the table a moment later.

"Drink, please."

"I'm not going to drink it."

"You saw me fill it."

"You're crazy. Both of you." She turned to the Captain, who watched with interest. "Help me," she said. She started to cry.

"Miss," said the Captain. "Maybe the boy's crazy. But what seems crazier to me is that you won't simply drink the goddamn water to get it over with."

She sobbed into her hands.

"I've been to a few interrogations," the Captain continued. "I haven't felt my middle finger since 1973 because some slant-eyed dink pushed bamboo under my nail. He didn't get what he wanted, either. Got to where I can tell a liar from a saint better than any machine. You're good, lady. Real good. You're not just a liar, you're a *trained* liar."

She stopped crying. When she brought her hands down, Jack thought, for an instant, that he was staring at a different woman. Gone was the gentleness he'd seen inside her. Gone were the tears. Her cold eyes regarded them, in turn, with something close to pity. It was Jack, now, who was afraid.

In a flash, Cole was at her side, the slim blade of a pocketknife pushed into her neck hard enough to dimple the skin. The woman didn't flinch. "I borrowed twenty bucks to buy a Swiss Army knife while I was out looking for pizza last night," he said to Jack. "I'll pay you back."

"As I recall, you won a bet," Jack said. His voice sounded like it was coming down a long tube.

"Empty her pockets," said Cole.

Jack reached, expecting the woman to pounce, but she remained still. Her breathing had slowed and he thought that was probably a bad sign. There was something in the pocket of her suit, cold to the touch. He brought it out. It was a stainless-steel object shaped like a bat's wing, with a red button on top.

"What's this?"

"A lighter," she said.

Jack pushed the button. Something shot out of the device. It looked like the wavy air you see around a jet engine when it revs up on the tarmac, that shimmer you catch on the horizon on hot days. And then the lamp on the other side of the room turned to dust. There was no sound, just that wave shooting from the gun, and then the lamp was atomized. He'd missed the Captain by a foot.

He turned the gun on the woman and nodded for Cole to step back.

"Now," he said. "Let's start with your name. And then you can tell me what the hell this thing is and what it just did to that lamp."

4 "My name is Christina Ferris," she said, that murderous look gradually dissolving from her eyes. "And that thing you're holding like a toy is a particle agitator. It uses compressed sound waves to pick apart objects at the molecular level. I was his father's partner. One of the Twelve Angry Men, as they're called. I was the first woman, so, you know . . . bit of a misnomer."

"My father's partner?" said Cole. "Why didn't he ever talk about you?"

"Everything we do is secret. I imagine your father was protecting you. Or me." She shrugged. "You know what they'll do to me when they find out I talked to you? They'll erase my mind. They'll put a microchip in my tooth, a little thing that broadcasts new memories just for me. They'll make me believe I'm a beautician in Iowa or something and I'll think that was me for the rest of my life."

"Christina," said Jack. "All we need is a little information and you can go. We won't tell anyone we ever spoke."

She laughed and sat back in the seat, regarding the kid. "How do you remember? Why didn't you forget?"

Cole knocked on the titanium plate behind his left ear. "I don't know how, but this thing dampens the signal."

"Fantastic," she said. "I know he loved you very much, Cole. He had pictures of you in his office. For what it's worth, I had nothing to do with what happened that day."

"Let's not talk about my dad right now."

Christina nodded.

"I want to hear about the Great Forgetting," said Jack.

"What do you want to know?"

"What was it all about?"

"We let something terrible happen and the leaders of the world decided we should forget. 'Forget the past to make a better future,' they said."

"But what, exactly? A genocide, right? But who? What race did we wipe out?"

"The Nazis nearly won World War Two. Who do you think they wiped out?"

"But . . ." Jack tried to make sense of it. Couldn't. Came up short.

"The Nazi gas chambers killed millions of Jews in Europe," the woman said. "The gas chambers they built in the Nevada desert after they invaded America killed millions more. They killed almost every Jew in the world and we let it happen. There was no Pearl Harbor. No D-day. No Hiroshima. The United States hid its head in the sand until Hitler had the entire Eastern Hemisphere. By the time we acted, it was too late. Ten million Nazis descended through the Bering Strait. Anchorage fell. Then Seattle, Portland, Sacramento. They pushed east all the way to Pennsylvania before the Resistance created the A-bomb, before we started to push back. By the time it was over, it was 1964, and half the population of the world was dead, and an entire race of people was utterly lost. Only three thousand Jews remained, scattered survivors. Endangered. And it was our fault. Wouldn't that be something you'd really want to forget if you could?"

"Make it make sense with what I know," said Jack, measuring his words. "I know Jewish people. And what about Pearl Harbor . . . I've seen photographs. My grandfather served in the Pacific Theater."

"So, it took a hundred years to build the Great Forgetting machine," she said. "A hundred years to prepare for it. During that time, we . . . reconstituted the Jewish people using techniques invented by the Nazi scientist Josef Mengele."

"Reconstituted?"

"Eugenics. A breeding program. On a scale you could not imagine. Baby warehouses on every continent. The antithesis of the gas chambers. We brought them back."

"Hubris," the Captain said. But his voice was filled with awe.

"By the time we were ready to flip the switch to forget, it was 2065. A new history was written for our minds. Memories of World

War Two as it had never been. Pearl Harbor. Our victory over Japan and Germany. They're stories, a fiction told by the digital code that comes out of HAARP. The algorithm allows each person's mind to create their own personal memories that correspond with an invented, shared history. Like separate instruments playing the same symphony."

"How much of what I know as history is actually true?" asked Jack.

"Does it matter?" she said.

"This is a perversion," the Captain said.

"It all happened before I was even born."

Jack shook his head. "And your job is to collect evidence of this world that existed before the Great Forgetting. Stuff that might clue people in to what we've forgotten."

"Yes."

"How do you know where to find these artifacts?" asked Jack.

"We're given assignments."

"By whom?"

"I'd rather not say."

"I'd rather you did," Jack said, gesturing with the atomizer.

"You don't understand. Just saying his name alerts the system. It's one of the code words the NSA listens for in outgoing e-mails and phone calls. Maybe you've heard of Echelon? Our data-mining system? Well, what it's really doing is monitoring any reference to the Great Forgetting. Saying this man's name brings attention to our conversation. The whole system will focus on us, record our voices, target us as a threat."

"Write it, then."

Cole pulled paper and a pen from his backpack and tossed it to her. She scribbled something and passed it to Jack.

The Maestro, it read.

"Don't say it out loud if you want to remain hidden," she said.

He passed it to the Captain.

"Who is he?" asked Jack.

"He's the man who maintains the algorithm. He lives in the

mountains with the Hounds, beyond the Grimpen Mire. I've never met him."

"The Great Forgetting was only supposed to be a one-time deal," said Cole. "But now somebody is using the machine to reset the calendar again. Little forgettings. Over and over. Sometimes a day. Sometimes a week or a month. Sometimes an entire year."

"It's true. Someone has hacked into the machine."

"Who?" asked Jack.

"We don't know."

"What? What do you mean you don't know?" asked Jack. "Who does?"

"The only one who really needs to know is the Mae—" she stopped abruptly, covering her mouth with one hand. "He writes the code. I just collect things."

"We should be going," said the Captain, putting a hand on Jack's shoulder.

Jack nodded. He backed up and motioned for Christina to stand. "There's something else I can't wrap my mind around," said Jack. "There must be some things that can't be manipulated by this algorithm. I mean, if the calendar resets at a full moon, goes back a week, wouldn't everyone, at least astronomers, realize the moon is full when it shouldn't be? The moon, and the position of planets and constellations in the sky, that's not something you can explain away like pages on a calendar. That's something that can't be ignored."

Christina smiled. In spite of her pathological nature, Jack found himself wanting to like her. "The first day on the job I asked Cole's father about that very thing," she said. "You know what he told me?"

"What?"

"He told me the moon changes, too. Nobody remembers how the moon works. If anybody knows, it's the people of Mu."

5   Christina waited until they were in the elevator and Jack's guard was down. He sensed a change, a shift in her demeanor, but was powerless to stop her.

"I'm sorry," said Christina. "They scan our minds every month. I can't just let you let me go."

"The fuck are you saying?" said Jack.

Christina closed her eyes. "The Maestro is in the mountain. The Maestro is in the mountain with the Hounds. The Maestro. The Maestro. The Maestro."

"Stop!" screamed Cole. "Shut up! Shut up!"

Jack pulled her close, a hand over her mouth. But it was far too late.

When she squirmed out of his grip, he did not fight.

"I'm sorry," she said. "I waited as long as I could. You have a two-minute head start. That's as much as I can do."

"Thanks, lady," the Captain said.

"I am sorry about your dad," she said to the boy. "He was a good man."

"He wanted to stop what's happening," said Cole. "You should, too."

"You can't stop it. It was built to last forever."

The doors opened with a ding.

"Go," she pleaded. "They'll be here soon."

They ran down John Street, then north on Nassau. Jack tried to flag a cab, but none stopped.

"Panama hat!" Cole yelled, glancing behind them as they neared Fulton.

Sixty yards behind and closing fast was a man in a charcoal suit and a Panama hat. The man's face was wrinkled in jaundiced creases like the Hound Jack had seen on his jog. Perhaps it was the same one.

They got across the street in time to cut off the Hound by the changing lights. They watched him across the river of traffic. He marked their passage with a slack face.

Jack led them down a thin alley that swung at ninety degrees behind bins of garbage, toward Broadway. He chanced another look. There were two now, bounding down the alley, gaining. As he watched, one of the sharp-dressed Hounds leaped onto a brick wall and used it as leverage to launch himself forward. The little display of parkour closed some of the distance between them.

"Don't look back," said Jack, quickening the pace.

But of course Cole did. "Holy fuck!"

They shot onto Broadway. To their immediate right a cab had pulled over to let out a pair of women. A man in a tweed jacket, the kind with cosmetic patches on the sleeves, waited to get in. As they approached, the man positioned himself to block them. The Captain barked at him like a Doberman. The man in the tweed jacket jumped back three feet, holding his hands in front of his face. "He's ill," said Jack. In a moment, they were inside.

"GO!" shouted Cole.

"Where, brotha?" said the cabbie, a young bearded man with a Quincy accent.

"Just fucking go!"

"Roger dodger." The driver accelerated into traffic. Jack spun in his seat to look out the window. Two Hounds watched from the shadows of the alley. One was on a cell phone. They didn't even look winded and their hats remained snug on their simian heads.

As the cab darted through narrow gaps in traffic Jack noticed the driver staring at them in the mirror. What he didn't need right now was someone recognizing them from the news. "What's up?" he asked.

"You guys media?" the cabbie asked.

"What?"

"CNN? The *Times*?"

"No. Why?"

"The attack. Just, everyone's going crazy. I've been jetting reporters around town the last hour."

"Attack?" the Captain said, leaning forward.

"Man, where you guys been? Check the monitor."

They looked at the small screen stuck into the back of the cab's partition. It showed a live news feed: a fire on the ocean, flames erupting from a jumble of twisted metal without shape. An urgent scrawl ran underneath, portending major shit. A red bug on the top right corner blinked: *Breaking News*. Cole fumbled with a knob, cranking the volume.

". . . according to unconfirmed reports. President Obama was alerted an hour ago, in Florida, where he was addressing a group of elementary students. He was moved by Secret Service to a secure bunker at an unknown location."

The summary came from the scrawl: *Terrorist attack! Cruise ship taken by hijackers, crashes into oil rig in Gulf of Mexico. 3,000 feared dead. Oil plume seen miles from explosion . . .*

"Who did it?" the Captain asked.

"They're saying al-Qaeda."

"What's al-Qaeda?"

"Some Islamic cult."

"They'll find a way to use this," said Cole, looking out the window as they headed south.

"What do you mean?" asked Jack.

"Whoever is running things. Whoever is causing these new little forgettings. They'll rewrite everyone's memories of this attack to fit in with their agenda. Don't you get it, yet? Whatever history is the last one written is the one that becomes true. The history we know right now may not be the one that ultimately survives."

The Captain looked out the window, at the skyscraper where the kid's father had once worked. Cole's father had worked in the north one.

"We used to joke about those buildings," the Captain said. "When we were flying into JFK."

Cole looked over at him. "The Twin Towers?"

The Captain nodded. "We used to joke about flying into them. Sick joke, really. They're just so goddamn big. Every pilot knows that, eventually, somebody's going to accidentally fly right into one. Some little Cessna, maybe, flying blind at night."

As the Twin Towers of the World Trade Center passed behind them, Jack gave the driver directions to the garage where they'd left the truck. In another hour, they were out of the city.

6 "There's the Gate House," said Sam as they turned onto a gravel road. She pointed to a castle-like building on the water, attached to the shore by a stone bridge. She parked the car in the lot across from it. Neither of them noticed the Franklin Mills cruiser that stopped at the turn in the road and slowly backed up into the shadow of a giant oak.

Nils climbed out and stretched his back, feeling vertebrae shift into place. The air outside was warm and fragrant with the honey-pollen of early summer.

They crossed to the Gate House, walking under the rock canopy of the bridge, the kind of bridge trolls hid under in fairy tales, all the way to a heavy wooden door with wrought-iron fixtures. Sam tried the handle and, finding it locked, tried the knocker. But no one answered.

"Let's walk around a bit," she said. "I don't know why, but I can almost feel him here. You know? Like Jack was standing right here a minute ago."

They walked the length of the reservoir road, about a half mile, then down its slope. They tried a jogging path that snaked through the woods and then around the edge of the water to a section of pavilions and restrooms where fishermen cleaned blue gill on a sheet-metal table. By the time they returned to the car, Nils had sweated through his vintage *Star Wars* tee and was huffing loudly.

"Take a breather," she said.

"I should call Debbie," he said, leaning on the fender.

"Need my phone?"

He nodded.

"It's in the cup holder," she said, tossing him the keys. She stood there fidgeting for a pace. Finally, she said, "I'm going to check the Gate House again," and started back up the hill.

The call was brief and heated and mostly pointless. "Where the hell are you?" "Pymatuning." "Why?" "I'm keeping an eye on Sam." "You should be keeping an eye on your wife." "She needs someone.

I'll be back soon." In the end, Debbie loved him. He knew this. And there were times she could be so kind, twisting her manicured nails through his nappy red Viking hair while they watched *The Walking Dead*.

When Sam didn't return after another five minutes, Nils walked up the hill. She wasn't at the Gate House. He walked across to get a look at the shore. But she was nowhere to be found.

7 "What now?" the Captain asked over a bowl of lentil soup. They were in a truck stop somewhere in Delaware. They hadn't talked much on the drive out of the city. All they could do was listen to the news reports on the truck's lousy speakers. Obama had reappeared at the White House around three for a brief press conference. He vowed a "swift revenge." There were no more updates about Jack's flight from authorities. Nothing except more footage of the attack on Deepwater Horizon. The nation had forgotten Jack Felter.

"I don't know, Pop," said Jack. "What do you think?"

"Everything Cole said was true."

Cole smiled around his sandwich.

"So, what, then? The island?"

The Captain nodded. "Where else can we go, Jack? Eventually this will die down and the feds will remember us. If we're lucky, we might have a week of relative anonymity. We best use our good fortune to get to Alaska."

"And Jean? Sam? What about them?"

"They're safer where they are. Better they don't know about any of this."

"It feels like we're running away just to save ourselves."

"For Christ . . . listen, there's nothing we can do. And, frankly, I'm not keen on living in a world that controls the minds of its citizens. I want to keep my memories, as fucked up as they are. My memories are what make me, me. Now, I'm too old to join any crusade. I've been through the hell of war. But maybe you should start asking yourself if you shouldn't be helping Cole and your old friend Tony. Maybe you should get to Mu and help him tear this thing down, stop all this, stop whoever is deleting history."

"If something could be done, don't you think Tony would have done it by now?"

"We won't know what happened to Tony until we get there," said Cole.

"I can't just leave Sam behind."

"You can and you will," the Captain said in a tone Jack had not heard for many years, that I-am-your-father commandment voice. "If she and your sister know nothing, the Hounds might leave them alone. If they come with us, they're going to get hurt. Or worse. And I don't even want to think about carting Paige across the country. Do you?"

Jack relented. This was the safest choice, to leave them behind. He was being selfish. But it tore his goddamn heart to shreds.

"I have to say goodbye."

"You'll say too much," the Captain said. "Don't."

"That's the deal. I can't let Sam think I left her without a second thought like her husband did." He didn't look at his father before he walked away.

Five minutes later he had a cheap prepaid phone from the rest stop boutique and was cowered in a corner by the restrooms, trying to look inconspicuous. Sam's cell rang three times before a voice came on that wasn't hers.

"Hello?" It was a man's voice, familiar. His tone was anxious.

"Hello?" said Jack. "Who's this?"

"Jack? Shit. Jack!"

"Yes?"

"It's Nils."

"Nils, what are you doing with Sam's cell phone?"

"Jack, I have some bad news."

He didn't think his mind could hold any more, but he asked for it anyway.

"Sam's gone, man," said Nils.

BACK THERE

1 Jack ended the call and put a hand on the grimy wall of the truck stop atrium to steady himself. There suddenly was not enough oxygen in the air. He fought for breath, for clarity.

"What happened?" the Captain asked. Cole bounced on his sneakers a few feet away.

It took Jack a minute to relay the news. When he finished, nobody said anything for a beat. They could all feel the flow of time pulling opportunity away from them.

"The Hounds took her," said Cole.

"You don't know that," said Jack.

"Well, it's either the Hounds or the police."

"We have to go."

"No fucking way," the Captain said. "You may be old and ugly, but I still outrank you. Driving back that way only gets you thrown in jail. I'll end up in hospice or something. Cole will end up in the nut ward by nightfall."

"I'm going," Jack said, his jaw set.

Cole raised a hand to draw their attention. "If it's the Hounds, I know where they'd take her and we wouldn't have to drive all the way back to Pymatuning," he said.

"I'm listening," said Jack.

Cole's father took the exit into Jersey. They were in his work car, that light brown thing that looked kind of like a jet and hummed like a vacuum cleaner. He parked it in front of a warehouse in Newark. Antolini's Bookshop, the faded red-and-white sign out front said. Inside were aisles of books on corrugated metal shelves stretching so far the rows appeared to curve. Boxes of paperbacks were stacked on endcaps. A dozen people milled about with shopping carts full of hardbacks. Cole followed his father to the counter, where a man with a corona of white hair sat on a stool.

"I'm Jonas," his father lied. "I called about the book?"

The octogenarian raised a finger, then bent and pulled a small tome from under the desk, which he placed on the counter. It had a funny title and on the cover was the image of a man on fire. It was listed for $2.50.

"Is it a good book?" the old man asked. "I haven't read it."

His father handed him exact change. "I don't read them," he answered. "I'm just a collector."

Cole opened the novel as his father drove north on 87. He read the first sentence out loud: "It was a pleasure to burn." He blinked and looked at his father. "That's a funny thing to say."

"That's the problem. Some of the books from before the Great Forgetting are just nonsense. They upset people. Why would anyone want to remember a story that upsets them?"

"I don't know," said Cole. But he was curious. Why was it a pleasure to burn? He had to read a little to find out. Except when he read two pages, some more questions popped up. And so he read a couple more pages. And then ten. And then he was halfway through already and so he might as well just finish it. It was a short novel anyway.

Cole finished the book before they arrived at Big Indian Mountain.

"Was it any good?" his father asked.

He wasn't sure what to say. "I think so."

"You think so? If you have to think about it, it must not be very good."

On a dirt road that wound up the side of the mountain, a sign with three arrows informed them that they were approaching a large bog called Grimpen Mire. There was a drawing of a hiker inside a red crossed-out circle. His father parked beyond the sign and they got out, Cole clutching the misbegotten book.

"This way," his father said. "Walk in my footsteps. You step into the mire and we'll have to work to get you out. A couple riders have lost horses in here."

Cole followed closely, stepping where his father stepped along a thin band of moss-covered earth that snaked between pools of fetid water choked with bracken and black timber. After a quarter mile his father veered off the path and went around a large oak tree. He pushed at the bark and a panel set into the tree clicked open like the door to the entertainment center they had at home. Inside was a keypad.

His father grinned. It was nice to see him smile again. He didn't smile much anymore. "We are the music makers," he whispered to his son. "We are the dreamers of dreams." Then he softly said the combination out loud as he punched in the code, just like Willy Wonka had done in the movie. "Ninety-nine, forty-four, one-hundred-percent pure." There was a hiss as a seal was broken. A door appeared in the oak tree and it opened on a hydraulic hinge.

"Stay close," his father said.

When the door shut behind them, everything went pitch-black for a moment and then a rope of orange light flickered on overhead. It wound down a tight staircase, which his father descended. The stairs went on forever, it seemed. Ten stories at least. Eventually they came to a wide concrete tunnel lined with cables and pipes. The air was cooler down here, but regulated; a light breeze tickled Cole's nose.

"This way," his father said, taking a right. A sign on the wall read SECURITY/GULAG/STORAGE. At a large junction they stopped for a moment. His father went to the wall and slid aside a metal panel, revealing an array of thin television screens. It was some kind of security system, the CCTVs showing different areas of the compound. Something that looked like a barracks. Another one showed a cafeteria full of men in boxer shorts and tees; hairy, muscular men.

"Are those . . . ," Cole asked.

"The Hounds? Yes. Don't worry. They're not close. But I had to check. They'd erase my mind for bringing you down here if they caught us. And when the Hounds delete your memories, they're not gentle about it. Some of their victims end up with a good dose of dementia when they're done."

They took another right. Some time later they came to a door set into the wall, the sort of door with a circular handle, like on a sub. His father unwound the wheel and it kicked open. They stepped inside.

"Holy shit!" said Cole.

His father sighed.

It was a great big hanger, a domed concrete bunker ten football fields wide, and it was filled with all kinds of forbidden junk. They stood on a wrought-iron platform overlooking the whole mess: cars with three headlights; bins of shiny coins, whole rows of them; city signposts for places that had been wiped from memory—20 MINUTES TO CAHOKIA, one read. There were clothes imbued with some magic that illuminated the fabric from the inside. And stacks and boxes and cases and racks of books. His father led him down the steps toward the library quadrant. There, among a hundred more, he placed the book with the strange title.

"Did you bring all these books here?"

"Most of them were voluntarily turned in before the Great Forgetting. But I've brought a lot of them, yes."

"Why not destroy them?"

His father shrugged. "It was part of the deal. A concession."

By the time they returned to the car it was dark.

"That library," said Cole. "And all the forgotten stuff. It's sad."

"Is it?" His father reached over and squeezed his hand. "Try not to think about it."

"If you can get me to Big Indian, we can find out if the Hounds have Sam," said Cole when he finished telling his story.

2   Jack walked to the map on the wall of the truck stop. They were just outside Wilmington. Big Indian Mountain, when he found it, was several hands away. "We're looking at a four-hour drive," he murmured, hands on his hips. "You," he said, pointing at the boy. "Follow me. Dad, we'll be right back."

"You going to jerk each other off in the bathroom? We're kind of pressed for time if you haven't noticed."

"I know it, Pop. Just give us a minute."

Jack pulled Cole along by his shirtsleeve, out a set of doors leading to a picnic area, then behind a row of snack machines. He looked into the boy's eyes. He'd perfected this stare the last few years. He thought of it as the teacher's version of a vampire's mesmerizing gaze. Under its spell no one could lie.

"You were not honest with me," he said.

"I know," said Cole.

"You knew more about the Great Forgetting than you told me."

Cole didn't say anything.

"You're manipulating me. You still have me on a gradient, don't you? You're giving me crumbs to follow and I don't know where you're leading me. No more gradients, Cole. You don't have to do that anymore. Aren't we starting to be some kind of friends?"

"Are we?"

Jack laughed. "Yes," he said.

Cole blushed.

"Is there anything else I need to know? If so, tell me, now."

Cole didn't say anything.

What was this boy after, really? Jack sensed another agenda, something other than finding Mu.

"You don't have to play it so close," Jack said. "I'm on board. I'm a believer. Why won't you trust me?"

For a moment it seemed like the boy was about to say something, but then he just stood there, staring back at Jack, the way so many of his students had.

This was leading nowhere. And the Captain was right. Time was running out. "Let's go," he sighed.

"Let's buy a gun," the Captain proposed as they walked back to the car.

"No," Jack said. "And fuck no."

"What if those Hound things come after us?"

"Then it's over anyway. We don't need to bring a Saturday night special to this rodeo."

"That's good," the Captain said. "That was good, Jack. You're learning."

Jack smiled. "Besides, I still have that woman's atomizer."

"You took it?" Cole asked, his eyes wide with newfound respect.

"It felt wrong to pitch it in the trash for the cleaning lady to find."

"Can I hold it?" the Captain asked.

"No."

On the highway again, Jack called Nils and relayed their plan. And though he tried to dissuade him, in the end Nils couldn't be talked out of meeting up with them at Big Indian. When he was done, Jack pitched the phone out the window.

3   Sam was in another interrogation room, not unlike the one she'd shared with the detective in Franklin Mills. Beige concrete walls, a wide mirror that must be one of those see-through-from-the-back kinds she'd seen on *Law & Order*. She was cuffed to a metal chair in front of a colorless table where two cups of coffee sat, long since steamed out. Sitting across from her was a man in a charcoal suit. At least she thought it was a man. But the man was, well . . . weird-looking. Like no cop she'd ever seen. Like no *human* she'd ever seen. He was a hairy motherfucker, dark coarse hairs sticking out from under his shirtsleeves and the top of his collar. And his fingers! Prunish things, long talons that looked like they'd sat in water for a week. She couldn't look at his face. That squashed nose, like it had been pounded into his skull by a brick; that thin, patchy beard, the kind high school freshman try to grow; beady eyes. He sat there looking at her, a smile playing at his mouth where there was but a hint of an upper lip.

After she'd left Nils in the parking lot at Pymatuning, she had gone back to the Gate House and found the door open an inch. She went in. Then she heard the voices below. The sound was coming up a winding staircase in the middle of the floor. She'd gone to find out who was there, knowing it must be Jack, had to be Jack, because who else could it be? "Hello?" she had called out. And then the voices stopped and she felt the first tingling of apprehension. When this man's wrinkled face appeared around the curve, she screamed. In a flash, he grabbed her, dragged her down to this dungeon room that looked like something out of a seventies cop shop. Ever since, they'd just sat here.

Finally, the door opened and a man—a real, recognizable-as-a-man man—entered, carrying a thin manila folder. He was dressed in a suit and tie but no Panama hat. His hair was blond and cut short, military-style. He appeared to be in his midthirties, the sort of rugged Texas-handsome guy Sam liked to dance with at the Boot Skoot in Brimfield on occasion.

"Afternoon, Ms. Brooks," he said. "Sorry to keep you waiting." He took a chair beside the man in the Panama hat and set the folder on the table. Sam could see her name written on the tab.

"What the hell is going on?" she asked.

The man smiled. It was an honest, friendly smile, and she felt herself relax.

"My name is Greg Carr," he said, uncuffing her wrist. She rubbed it, hesitantly. "I work for the NSA, the National Security Agency? Probably you didn't know this, but the Gate House is federal property. You were trespassing. This is Scopes. He's in charge of security for our small department."

"Scopes?" she asked, looking to him. He didn't blink.

"He's a . . . private contractor."

"Okay," said Sam. "I didn't know I was trespassing. I was only trying to find a friend and . . ."

"Jack Felter?"

"Yes. How did you know?"

"Because we're looking for Jack, too. He kidnapped an NSA agent in New York earlier this afternoon."

She was stunned into silence.

"It's terribly important we find Jack, Ms. Brooks. We don't want anybody getting hurt."

"That can't be right. Jack wouldn't kidnap anyone."

"I assure you, what I'm telling you is the truth. All I ask, in return, is for you to do the same."

She nodded.

"What do you know about this mental patient, the boy, Cole?"

"He was my husband's patient. Tony Sanders."

"What do you know about the boy's condition?"

"Condition?"

"His delusion."

"Nothing."

"Let me speed this up," Agent Carr said, wiping his forehead. "What do you know about the Great Forgetting?"

"The what?"

"Don't be coy."

"I don't know what you're talking about."

The man in the Panama suit grunted.

"What do you know about fluoride?" Agent Carr demanded. "What do you know about HAARP?"

Sam saw it then. Tony really had stumbled onto something. There was some nugget of truth in the boy's strange stories. Certainly the whole thing couldn't be true. But a piece of it? Could the kid have picked something up from his father, the details of a covert NSA program or something? Whatever it was, she knew her best chance of walking out of the Gate House was to play dumb.

"I don't know anything," she said. "I promise."

Agent Carr sighed. "Have it your way, Ms. Brooks." He reached into his jacket and pulled out what appeared to be a Walkman cassette recorder attached to a tiny handheld radar dish. He put the seashells in his ears and lifted the device so that it pointed at Sam's head.

"What's that?" she asked.

"A forgotten toy."

He fiddled with a knob on the Walkman, and then, suddenly, Sam's head filled with a palpable hum. It felt like she was standing in front of a tall speaker that was pointed at a microphone in some punk rock club, as if her thoughts had folded back on her in a loop, building feedback behind her eyes. Agent Carr dialed down the knob and the pressure slagged off a bit.

"What do you know about the Great Forgetting?"

"Nothing, I told you," she said. But then an image flashed in her mind. She was back in Dr. Kimberly Quick's office. *Did you ever hear Tony talk about a place called Mu?* she had asked. And that's when Quick had told her the basics of Cole's theories, how the government was brainwashing people with chemicals and rewriting their memories through radio broadcasts, about a secret island off the Alaskan coast.

"You lied to me, Ms. Brooks," said Agent Carr.

"You read my mind," she whispered.

"That's right." He pulled out the earbuds and secreted the radio back into his pocket. He opened her file and wrote some notation in the margins of his report.

"Can I go?" she asked.

Agent Carr laughed. "No."

"I'd like to call a lawyer, then. I have rights."

"This is a United States military tribunal. You don't have any rights."

"Am I being charged with something?" she asked. Her heart thumped rapidly against her chest. She could see her blouse rising and falling with its momentum. Her underarms dripped perspiration.

"Treason," he said. "Your sentence is 'identity modification.' Effective immediately."

"This is some kind of joke."

Scopes grunted.

"No joke, ma'am." Agent Carr finished writing, then crossed to her chair and cuffed her hands together. "Come with me," he said. He pulled at her shackles, leading her out the door. Scopes followed.

Tears welled up. This was a bad dream. She would wake up soon, back in bed, sweating with fear, thankful to be home.

"Who was the man who came with you?" asked Agent Carr as they walked down a wide concrete corridor lit by flickering fluorescents. "That fat guy."

"His name is Nils," she said.

"Well, we had to kill him, I'm afraid. He tried to break down the Gate House door. Put up quite a fight for a minute."

She started to cry. Agent Carr pulled her down a thinner hallway that ended at a door with a frosted-glass window. Upon it was etched DELIVERY/PICKUP. He brought her inside.

It was some kind of post office, a small room crammed with boxes and envelopes. Laminated memos were taped to the walls. A poster near the counter showed Uncle Sam towering over a ruined city. NEVER FORGET WHY WE FORGOT! it read.

Set into the wall beside the counter was a giant glass tube running through something like an MRI machine lined with panels and readouts. Agent Carr pushed a button and a door opened on the tube with a hiss of trapped air. A long bed lay within. Not an MRI, she realized. It reminded her of the machine she used to pick up her prescriptions at the twenty-four hour drive-thru in Ravenna. It was a vacuum tube. Big enough for humans.

"No," she said. She was no longer crying. She was much too terrified to cry.

"Get in," he ordered. Scopes pulled a revolver from a holster and aimed it at her chest.

Sam stepped up to the tube. Scopes pushed her, hard, with the barrel of the gun.

"Lie down," said Agent Carr.

Sam climbed inside and lay flat on her back. "Please," she said.

But Agent Carr was done with her. He sealed the lid. There was a loud *FOOOOMP!* and then she was being launched down the tube at something near the speed of light, or so it felt to her.

4   A fisherman found the fat man's body and called ranger Bat Hadley. By the time the ranger got to the Gate House there were a dozen smelly anglers moping around the remains, taking pictures. That was all he needed, a photo of a dead guy in his park.

"Christ," he said when he saw the body sprawled beside the creepy wooden door of the NSA outpost.

"You know him, Bat?" asked a woman with a chipped front tooth.

"Yup," he said. "It's that cop from Franklin Mills."

The detective had been shot at close range, between the eyes. But something funny had happened to his arm. It looked gray and deformed, and when Bat kicked it with his boot it dissolved into fine ash and blew away in the breeze.

5   They met at a rest stop at the base of Big Indian Mountain, a green child of the Catskills range. Nils transferred their gear into the trunk of Sam's car and then climbed in the back. They left the truck behind. Jack was touched to see that Sam had gone through the trouble of boiling eight gallons of water. That would come in handy if they really were traveling all the way to Alaska.

He drove the winding switchbacks of Big Indian with Cole riding shotgun so he could navigate the TacMars. For a while the road was paved and lined with heather and Russian thistle. Great maples provided a thick canopy. Streams meandered down slopes, feeding Esopus Creek. There was a path on the side of the road for hikers and riders. Soon deciduous trees gave way to knotty pines. At a dirt trail nearly hidden by ferns, Cole told Jack to turn.

"We used to get this feeling in the bush, sometimes," the Captain said quietly. "That feeling in your gut that says to turn around. The men who ignored it and pushed on usually stepped on a Bouncing Betty or something and that was all she wrote. Like the voice of God shaking your insides and telling you to go home."

Jack didn't stop. A little ways down the trail, the road got muddy and threatened to suck in the tires. Jack parked and they got out. It would be completely dark in three hours. He wondered if there was enough time to find Sam and get back before sunset.

The path ended in the mire, a great flat bog that smelled like damp death. Dead lumber jutted from stagnant pools like the rotted teeth of the mountain herself. A thin, noxious mist obscured their feet. A million crickets played a discordant lullaby. Nils picked up a rock the size of a baseball and chucked it into the nearest mud pool. It hit the earth with a wet smack, like a lover's kiss, and then disappeared.

"That's not good," said the Viking.

"I remember the way," said Cole. "Stay close. Walk where I walk." The boy stepped onto a patch of high grass. Jack took the Captain's hand, lending support, and Nils followed. Their progress was measured in inches. A couple of times Cole muttered a curse and made them double back. Jack sensed they were coming to the other side, when the Captain stepped into the mire.

"Fuck a duck!" he shouted.

His father's right leg was sunk up to the knee. The earth belched and his leg slipped deeper.

"Help me!" Jack yelled. He pulled at the Captain, both arms wrapped around the old man's delicate torso. Cole grabbed the back of Jack's shirt with both hands and tugged. Nils bent at the Captain's legs and yanked, hard.

"Ow!" the Captain said. "You're going to pull off my foot, you dumb ox!"

For a long, terrifying pause, nothing happened. Then, slowly, the Captain's leg began to slip free. They repositioned and pulled again. The leg popped out all at once, sending them backward, onto the ground in a pile.

Jack let out his breath and began to laugh with giddy relief. Nils and Cole laughed, too. The Captain suppressed a smile. "I feel like a scoutmaster again," he said. "In charge of one of those 'special troops,' the ones that take the short bus to camp and sing shit in the middle of lunch when nobody wants to hear them sing."

Cole found the tree five minutes later. Jack could see that it wasn't a normal oak. The bark was too polished. Plasticine, maybe.

"You guys realize who we are?" asked Cole.

"What are you talking about?" said Jack.

"We're the characters from *The Wizard of Oz*. The good guys from the story? The Scarecrow," he said, pointing to the Captain, "who needs a new brain. The Tin Man," he said, pointing to Jack, "who needs to get his heart back, and the Cowardly Lion," he said, pointing at Nils.

"Hey!" said the Viking.

"So who does that make you?" asked Jack.

Cole shrugged.

"He's a friend of Dorothy's," the Captain grumbled. "Hey, Toto, open the goddamn door so we can see what's inside."

Cole pushed the panel. It clicked open easily. "We are the music makers," he whispered, typing the code. "We are the dreamers of dreams."

"For fuck's sake," said the Captain.

"Uh," said Nils, "I'm taking a lot on faith here. But could someone please explain to me who built a fake tree in the middle of a swamp?"

6 Here was the long corridor Cole had traveled with his father in some long-ago, better world. It stretched forever both ways, a current of cool air ripping through the tunnel, black cables snaking down the walls like veins. They followed the boy, quieting their footfalls with careful steps, afraid the sound would carry to the beasts that lurked inside.

Cole felt crummy for manipulating Jack. He did. But he knew if he had told Jack what he really wanted he could never have gotten him to bring him here. He'd had three years to plan it and he'd played him good: pushing them eastward by feeding Jack scraps of information, getting him to New York. He knew that if he got Jack to New York, he could talk him into coming here. Sam's kidnapping, that was serendipity.

They came to the intersection of a long-abandoned reception area. A sign on the wall read SECURITY/GULAG/STORAGE. Somebody had scribbled black Magic Marker over SECURITY and had written *Maestro* above it. Cole went to the panel in the wall and pushed it open, revealing nine CCTV screens that showed live feeds from different sections of the Underground.

"Do you see her?" asked Jack, peering over Cole's shoulder.

There was only one place Sam could be. Cole found her immediately. His heart sank. Now Jack would want to run to rescue her, and they couldn't. Not until he got what he'd come for. He might never get another chance.

"There," he said, pointing at the corner screen. The feed was in shades of green and white. It showed a sterile room. In the middle was a dentist's chair surrounded by medical implements. Two men were strapping Sam down with some effort.

"Oh my God," said Jack. "Where is this?" He looked at the display under the screen. "Identity Mod? What's that mean? Where is this?"

"What the fuck?" asked Nils, pointing to another screen, which showed a cafeteria. Two Hounds were playing Ping Pong. Their bare chests were strangely shaped and hairy. They did not look entirely human.

Cole did the first thing that came to mind. He nudged Nils. "Look," he said, pointing to the defaced sign above them.

Before Jack could stop him, it was out of Nils's mouth. He didn't know any better. "Who is the Maestro?"

At the sound of the word all the screens abruptly changed. All nine monitors now showed their group, footage taken from a camera hidden in a corner above. A mechanical alarm sounded, the kind that builds in intensity as if cranked by hand. "Intruders," a calm female voice announced from hidden speakers. "Section 9-G." *Wooooop!* "Intruders, section 9-G. Security breach. Grimpen Mire stairwell." *Wooooop!* "Unauthorized discussion of state secrets. Keyword: Maestro." *Wooooop!* "This is not a drill." *Wooooop!*

"What did I do?" said Nils.

"Come on," yelled Cole, darting down the corridor, away from the exit. "This way! Hurry!"

They ran. For at least a mile they ran, Jack supporting the Captain with a tight arm around his waist. At another intersection Cole halted briefly, getting his bearings. Behind them a group of Hounds (would you call them a gang, Jack wondered, or a shrewdness?) bounded after them, pushing off the walls for extra momentum.

"Jesus Christ!" the Captain shouted.

Cole led them to the right and immediately down another hall to the left. It was a dead end.

"Shit, man. We're trapped!" yelled Jack.

"No, we're not," said Cole. He stepped to a beige panel set into the concrete wall. It was a call box, the kind you might find outside a cheap apartment building. He pushed a button. There was a sharp buzz and then an automated voice, the same pleasant feminine voice that had alerted the Hounds to their presence.

"Password," she said.

"Open sesame," Cole replied.

There was a click and another buzz and then the wall slid into a niche in the concrete with a sound like Lazarus's tomb unsealing. They ran inside and Cole touched another button that caused the wall to slide back. There was a *thunk* as it closed, and then the *clankity-clunk* sound of heavy locks falling into place.

They stood there, panting, against the door. And then the occupant of this room addressed them. It was a voice Cole had not heard in a long time.

"Hello, Cole," said the voice, a man's voice, though slightly effeminate—the voice of a poet. "We knew you'd come back. We just didn't think it would take three years."

Cole turned, the atomizer he'd stolen from Jack in his right hand. He pointed it at the Maestro. This. This was all he'd ever wanted. Murder. Justice. Revenge.

FIVE

TO SERVE MAN

1 *"Wake up."*

Cole rubbed his eyes and looked at the clock beside his bed. It was 4:00 a.m. His father was a shadow in the dark room, outlined by the light through the open door. "What's going on?" asked Cole.

"Get dressed. Don't wake your mother."

Cole pulled on a T-shirt and jeans and looked out his window to the void of the Atlantic Ocean. Not even a hint of sunlight on the horizon. They'd gone to see Wicked last night, for something like the fifth time—his father was suddenly nuts about it—and had eaten a late dinner at Gaby's.

As they stepped into the early morning, his father ruffled his hair the way he used to when Cole was little. His dad was dressed not in his suit but in khakis and a simple polo. "We've got a long day ahead of us," he said.

"Where are we going?"

"Back to Big Indian." His father handed him a coffee, another sign that all was not normal. He didn't like Cole drinking caffeinated beverages or anything with a lot of chemicals in it, really. They took 95 through the Bronx,

then across the GWB into Jersey. A schooner sat on the Hudson, sails wrapped in white string lights. It had been forever since they'd sailed.

"Lots of people get lost in their jobs, I think," his father said. "Things become routine. You do what your boss asks because that's what you get paid to do, right? You don't question it. There were young men who guarded the Jews at Sobibor. When they signed up to work there, it was just another labor camp. By 1942, they were gassing the prisoners with carbon monoxide. Their job didn't change overnight, it changed slowly. It became the new routine. Like every job, it must have even seemed boring to some. See what I mean?"

"What are we doing?" asked Cole.

His father sighed. "I think we made a terrible mistake. I think we were wrong to forget. I'm not helping anybody. Cole, I think I'm the bad guy in this story."

"You're not a bad guy."

"You wait and see what happens to the world after another thirty years of this, of all these terrorist attacks and retaliatory wars. If we'd remembered we'd already done it, maybe we wouldn't be so eager to kill each other again."

"Where are we going?" asked Cole.

"We're going to talk to the only man who knows how to stop it."

Up the mountain, through the mire, into the Undergound, its catacombs lit with dirty light. Cole followed his father down the corridor and around several turns. They walked for half an hour before they reached the intercom. His father chuckled. "The most important secrets in the world are kept behind this door and they picked the oldest password in history." He leaned to the panel. "Open sesame," he said.

The light inside was warm, the harsh world of concrete and fluorescence shut away as the door closed behind them. They were standing in someone's cherrywood den, an expansive room of plank floors and leather couches. Hardback books lined deep shelves on every wall, old tomes, fragile and fragrant with glue. Someone, somewhere, was cooking bread.

"Hello?" his father called.

A head peeked around the corner of a doorway. A man's head, fortyish, *skin waxy and grayish, almost sickly, the way a vampire might look after decades of night.* "Ah! What a pleasant surprise!" *he said.*

The Maestro stepped into the den. He wore black pants and a gray sweater. A white apron hung around his waist. LICENSE TO GRILL, *it said in black letters. The man's body bent forward slightly, a hunchback's bony knob pushing his sweater into a mound behind one shoulder.*

"And who is this?" *asked the Maestro.*

"This is my son."

"Well, hello. Won't you come into the kitchen for some cupcakes? We've just made some red velvet. You must try one. This way." *There was something simply magical about this man, like an old wizard. The boy was too thrilled to speak.*

They followed the Maestro into a kitchen bathed in pale blue-and-white light. A plate of cupcakes cooled on the island. The Maestro motioned for them to sit on wooden stools, then nodded to the treats. On top of each cupcake was a white marzipan aspen leaf. Cole ate greedily. They were wonderful, soft and moist.

"And what is your name, young prince?"

"Cole," *he said around bites.*

"Cole, you can call us the Maestro. It's all right to say it in here. The Hounds can't come in. Not without proper cause."

"Nice to meet you."

"Our pleasure. We haven't seen a child in fifty years." *They turned their attention to his father then.* "A break in protocol. What if the Hounds found out?"

"I'm beyond that now," *his father said.*

"Do tell."

"All the time I've known you, you've never much liked what you do. You hate the Hounds . . ."

"Animals. Don't get us started."

"So why are you helping them?"

"We maintain the algorithm. It's what we were made for."

"But the founders wouldn't have supported these new forgottings. Right? We should stop it. All of it. People need to remember."

The Maestro smiled. "Consider what would happen if the signal from

HAARP suddenly cut off and six billion people woke up to the real world. If they weren't ready for such a thing, it would drive them mad. They might become more afraid than they already are. Then they would truly be dangerous."

"So then what do we do?"

"They have to want to remember."

"What does that mean?" his father asked.

"It means we can't simply turn the machine off. The people have to want us to. But . . . perhaps we can nudge them in the right direction. Allow them the choice of remembering."

"How?"

"Give them reason to question this version of the world. Show them part of the machine. Hint at the truth. That way, they come to it gradually."

"Show them part of the machine?"

"Expose a relay," the Maestro said.

"How?"

"Blow off its shell."

His father rubbed his chin, considering what the Maestro was suggesting. Cole could tell it was a weighted decision, the kind of decision you can't back down from. Then he patted Cole on the back. "Come on," he said. "Time to go."

The Maestro walked them to the door.

"You've come a long way, Stephen," the Maestro said. He looked down at Cole. "Whatever happens today, you've already inspired others to remember. And that's a real start."

Back in the corridor, Cole's father zigged right, down a narrow hall where another blast door was located. A sign above this one read BATTERY. He spun the wheel and it clicked open on a room filled with rows of metal lockers. The place reeked of oil and grease and the sweat of large beasts. His father went to a locker and pulled it open. Inside were guns placed in gray foam. He took one, considered a moment, and then removed another, which he handed to Cole. It looked like a toy ray gun and felt as light as a television remote.

"Here's the safety. Here's the trigger," his father said. "Keep the safety on unless you mean to use it. Hold it steady when you fire. It won't kick, so don't flinch. Keep your eyes open when you shoot, okay?"

Cole felt his heart beating in his neck.

"It's just a precaution. You probably won't need it." His father went to another locker and removed five bricks wrapped in thin, powdery paper.

"What's that?" asked Cole.

"Bombs," his father said.

Just after noon his father pulled the strange jet car into the public parking decks below the North Tower of the World Trade Center. "It's like this, sometimes," his father explained. "Everyone wants to live in a time when all they have to do is live, to live their lives and not rock the boat. But sometimes . . . sometimes you realize you have a responsibility to change things for the better and not just for you but for everybody. And the only way to do that is to risk your own peace. It's a choice like everything else. Do you understand?"

Cole didn't. But he nodded. If his father—and the man he called the Maestro—if they believed this was the right thing to do, then it must be. He'd never known his father to make an impulsive decision.

The Twin Towers, his father explained, disguised relays that blanketed all of New York City with the forgetting broadcasts. If they could blow apart the shell of one of the towers, the relay would be revealed. In the face of such technology, the public would question its purpose and function. The signal itself might weaken all over New York, too. It was a start.

The parking deck was claustrophobic and every sound they made bounced back to them from the walls in a way that made his fillings tingle. Cole felt the gun as a bit of pressure against his thigh. Could he actually point it at someone and squeeze the trigger if he had to? He didn't think so.

They began a circuit of the parking garage. His father paused at a key column of concrete and placed a brick of C-4 against it while Cole watched for cars. They continued around the lot and placed another. They had placed only two when a young man in a sharp suit came out of the elevators and spotted them: "Hallo there!"

His father tucked the explosives into the bag and put an arm around Cole's shoulders. "Greg!" he said.

"Hey, man, where ya been? We missed you at the conference this morning."

"My son caught a cold," he said. "I had to pick him up from school."

The agent looked to Cole. The boy blushed, beads of sweat gathered at his hairline.

"Oh," said Agent Greg Carr. "This your boy?"

"My one and only."

Greg waved. "Hey, kiddo. Well. I'll just, you know, head back up."

Suddenly one of those ray guns was in his father's hand. It had appeared so quickly, Cole hadn't even seen him reach for it. He pointed it at Greg. But Greg was already ducking behind a minivan. His father fired. A wave of energy shot from the barrel, rippling the air like the wake behind a boat, and then the minivan was a pile of blue ash. Greg crouched in the open space. He raised his hands. "Hey, man. Think about it. What are you doing?"

"Get out of here, Greg," he said.

The agent ran for the street. As soon as he was out of range, they could hear him shouting into his walkie-talkie. "Breach! Parking lot! It's a breach! Evac!"

"Run!" his father screamed, shoving Cole toward a set of stairs. Thirty feet away, a Ford Taurus vaporized in front of them. Cole turned to see three Hounds jumping over a row of cars, launching off the metal roofs like acrobats. His father reached into the pocket of his suit and came out with a thin metal tube with a red button on top. He pressed it, hard.

Cole felt the blast before he heard it, a wall of hot air lifting him off his feet like a wave breaking against him. He was lost in it, unable to tell up from down, left from right. He collided with a red sedan, crumpling the back door. The world was filled with a cacophony of hurtful noise and shrieking metal. The sound registered as pain before it differentiated into separate tones to be heard. Then the heat: a numbing fire, as if he'd bent close to a grill. Cole tried to breathe but his lungs were empty, the fire had stolen his air. A rush of wind as the blaze consumed oxygen, became a living thing. The crash of girders against concrete, raucous music of architecture, a symphony of destruction.

A Hound, its hair on fire, rolled on the ground six feet away. "Hoo, hoo, hoo," it shouted. "Help! Ha-elp!"

Cole watched it succumb to the fire, flames rippling around its humanoid lips as it inhaled its last breath. The Hound's body curled against itself, a charred black mummy. Cole tried to stand but collapsed back to the ground. Great clouds of noxious smoke rolled like dirty cotton balls on the ceiling.

His father appeared behind another car. His face was covered in soot and an open gash ran down the left side of his face. "Cole!" he shouted. He started to run for his son but then a hairy arm wrapped around his father's neck.

"You!" the Hound screamed. It shoved his father against the car and pointed a gun at him. This was no atomizer. It was a nine-millimeter. As Cole watched, the Hound fired two bullets into his father's chest. His body slumped to the ground.

The Hound turned his attention to Cole then. And for maybe the third time in his life, the boy prayed.

If someone's listening, he thought, please don't let me die.

He never heard the shot. There was a little pressure in his head, like he'd been hit with the worst migraine of his life, and then . . . nothing. The next thing he knew, he was coming out of sleep, bit by bit, becoming alive in fractured memories. He was in the hospital.

He'd been in a coma for two weeks. By the time he woke, they'd already buried his father. His mother told him that they'd been in an accident on Church Street; a taxi had pushed their car into a Sephora. She showed Cole pictures of the accident, color photographs of what looked like his father's car smashed into a display of expensive makeup.

"What about the explosion at the World Trade Center?" he asked.

"You mean the bombing in the parking garage? That happened in 1993, nineteen years ago," she said.

The Maestro had rewriten the algorithm. The altered code had gone out from HAARP to the relays, out to the minds of humanity, altering memories of the attack to fit a new truth. Instead of becoming the spark that illuminated the world, his father's insurrection was rewritten to further darken history. Another terrorist attack. A story to make people more fearful. The day Cole came out of the coma, three men in Alabama lynched a Muslim girl walking to school in a burka.

Cole felt sick. Too frustrated to cry. And who to blame?

If the Maestro had simply shut off the signal, his father would still be alive. Instead of turning off the machine, the Maestro let his father try to do it the hard way. The Maestro had made him a target. It was cowardice. It was evil.

At first Cole tried to convince his doctors what was really going on. Cole *told them about the chemtrails and the fluoride and the TacMars and they locked him away in the psych ward for so long his mother was forced to consider long-term care. It didn't matter. They could ship him off to Ohio. Eventually, Cole knew, he would convince someone that he was telling the truth. It was just a matter of finding the right words, the right story to tell. He thought back on his meeting with the Maestro. That idea about gradual change. Gradients. That was an idea he might use to his advantage.*

Eventually there came a day when a new doctor arrived, a tall doctor with shaggy brown hair and glasses, a skinny man with a nice smile but some kind of darkness behind his eyes. Cole thought he recognized something there.

"Cole, I'm Dr. Sanders," said the man in the white coat. "Tell me your story."

2 "You killed my father," said Cole, stepping toward the Maestro, the gun leveled at the sickly man's torso.

"No, Cole, we tried to help him," he said. "What happened after he left this room we could not have predicted. There were too many possible outcomes."

"Put the gun down, kid," the Captain said softly. "You're about to kill the only person with any answers."

Cole's bottom lip trembled with warring emotions. He stepped forward. "Why didn't you just turn off the signal?"

"Freedom can't be granted," said the Maestro. "It must be won. It must be fought for. Tell him, Jack Felter. In the history of the world has there ever been a society that has won lasting freedom without rising up and taking that freedom from the hands of their oppressors?"

Jack shook his head. "No."

"You're not going to kill us," the Maestro said. "You don't have murder in your heart."

"My heart is broken!"

"This is bigger than you," said the Maestro, his eyes full of patience. "We're getting to the end, we are. But you and your friends here—and us, even—we are only single characters in a much larger story. If you could only see . . ."

Something large collided with the door to the Maestro's lair. The barrier held, but the Maestro suddenly seemed distracted. Annoyed.

"If you want the Hounds to leave, I should talk to them," he said.

Cole didn't move. His mouth twisted in thought, his eyes barely holding back tears.

"Set the gun down. We'll talk. Let's talk."

Cole felt his vengeance breaking, his confidence dissolving. He knew he was failing his father, that somewhere his father looked on him with disappointment. The gun went limp in his hand and he passed it to the Captain before it could fall. Then he went to Jack and buried his face in his chest. Cole didn't cry. He just sighed, a coldness draining from his pores. He closed his eyes and wished the world away. Jack held him tightly.

The Maestro walked to an intercom and pressed a button. "Scopes? Is that you?"

"Open up, Maestro," came a shrill voice.

"You know how this works," the Maestro said. "These rooms are sovereign. It is a separation of powers spelled out clearly in the founders' laws."

"Don't quote canon to me," said Scopes. "And don't assume the law is guaranteed forever. The founders are long gone. Nobody remembers them."

"We remember," the Maestro said.

"We'll wait," came the reply.

The Maestro turned back to them and smiled. "Well. Now that's done, who wants pie?"

3   "Get up!" the Hound shouted as Sam collapsed to the concrete floor of the debarkation room, another tidy space that resembled a suburban post office.

Sam's legs had fallen asleep inside the vacuum tube, and when she stood, it was like a thousand sewing needles jabbing into her muscles. She looked at the Hound before her. He wore a familiar uniform, that gray suit and Panama hat, a G-man on vacation. But this one was fatter. He didn't seem to have a neck.

"Step to the line," he said, pointing to the floor.

Thin trails in different colors were painted on the concrete. One blue. One green.

"Green," he said when she raised an eyebrow.

She followed the green line through the door. Beyond was another branch of that familiar endless corridor. They walked for so long Sam lost track of time. Her mind wandered, remembering the day at the fair when Jack had looked at her as if she was worth something. Eventually they came to a steel door marked MOD-1, where a young man in a dark suit greeted them.

"I'm Agent Snowden," he said, shaking Sam's hand as if he were an ob-gyn on a consult. "Come in, come in."

She stepped inside. The Hound closed the door and removed her cuffs.

"Sit, please," said Snowden, gesturing to a dentist's chair that waited in the middle of the concave room. Her heart shuddered at the sight of the tools waiting on the tray beside it. "Don't worry. This isn't torture, Samantha."

"What is it then?" she asked.

"Just a filling," he said. "Painless. In, out, you're on your way."

She didn't move.

"Here," said Snowden, his voice gentle, the good doctor easing the anxious child into the chair. He picked up a tiny square of electronics and held it in the palm of his hand for Sam to see. "That's all."

"What is it?"

"Tiny transmitter," he said. "Your own little radio station. We write your new history here . . ." Snowden pointed to an antique green-screen Apple II personal computer sitting on a desk. "And it gets broadcast to your brain, from here . . ." He wiggled the relay in his hand. "Your own personal Forgetting. It's a mod. A programming patch, like an update for *Candy Crush*."

Sam looked at the fat Hound. He glared back at her from under the brim of his stupid Panama hat. His hand rested on the butt of the nine-millimeter in his holster.

"Painless," Snowden said again.

Resigned, she climbed into the chair and looked up to the drop ceiling, where Snowden had hung a poster of a kitten dangling from the branch of a tree. HANG IN THERE, it said.

"Now," said Snowden, sitting on a rolling stool and swinging around to face her. "What sort of person would you like to be, Samantha Brooks?"

4   "So are you like a hunchback or something?" asked Nils between large spoonfuls of homemade cherry pie. They were in the kitchen, a wide expanse of robin's-egg-blue backsplash and granite countertops, standing around an island made of wood. Everyone ate except Cole, who glowered silently and leaned against the stove.

Jack felt guilty eating this pie, which was delectable, its crust made with some heavy lard, while Sam was imprisoned somewhere within this labyrinth of concrete. They were wasting time.

"I'm not a hunchback, no," the Maestro said. The strange man watched them eat. Jack noted how pale his skin was, whiter than an albino, he thought. Nearly translucent.

"So what's wrong with you?" asked Nils, with open curiosity.

The Captain shook his head.

The Maestro laughed. "It's all right. I like a man who isn't afraid to ask questions. And it's a story I rather like telling. But first things first. There's something I want to show you when you're done with the pie, an artifact from before the Great Forgetting that might explain a lot."

"We have to get Sam," said Jack, setting his plate in the sink and checking his watch, Tony's old watch, its tribute to him forever engraved on the back.

"Sam's freedom is Sam's to earn," the Maestro said with an unnerving finality. "The story of her life has brought her to where she is and it has given her the means of escape. Faith is her lesson. Let's hope you've taught her how to trust people, Jack, because so much depends upon her next move."

"I can't just leave her there," said Jack.

"It's not your choice," the Maestro replied. "The door to the Underground is shut to you forever."

"So we're prisoners?"

The Maestro laughed. "You can leave if you want, but not that way. You can leave through the west exit, which will take you to Alaska and the end of your misadventures."

"Not without Sam."

"Then you must wait here and see how her story plays out."

Jack started to say something else, but his father placed a hand on his arm. "Shut up, son," he said. "We're in enemy territory. No offense." The Maestro shrugged. "So take some time and learn a thing or two about your opponent before you start dreaming up ways to rescue your girlfriend."

Jack nodded.

"Follow us," the Maestro said. He led them down a hall and into a library. Each wall was lined with bookcases that reached to the twelve-foot-high ceiling. A large globe rested on a stand in the corner. Several long leather sofas faced a blank wall. On the ceiling was a cracked fresco depicting some fierce battle amid a cityscape aglow with fire. A general on horseback led a charge against twenty German panzers, waving an American flag beset with sixty stars. The Maestro motioned to the sofas and then walked to the front and pulled down a white screen.

"Are we watching a movie?" asked Nils.

"A newsreel, actually," the Maestro said. He pushed a button on the wall and the room went dark. So dark, Jack couldn't see his nose. He pictured the Maestro baring hidden fangs and leaping at them in the dark. He felt like the stupid trick-or-treater who accepted the weird man's invitation to come inside.

Then the projector clicked on and he could see the Maestro in the glow, looking on.

Trumpets belted out a patriotic tune. A title card read *An Official United States Civil Defense Film*. The image jumped out of the frame and then settled as it spun through the sixteen-millimeter projector in the wall behind them. *The Great Forgetting. Produced by Aspen Films. Copyright 2043.*

Then: an image of a sweeping plain, blackened to carbon. "This is all that remains of DeCapua, Indiana," the narrator said in a grave voice, the sound of open wind behind him. "Sand and glass. The dead tree gives no shelter. What was once a capital city is now a handful of dust. Like Cahokia, Miakoda, and St. Pease, they—and all who lived there—are gone, forever." Grainy pictures of a teeming metropolis where people walked to work under the shadow of a giant glass pyramid. Another cityscape showed granite buildings linked by metal catwalks. "A billion dead. All of humankind suffered. None more so than the Jewish peoples."

Black-and-white film of naked, emaciated women standing in front of a long, low building. "At first they called it the Final Solution. An experiment in evil." A series of pictures: Mengele in SS uniform looking like some gentle math teacher, his bushy black hair combed, slick; Mengele pulling on a plastic glove in front of a gurney where a dead body lay, half covered; Mengele injecting medication into the arm of a man wearing a jacket emblazoned with a star patch and the word *Juden*. "Our leaders knew what the Nazis were doing. They knew what the concentration camps were for. And they lied to us. They told us made-up stories to keep us from being afraid."

Film of an unfamiliar man in a sharp suit standing before the houses of Congress as the narrator continued: "President Bertram Huckley explained that the war was an Old World war, that Hitler had no desire to attack America. We were told our Jewish friends were only being temporarily relocated. Only later did we learn that President Huckley had negotiated a secret truce with the Führer. We would not assist Great Britain. In exchange, Hitler would not invade the United States."

Here, footage of mass protests on the mall in Washington, D.C.

Women in full-length dresses, hair done up in buns, and men in three-piece suits and dark hats waved homemade signs with slogans such as THE FINAL SOLUTION IS A JEWISH MYTH and PROTECT AMERICA FIRST! The narrator returned: "When we finally learned the horrific details of the concentration camps, conservatives assured us it was a twisted exaggeration of the truth. The Jews were lying. They only wanted to pull us into their war. But the war was Europe's problem. Not ours." Photographs of a fleet of U-boats approaching the Santa Monica pier, great zeppelins hovering over downtown Los Angeles. "We ignored the war as long as we could. But the war did not ignore us."

The first color footage was presented as the music swelled. In it, President Huckley walked back to his car through a mob of people. He had a team of Secret Service, but they were overpowered. The mob ripped the president from the arms of his protectors. He was strung up from a light pole on Pennsylvania Avenue, the Capitol dome rising behind his swinging feet. "By the time we mustered an army, Hitler had taken the West Coast and the Wehrmacht were pushing into the Rockies." Video now, shaky handheld color images of great metal tanks the size of semi trucks pushing over a hill, bison stampeding before them, a phalanx of Indians on horseback riding to meet them. "The Seven Nations were no match for such weaponry. California fell in 1955, decimating the Cree and Chippewa nations." An Indian stood by the roadside overlooking a valley of fire, a single tear streaking down his wrinkled cheek.

More trumpets. A photograph of a handsome man in uniform atop a black steed, holding a flag that flapped in the gale-force wind of a nuclear explosion. "On July ninth, 1959, after a battle that claimed the lives of eight hundred thousand American souls, General John Francis Halloran, a former schoolteacher, led a contingency of National Guardsmen to victory over Nazi storm troopers in Cleveland, pushing Hitler's army into Canada. Halloran had a secret weapon, a device of mystery created by the scientist Nikola Tesla. This 'atom bomb' could harness the elemental properties of the sun. 'Now I am become Death, the destroyer of worlds,' Tesla remarked upon seeing the devastation unleashed by his creation."

More footage of Halloran's troops chasing graysuits through city streets, Nazis crucified on the sides of midwestern dairy barns. "Following the repatriation of Decatur, the Nazis retreated from America, running back toward the fatherland. We followed."

Halloran and a hundred men pulled at thick rope attached to a tall statue of Adolf Hitler. It fell to the street with a crash of stone and dust to the hails of many men. "On June nineteeth, 1964, Berlin fell. On General Halloran's command, Hitler was stoned to death outside the Palace of Justice in Nuremberg." A small girl with curly blond hair chucked the first rock at the Führer. It hit him high on his cheek and he began to bleed.

Footage of giant cranes in the streets of New York, lifting the steel girders of the Chrysler Building. "We tried to move on. We tried to rebuild. We buried our dead cities and drowned them beneath man-made lakes, wiping them from our minds, our memories."

Photographs of a giant pile of bodies beneath a bridge in Pittsburgh. "But our resolve was broken. Why did we deserve freedom? Why did we deserve to go on when we had turned our backs on a nearly complete genocide? The world fell into a Great Depression, a period of four years when the suicide rate climbed as we came to terms with the consequences of our ignorance and apathy.

"It was at the second council of the United Nations that a young scientist named Stephen Hawking came forward with a plan." Video here of a wiry man in a dark suit walking to a podium in front of a collection of world leaders. He looked about nineteen, his cowlicky hair sticking up in back, nervous but determined. "We can forget," he said, his voice echoing inside the great hall. "If you want to, we can forget."

Hawking stood before Congress as they rose in ovation. "Dr. Hawking had developed a machine that could rewrite our memories. He knew ways to bring back the Jewish people. The support for Hawking's Great Forgetting was nearly unanimous."

Footage of a large tribe of Indians taking down teepees on a vast plain overlooking a wintry river. "The Seven Nations resisted. Chief Crooked River warned the UN that forgetting would allow the evil to return—an ignorant, pessimistic view we now know to be without any basis in fact. Concessions were made to the savages so that the Great Forgetting could go forward: we could not destroy artifacts of culture and the Seven Nations would be given a continent of their own, the semihabitable island of Mu. Residents of Mu would be exempt from the Great Forgetting, but they could never leave. They chose to remember, alone."

Hawking stood before a line of bulldozers as the machines leveled a forest of pine trees—Jack thought it looked like the Alaskan frontier. Further photographs showed an array of radio telescopes—HAARP. "It will take a hundred years to build the infrastructure for the Great Forgetting and it will be the most expensive public-works project in history—a small price to pay for a better future. But we are getting close. Our top scientists, led by Dr. Hawking, along with the most brilliant minds captured from the Nazis"—here, a couple of photographs of Mengele, smiling into the camera in front of a chimpanzee cage—"are hard at work readying the custodial team that will ensure we never remember what we choose to forget."

Color video of schoolchildren gathering history textbooks, placing them into boxes. The boxes are loaded into trucks and carted away. "Everyone must do their part. Evidence remains that should be collected. Please comb through your attic, your basement, your closets. Collect anything that reveals the world as it was during those terrible years. Pay special attention to anything with an exact date as well as photographs taken in cities that no longer exist."

A man dressed as Uncle Sam takes a box of books from a young boy and places it into the back of a truck. Uncle Sam drives away. The boy waves as the truck disappears into the sunset. "Only together can we truly forget."

The film reel ended with a clicking of crumpled film stock snaking through the projector, and then the Maestro turned the lights back on.

For a moment, nobody said anything. Then Nils clapped enthusiastically. "Far out, man! Far fucking out!"

5   "You can be anyone you like," said Snowden, handing Sam a binder of personality templates arranged like a book of haircuts in some high-end salon. She flipped past pictures of women in uniform, women in expensive dresses walking red carpets, women sunning on the decks of luxury liners in the Mediterranean.

There was a time when this was exactly the fantasy she'd needed, the ability to forget her troubles, to become someone new. Someone *clean*. Where had these secret government agents been when she was thirteen and needed a new family?

Snowden handed her a tissue. "Shh," he said. "This doesn't need to be sad. Think of it as a gift. Everyone wishes they could have a better life."

"I'm pregnant," she said. "I haven't even decided if I'm keeping it. But . . . Will it . . ."

"Your child will be just fine. It doesn't have any memories to adjust."

She felt herself giving in. What choice did she have? The Hound stared at her with disregard. There was so much hatred in those close-set eyes. Why not take what this nice man was offering? Wouldn't forgetting be nice, after all? Wouldn't it be sublime to wake up as somebody new?

"I want a safe place to raise a family," she said. "A safe place away from people."

Snowden nodded and swiveled on his stool. He scooted to the Apple II and punched a few keys. "Good," he said. "Most people, all they want is ten million dollars and a mansion on the ocean."

"I want to live in a cottage. Not Ohio. Somewhere in the middle of nowhere so I can get lost and never be found by anyone I ever knew."

"That's the spirit, Sam," said Snowden, typing quickly.

"Will I forget everyone I know?"

"Is there anyone you wish to remember?"

She thought about it for only a moment. "No," she said. "I'll forget them all. All the men who've ever hurt me . . ."

"Yes."

"All the men who've ever left me . . ."

"Yes, of course."

"And everything about that boy who told my husband about the Great Forgetting and then stole Jack away from me."

Snowden stopped typing. "What boy?" he asked.

"Cole," she said, waving a hand at the name as if she were dismissing him. "The kid who convinced Jack to run away with him to some secret island."

Snowden turned to her and for a moment said nothing. He looked at the Hound and then back to her. "This boy," he said at last, "was he from New York?"

"The city," she said. "He went crazy after his dad died and so his mother shipped him to a mental hospital in Ohio. It was my husband's bad luck that . . ."

Suddenly a scalpel was in Snowden's hand. He looked at the Hound and motioned for the guard to come to him. "Hold her down," he said.

"Wait," Sam screamed. "Wait! Isn't there novocaine or something?" She crawled up the chair as the Hound drew near. His long hairy arms reached out for her. And that's when the scalpel slid under the Hound's flabby chin and Snowden opened a large gash there. Pints of warm blood poured from the Hound's neck onto Sam's blouse.

Snowden looked at the scalpel in his hand as if it had acted of its own accord. There was fear in the man's eyes. A growing, dawning fear.

The Hound collapsed on the floor, expelling a final breath through thick gurgles. Sam screamed.

"You have to get out of here," said Snowden, unstrapping her from the chair.

"What did you do?" asked Sam. Her mind was a whir of confusion.

"I killed him," said Snowden, as if explaining it to himself. He opened the steel door and checked outside for more Hounds. There were none. For the moment. "I knew Cole's dad. Stephen Monroe. We worked together a couple times. He didn't know it, but I'd been helping the Maestro push him toward action for years. Editing his memory. Something had to change. I . . . I thought Cole had forgotten like everyone else." He held Sam in place with one hand, gripping tightly with fear and something else. Hope? Earnest, terrifying hope? "But if Cole remembers, he can get your friends to Mu. You have to help him. You have to get him there before the Hounds stop him! Go!" He dropped his hand and held the door wide for her. Just then an alarm sounded, blaring from overhead speakers.

What was this now, at the eleventh hour? Another man to blindly trust. And what had her life taught her? That a man could never be trusted, not even those you know the most. She had been taught that men are animals who run on instinct and fear and you can never ever trust anybody. But that wasn't exactly right, was it? That wasn't all of it. There *were* good men. She'd met a few. There had been a man named Stan Polk who had loved her like a daughter, like a father should love a daughter. And Jack. Jack, whom she had not trusted to love her forever and so she'd let Tony lead her away. Those men were better than instinct. They battled it. For her. And for the first time Sam sensed something greater than the nature of men. A twinkling on the edge of things, a promise that things might be fine, that all manner of things might be fine. That things could be *right* again, that it wasn't ever too late. It was a word she had never used because it made no sense to her, and it swam up from the deep recesses of her mind and announced itself, a shadow on the wall: grace.

"I almost forgot," said Snowden. "You'll need the password."

Sam listened. And then Sam ran.

6   "The tour continues," said the Maestro, leading them down the hall toward another doorway, outlined in a pale blue glow. "My office," he said.

It was a rich music mogul's private editing suite, lined with red carpet and black sound panels. Jack counted fifteen wide-screen monitors. A leather chair faced the largest screen, on which computer-generated wave patterns trailed along like the readout of a heart monitor. Below this was a soundboard full of dials and knobs and faders. There was also a keyboard and a metal box with a toggle that looked like something from a 1950s sci-fi flick.

"This is Clementine," the Maestro said, nodding at the computer.

"Can you play *Warcraft* on that thing?" asked Nils.

"What the hell is all this junk?" the Captain asked.

"This is where we compose the code for the algorithm, the message that's broadcast from HAARP. It's really just one long strand of code on a repeating loop."

"Broadcasted like music on the radio?" the Captain said. "Bullshit. There's got to be more to it."

The Maestro smiled. "Sound can be very powerful. The Nazis were fascinated by the properties of sound. They had weapons in the war that used only sound, weapons that could tear a man apart." He walked to a flimsy card table in the corner. A large speaker had been placed beneath it. Next to the table was a box of blue sand. The Maestro scooped out a handful and let it fall from his fingers onto the shiny laminated surface of the table. Then he walked to the soundboard and turned a key. The speaker began to emit a tone. The Maestro slowly increased the volume.

The grains of sand on the table vibrated and then arranged into a geometric shape: a perfect circle. The Maestro dialed back another knob and the tone changed to a higher pitch, and suddenly the grains of sand scooted around to form more complex shapes: a damask pattern, the kind with shapes that look like the faces of fat dragons.

"Would you like to see the algorithm?"

"Is it safe?" asked Jack.

"I'll just play a portion," he said. The Maestro turned another key. What came out of the speaker sounded to Jack, at first, like one of those aboriginal music pipes, a didgeridoo, but then it morphed into a song that reminded him of the sound humpback whales make when calling to their calves. A new shape formed on the table, a strangely familiar and specific shape.

"It's a leaf," said Nils.

"An aspen leaf," Cole corrected.

The Maestro smiled. "Yes. The physical representation of the algorithm's wave." After another second he turned the speaker off. Jack was glad. The tones had started to make his fillings hurt.

"We don't compose much anymore," he said. "Mostly we just write new deletion commands so that the calendar resets a day or two. There hasn't been any significant composition since the Great Forgetting. In the beginning, we had to write a complete alternate history, a shared history where America joined the war and defeated the Nazis before the Jews died. We composed an algorithm in harmony with every human mind. It was . . . elegant."

The Maestro's eyes wandered to some distant memory, then refocused on his guests, who looked back with a mixture of vague comprehension and distrust. He fiddled with a fader on the soundboard. "There was this family, once, went camping at Yosemite. The teen boy crawled into a cave and discovered a buried skyscraper from the old city of Miakoda. We buried these dead cities under mountains and built parks around them so that no one could ever dig them up. This kid went in the cave and found a forgotten metropolis. Part of an office building, empty cubicles preserved under a hundred feet of clay. He brought his dad back inside. They took pictures. How do you explain that? I had to make all those people forget again."

"What about the new forgettings? Who's resetting the calendar now?" asked Jack.

The Maestro pointed at a black rotary phone resting on the desk.

"That phone was put here in the beginning and I was instructed to obey the person on the other end," the Maestro said. "If anyone ever called and they had the password, I was obligated to do what they told me to do. It started ringing again about seven years ago. It rings all the time now. They tell us what to change. Sometimes the change is big. Other times, it's silly little stuff."

"Who is it?"

"Two capitalists from Wichita," he said. "Brothers. Their father made some money off oil. Filthy rich. The one percent of the one-percenters, you know. They got involved in politics. Wanted to change things, manipulate law with their money."

"Who gave them the password?"

The Maestro shrugged. "One of the Hounds, most likely."

"But why do you do it?" asked Jack. "What power do they have over you?"

"I checked the law, the law that was passed by the people of the world. There's nothing in there about a time frame. Nothing in the language says when I must stop taking instructions after the Great Forgetting. We were made to serve man. It's our job to obey the man on the other end of that line."

"Goddamn your job," the Captain said.

"Yes," he said. "But it's not like we haven't tried to stop it."

"What do you mean?" asked Jack.

"We . . ."

The phone rang, a shrill clatter of heavy plastic and metal bells shaking. Everyone stared at the phone as if it was some poisonous thing, a snake with fangs, coiled and poised to strike.

"It's that thing in the Gulf, the oil rig," the Maestro said. "We were expecting this."

"Don't answer it," the Captain said.

The Maestro ignored him and picked up the receiver. "Hello?" He listened for a moment and then a wave of relief washed over his face. He smiled. "No thanks," he said. "I'm happy with my current long-distance plan. Please take us off your list."

7 For a long time, nobody spoke. What more was there to say?

"Who needs a drink?" the Maestro asked, leading the march. "I have spirits in the living room."

"Ghosts?" asked Nils, looking excited.

"He means liquor," said Jack.

"Oh," Nils whispered, unable to hide his disappointment.

They followed the Maestro to the large cherrywood room and sank into leather sofas. Jack felt his body relax, imploring him to lean back his head and doze. He couldn't, though, not yet. Not when Sam was still with the Hounds.

The Maestro stepped to a cabinet in a wall, a part of the bookshelf that pulled away to reveal an icebox. He gave Cole a Yuengling. Jack, too. Then he handed a strangely shaped bottle to Nils. "Mead," the Maestro said. "Sweet," said Nils. Finally, he walked over to the Captain with two tumblers.

The Captain read the label: "Jameson, 2047?"

"It's sixty years old," the Maestro said. "Evidence, technically. But nobody said we couldn't drink it."

The Captain poured two fingers each. "To the end of the world as we knew it," he said, clinking his drink against the Maestro's.

At the moment their glasses touched, a red light suspended in a corner began to strobe on and off.

"What's that?" asked Cole.

"Company," said the Maestro.

From the other side of the door they heard a familiar voice shout, "Open sesame!" then the wall was sliding open. Jack nearly collided with her as she ran inside. It was so unexpected, this reunion, that for a second his brain would not make sense of it. His eyes protested and it was like he almost couldn't see her. Sam was here, in his arms, but he knew it could not be true.

"Jack!" she screamed into his ear.

It was the smell of her that brought him back to reality, that simply Sam smell. Sweat and sawdust and linseed oil. Her blouse was covered in blood, but it didn't appear to be hers. He gripped her tightly and laughed.

"Close the door!" the Captain shouted. The Maestro pressed a button on the wall and the door retracted. As it did, Jack caught sight of five Hounds racing down the hallway, guns raised. The Hounds fired a few shots, but their projectiles went wild. The door closed with a shudder and sealed them away.

Sam looked around the room. When she saw Nils, she gave a little shout. "They told me you were dead!" she screamed. Nils hugged her, but winced as if his arm was sore. She hugged everyone. *Home.* In the strangest of places, an apartment inside a mountain.

When the conversation finally died down the Maestro showed them to their rooms. There would be rest before they continued. Just a few z's and then out the back exit. That was the plan. All told, there were a dozen apartments in the Maestro's house, decorated like posh hotels from the sixties: robin's-egg-blue walls, avocado-green bathroom fixtures, shag carpeting, silk bedding.

"Looks like the goddamn honeymoon suite at the Tropicana," the Captain remarked.

They all enjoyed hot showers that night. Sam threw her bloody clothes away and put on a gray T-shirt from the supplies Jack had brought along. And after they were in bed Jack tried to get Sam to tell him what had happened on her journey through the Underground, but she grew quiet the way she used to when they were kids, and he let it drop. It didn't matter. Not anymore.

PASSAGE ON THE *LADY ANNE*

1 At first Nils thought it was just a piece of concrete shrapnel that had ricocheted off the wall and hit his shoulder. It happened in that moment when Sam had come through the door. Felt like being stung by a yellow jacket, and now he could feel something under his skin. While the others slept, Nils went to the bathroom mirror and pulled up the sleeve of his *Star Wars* T-shirt and had a look.

He could see a little cut, a quarter-inch long. He felt around but couldn't locate the foreign object. It was kind of cool, actually. He'd been wounded in battle by otherworldly creatures.

But he felt cold suddenly, shivering cold, even though he'd gotten the pale blue comforter out of the linen closet in the hall and cranked the thermostat in his room to 85. His forehead was hot and clammy and there were dark bags under his eyes that had not been there before. Quietly, he went in search of some aspirin.

The lights in the hall had dimmed. He could hear the Captain snoring, a deep resonant growl that made the place seem more like home. Nils started for the kitchen but stopped short when he noticed

light under the Maestro's bedroom door. He heard soft music playing on the other side. A ballad, but not one he knew.

Nils knocked lightly.

The door opened a crack. The Maestro's face appeared, colorless
and tired. "Yes, Nils May? Is everything all right?"

"I don't feel so hot," he said.

"Oh, dear," said the Maestro. He opened the door and ushered
Nils inside. "Sometimes the Underground does not agree with one's
consitution. A lack of vitamin D can leave a person feeling quite
crummy, I'm afraid."

The Maestro's bedroom was spacious, by far the largest room in
the complex, a wide suite that would have made Liberace blush.
Modern art in expensive frames leaned against the walls. Objets
d'art were displayed in shallow lighted alcoves. Volumes of books
waited in cherry cases. A king-size bed was made up with thin-weave
blankets below a fresco of a wide glen.

The Maestro was dressed in a long nightgown and Nils gasped
involuntarily as the man turned. Through the sheer fabric of the
gown, two eyes stared back at him. The Maestro's hump was a second head.

"'*Zwillinge!*' he yelled when he saw us," the Maestro said as he
fiddled in a cabinet beside his bed. "That's German for 'twins.' He
was so excited, you have no idea." The Maestro turned to Nils and
handed him a white-labeled generic bottle of cold medicine.

"Wha . . . ," Nils whispered.

The Maestro smiled. "Mengele," he said. "Josef Mengele. The
Nazi scientist who created the Hounds. This was years before the
Great Forgetting. During the war. My brother and I, we were lieuten-
ants in General Halloran's army. Led an incursion into Denver. We
were both captured. And when the Nazis noticed we were identical
twins, they brought us to Mengele. He had a thing for twins."

Nils looked at the bottle in his hands. It was something called
Zyklon F. "What did he do?"

"He experimented on us," the Maestro continued. "Identical
twins make the best transplant patients. No organ rejection. By the

time he met us, Mengele had successfully grafted the head of a dal-
matian onto the back of a German shepherd. He wanted to try it on
a human."

He led Nils to the door and patted him on the back as he stepped
out.

"And that's what became of Isaac and Ismael Schmidt," said the
Maestro at the door. "It was a blessing, in a way. After all, we're the
only person in the world with the brainpower to code the algorithm
that makes the Great Forgetting possible. Someone had to do it."

Nils did not sleep that night.

2   At breakfast the next morning Jack posed an important question. "So, there's this chunk of a hundred years missing from history," he said to the Maestro. "A hundred years we forgot. What
happened to all the music and movies and books and art that people
created in those hundred years? Wasn't there anything we would
have wanted to remember?"

"That was our favorite part of the job, actually," the Maestro
said. They were in the kitchen, seated around the island, eating
scrambled eggs and toast. "We had a Department of Artistic Preser-
vation, a committee of artists and writers who decided what would
be kept and what could be forgotten. In the end, they came to us with
a list of songs, books, artwork, and films that they wished to preserve. We were the curator of these things. What we had to do was
hold on to these treasures and then reintroduce them back into the
world after the Great Forgetting. We became a muse. We searched
for creative individuals to whom we could impart the stories over
the ether. Whole novels sent by radio waves into the minds of authors
who believed they had come up with the idea themselves. How often have you heard some writer say, 'This book wrote itself'? Well, in
some cases, that's exactly what happened. We gave Stephen King
The Shining. We liked *The Corrections* so much we gave *Freedom* to
Jonathan Franzen even though it was really written by a guy named
Joshua Price, seventy years ago. The entire library of Beatles music

was written by a black man who climbed the charts a decade before the Great Forgetting. I still have a thousand works to filter back into the world."

Later, Jack visited the room at the very end of the long hall, where the Maestro had assembled artifacts from before the Great Forgetting in a kind of small museum. The room was filled with incongruous artifacts: a copy of *A Man in Full* written by some guy named Ron Sweed; a framed copy of the *Times*, dated March 30, 2021, headline: "Browns Win the Super Bowl!" There was a soda machine standing in a corner that accepted the Nazi-American quarter Cole's mother had given him and spit out a bottle of something called Umami Pepsi that tasted like beef broth and stung the top of his tongue.

The declaration came just before noon. Cole had just stepped out of the shower, when everyone heard an odd percussive *FOOOOMP!*, and then a message landed in a tube beside the front door.

"Hmm," said the Maestro. It was one of those pneumatic tubes some banks still use to make transactions from your car. The Maestro walked to it and withdrew the rolled-up parchment from the container. It was a single page. From where he stood, Jack could see it was notarized.

"Clever," said the Maestro as he finished reading.

"What?" asked Jack.

"Scopes found a loophole. My chambers are sovereign. A place the Hounds cannot trespass without invitation. But it seems every twenty years the Hounds may audit me."

"Audit you?"

"Yes. Well. You know. Inventory my computers, tally my expenditures, subtract any contraband. Oh, dear, they'll probably take my whiskey."

"What does this mean for us?" asked Sam.

The Maestro coughed nervously. "I'm afraid it means the Hounds are on their way with instruments they will use to lobotomize you. Come with me, I expect we have only a few minutes before they blast the door down."

3   As quickly as they could, everyone returned to their rooms for their belongings, what little there were. They regrouped in the hall and followed the Maestro into the museum. The Maestro went directly to the Umami Pepsi machine and pushed it aside with some effort. Behind it was a thin metal door and another keypad full of buttons and arrows. Jack watched as the Maestro typed in the code: Up, Up, Down, Down, Left, Right, Left, Right, B, A, Enter.

"You're kidding," said Jack. "That's the code I used to get extra lives in *Contra* on my Nintendo. It's the Konami code."

"It's my code," said the Maestro, opening the hatch. "There were video games that needed to be reintroduced after the Great Forgetting, too. *Pac-Man, Skyrim, Polybius* . . ."

The door opened onto a concrete tunnel. Jack took the rear, listening for the sound of the front door collapsing and hoping they were not too late.

Another fifty yards and they entered a great chamber decorated with ornate sculptures. A statue of General Halloran upon his horse, shotgun raised, sat on a shelf above the door. The air inside this empty space tingled with ozone, as if thunder and lightning were planning another war.

"Whoa," said Cole, eyeing the contraption resting on tracks in the middle of the room. Jack pulled Sam close.

It was a simple rectangle of glass, ten feet tall and sixty feet long. Most of its surface was transparent and they saw plush seats arranged inside. To Jack, it looked like a piece of modern art, some minimalist's idea of the form of something.

"Is it a train?" asked Jack.

"It's more like an elevator," the Maestro said.

Nils smiled. "A great glass elevator."

"The *Lady Anne* was created to serve as an escape capsule in the event that we ever had to flee the Underground. This track leads all the way to Washington State, just south of Seattle. It's a long journey but it's quite comfortable inside."

"Wait," the Captain said. "We're supposed to ride this thing across the entire country? *Underground?* How do you know the track isn't crushed somewhere down the line by a cave-in?"

"The tunnels were built to last millennia," the Maestro said. "Your only other choice is to surrender to the Hounds."

"The Great Glass Elevator it is," said Jack.

The Maestro pushed a button on the side of the craft. The interior of the cabin filled with a warm purple glow. Above the door, a liquid crystal display clicked on, flashing green letters: *Ariel Express.* A door slid open with a gentle *WHOOOSH!*

Nils was first to enter. Then Sam and the Captain and Cole.

"Here," said the Maestro, handing Jack a round tin. "Some cookies for your trip."

"Aren't you coming?" asked Jack.

The Maestro shook his head. "We have to maintain the algorithm," he said. "Nobody else can. The Hounds won't kill me. They can't."

"Thank you," said Jack. He turned to join the others already inside, but the Maestro grabbed his arm.

"Jack, over the last century we've come to know what a man is capable of. We are constructs of our past experiences, of the stories we remember. And we know each of you and your memories so well, we have a sense of how your stories will conclude. It's not seeing into the future. It's a calculation of your probable outcome."

"You know what's going to happen to us?"

"We know what will *probably* happen," the Maestro corrected. He dropped his voice low so that only Jack could hear. "There are many ways your story could end. In most of these endings, all but one of your group dies. But there is the possibility that you can save somebody else. A small chance. It requires you to recognize the lessons of your life. You must learn."

"I don't . . ."

The ground shook violently beneath their feet. Thunder rumbled as the doors to the Maestro's lair were blasted apart. In moments, the Hounds would be upon them.

The Maestro pushed Jack inside. Immediately the door slid shut.

The cabin filled with an electric hum and the *Lady Anne* lurched forward as a conveyor belt engaged. Crew and cabin soared sideways down a tunnel, into the dark.

4   There was room enough inside to spread out and get cozy. Jack counted twenty-four plush seats, the kind you might find on a Greyhound. Everyone found a place to sit. It was a smooth ride, but the transparency of the walls was disconcerting. It gave them a sense of how quickly they were traveling through the earth and it made Jack's stomach roll.

Sam was full of the same ragged energy she'd given off that day at the fair when they were kids, when she had sat inside a different glass cage. He took her hand and caressed her fingers. The Captain sat in a chair facing them, wincing at the pain in his knees.

Sam rubbed her nose against Jack's neck, a simple gesture that warmed his body. She pushed closer.

"My dad mentioned Ariel once," said Cole from his seat across the aisle. "It was a kind of branch office for the Collectors. Four of them used to work there, gathering artifacts up and down the West Coast. But then, around 1990, there was a mutiny among the Hounds. This one Hound, Scopes, overthrew their leader, Titano. To consolidate power, Scopes pulled everyone back to New York. He exiled the old boss to Ariel. He might still be there. We should be careful."

"Do you really think you can get us to Mu?" asked Jack.

"I think so, yes," said Cole. "I know someone who can take us there. But he might need a little convincing. He's forgotten who he is."

5   Ten hours into their journey a gentle bell chimed and a female voice announced, "Miakoda: City of Spires." Outside the transparent glass, the tunnel gave way to an enormous cavity in the earth that held a silent metropolis. Great spotlights snapped on as they flew along a raised conveyor. Jack shook the Captain awake.

Their capsule turned toward the city and rose, slantways, into the air. They swayed slightly as hidden gimbals allowed for a balanced ascent. Jack felt his guts drop inside his body as if he were on an elevator that was rising too quickly.

Miakoda was an empty city of glass and concrete. Skyscrapers twisted like tops of ice cream cones in configurations that reminded Jack more of Whoville than Cleveland. Spotlights illuminated a great park in the center, a perfect circle decorated with bronze statues and empty fountains. A preserved billboard advertised Lawson's All-Dressed Potato Chips. Behind them the spotlights turned off in their wake, sealing Miakoda in darkness once more.

"What happened here?" asked Jack. "It doesn't look damaged at all. Why did they bury the whole city?"

"They used neutron bombs in the war," said Cole. "Kills the people, leaves the buildings. But the neutrinos stick around for a few hundred years, blasting microscopic holes into everything organic. You'd be dead in a minute if you stepped outside."

"But where do you bury an entire city?" asked the Captain.

"Look there." Jack pointed beyond Sam, through the window, to the domed ceiling. A round hole blinked open and then closed, like an eye. "What was that?" he asked.

It was the voice of the computer that answered. "Directly above you will see the exhaust port that regulates the immense heat generated by the stray neutrinos that have made this city uninhabitable. The temperature is regulated by tubes of circulating water that must be vented periodically."

"Old Faithful," the Captain said. "We're under Yellowstone."

"Correct."

The elevator passed over an empty coliseum, its Astroturf proudly advertising the Miakoda Tornadoes, and then into another tunnel, heading west once more.

SEVEN

THE MIND AND THE MATTER

1 They arrived at the western terminal fourteen hours later, and the Captain nudged the boy awake. Cole had been dreaming of his father. The closer they got to Mu, the more he felt the weight of responsibility on his shoulders. His father had never meant for this task to be his.

The glass elevator came to a jarring stop at an abandoned subway platform wrapped in hanging white moss. The doors opened with a wiff of compressed air. "Ariel," the female voice intoned.

Cole accepted the Boy Scout backpack from Sam. The Captain carried two gallons of pure water, all that was left. He followed the others into the dank cavern. The doors closed behind them with a shudder and the capsule pulled back into the dark tunnel and disappeared from their story forever.

The floor, walls, and ceiling of this way station were a single tiled mosaic that depicted an army of Indians on horseback engaging a division of German panzers. A red-skinned warrior stood atop a tank, pulling a Nazi from the open lid by his blond hair, knife raised for scalping.

Cole fished a flashlight out of the backpack and shined it around until he found a wide staircase concealed behind a curtain of moss. Jack went first. After a hundred steps the staircase ended at a blast door.

"Oh, good," said Nils. "Another creepy fucking door."

Cole tried the wheel, but it was rusted tight. He backed up and let Jack have a go. The history teacher put his back into it and slowly it turned, depositing a scrim of red dust onto the floor. The stairway was suddenly filled with the warm light of the western sky.

One by one, the travelers stepped out, shielding their eyes against the bright summer sun. They emerged from a concrete shack disguised to look like part of a water treatment facility, large domes of steel and fiberglass on the edge of a wide lake. This was where fluoride was mixed with the water of Lake Merwin before it was sent along to the residents of Cowlitz County, Washington. The air was thick with evergreen mist and the fragrance of the thimbleberries on the edge of the forest. Foothills rose around them, crowning the still waters. In the distance they could see the blasted top of St. Helens, blue and hazy on the horizon.

"Now what?" asked Sam.

"We need to find a library," said Cole.

2   Two hours later, Jack and Cole walked into the small library that was part of the new strip mall in Battle Ground, just south of Ariel. They had taken a cab, which had dropped off the others outside a Menchie's around the corner. The Captain was after a yogurt topped with toffee chips.

Cole made his way to a bank of computers across from circulation while Jack walked around the library, keeping an eye out for Hounds. He busied himself by reading the framed historic newspaper clippings that hung on every wall. Battle Ground was the site of an uprising by the Yakima Indian tribe centuries ago. Their leader,

Chief Umtuch, had died here under mysterious circumstances. Ariel, he learned, was known for two other mysteries: D. B. Cooper and Bigfoot.

The day before Thanksgiving 1971, a man calling himself Dan Cooper purchased a ticket for Flight 305 out of Portland to Seattle, a thirty-minute hop on a 727. There were few passengers on the jet that afternoon. As soon as they were at altitude, Cooper gave the stewardess a note claiming he had a bomb and would blow up the plane unless they gave him two hundred thousand dollars and four parachutes. The pilot landed at Sea-Tac and the feds gave Cooper the money and chutes in exchange for the passengers. Then the pilot took off again. Somewhere over Ariel, Cooper jumped out the back of the plane with the money, never to be seen again. To this day, it remains the only successful American hijacking.

Some of the more colorful residents of southern Washington believe Cooper landed near Lake Merwin, where he was promptly eaten by a Bigfoot.

Bigfoot was popular in this part of Washington State. At least a dozen news articles dating back to the sixties showed grainy photographs of the Sasquatch, spotted by hikers in the woods around St. Helens. One high-res photo, taken in 2005, captured the creature drinking from a river. Jack grinned. There was no mistaking the monster in the picture. It was a naked Hound, bathing himself in a stream.

Cole stepped up behind him. The look on his face was troubling.

"I've got good news and bad news," the boy said.

"Uh, good news first, please," said Jack.

"Well, I found him. The guy from Mu. He's alive and he's still a pilot. So . . . you know, we've got that going for us."

"So what's the bad news?"

"We've got a little farther to go."

3   Scopes stood on the beach and watched the waves deposit globs of crude oil all around him. *Fuck. Fuck fuck fuck.*

Al-Qaeda had destroyed Deepwater Horizon and now the ocean floor was bleeding crude and the waves were poisoning the shore. Oil stocks were tanking. That was bad enough. But Deepwater was also a HAARP relay and now half of Louisiana was getting a weakened forgetting signal. It would be pointless to have the Maestro reset the broadcast again until a new relay was built and that might take months.

These attacks were coming in waves and Scopes could barely keep up. Oklahoma City. Fort Hood. Boston. Terrorist cells, each trying to expose the Great Forgetting. He didn't know for sure, but Scopes thought these terrorists might be the Maestro's pet projects. What new memories was the Maestro sneaking into the code?

Sometimes Scopes wondered if something was wrong with the algorithm itself. Maybe there was a bug in the system. A virus. That would be bad. Scopes needed it to continue long enough for the Wichita brothers to make a perfect mess of things. The Great Forgetting needed to hold together until then.

His phone vibrated loudly.

Scopes answered.

"How bad is it?" It was the eldest brother.

"It's bad," said Scopes.

"Well. Leave it. I can handle things down there for a couple weeks. I need you elsewhere."

"Where?"

"Malaysia. That group from Franklin Mills just surfaced in Washington State. They bought illegal passports from an asset in Seattle. Then Jack Felter booked a flight to Kuala Lumpur. They left before I could flag their new IDs."

Damn it. *Cole.* Somehow the kid knew about Zaharie Shah. Probably his father told him. That was unfortunate.

"Why are they flying to Malaysia, Scopes?" the man asked.

"That's where Cole's father relocated a prisoner of war. We

cooked his brain, made him forget. But he was from Mu. And the kid can make him remember how to get home."

"Stop them."

Scopes nudged a glob of oil, rolling it back down the beach, into the water.

4 Zaharie was returning from the Pasar Malam on Petaling Street, swinging a plastic bag full of red snapper and artichokes, when he noticed the American boy watching him from across the street. There were Americans in this section of Kuala Lumpur, quite a few. But most were IT types or ESL teachers. This kid was different. Uninitiated. Like his left foot was still firmly set in Manhattan. He blinked at Zaharie. Zaharie smiled and continued on. His car was parked around the corner.

The red snapper was a present for his wife. She hadn't spoken to him since they'd quarreled two nights ago. A stupid argument about fixing the drainage behind their home. She liked the way he prepared snapper. Just olive oil and cracked salt. He'd use the charcoal grill with the mesquite he'd saved. The sun was setting, casting a rose glow on the Petronas Twin Towers in the distance. It would be dark soon. They could eat by candlelight on the patio.

"Excuse me?"

Zaharie stopped. The odd teenage boy was directly behind him now. His dark hair was messy like he liked it that way. A very American look. Something about his demeanor set off alarms in Zaharie's mind, like an abort warning on approach.

"Can I help you?" he asked. "Are you lost?" There was a hostel on Jalan Thambipillay, not far from here. The kid was probably staying there.

"You're Zaharie Ahmad Shah."

"Yes. Do I know you?"

Suddenly, two men jogged out of the alleyway behind him. One was a thin gentleman with overlarge ears, a normal-enough-looking fellow, but the other man was a giant, a red-bearded beast like a

Viking from some myth. They grabbed him and before he could shout for help, they'd pulled him down the alley and around a trash bin that smelled of oily *nasi lemak*.

"What do you want?" asked Zaharie.

The boy pulled a pair of pliers from his jeans pocket. "We want to help you remember," he said. The Viking pulled Zaharie down to his knees and held him there. The other man kept his head still. The boy stepped forward and then the pliers went into Zaharie's mouth. The tool tasted like gun grease.

Zaharie screamed. But only for a second.

The boy held the pair of pliers before Zaharie's face and in its teeth was a tooth, a nerve still dangling underneath. The pain was numbing, excruciating, but Zaharie stayed quiet. That wasn't a nerve dangling from the bottom, he realized. It was a bit of copper wire and it was attached to a tiny transistor someone had plastered into a crevasse of his tooth.

"What . . . ," he began.

And then the memories hit him like a tsunami: the dumb birds that lived on the beach outside Peshtigo; the great geodesic dome in the center of the forgotten city; the lonely mountain capped in snow; the herds of purple buffalo moving across the plains of Ende. Mu. Then: the plan, his capture in New York, the interrogation by that Hound, Scopes, and the agent who looked like an older version of this boy before him.

"Do you remember?" the boy asked.

Zaharie nodded. "Yes. I do. Tell me. Has it happened yet?"

"What?"

"The end of the world."

5 Sam stood on the back porch of Zaharie's home, leaning against the railing. She watched the jets circle KLIA, Kuala Lumpur International Airport. Malaysia. It was all so alien: those weird towers, like something from a kid's book about the future, the strange smells of the wet markets, the hurried clip of the language. She didn't consider herself ignorant. She managed her own business. Had married a doctor. But when Cole had told them that they must travel to Malaysia she'd realized she had no idea where that even was.

"Same neighborhood as Vietnam," the Captain had said, as if that should make her feel better.

That was three days ago.

That was another thing that troubled her, the speed at which everything was happening now. Like she'd been thrown from a raft and was being carried along by a current, faster and faster, toward a waterfall. Cole often spoke about gradients. Jack had explained it as an uphill battle, this urge to understand the Great Forgetting. But gradients could be downhill, too, they could be declines. And that's more like what this was. She was trapped inside a car with no brakes, steered by men, careening downhill toward who the hell knows what, in complete darkness.

Jack got passports for himself and Cole in Seattle, off a Russian man he'd found on Craigslist. The Boy Scout, the history teacher, breaking the law again. So quickly he'd set aside long-standing morals. The Russian, when they met him at a Tim Hortons, was just some kid. A nerd. He gave them two new identities. Until they got to Mu, Jack was "Christian Kozel." Cole was "Luigi Maraldi."

It worked. Of course it worked. They put the plane tickets on Sam's business card. Coach from Sea-Tac to Kuala Lumpur. Five seats. Three thousand dollars through Priceline. And now here they were, on an alien island, just not the one they were looking for. One last detour.

Sam thought about the night she'd first kissed Jack, three days after the fair, on the shore of Claytor Lake. How she felt safe for the first time. The touch of his hand on her cheek. How the fireflies were like connect-the-dots in the air.

The patio door slid open and Jack came out and handed her a blue beverage, something called *aiskrim* that tasted like lime and milk.

"It's set," said Jack. "We leave tomorrow morning. Early."

There was something different about Jack, a hardness she didn't care for. He was becoming as single-minded as Tony ever was. All he could see now was the way to Mu. When he looked at her it was as if he was simply counting her, checking her off his list of responsibilities.

"Fuck you," she said.

He winced like she'd slapped him. "What'd I do?"

"I just wanted a good life," she said. "A simple life. That's all I ever wanted. I fucking deserve it, too. What the hell are we doing here, Jack? Why aren't we home in bed? What we should do is use your passport and keep going, to Australia or somewhere. Start over. It doesn't matter if we find Tony. I don't think it matters anymore. We could be safe again. The police will never find us over here."

He went to her and put his hands on her arms, but she tossed them off.

"The forgettings go all around the world," he said. "It's not just the United States. What if you wake up tomorrow and don't remember who I am or that we ever met?"

"We're not going to be any happier on Mu, remembering."

Jack sighed, looked out at the city of blue-and-white light. "All the answers are on that island. Zaharie says there are people there who can help us. It's the only place that's safe anymore. It's the only place the Great Forgetting can't reach."

She grabbed his shirt, pushed him back, then drew him near and held him close. "This is a crazy fucking plan," she said.

"It's a crazy fucking world."

6 Late that night, Jack went for a walk. His mind was racing, clicking down the list of everything that might go wrong in the next few hours. As crazy as the plan sounded, the risk was minimal. Or at least as low as it would ever be. But Sam's derision eroded his confidence, leaving him anxious and paranoid. Maybe she was right.

Zaharie's home was in that tony section of Shal Alam on the outer rim of Kuala Lumpur, near the golf course. It was a gated community, safe. Jack passed the main gate and took a turn down the running track that led along the Sungai Damansara, a muddy tributary, drainage for the monsoons. It was just after sunset and he could feel the trapped heat of the dirt trail evaporating into the night around him.

"Hello, Jack," came a high-pitched voice directly behind him.

He whirled on his feet, nearly falling. And there it was. The Hound. Not just a Hound. The big guy. The one they called Scopes. Their leader. A foot away from him. Caught! And so close. Another three hours. That's all he would have needed. He thought of running but saw the revolver in the holster at the Hound's hip and knew that it would get the draw before he'd taken three steps.

"Easy," said Scopes. "I'm not here to kill you."

"What do you want?" he asked.

Scopes looked to the river. On the far shore a man was trolling the bottom for carp with a homemade rod and reel. "I thought we could talk."

"You came all this way just to shoot the breeze?"

The Hound's eyes sparkled under the brim of his Panama hat. "I'm going to let you go to Mu. You and your family. You deserve it. To be happy. To be safe. It's the last happy place on earth, didn't you know? Better than Disneyland. Hell, I'll join you there soon. We'll drink lemonade on the beach and talk about our adventures."

Jack steeled himself, waited for the inevitable "but . . ."

"But I want you to stay there. Don't leave Mu. Don't come back."

Jack looked closely at the Hound. He seemed sincere, earnest. What Jack really sensed was a sadness. A deep, old, stubborn sadness. Weary and tired.

"How would I deserve that happiness if I knew that everyone back home was living in a world run by a couple capitalists who can rewrite our memories with a simple phone call? That's not freedom."

"You think people want freedom? Everyone is scared. They don't want freedom. They want to forget. They want to forget all the bad, scary things."

"The Great Forgetting was wrong," said Jack. "But these new forgettings. Nobody voted for them. Why are they doing it? Do they think they're making the world safer for us by making us forget again?"

Scopes laughed. "They don't care about making the world a better place. It's not that complicated. All they want is money. Money and power. And power comes from money, so really, just money. Just money. Something out there messes with the price of oil, they make people forget. That simple. A storm in New Orleans wipes out a couple refineries? Boom, gone, forgotten. A sex scandal involving subcontractors in Iraq? Pick up the phone, tell the Maestro to delete six billion memories. It's greed, Jack. Simple greed."

"So why are you helping them?"

"Helping them? I own them. I told them about the Great Forgetting. I gave them the password for the Maestro."

"I don't understand."

"It's greed we should have forgotten. Not history. That's what the founders didn't understand. We forgot about all those bad things, but we left greed in the box and that's why it didn't work. Every war, every act of terrorism we've seen since we hit that reset button, it was all based in greed. It'll never stop. The only thing left is to let greed run its course."

"Run its course?"

Scopes nodded. "I found the two greediest men in the world, two brothers who want to control the world with their oil money. Buying influence. Stealing elections. They sank a hundred million dollars into the Tea Party last year, not because they're patriots but because the Tea Party will do away with all regulation, the only thing keeping greed in check. Then corporations will run the world. They're close. Very close. They control the Supreme Court, Congress. They'll have the White House. It's going to happen. And it will work. For a few years, it'll work brilliantly. They will be rich beyond even their dreams. It'll work right up until their laborers begin to starve to death. When that happens, the workers will finally rise up and murder everyone at the top. It will implode. *Everything.* The world will fall. And the only culture remaining will be the one that never forgot, the culture of Mu. We can rebuild then. We'll have our history back, all of it. Because, Jack, and here's the thing: the only thing that could ever keep our greed in check is the horror of our shared history."

Jack took it in. The idea overwhelmed him. It was so dark. And yet hopeful. Seductive. Perverse. "How many people will die when it all comes apart? Do you have any idea?"

The Hound shrugged. "Something like three billion. Give or take a hundred million."

Jack's heart raced in his chest. Was this some kind of grand decision he alone was faced with, here, now? No. No, this couldn't be his decision to make. Not really. He couldn't believe that. Nothing he could do could have an impact on the future of the human race. That was ludicrous. But what else were they discussing?

"Why don't we just let them remember?" asked Jack. "Maybe if they remembered before all that other stuff happened . . ."

Scopes shook his head. "They're not ready for that."

Jack looked back at Zaharie's house. He could just make it out on the hill, behind a row of langsat trees.

"Here," said Scopes. He had two belts crisscrossed around his waist like a gunslinger. He disconnected the buckle from one and handed it to Jack. It felt heavy, heavier than it should.

"What's this?"

"It's a bit of the forgotten tech we had from Before. The marines called them ripcords or boomerang belts. Something to do with quantum entanglement. Whatever. Essentially, the buckle is still attached to the belt and always will be. You click this button—" Scopes turned the buckle around in Jack's hand and on the back was a red button—"and it will bring me to you. When you get to Mu, bring me over."

For a moment, Jack said nothing. Then, gritting his teeth, he threw the buckle into the river.

"No," he said. "I won't do it your way. I won't just watch the world destroy itself. I'd rather you killed me first."

Scopes surprised Jack with a smile. "Maybe," he said. "But not today. You still might change your mind." He tipped his hat to Jack and walked away, toward the night markets of Kuala Lumpur.

7   Later that night, back at Le Meridien, in a suite overlooking the sea, Scopes sat on the edge of his bed, the nine-millimeter in his hairy hand. He'd thought of doing this before. Tonight was as good a night as any. Jack had proved it to him. Nothing ever changes.

When he was little his name was Yohance and his mother played music to him in their apartment at night. It helped with his headaches, which sometimes felt like fire inside his skull.

Memories: a gentle hand that smelled of tallow; the sound of her cotton dress swishing over her legs; her music—she plucked at a wooden saucer with bent metal keys that sounded at once like a piano and a steel drum. Music of his mother's father, who had constructed the instrument from the trunk of a tree at the edge of a forest.

Yohance lived with his mother in a brown and yellow apartment on the hospital grounds. Sometimes when he thought about what they were doing to him, he cried so much his eyes burned.

"Why?" he asked her once.

"It's a very pointless question," she said.

He didn't like school. The old priests wouldn't look at him. The priests were afraid of them. Of Yohance and his classmates.

There was no arguing the essential truth: he and his friends were special. But he most of all. Because of his mother, Ambala. His mother was a bright light in the hospital. The staff called the other mothers "bush babies," but not Ambala. She was smarter. Smarter than some of the doctors, he thought, though she had never gone to school and had been abducted from the bush like the rest of the women.

Maybe it was the music, he'd wonder later.

Yohance suspected the migraine headaches that plagued his childhood came from the stuff they injected him with. The doctors wanted to know what side effects the medicine would have. Maybe suffering these headaches had

saved countless people from enduring their own migraines during the Great
Forgetting. Probably that was the case. Why else would they have done it?
And for so long?

Memory: a sunlit morning, amber light through the window. His mother
was packing, tossing clothes into a potato sack. She stopped when she saw
him and came to him and placed her long hands on his wrinkly cheeks. That
dark skin. Flawless. Warm to the touch.

"Yohance," she said. "Yohance, we must flee."

"Why?"

"The doctors lied to us. They want you to protect them after the Great
Forgetting. They want to continue using you. There will be no freedom for
you in their new world."

"But . . . why?"

"They don't see you as human. But you're no more an animal than any
of the men. You. Are. Human."

"I don't feel human."

"You will know grace. That is being human. Come."

They ran. Out into the world that was hot and loud and full of people
who looked at him as if he were diseased. They fled from village to village,
over the road that led back to Ambala's people. There was war everywhere in
those days. Tribes fighting tribes over a tiny well or a truckload of rice.

The doctors caught up with them outside Otukpo. A group of six men in
white jackets led by that German with the slick hair. "Guter boy," said
Dr. Mengele. "Come wit me." And they put him in a Jeep and he never saw
her again. Ambala.

The doctors paid special attention to Yohance after that. Mengele recognized that he was different, that Yohance understood their numbers and ab-
tractions. Algebra. Geometry. And language. Mengele brought him books of
poetry. Keats. Tennyson. Eliot. His favorite, Angelou, reminded him of his
mother. He devoured the literature.

For a time, Yohance was Mengele's favorite. And then one day Mengele
brought with him a man with a strange voice and an odd hump on his back.
Yohance did not like this man. He had just enough brains to be dangerous.
Yohance made fun of the humpback. He called this man "Maestro." It was
supposed to be ironic. But he didn't get it. The weird man loved it so much

he told everyone to call him Maestro. And in return, he bestowed nicknames on Yohance and his kind, naming most of them after apes from silly comic books and movies. He called Yohance "Scopes," because he thought it was funny. But it wasn't funny. Or at least it wasn't smart humor. All the more unbearable because the Maestro thought he was being gracious. Eventually the Maestro figured it out, that Yohance had been making fun of him. And from that point on, they were all called the Hounds. And even Yohance knew where that had come from. He'd read Bradbury.

Came a time when the great scientist Stephen Hawking visited Lagos. The young scientist was the architect of the Great Forgetting and he wanted to live for a hundred years to see it completed. He tested his longevity drug on the Hounds first, Scopes being one of them. They put it in their Kool-Aid. Now Scopes would live forever in a world with no place for his kind. And when the Collectors were all retired and the Maestro had nothing more for them to do? Where would they go? Who cared?

The time of the Great Forgetting arrived at last. As Yohance boarded the helicopter that would take him to the staging area, he watched a marine with a flamethrower torch the bundle of reeds that covered the warren where two male bonobos lived. Was one of them his father?

The last thing Mengele did was make Titano their leader. Titano the brute. Titano the simpleton.

"Why?" Yohance asked Mengele when they were alone on the eve of the Forgetting.

"Because you think you're better than us."

Years. Years watching over the Collectors, hiding under the mountains. Years watching humanity corrupt the vision of the Great Forgetting, babies shitting in their cribs. Three short years after they reset the calendar to 1964, America found its way back to war. This time in Vietnam. Like they couldn't wait. And Yohance was smart enough to see that this war, like all wars, was not about peace, but money. Wars create billionaires out of the men who own the companies that make the guns and bullets. Greed was an instinct that humans had not evolved beyond. It was the virus in their code.

But Yohance had a secret. He had learned to translate the code that went out from HAARP. The read-only files that contained the bits and bytes of the Maestro's algorithm were accessible from any computer in the Underground if you knew where to look. He taught himself to interpret its structure, to appreciate its elegance. And so when the Maestro began fucking with it, Yohance noticed right away. He spotted the broken fractals jutting from the original algorithm like melanoma. The Maestro had come to see the folly of human redemption, too, it seemed. And he'd begun to take measures to fix it.

The Maestro was trying to wake people up to the Great Forgetting, give them a chance to bring it down themselves. What would that accomplish? They'd already showed they had no capacity for transcendence. Truth: humans love to forget.

As he'd predicted, the Maestro's meddling went awry. Tim McVeigh had seemed like a safe bet. Intelligent. Gulf War vet. The Maestro recruited him, told him about the Great Forgetting, showed him how to keep his memories safe. Guy went fucking nuts. Blew up a relay but killed 168 people, and how many of those were children? After that the Maestro trod more carefully. He used a gradient. It would go on and on until the Maestro finally succeeded. And when that happened, if there was something like a Great Remembering, what then would humanity do to the Hounds? He knew. He had only to remember the men with American flags on their sleeves torching the primate cave.

There was only one chance for the Hounds: a clean slate. No money to fight over. Everyone equal again. Those who survived, anyway. The world was bent on destruction, anyway. Why not give them a little push?

And when the world began to fall, he'd retire to Mu and watch the mushroom clouds from the beach, and when the smoke cleared he might return and do a little better.

Scopes set the gun down.

EIGHT

THE LAST FLIGHT

1 The Captain called it a Triple-7, but to Jack it was just another big damn jet. They watched it taxi to the gate from their seats in the terminal. Zaharie was speaking quietly with the steward at the ticket counter, arranging their seats for the red-eye to Beijing, even though China was no longer their destination.

"I feel sick," said Nils, holding his head between his large legs.

"That's normal," the Captain told him. "Nerves."

As soon as the jet parked outside, the passengers formed a line at the door. Most were Chinese, Jack noticed, on a simple flight home.

Sam gripped Jack's arm and whispered in his ear. "We're going to scare the shit out of these people."

"Maybe," he said. "But they'll forget it all. Quick detour to Mu. Then on to Beijing. When they get home, HAARP will wipe their memories. For once we get to use the Great Forgetting to our advantage."

"Boarding has begun for Flight 370, nonstop to Beijing," the steward said into the mic. He took an old man's ticket and waved him through the open door and down the ramp.

Zaharie returned with their tickets. He was dressed in his black-and-white pilot's uniform. He'd left his family behind. The flight was not without risk. One day he'd come back.

"Ready?" Zaharie asked the Captain.

"Ready," he said.

Zaharie had arranged first-class tickets near the cockpit. Jack sat by Sam. The Captain and Cole took seats across the aisle. Nils ended up nearer to the bathroom. The big guy looked pale. Was it really nerves? Jack pushed the thought aside. There were more important things to worry about than Nils's upset stomach.

The other pilot arrived and Zaharie shut the cockpit door. A stewardess closed and latched the entrance. Then the jet pulled away from the gate and rolled toward the runway. It was thirty minutes past midnight according to Tony's watch.

2   As soon as they were in the air and the seat-belt light came on, Nils stood and walked to the bathroom. The first-class amenities were larger than those in coach, but still, he was a tight fit.

I should have told them, thought Nils, looking at himself in the frosted mirror.

He lifted his shirt. His chest was mottled, marked by dark patches like bruises. He moved his fingers across a black circle near the center of his chest. He felt another fiber poking out of his skin there. He took it by his fingernails like he'd done in the bathroom at Zaharie's mansion. Grabbed it and pulled. It was another corkscrewed fiber, nine inches long, green like the inside of a kiwi, rigid like a steel spring. He tossed it in the toilet. Since yesterday, he'd pulled twenty of them out of his body. Mostly from his chest and underarms. But he'd also found one in the skin beside his balls.

What's happening to me?

That day in the Maestro's house when Sam had come through the door. The Hounds had shot at them and he'd thought a bit of

shrapnel had hit him. That was when it had started. He'd felt fever-
ish that night. One of the damn Hounds had shot him with something. Something poisonous, or worse.

He didn't want to bother anyone until this next part was over.
Everyone else had so much on their minds already. He could wait
another four or five hours. Then he would tell them. There would
be doctors on Mu, right? Someone who could help him. Maybe
someone there could tell him what the fuck he was dealing with.

He looked at the fiber in the toilet bowl. It was a parasite's egg,
he knew. There was no other explanation. There were things crawling around under his skin. He could feel them sometimes, moving
like thin fingers along his chest. These were eggs. Had to be.

Nils closed the lid and flushed away the matter. He stood there
and shivered.

3   An hour into the flight, Jack felt the jet buck a little, as if they'd
flown through a patch of turbulance. Then the cockpit door opened
and Zaharie stepped out. There was a stewardess in the front alcove,
microwaving bowls of minced pork noodles. She turned to him,
alarmed to find the pilot out of the cockpit, unannounced. They
exchanged whispered words and then she nodded and walked through
the curtain into coach.

"This is it," Zaharie said. "Let's hurry. She'll be back in a moment."

Jack followed Zaharie into the cockpit. It was tight inside, barely
room for three. There were knobs and readouts and toggles everywhere and Jack was overcautious with his movements, fearful that
he might brush up against a self-destruct button or something by
accident. The first officer was asleep in his chair. Not asleep, really.
Zaharie had dosed his coffee with Ambien. Jack and Zaharie pried
the copilot from his chair and carried him back to the Captain's seat
in first class and strapped him in.

Sam touched Jack's arm and he kneeled to her and kissed the top
of her head. Then he helped the Captain to the cockpit, where his
old man took the first officer's chair. Zaharie pulled out a hard plas-

tic shelf from a cache in the wall for Jack to sit on, then he shut the cockpit door, locked it tight, and climbed into his seat.

"I'm taking her off auto," said Zaharie.

The Captain's hands responded by muscle memory, drifting over the console around him, flicking switches and dialing down knobs. He opened a compartment between their seats and turned a key. "Transponder is off," the Captain said.

Through the windows Jack could see a full moon reflecting gray light off a scrim of clouds below them. It was peaceful, dreamlike. Zaharie slowly banked the plane north-northeast.

There was a single runway on Mu, Zaharie had told them. The Germans had it constructed during the war for the Luftwaffe. "It's where I landed in 1985," he'd said to them at his kitchen table. "I was a surveyor for the Forest Service out of Juneau, flying a Cessna Citation. Squall come up. Tossed me around. Shorted my instruments over the open sea. Too dark to get a read on direction. No sun, no stars. Was about to run out of gas. Figured I was in for a freeze and a drowning. And then I saw the lights on the horizon. A city where no city should be. And just outside the city was this old airstrip." Zaharie had lived on Mu until 2009, when he and four other revolutionaries had returned to take down a relay. They were caught by the Hounds. He had no idea where his friends were now. If they were not executed, their minds were wiped and they had no idea who they were anymore.

Jack realized he was holding his breath. He let it out and tried to calm down. He looked to the horizon, searching the night for the lights of Mu's great city.

4   Nils was back in the bathroom. It was getting worse. Perhaps it was the stress of their current predicament accelerating the disease. He looked at himself in the mirror, horrified by what he saw. There was a purple boil under his right arm, a dark boil in his armpit that was getting bigger, expanding every second. Carefully, he probed it with one finger. It exploded with an audible pop. Pus and blood spattered the mirror and a thousand long green fibers fell from the abscess, dropping upon the sink, the counter, the floor.

Nils began to scream.

5   The scream was loud enough that Cole heard Nils from seat 2D. He clicked off his seat belt and raced to the door of the bathroom. It was locked.

"Nils?" said Sam, appearing just behind him.

The screaming stopped and something very large fell against the door. For a moment it buckled out. Cole had just enough time to pull Sam back before the door broke apart and Nils's body collapsed into the aisle. His shirt was half off and he was covered in blood. Green fibers covered his legs. And the smell . . . like a fruit basket left to rot. Putrid sweet.

"Oh, shit," said Cole. "It's Morgellons."

Sam couldn't respond. She stood over the body, her hands covering her nose and mouth.

Cole leaned down and checked for a pulse. "He's alive," he said. "But he doesn't have long. Fuck!"

"What the hell is Morgellons, Cole, and how did he get it?"

"One of the Hounds must've shot him. Maybe when you came through the door. Or in New York. It's a parasite. Nazis weaponized it during the war. I only know what my dad told me, but he said it wasn't contagious. It has to be injected into your blood. Little worms that eat you up from the inside, leave egg cases everywhere, these fibers. If we can't get him the antidote, he'll be dead in six hours."

Another passenger, a Chinese woman from the row behind them, was leaning into the aisle, watching. She asked them something in Mandarin, and when they didn't answer, she keyed the button for the stewardess.

"What kind of medicine does he need?" asked Sam.

"There's only one cure," said Cole. "A kind of ambergris."

"What?"

"Juice from the belly of a diseased bird."

"What bird?"

"The dodo," said Cole.

"But the dodo is fucking extinct!"

"Not on Mu."

6   A red light clicked on above the cockpit microphone, an alert from the stewardess. Zaharie pressed a button. "What?" he said.

"We've got a situation in first class," the stewardess said. "There's a guy out here. I think he's dying."

"We're three hours out," he replied. "Do what you can to make him comfortable."

"We should be on approach to Beijing in fifteen minutes."

"I am diverting the aircraft to another airport."

There was a pause. When the woman spoke again her voice was confused, suspicious. "Why?"

"I have been instructed to continue northeast of Beijing."

"Zaharie, why is Fariq asleep in first class? Where is the passenger from seat 2C? Zaharie, have we been hijacked?"

Zaharie looked to the Captain. "We have not been hijacked, Melissa. I am in control of the plane. I'll explain on the ground. Keep everyone calm back there."

7   It took some effort on their part, but Cole and Sam finally got Nils back into his seat. Sam cleaned him off the best she could and slipped two pillows behind his large head. He was snoring now, a sound like a Husqvarna chain saw. Cole watched him from where he sat. Sometimes the worms moving under the Viking's skin rippled the flesh around his neck like waves.

Time passed in a haze, like a shared delirium. The passengers became anxious. Why had they not yet arrived in Beijing? Was there a problem with the engines? The stewardess did her best to keep them calm. Their flight had been diverted to another airport, she told them.

Around 5:00 a.m., the aircraft shuddered as the autopilot kicked off. They were descending. Finally. Cole turned, lifted the blind on his window. Sam leaned over him to see, too.

It was sunrise and the tops of the clouds glowed with a warm pinkness, and then they were flying into them, through them, and for a moment they could not see. Then they shot out of the clouds and there, on the horizon, was Mu.

It was a vast island, larger than Cole had ever dreamed, the coast of a continent rising out of the Pacific. Blue glaciers hugged the shore. Cliffs, a hundred feet high, rose from the waters. There was a great plateau and in the distance a single peak, the Lonely Mountain, capped in snow.

"There's nothing there," said Sam. "You were wrong."

"You're experiencing what's called inattentional blindness," explained Cole. "I can see it clearly. It's right there." He pointed. "Give yourself a minute. Trust me when I tell you it's there."

"I don't . . ."

Suddenly, Sam started in fright. She let loose a short scream before she covered her mouth. "What is that?" she whispered around her fingers.

There was a vast city on the southern plateau. She could see it now. Everything. The island. The mountain. The plateau. But it was the city that frightened her. Something about it scared Cole, too.

The city was a perfect circle of skyscrapers divided into equal slices, outlined by cobblestone streets. The buildings were made of steel and glass and reflected the light of the morning sun with a brilliance that caught in your throat. In the center was a great geodesic dome, a white sphere like the one at Epcot, only bigger, much bigger.

It was the symmetry of this city that frightened them. It was orderly to a frightening degree, the suggestion of a culture rigid in mind-set, devoid of beauty, of mistake, of forgiveness. Relentless.

"Cole," she whispered, gripping his arm. "Who are they?"

8 "I've got a bad feeling about this," said Jack, looking out at the city, which Zaharie called Peshtigo.

"Where's the runway?" the Captain asked. His hand was on the throttle, helping Zaharie guide the 777.

"There," said Zaharie, pointing east of the city. Jack saw it. A long swatch of concrete and . . . "Oh, shit."

"What the hell is that?" the Captain barked.

"It's a goddamn park," said Zaharie. "They built a goddamn park in the middle of the runway."

A square patch of trees and shrubs divided the runway in half. Jack could even see the statue in the middle of the park, a tall granite sculpture atop a fountain.

"Dump the gas!" the Captain shouted.

"What?" said Jack over the whine of the engines. "We need the rest of the gas to fly the passengers back home!"

His father turned in his seat to look at him. Jack recoiled at the fear he saw in the Captain's eyes.

"We're going to hit that statue at sixty miles an hour and this bird is going to break apart. We can't have it turn into a fireball, too." He looked at Zaharie. "Dump it!"

Zaharie pressed a button, twisted a toggle. "There!" he said. "Help me bring her in."

The Captain took the wheel and pushed forward with Zaharie. The nose of the plane tilted downward and they were coming in. Coming in fast. Jack tightened his seat belt.

Zaharie clicked on the intercom. "This is your captain speaking," he said. "Brace for impact!"

PART FOUR

THE LATENESS OF THE HOUR

There are weapons that are simply thoughts . . . For the record, prejudices can kill and suspicion can destroy.

—ROD SERLING

THE INVADERS

1 The psychiatrist leaned back in his chair and listened to the round woman explain why she wanted to leave her husband.

"I can't look at him," she said. "I'm tired of his fat face."

"Why are you tired of looking at his face?" he asked.

The doctor was a rough-looking man in a sharp suit, a cleaned-up hit man from a daytime soap. His face was gaunt and lined with long wrinkles, and a black velvet eyepatch covered his right socket. His hair was mostly gray. He'd have been all-around intimidating if not for that single sea-blue eye that demanded your attention and held it, warmly.

"I just can't look at it anymore," the woman said.

She was round but not unattractive. Dark hair, dark skin. She was forty-five. A Navajo. Full-blood. One of the librarians from section twelve. Biographies.

"We weren't made to live like this."

"What do you mean?" asked the shrink. He'd had this conversation a hundred times before with a hundred different clients. It was epidemic, this ennui. The doctor opened his eye wider so that she would feel that he was paying attention. Outside his office window, a squat bird with a comically large beak waddled up to its reflection, pecked the glass, and then sauntered away, back toward the ocean.

"We weren't meant to live this long."

"Yes," he said. "That's true. When you married Catori you promised to love each other till death do you part, but . . ."

"But I had no idea how long that would be."

The doctor nodded. "How old are you this year?" he asked.

"Goodness," the woman said. "One hundred and seventy-four."

Just then the door to his office opened and a teenage girl stepped in.

"Guten Morgen, fräulein," he said.

Becky was no more German than he was. But they pretended. She was thirteen, tall for her age, a blonde with skin the color of meringue. She was dressed in a dark smock. Same as always.

"Dr. Sanders!" she said excitedly. "A bunch of people just crashed a plane through the park. A whole plane!"

The doctor grimaced and set down his notebook. Becky was hopping up and down, waving her hands at her sides, barely containing her excitement.

"Where are they from?"

"Home!" she said. "And they ask for you by name!"

2   Scopes pulled up to the guardhouse outside Area 51, in southern Nevada. There was a man in uniform on the other side of the bulletproof glass and he regarded Scopes only a moment before retracting the gate. The guard knew him well.

Groom Lake, they called it. Conspiracy nuts believed this isolated base in the Nevada desert was where the United States military kept crashed UFOs. In reality, Area 51 was operated by the NSA. It was a warehouse for forgotten tech, storage for strange machines made before the Great Forgetting, stuff meant never to be remembered.

Scopes parked and walked inside. He had a small office in the main hangar, a black dome so expansive and tall that microclouds gathered at the rafters and sometimes sprinkled the floor with a misty rain. There was a platoon of Zerstörer mechs in the corner, nine-foot-tall humanoid robots the Nazis had used at the Battle of St. Louis.

Inside his office, he powered on the Apple II while he boiled water for tea on a hot plate. The greenish-yellow screen came on. *CLEMENTINE*, it read. *PRESS ENTER TO ACCESS MAINFRAME.*

Scopes pressed Enter.

A crude desktop came up. He used the flat, square mouse to move the cursor to a folder titled *READ ONLY FILES, ALGORITHM: ASPEN.*

He held the tea in his hands, reading over the data that appeared on-screen. On his mug was the logo from the 2026 Winter Olympics.

"Okay, Maestro," he said. "Let's see what you're up to."

3   "We're here to see Tony Sanders," Jack said again, this time a bit slower. But the robot remained still.

Jack was standing on the broken tarmac of Mu's only runway, the remains of Flight 370 smoldering behind him. The statue had sheared off the right wing, just as the Captain had predicted. The jet had rolled then, and the impact had snapped the fuselage in half. It was a good thing they'd dumped the fuel. Miraculously, no one had died. There were, however, a dozen injured Chinese businessmen lying on the grass. Most had concussions and one had broken his leg.

This robot was whatever passed for a welcoming committee on Mu. It was four feet high, nothing more than a tin cylinder with a dome head that swiveled back and forth, watching them with a single camera eye. It had rolled out of a decrepit hangar like an oversize Roomba while Jack was pulling passengers from the wreckage.

Sam stood beside Jack, squinting her eyes at the machine. Nils's body was strapped to a makeshift gurney behind her (a seat cushion tied to thin steel girders from the wreck). Cole crossed the runway and joined them.

"Looks kind of like R2-D2," the boy said.

"More like a Dalek," said the Captain, who had made sure each of the 240 displaced passengers was off the plane before he walked away from the broken bird.

Jack gave his father a puzzled look.

"*Dr. Who*," the Captain explained. "What kind of a nerd are you?"

"*Folgen Sie mir!*" the robot said. Its voice was modulated and shaky, a very old computer program shaking off dust. Then it turned and rolled back toward the hangar.

"What did it say?" asked Sam.

"It said, 'Follow me,'" the Captain replied. "In German."

Fifty feet away, Zaharie held up his hands. *"Dàjiā bǎochí lěng-jìng!"* he shouted to the Chinese passengers of Malaysia Airlines Flight 370. *Remain calm.*

"Come on," said Jack. He followed the robot. Sam, the Captain, and Cole walked behind him. The robot rolled along on thick rubber wheels, deftly avoiding potholes and puddles, and led them through the open door of the hangar. Inside, it was dark and dingy and smelled of spilled oil. They followed it across the empty garage and through another door, into a tiled hall.

"What's this?" asked Sam.

"Looks like a shower," said Cole.

It was at that moment the door to the tiled hall closed and they heard a lock turn loudly. The robot spun around and regarded them coolly.

"*Ausrotten*," it said.

Jack looked up to the ceiling. Long pipes ran overhead, from one end to the other, attached to round spouts like the kind used for fire sprinklers in hotels or . . .

"What did it say?" asked Cole.

The Captain was thinking. "Uh . . . my German's rusty . . ."

"*Ausrotten*," it said again.

"*Ausrotten*," the Captain muttered. "Uh . . . uproot . . ."

"Uproot?" the boy asked.

"Uproot . . . destroy . . ."

"Exterminate," said Jack. He pointed to the ceiling. Painted on the tile behind the pipes was a black swastika. "We're in a gas chamber."

But before anyone could scream for help, the door at the far end clicked open and a man stepped into the room. He was tall, with gray hair. A surgical mask obscured his face below a dark eyepatch. He looked at the robot and put his hands on his hips.

"Damn it. I thought we got rid of all these guys."

"*Ausrotten!*" it said.

"Yeah, yeah," the man in the mask said, waving a hand. "We heard you." He looked at Jack. "Don't worry," he said, his voice muffled by the mask. "It's just replaying old programming. None of this stuff works anymore."

"We need to find Tony Sanders," said Jack.

The man's good eye gleamed. And then he pulled the mask down around his chin.

Jack gasped in surprise. His old friend stood before him, but there was little resemblance to the boy he once knew. Those wrinkles. That eyepatch. There was a nasty scar snaking out from under it. And he'd lost so much weight. He looked older than he should, as if he'd skipped forward ten years.

"Do I look that bad?" said Tony. He smiled wryly and shook his head. "Jesus, Jack. You brought everyone. Sam, Cole, the Captain . . . and a couple hundred red Chinese for good measure, I see."

"And Nils," said Jack.

"I saw. What's wrong with him?"

"Morgellons," said Cole.

"Damn it. Okay. Let me see what I can do." He turned to leave.

"Wait," said Jack. "Where the fuck are you going?"

Tony turned back to them. "They've got something that might help Nils. I have to go into the city. While I'm gone, you should gather everyone in the hangar. You've been placed in quarantine for a bit. Don't worry. I'll have food and water brought down. We'll have you out in a day or two, tops. Procedure. There was a shipwreck back in the seventies. Someone brought measles. Wiped out a quarter of their population. I'll be back."

Before he left, his last eye found Sam. He nodded at her, then he disappeared out the door.

4　It was a long drive from Nevada to Big Indian Mountain, but Scopes didn't mind. He loved traversing the country by highway. He loved the way the culture of America evolved from town to town. The more miles you traveled in a day, the easier it was to notice the quaint differences from one place to another. The way prairie dogs got fatter as you drove east. The way French dressing got sweeter the farther you went west. How people said "slippy" instead of "slippery" the closer you got to Pittsburgh. Or how, as you drove south, there were advertisements for "pop," and then "soda," and then, simply, "coke." People were dangerous animals but also infinitely fascinating.

Also, Scopes liked his car. It was a 1964 Chrysler turbine, made the year of the Great Forgetting. The last mass-produced turbine-engine car in the world. It was quiet as the wind and could run on anything in a pinch: cooking oil, whiskey, Chanel No. 5. They don't make 'em like they used to. How could they? They'd forgotten how. The radio was AM and he liked it that way. In the summers he could pick up ball games from Tallahassee to Akron. There was nothing more American than listening to a ball game in mono, the crack of the bat like a smack in the face.

He needed to talk to the Maestro, but he also needed time to figure out what to say. What Scopes had discovered lurking in the algorithm's code was concerning. The Maestro was sneaking software patches into the resets, bits of code that targeted Jack and Tony and their friends. He was actually rewriting their memories as the group progressed, tweaking their personal backstories to motivate them. But motivation toward what end? For instance, what did drawing out a love affair between Jack and Sam and Tony have to do with the bigger picture?

It made Scopes nervous. Could be the Maestro had learned something about the human condition. Had he found another way?

It was time to confront the Maestro about what he knew, but for the first time Scopes was no longer sure that he was smarter than the old man in the mountain.

Scopes realized he was gripping the wheel too tightly. He had to control his anger by the time he got to Big Indian. The anger shamed him. Such a human emotion. He was better than that. More evolved.

He made himself remember Ambala. Her night music. And slowly he relaxed.

5   When Tony returned, he had no mask. He carried a wooden box, two inches square, inlaid with a dark design, like henna. The Chinese, who had gathered in the hangar, quieted and parted to let him through. He walked briskly to where Nils lay on the floor, and then kneeled beside his body and opened the box. Inside was a tar-like paste that smelled distinctly of treacle.

"What is it?" asked Sam who sat beside Nils's head, a hand on his hair.

"Dodo juice," said Tony. "Gunk from their stomach."

"So there *are* still dodo here?" asked Cole, eyes wide.

Tony looked at the boy with his good eye, "There are all kind of things here," he said. "On the other side of the mountain there's a herd of triceratops."

"Bullshit," the Captain said.

Tony winked at him and then used his fingers to scoop out a glob of the ambergris.

"He can't eat anything," said Sam.

"It doesn't go in his mouth." Tony gently nudged Sam aside and straddled the Viking's body. Then he distributed the black goo evenly between the fingers on both his hands and pushed them into Nils's ears. He used the pads of his hands to squeeze the mess deep into the man's ear canals. When he was finished, Tony pitched the box to the floor and stepped away from the body. "Back up a bit," he said. "It works fast."

Faster than anyone expected. As soon as Jack was out of the way, Nils opened his eyes. They were so shot with blood that all the white was red. He looked possessed, and in a very real way, Jack realized, he was. His breathing became ragged, lungs full of mucus. Then he sneezed. And sneezed. *KA-CHOW! KA-CHOW!* Again and again he sneezed. Finally, Nils sat up and, feeling another sneeze come on, squeezed his nose tight with two fingers. The force of the caged sneeze caused a thousand, ten thousand, a million fibers to erupt from his body simultaneously though the pores of his arms and legs and chest. Green fibers shot from his skin like gruesome party streamers. "Gaaaa!" said Nils. "That was so fucking gross!"

6   Since Tony had breached the quarantine, he was in with them for the night. He sat against the tin wall, and the others from Franklin Mills gathered around him in a tight semicircle. He felt awkward, insecure. There were things they should know and things they should not know, things they should never know. But they'd come so far for him. It moved him to tears.

"You're a real sonofabitch," said Jack.

"Fuckin' asshole!" said Sam.

"You're a great big asshat," said Cole. "How long were you gonna let me rot in that loony bin?"

"One at a time," he said, raising his hands in defense.

The Captain shook his head and said simply, "The fuck happened to your eye?"

"I've missed you, Captain," he said. "So, yeah, the eye . . . uh . . . after I put Mark's body in the lake, I borrowed his car. Drove it to the Gate House. Underneath Pymatuning I found a room with a weird vehicle, this thing called a water cart. Kind of like that log ride at Cedar Point? The one where you sit in the cart that gets pushed down the track by water? Like that, except the cart was sealed so the

water couldn't get in. Like a train car, kinda. I traveled three thousand miles down a tube of water. All the way to California. Or would
have, if the track hadn't blown up halfway through, I mean . . ."

Tony was dozing inside the water cart, rushing along the tunnel toward the
West Coast, when it happened. It began with an odd sound. Like, if you
were swimming underwater and someone cannonballed right next to you. A
percussive, dull GOOOOOSHH, and suddenly the bullet-shaped four-
seater car Tony was traveling in slowed as water rushed backward around it.
It stopped for only a moment, and then he was being pulled faster down the
tunnel. The water sloshed violently, bumping the cart against the Plexiglas
tube. Tony tugged at his harness, pulling it tight around his chest. A second
later, the water cart launched out of the tunnel through a giant gaping hole.

For a moment, he was weightless, falling through the black void, and
then spotlights came on high above, painting his surroundings with a harsh
yellow light, and Tony saw that he was falling into some abandoned city, be-
tween tall pylons that held the tunnel aloft over a street lined by brownstone
apartments.

Impact! His whole body jolted forward, but before he could crush himself
against the console, the cabin filled with pink foam that transferred his poten-
tial energy and converted it to kinetic waves within itself. It felt like Jell-O
and smelled faintly of burned rubber. Just as Tony began to wonder if he might
suffocate, the windshield retracted and he came spilling out. He rolled away
from the water cart inside a wave of foam that quickly dissolved into a pool of
pink water.

Hesitantly, Tony stood. His mind reached out to his organs and extrem-
ities, to ascertain the location of any injury, but he found he was unharmed.
Whatever that pink goop was, it was probably something we should not have
forgotten.

He walked away from the spume of water falling from the blasted tube.
More spotlights clicked on, responding to his progress, revealing the city in a
hundred-foot radius around him.

Tony had never visited Europe, but he'd seen pictures of London on
album covers, and that's what this city looked like to him. An old city. Older
than Cleveland. The apartments were made of hand-laid brick and rock and

wood, packed so closely together he thought they might share common attics, like in those novels about children who wandered into other worlds. The street he was on ended at a great cathedral, the junction of rue Nibi and rue Giizis, according to the street sign on the corner.

He was about to call out. Call out "hello" or "hey" or something, when he heard the sound of running footsteps. His first thought was to hide. Hide behind the church or the side of that brownstone over there, but he didn't know what he was running from and hadn't he been about to call out for help anyway?

Spotlights clicked on around a corner, and as the sound of the running feet grew louder, Tony marked the person's progress by the approaching lights. Then the lights and the noise and the runner turned the corner onto rue Nibi and Tony saw what it was.

Cole had described them, but still Tony was frightened by its appearance. The hair, all that hair, made the Hound look like a werewolf. Cole had warned him that they would come for him. This one wore two belts crisscrossed around its waist like some cowboy.

Tony ran for the church, but even before he got to the door, he knew it would be locked. And it was. He reached out for the brass aspen leaf knockers, but by then the Hound was at the bottom of the stairs, looking up at him.

"Come here," the Hound whispered.

"What do you want?" Tony asked.

"Shhh!" the Hound said, looking around nervously. He waved at Tony to come down.

What else was there to do? Readying himself for a fight, Tony walked to the Hound.

"You blew up the tunnel," Tony whispered.

"Yes."

"Why?"

"Because you're trying to get to Mu," said the Hound. "I want to know why."

Tony didn't say anything.

"You can tell me or I can read your mind. Save me the trouble."

"I have to stop the forgettings. Stop whoever is resetting the code."

The Hound grunted.

"Why are we whispering?" asked Tony.

"Because things still live in the heart of this city."

"What is this place?"

"Na'Duli," said the Hound. "It was once the capital city of the Seven Nations. It's irradiated now."

"Irradiated?"

"Don't worry. You can survive down here for quite a while." The Hound motioned for him and turned back down rue Nibi. "Come."

Tony didn't move. He looked back down into the darkness where downtown must be. He thought about running.

"Bad idea," the Hound whispered.

"I can't let you erase my mind," he said.

The Hound reached for him and that did it. Tony ran. He ran so fast down the dark street that he was at the edge of the spotlight's cone before the next one clicked on. He ran for a quarter of a mile before he realized the Hound was not chasing him. The Hound remained by the cathedral, under a spotlight of its own, separated from Tony by the void between.

"What do you want?" Tony shouted, loud enough for his voice to cross the distance.

Suddenly the Hound was jumping and waving, signaling him back.

And that's when he first heard it. A low rumble. The sound a rubber ball makes rolling down a flight of carpeted stairs. Except it sounded like a thousand rubber balls. A million. Tony looked behind him, into the dark heart of Na'Duli. A spotlight clicked on a half mile away, silhouetting a skyscraper that appeared to be something between an office building and a castle.

"Run!" yelled the Hound.

Tony obeyed. He ran back toward the Hound, who was already jogging back the way it had come.

That awful sound, that sound of some single-minded horde, grew louder and louder until Tony could feel the vibration in his jaws. Something hit his right leg and he almost fell onto the cobblestone street. "Don't stop!" shouted the Hound.

He couldn't flick it off. It was heavy. It clung to his jeans. Still running, he reached down. *His fingers found thick, coarse hair and then something bit into his palm. A bright pain, full of needles. He screamed and stopped and yanked his hand away.*

It was a rat. A fat rat the size of a cat, with blind, milky eyes. It hissed at him and dug its claws into the meat of his calf. Tony screamed again, and then the Hound pulled the monster off. It drop-kicked the rat down rue Nibi, back toward the rapidly approaching spotlights and the noise, toward the stampede.

"Faster!" said the Hound.

Tony followed, past more brownstones and then into a district of tall warehouses. Then he was hit again, this time in the square of his back, and he tumbled to the ground. The creature scampered over his exposed face, sensing where the vital bits were. Before he could grab it, the rat raked a talon up his left cheek and snagged its claws deep into his eyeball. It felt like someone had fired a gun into his brain. It was a pain he'd never experienced before. The pain enveloped him.

Distantly, he was aware of the Hound again. It punted this rat, too. Then the Hound picked Tony up. It draped Tony's body over its wide shoulders and, quite unexpectedly, bounded into the air and onto the fire escape of a warehouse. It flew up the stairs as the rumble of the million rubber balls became a din of claws against brick. He listened to their squeaking as the creatures began to climb after them.

Five stories and they were on the roof. The Hound rolled Tony off its shoulders and onto the white gravel there. He took off one of the belts and wrapped it around Tony's waist.

"What are you doing?"

"I'm saving your life," the Hound said in a way that told Tony it was a little unsure of its own motives. "In a moment you're going to appear in the back room of a bar, near Seattle. You tell the woman there . . . Listen! You tell her, 'Scopes said to get me to a hospital.' You got that? Tell her it's a direct command from Scopes."

"Why?"

"Because," said Scopes. "You're right. Something needs to change. But the people of Mu can't help you. They're the worst sort of humans. They're pragmatists."

The Hound pushed something into Tony's hand. It was hard to concen-

trate, because his head screamed with such agony, but it felt like a belt buckle.

"You go to Mu. Go and see for yourself. When you've had enough of their talk, you can bring me over with this. And then we'll fix it together."

Scopes pushed a button on the belt wrapped around Tony's body, and suddenly Tony was weightless.

"I woke up in the back of a bar in Ariel, Washington," he said. "The woman who ran the place knew the Hounds. Husband was a Collector back in the day. She got me to the hospital. I gave them a fake name. Spent a month recovering. Lived out of a homeless shelter in Seattle until I got my mind right again. Then I made my way to Dutch Harbor, in the Aleutians. Hijacked a crab boat to get me here. This guy named Phil was the boat captain. He stayed here, too, once he saw what it was all about. You'd like him," he said to the Captain. "Grumpy just like you."

"What about the belt buckle?" asked Jack.

"Hmm?"

"The buckle the Hound gave you? What did you do with it?"

"Oh. I dunno. There's a whole cache of those belts in Peshtigo. Nazis left behind all kinds of dangerous shit."

"Okay," said the Captain, "so what the fuck have you been doing for three years?"

"Well, first of all it's been more like five years, not three. That's how much the new forgettings have fucked with the calendar. You know they can reset only so many times until the seasons start to get all out of whack and then they have to leap forward like nine months to make it right again. But what have I been doing? I work. Yada yada yada . . . from each, according to their ability, you know? I talk to people about their problems. Listen to their stories."

Cole was looking at Tony as if he were an alien.

"People here, they've got everything solved. Everything except boredom. The vitamins everyone takes allow them to live for hundreds of years, but, man, they're so afraid of getting hurt outside the city, nobody ever leaves."

"Did you even try to fix anything?" asked Jack.

Tony looked to his old friend. "Fuck you, okay? I tried. I did. But nobody wanted to help. And, you know, why leave? We're safe here, Jack. We can stay right here forever and everything will be okay."

"For you," said the Captain. "But what about the six billion people who don't live on Mu?"

Tony threw up his hands. "What do you want me to say? They're fucked. They're totally fucked. But they brought it on themselves, didn't they?"

The Captain glared at him. "You've been given more chances than you deserve, you little snot. You're indebted. To the world that took care of you after your dad went crazy. To the people who cleaned up your mess after you left. Understand? You pay it back because that's the way it works. Sit back and watch the world go to shit? Nuts!"

"Dad," said Jack, his voice calm, calming. "Easy."

The Captain grunted and walked away.

7   A Native American fellow with a long ponytail arrived later that night in a big school bus filled with fruits and vegetables and dried fish. Jack and Zaharie organized a buffet, and while they served the passengers, Sam slipped away and walked the mile to the beach along the southern shore of Mu. She walked a narrow footpath to the sand, still warm from the sun even though it had set an hour ago. The grains smushed between her toes like moon dust.

She walked a bit, the white lights of Peshtigo a shimmer on the horizon. The Milky Way was a river of stars above the sea. Maybe she shouldn't be exploring this island in the dark, she thought. She didn't really believe Tony's stories about dinosaurs. But still.

A shadow moved beside her feet and she jumped, startled.

"Heya, Sam," said Tony.

He was sitting on the sand, smoking a short pipe. He looked up at her with his good eye and patted the ground beside him. She sat and he offered her the pipe. It was marijuana, or like marijuana in the way a freshly picked berry from the forest is like store-bought fruit. This was uncultivated, wild pot. It smelled of damp earth and time. If history had a smell, thought Sam, it would smell just like this. She held in the smoke and then let it out slowly like he'd showed her to do when they were kids.

"You're an asshole," she said.

"I know."

"No. I mean it. You're an asshole."

"Yes."

"You could have left a note."

"I couldn't tell you where I was going," he said. "Not without putting you in danger. But I left you the insurance money."

"I never got it. I couldn't declare you dead because it was so obvious you'd run away. You had me stealing money from Haven."

"We were only borrowing the money. I meant to pay it back," he said.

"What was it for?"

"I spent what was in our checking on stuff for the trip here. Ion-filtration system for bottled water, night-vision goggles I thought might help me see the island . . . I thought the police would go looking in the lake after a while. I was sure you'd think I'd committed suicide and tell them to send a diver down. I tried to make it look like . . ."

"You really thought putting your watch on my brother's wrist was enough to fool anyone?" she said.

"I thought the lake was too deep for them to bother with the body. I figured they'd send a diver down for my personal effects." He shook his head. "I don't know. It was the best I could do."

The light of the stars was enough for her to see the outline of his body and she watched him lean forward, tilting his head. She drew back.

"No," she said. "Are you crazy?"

"Are you my wife or what? Where are we with that?"

Sam laughed. "I *mourned* you. I got over you years ago." And then she leaned into him, pushed her lips against his, opened his mouth and found his tongue. He tasted like ash from the pipe. Gritty. Warm. His hands found her, drew her closer. He put a hand on the back of her head and held her tight while he kissed her.

She twisted away from his grip and wiped her bottom lip. "I should have been with Jack from the beginning."

Tony scooted closer. "You hated the way Jack always walked on eggshells around you because of what your brother did to you. He didn't want to break you and you hated how careful he was with you."

He leaned in for another kiss, but she caught him, held his face with one hand and looked into his eye. "If you ever try to kiss me again or even look at me like you want to, I will leave and I will take everyone who ever loved you with me."

8   Jack leaned on the bus and picked apart a pomegranate. Hundreds of rinds littered the ground around him. The Chinese had eaten their fill. He looked up at the sound of feet on the macadam. Tony was walking back to the hangar, head down, leaning forward.

"Hey," called Jack.

Tony looked up, then walked over, straightening himself as he came nearer. He stopped when he was still a foot away.

"You want to punch me or something?" Tony asked.

"Come here," said Jack. He reached out and grabbed his shirt and pulled his friend to him. He hugged him tightly. "I'm glad you're alive."

When he let him go, Tony slipped a finger under his eyepatch and wiped away the moisture that had collected there.

"This is yours," Jack said at last. He unclasped the watch and handed it to Tony.

Tony turned it over in his hand, reading the new inscription by the light of the stars.

"Cool," he said. He put it on his left wrist and then looked at Jack a while longer, not saying anything. Jack remembered a time when they were children, a night during the heat wave when they had stayed up until 4:00 a.m. to watch the Perseid meteor shower. He had never felt so close to another human being.

9 In the morning, they awoke to a brilliant sunrise. The sun was a ball of red fire above a sapphire sea. Another bus arrived after breakfast. The driver was a young Cherokee in a black tunic. He spoke to Tony in broken English.

"So, we've got a meeting in the city," Tony said to Jack. "Just, you know, us, everyone from Franklin Mills. They'll bring the others in later today."

"Are we in any danger?" asked Jack.

"No," said Tony. "No way. Trust me."

Cole laughed at him.

"You were always a little snot," he said to the boy, with a smile.

Cole gave him the finger.

After Jack spoke with Zaharie, he and the others boarded the bus and soon they were driving toward the city. Jack looked out at the airfield as they passed by. A hundred boxy robots were making fast work of the crashed jet. Self-directed cranes hauled away sections of the wings. A dozen round drones hovered over the fuselage, using thin lasers to divide the hull into movable pieces. A platoon of cylinder machines was putting the statue back on its pedestal, no worse for wear.

Immediately beyond the airport their group passed through a deserted village. The architecture suggested a German influence. An outpost, Jack realized, from World War II. Just twenty homes along either side of the street. A wide barracks. And, on a hill, a great white mansion.

Twenty minutes later, the bus entered Peshtigo along a street called Chankoowashtay. The road was narrow, made of jointed rock, and the tires hummed pleasantly as they traveled along. To either side, great skyscrapers reached to the blue sky. Each building was exactly the same: twenty stories, glass and steel, angled slightly toward the middle of the city, where the sphere waited, ominously. The geodesic dome was like a second moon and seemed nearly as large, though Jack understood this was only his perspective. It did look like Epcot Center, but ten times bigger, at least. It appeared to be their destination.

"What the hell is that thing?" asked Sam. She was sitting beside Jack and holding his hand tightly.

"It's a library," said Tony. "Biggest library in the world. Every book ever written before the Great Forgetting."

Cole turned to them in his seat. "Why can't they just, you know, digitize everything? They could really save some space."

"They believe humanity will destroy itself," said Tony. "And soon. One last great war. When the A-bombs fall, they'll fry all electronics. All your eBooks will disappear, your Nooks and Kindles will be worthless paperweights."

There were no storefronts, Jack noticed. No Starbucks. No Duane Reade. No Au Bon Pain or Tim Hortons. No advertisements, even. Just a thin sidewalk and few entryways. The buildings were linked together by bridges of glass and he could see people walking through them. On their way to work? Did they clock in somewhere at nine?

"Tony," said Jack. "Where does everyone live?"

"Here," said Tony. "They live here. And work here. Eat, drink, and sleep here. All in the skyscrapers. They're too scared to go outside. Outside is risky. It's pretty rad. Each apartment has these things called memory rooms . . ."

"But what do they do?" Sam interrupted, peering out at a Peshtigan who stood behind a window, watching their bus pass by. It was an old man. Native American. Mohawk, if Jack had to guess.

"Ah, most of them are scribes," said Tony. "They sit at tables all day and rewrite the old books, the ones that are disintegrating. Some others are binders. They bind the books. They don't believe in copiers. It's a sort of religious deal for them. Self-flagellation, kind of. There are maybe a hundred thousand of them and they work seven days a week. Barely keep up."

"Sisyphus," whispered Nils, clearing his throat.

"What's that?" said Sam.

"An old story," said Jack, patting Nils on the shoulder. The Viking smiled back at him. "A long time ago, a certain king thought he was more clever than anyone else. He was punished by the gods for his hubris. They made him push a boulder to the very top of a hill to gain his freedom. Only, it would always roll back down before he reached the summit. So he kept rolling that boulder up the mountain. Forever and ever."

10 At the point where the great sphere touched the ground, at the intersection of the twelve roads that sliced through Peshtigo, there was a single door. It was a plain door of ash with a gold knocker in the shape of an aspen leaf. Inscribed upon the door was a saying, which, Tony explained, was Navajo. *Hozo-go nay-yeltay to, A-na-oh bi-keh de-dlihn:* May we live in peace hereafter, we have conquered all our foes. As they approached, the door opened.

Tony, at the head of the group, was the first to step inside. The others followed. A thin staircase wound upward, lit by thin fibers in all the colors of the rainbow. One by one they ascended.

The staircase ended several floors above, at a granite hall lined by statues. At the end of the hall was another door.

"There's going to be a giant floating head behind that one," said Cole, finding Sam's hand and holding it without really being aware he was doing so. "And a little man behind a panel of wheels and buttons."

"Shh," she said, though she didn't know why. Surely they were expected.

As they continued down the hallway, she glanced sideways at the statues. Some were strangely familiar, as if they were renditions of people she once knew. One looked kind of like her foster father Stan Polk.

"Did you see that?" whispered Cole. "I think that statue was Mrs. Rice, from Laurel Hill."

"Was she famous?"

"She was the librarian."

It was Jack who opened the door. He hesitated just a moment. Then he pushed it open and walked inside.

Someone was waiting for them. But it wasn't a crazed wizard behind a console operating a holographic head. It was a woman in a long lavender gown. She stood behind a wide desk, her hands spread out on its surface like she was navigating some map.

The room. He knew this room.

"Uh . . . ," said Nils.

"It's the goddamn Oval Office," the Captain said.

11 "Everything you've ever seen, everything you've ever been told, is only the echo of an older story," the woman began. Her voice was like a hug, like an Amish quilt on a cold day. She was beautiful, sure. But more than this, she was strong. She was not Native American. Or not entirely. She was a mix of their best features, awash with the hints of many other cultures. The high cheekbones of the Cree. The close-set eyes of the Nordics. Her ears, elf-like, could only be Irish. Eyes that called to the clear dark skies of the Serengeti. She motioned to the couches situated in front of her desk. "Sit."

They sat in the two couches at the center of the oval room, and then she came around the desk and took a chair between them.

Cole felt overcome. This woman was too much to draw in, to look at, to listen to. He felt his heart would burst if she said anything else. She reminded him so much of his mother. Perhaps it was the gentle poise. Grace. But no. More than that. This woman radiated love. Unconditional love. He felt his face flush, undeserving. His eyes watered, but he held back the tears. He looked at Jack. And Nils. And Sam. It was the same for them.

"Are you their queen?" the Captain asked, finally.

She smiled. "No," she said. "We have no queens or kings. No bosses, no laborers. I'm their voice. For now. Just a voice. My mother and father called me Constance. You can, too, if you'd like."

"What . . . ," stammered Jack. "Well, I mean . . . what do we . . ."

"There's the issue of what to do with the two hundred people you brought to this island," she said. "And then what to do with you six."

"Yes," said Jack.

"The doctor here," she said, nodding at Tony, "can see to sheltering these people. There's plenty of room in section three. Room to grow. We'll find them work. But they can never leave. I'm sure you knew that."

Jack swallowed.

"What about us?" asked Sam.

"What about you?" the woman said. "What would you like to do, Sam Brooks?"

"I don't . . . I guess I don't know," she said. "It was all about getting here."

"We need to go back," said Jack. "End the new forgettings. Tell everyone what's going on. Wake them up. Isn't that it? Isn't that what we came here to do?"

"We came here to find Tony," said Sam.

"And there he is," said Jack. "And everyone back home has forgotten we ever existed. Right? Or hasn't that happened yet? Do we have another day or two? Does my sister still remember us?"

"We're going back," the Captain said. "We're going to tell people what's going on. We'll take down a few of the relays, wake up the world."

The smile on Constance's face faltered and she looked grimly at Tony. Cole was suddenly afraid.

"I've been the voice of the people of Mu for twenty years," she said. "I've sat here, in this room, and had a variation of this conversation a dozen times. I let each of them return to the world. And until now, none of them have made it back. Zaharie was the first. And even he failed to do what you propose. It won't work. It will only jeopardize what we've protected here."

"Let's just wait it out," said Tony. "I really think it's close."

"What's close?" asked Nils, curious.

"The end of the world," said Tony. "The day they finally drop the bombs. We can wait another year or two and then go back. Rebuild. Make something better."

"You're talking about sitting back and watching three billion people die!" Jack shouted. "When we have the chance to save them all?"

"What makes your group any different from the last twelve?" asked Constance.

Jack didn't have to think long. He pointed at his own head. "Our memories," he said. "Everything we've been through. To get here. We fought for it. And not just the journey here. Our lives. We fought all our lives for this moment, even if we didn't know it. Tell me that doesn't count for something."

"It does," said Constance. "Of course it does."

She stood then and went to the window. From here, Cole could see the Lonely Mountain and the little German village by the runway. Finally, she turned to Tony.

"Is this what you want?" she asked him.

Tony gritted his teeth. He looked at Jack. And then back at Constance. "Yep," he said. "I guess that's about the sum of it. Damn it all."

"You'll need three more, I think," she said, which was odd, Cole thought, because none of them knew yet exactly what it was that they were meant to do. Or how they might find their way off the island again. "Nine. You can take nine. No more."

"Thank you," said Jack.

It was clear that it was time to leave now, and the others were beginning to stand. But Cole had thought of something. A question. And probably only this woman would know the answer. Except he was so afraid of her—of her beauty and strength—that he could barely make a sound.

"Be safe," said Constance, as a farewell.

And now everyone was standing and Jack was moving toward the door.

"Wait!" Cole said, and he was so surprised by his presumption that for a moment his mind went blank and he forgot what it was he had to say.

Constance smiled at him, a warm, open smile that showed her teeth, the front two larger than the others and not quite straight. It made her look human for the first time. Less like a character from some fairy tale.

"I have a question," he said.

"Yes, Cole Monroe?"

"The moon," he said. "My dad never found out how it worked. With all the forgettings and all, the moon changes, too. It can't possibly reset with the calendar and somehow it does. I was wondering . . . how does the moon work?"

"A good question. A very good question. But I'm afraid you won't like the answer."

"I would like to know," he said.

"The moon," she said, "is only a story."

"I don't understand."

"Stories are magic, Cole. More than you know. Words have the ability to shape reality. History is just another story, and look how it's shaped our world. Look how the wrong history has altered your own. Stories are magic, and that is why the first thing any dictator does is to ban the stories that do not agree with him. It's always only ever been stories that really change anything. The stories we told each other across the campfires when we were still learning to walk upright, those stories have stayed with us ever since, in our hearts. Do you know what the Christians call their God? They call him the Word. The moon is a story, Cole. As are you. And me. And everything that is the Great Forgetting. We're nothing but stories, all of us. Characters in a twice-told tale. And also storytellers ourselves. It's an endless spiral. Around and around and around we go. Have a little hope that, over time, we might tell better stories."

—————

FIVE CHARACTERS
IN SEARCH OF AN EXIT

1   The bus was gone when they stepped outside the geodesic dome, and in its place was something that looked like a long golf cart with no wheels. It hovered silently two inches above the ground. Tony climbed in the front and waved the others over. "It's safe," he said. "Don't ask me how it works. It's sciency. Like all their stuff. But it looks like magic, right?"

"I dunno," said Nils, considering his gut.

"You're fine," said Tony. "This thing can carry a ton."

Jack sat up front, too, with Sam in the middle. When they were all in, Tony waved his palm over the dash and the vehicle turned smoothly and then accelerated toward the nearest building, one of a hundred identical skyscrapers. They were heading directly toward a wall.

"Don't worry," said Tony.

Just as it seemed like they were about to crash, a door slid open and they were suddenly inside, moving along a marble hall that wound slowly upward around the perimeter of the tower.

"Can you slow it down, please?" said Sam.

Tony waved his hand again and the tram slagged a bit. Halfway up, it turned right, into a glass tunnel that connected to another building. In the next skyscraper, they passed through a wide, brightly lit expanse full of long desks behind which sat hundreds of Native Americans leaning over tall books. Jack saw that they were copying pages by hand. Nobody looked up to see them pass by.

"Busy, busy, busy," said Tony. "Sad little busy bees."

The next skyscraper was a giant indoor park. Oaks trees towered over them, fed by sunlight radiating through a ceiling of glass. A dozen Choctaw jogged along the edge of a lake. A family of Abenaki walked briskly toward the nearest exit. It was beautiful, but Jack noticed that no one was looking up at the trees or tossing rocks into the lake.

In the next skyscraper, a room full of Onondaga worked an assembly line that spit out bound novels. After this, there was another writing lab, another park, and another bindery.

"The whole city is basically a fractal," explained Tony. "It's all the same, really. Just more compressed the closer you get to the sphere. Nobody has more than anyone else. But what we have is a lot. We're almost home."

The tram turned down one last tunnel and then slowed to a stop at a T-juncture lined with tall doors made to look like the entrances of Manhattan brownstones. A young white-skinned girl in overalls waited for them on the stoop of number 42. Her eyes grew wide when she saw Sam and her face broke into an unabashed smile. She made a sound like a mouse.

"Sam," said Tony, motioning to the girl, "this is Becky Cooper. She helps in my office. Brings me coffee, organizes my schedule. Smart cookie."

Becky leaped from the stairs and hugged Sam tight.

"He talks about you, like, all the time," Becky said.

Jack put an arm around Sam.

"I'm Jack," he said. "Good to meet you, Becky."

"Well, this is awkward, right?" the girl announced, swaying on her feet. "Your husband disappears for five years and you fall in love with your high school crush again. That's some Danielle Steel stuff, huh?"

"Come on inside, guys," said Tony, opening the door to his apartment. "Lots to talk about."

2 Becky's story came first. While she boiled coffee on the electric stove in the kitchen, she spoke in a frenzy of words with barely any punctuation. Tony listened with a kind of older-brother pride.

Becky's mother was a scientist, she told them, a professor of anthropology at Miskatonic University in Massachusetts. She was published. Wrote long papers identifying subconscious Jungian archetypes hidden within pop culture. She became convinced that Led Zeppelin's fourth album contained allusions to the mythical lost continent of Mu. That was the album with the strange symbols that supposedly represented the members of the band. The symbol Robert Plant picked, the circle with the aspen leaf in the center, was actually the ancient Mayan pictograph for Mu.

"And she was right!" said Becky, filtering the coffee grounds through a sheer cloth. "She found it. Of course her helicopter crashed when the compass got all wonky near the island, killing the poor pilot, so she couldn't ever go back. Not that she wanted to. She fell in love with my dad in Peshtigo. He's just next door. You'll meet him later, I'm sure."

"And your mother, too?" asked Sam.

Becky kept her eyes down while she poured the coffee into ceramic mugs. "She died. Lung cancer. They have, what do you call it—chemo? They have chemo here, but it didn't help. Not even their robots could make her better again. If she'd grown up on the vitamins here, maybe."

When Becky handed her a cup, Sam reached out and touched the side of her face, comfortingly. The girl smiled and, blinking, continued around the room.

"I'm an apprentice shrink," she said. "It's pretty much the only thing they don't have here. So Dr. Sanders is teaching me. I'm pretty much always at his office."

Tony led everyone to a sitting room with egalitarian furniture: a rocking chair, a cherry bench covered with a thick horsehair blanket. The walls were liquid-crystal screens that currently broadcast high-res video of the long plateau outside Peshtigo. It was as if they were having coffee outside, surrounded by nature. Tony went to a device on the wall, brushed his hand over it, and then the scene dissolved into wallpapering, the kind with those dark damask patterns.

They all looked at him, waiting.

"So," said Tony finally. "Anybody have an idea about how we're supposed to save the world?"

Cole sat on the stoop outside the fake brownstone and watched people come home from work. If he tried hard enough he could make himself believe that he was in Manhattan again. Gramercy Park.

"It's weird, isn't it?" It was Becky. She sat on the step beside him and looked out at the people walking along the tunnels.

"What's weird?"

"The truth. When you finally hear it, it's never quite what you expect. It's always a little worse and little better than you could have imagined."

He turned and looked through a narrow window at his friends inside. They were in the sitting room, arguing about what to do next. Jack was pacing, waving his hands excitedly.

"We're in what's known as 'section three,'" said Becky. "It's where they put all the castaways, people who got lost on the sea and wound up on Mu. Or crashed here, like my mother. It's not like they look down on us or anything. We just kind of like to stick together."

A brawny man was walking toward them. He had a thick gray cap of hair and looked to be about seventy, but he was still toned like a dockworker.

"That's my dad," said Becky.

They stood as he came near. He regarded Cole with a suspicious smile. "Who's this?"

"New people. From Dr. Sanders's hometown."

"Cole Monroe," Cole said. He held out his hand and the big guy took it, shaking it firmly.

"Dan Cooper," he said. "But all my friends call me D.B."

3 "Even if we managed to take down one relay," said Tony, "nothing would change. The system is built with redundancy in case a relay is lost during a natural disaster. The relays crisscross the entire planet. There's too many."

"So we take out a couple at the same time," said Jack.

"You'd need more than a couple."

"Why are you being so obtuse?" said Jack. "I thought you wanted to stop this."

"I do," said Tony. "But we need time to come up with a better plan."

"You had three years," the Captain said. "Wait. Five, right?"

"How many times do I have to say I'm sorry?"

"I don't know," the Captain said, his cheeks red. "A couple hundred more times seems like a good start."

Sam sat up. She had a mischievous look about her. A hunger. "Tell us more about the relays, Tony," she said. "Where are they?"

"All over the place. They're hidden in plain sight, disguised inside landmarks and buildings. The Sears Tower, the Washington Monument. You'll have to bring down the entire goddamn building to kill the relay, and how are you going to do that? You got a dozen sticks of dynamite somewhere?"

Sam laughed wryly and sat back. "What's it matter?" she said. "We can't get off this island anyway, right?"

Tony cleared his throat. "Actually, that's not entirely true."

4   On the floor below Tony's apartment was a museum. Before
she died, Becky's mother had volunteered as a curator there. It was a
retrospective history of the island from before the Great Forgetting.
Becky and her father led the group through silent wings full of Mayan
tablets and Egyptian sarcophagi toward the more modern section in
the back. There, tucked into a corner like a sleeping bird, was a
1936 Lockheed Electra.

"This was my wife's favorite piece," said D.B.

"Ho-lee shit," the Captain whispered.

"Amelia Earhart," said Becky. "She crashed on the beach in 1937.
She and that man Noonan. They never left. She defended the island
at the Battle of Mu when the Germans invaded in '45. Single-
handedly killed twenty SS officers before they got her. That's why
they put her statue out at the airfield. My mom's idea."

Jack looked at his father. "Could it work?"

"If the Germans kept petrol at the airfield, it'd be close enough
to avgas to at least get to the mainland," the Captain said. "If the
Wasp engine is sound and can mix oxygen, still . . . Yes. Yes, this
could work."

5   Sam awoke to the sound of her own voice and for a moment
thought she was still dreaming. She lay beside Jack in one of Tony's
spare bedrooms, on an expansive mattress with silken sheets. The
air was cool but the blankets were heavy and it had been the best
sleep she'd had since Franklin Mills and all she wanted to do was sleep
some more, but that voice filtering down the hall, just above per-
ceptible levels . . . It sounded like her own.

Quietly, she slipped out of bed and walked barefoot to the door.
She opened it gently. Now that voice was louder and she could make
out some of what was being said.

You are beautiful, you know that? You make me happy.

Sam brought a hand to her mouth. That voice coming from the
front room was definitely her own. She was positive now, because

she remembered saying those very words once. Was she dreaming? She must still be dreaming.

Slowly, she walked toward the voice.

Do I make you as happy as you make me?

Yes. This voice was a man's voice. Tony's voice.

She came around the corner and peered into the living room. Tony was asleep on the sofa. The walls around him played out a scene from their honeymoon. It was the hotel in Boston, by the aquarium. Sam saw herself, naked, lying across Tony's chest, smiling down into his blue eyes.

Tony shifted on the sofa, mumbled something, and the walls flickered a bit and then reset.

You are beautiful, you know that? Sam on-screen said. "You make me happy."

It was a memory. The walls were replaying the memory Tony had fallen asleep to.

After a minute, Sam put a blanket over Tony and returned to bed.

6   Someone was shaking him awake. Jack opened his eyes. His father's face was so close that he could smell the Scotch his old man had found in one of Tony's cupboards. For a terrible moment, he flashed back to the house on SR 14 and believed his father was about to strangle him to death once and for all.

"Johnny!" he said in a loud whisper.

"What? What's going on?"

"I figured it out," he said. "We can do it all. We can save our-selves. And we can save the whole motherfuckin' *world*."

PART FIVE

NIGHTMARE AT 20,000 FEET

The worst aspect of our time is prejudice. In almost everything I've written, there is a thread of this—man's seemingly palpable need to dislike someone other than himself.

—ROD SERLING

ONE

ON THURSDAY, WE LEAVE FOR HOME

1 There was blood on his hands, and for a moment Scopes couldn't remember how it got there. He stumbled on his feet and then kneeled down and wiped the blood on the grass. He looked back over the Grimpen Mire. He thought maybe he wouldn't come back this way again. He didn't like it here.

The Hound walked past the abandoned truck Nils had left behind and climbed into his Chrysler Turbine. When he turned the key, WKNY from Poughkeepsie was just finishing a test of the Emergency Alert System. Leaning out the window, he drove in reverse until he found the main road leading down Big Indian Mountain.

He could hear his heart beating a rhythm of murder in his ears. *What did I do? What did I do?*

"You helped them!" Scopes shouted at the Maestro. He sat at the kitchen table, eating the man's cold lasagna—which was, he had to admit, the best fucking lasagna he'd ever had. "Why are you helping them?"

"I'm only giving them a choice."

Scopes swallowed another forkful. "Talking to you is impossible. It's like a goddamn riddle talking to you."

"Riddles are the best kind of stories."

"I don't understand your obsession with children's stories and riddles and fairy tales. Josef never did, either."

"There is great truth in fairy tales," the Maestro explained. "'Hansel and Gretel,' 'The Three Little Pigs,' 'Goldilocks.' They are stories we never forget. We feel them, the lessons beneath them. They are reminders to us about how to live. Don't get lost in the woods. Don't trespass. Treat other people the way you want to be treated."

Scopes grunted, looked at the new painting on the wall, the one that hadn't been here the last time he'd bothered to visit. "What's that?"

"Do you like it? We painted it ourselves."

Scopes shrugged. "What is it?"

"It's an aspen leaf."

"So?"

"You ever notice the little marks the humans put on their things? The little c in a circle on books and things?"

"Yes."

"It means 'copyright.' It's a reminder to them that the thing is their creation. That's what the aspen leaf is. Whenever I rewrite a memory, I insert the aspen leaf into it so that I'll know it's a story I created. There are no real aspen trees. We invented them. If someone remembers seeing an aspen leaf, it means I've edited that memory for one reason or another."

"'Pride goes before destruction, and a haughty spirit before a fall,'" said Scopes.

"Maybe."

"What are you doing with Jack?"

"I'm just giving him a chance."

"We want the same thing. Don't you know that we're on the same damn team?"

"No, we're not," said the Maestro. "You want to bring about the end. Help it along. Well, we think there's another way."

There will be no freedom for you in their world, his mother, Ambala, had told him.

"And if the world does remember everything?" said Scopes. "What will happen to us then? You and me? Have you thought of that?"

The Maestro laughed.

"What the fuck's so funny?"

"This is not our world, Scopes. It's theirs."

"Goddamn it," he said, standing up. "There should have been a place for us. The tribes got Mu. Why isn't there a place for us?"

"They forgot to give us one," said the Maestro. "Like you, they were too busy thinking of themselves."

"Well, it's not fucking fair."

"The world is not fair, Scopes. It's indifferent."

"Stop calling me that. I hate that name! I hate it! It's a joke. Don't you think I know that?"

"But we forgot your real name."

The Hound grabbed the knife from its place above the sink and sank it deep into the Maestro's chest. The blade pierced the heart cleanly. "My name is Yohance!" he shouted.

The Maestro collapsed to the floor.

"You stupid monkey," said the Maestro. "Who will update the algorithm now?"

Scopes let the knife drop to the floor, his rage dissolving into shock. "You think we can't learn?" he said. "I learned. I had forty years to learn. I know how the code works. I can reset the algorithm. I don't need you. You're nothing special."

There would be a place for the Hounds after the world burned, Scopes assured himself, shaking off the memory of the Maestro's murder. He was nearly to Oneonta. He could see the lights in the distance.

This was the only way to make the world a better place: let their greed destroy them and then start fresh. And that new world would need a strong leader.

An emergency news report cut through the jazz playing on the radio. Scopes's hair bristled. It was another school shooting. This time in Newtown, in an elementary school called Sandy Hook. Sce.

They couldn't wait to kill themselves. Why not help them along a little?

2   On their sixth day on Mu, while they ate lunch—fresh tomatoes and greens—around a table situated on the tarmac of the Nazi airport, Jack noticed something about Sam. She had changed, a deep, elemental shift. She was radiant. She was a presence, persisting everywhere. She filled up the empty spaces with her voice and her laughter. It took Jack some time, but eventually he sussed it out. Sam was no longer afraid. He'd never known her to not be afraid of something. Kids at school. Her brother. Police. Human-ape hybrids. You know. Always something. But now. Now Sam held her own. And to say she was merely confident would be missing the point. It was more than that. There was grace in her being that belied the anger boiling deep down, and there was great beauty in that.

He stood and offered his hand. "Come with me," he said. "There's something I want to show you."

"Is it about what Walter's building in the hangar?"

"Yes."

"He said we should meet him there after lunch," said Sam.

"We'll only be a few minutes late. He can start without us."

Tony was waiting for them on a hover cart at the end of the runway. They climbed in behind him. Tony waved a hand over the dash and they were off. They shot past a row of German bunkers and into that old village they had spotted on the way to Peshtigo. Around a Tudor, half demolished by a fallen tree, the tram veered down an alley. The alley became a dirt road that led up a steep hill. Atop the hill sat a gigantic Colonial mansion in disrepair. The side that faced north was scraped free of paint. It was the color of storm clouds. Part of the roof had collapsed, leaving a gaping hole the size of a compact car.

"Looks like that famous house," she said. "The one where Gatsby lived."

"It was Hitler's retreat," said Tony. "He vacationed here in the summers for a couple years."

Sam shuddered against Jack as the tram slowed to a stop outside the front doors. They stepped into knee-high crabgrass and ascended the stairs. Tony opened the great oak doors.

It was dark inside and Jack could feel the emptiness of the wide corridors along the front. In the low light from the open door, Tony found an ugly red-and-black bit of machinery that sat in the foyer collecting dust. It had a metal wheel with a knob, which Tony grabbed and cranked furiously. The machine coughed twice and then began to hum. Most generators Jack had seen had belts that grated loudly when activated, but this one just hummed like a nest of honeybees. The fixtures above, the ones that remained, came on slowly and cast a dim amber light.

A wide staircase wound round the foyer to the third floor. Thick cobwebs draped from the crystal chandelier like Spanish moss. To either side, a wide hall extended to the ends of the house. There was a crumbling plaster smell and the ghost of something else. Tobacco, maybe. Of a subgenus that didn't exist anymore.

"This way," said Tony, stepping over a pile of rodent scat and walking down the hall to the right. He passed several doors and then opened the one at the end and motioned for Sam to come inside.

This room had weathered the span of time. It was a high-ceilinged office, a long room stretching to the back bank of windows that looked out to the mountain. The walls of the room were tall cherry bookcases stuffed with bound tomes, unreadable to Sam because they were in German. Tony pointed at the wall behind them, through which they had passed. It was plaster, and upon it had been rendered a floor-to-ceiling mural. It showed a row of German robots, like the one that had greeted them at the hangar, advancing over a hill, the Golden Gate Bridge behind them. A blond soldier in the foreground *sieg-heil*ed to someone beyond the borders of the painting.

Tony picked up a long metal rod that ended in a hook and used it to pull down a rolled map. It revealed Germany's empire in sunset red. Vermilion ink covered all of Europe and the Middle East and stretched across Russia, northern China, and over the Pacific to a continent that could only be Mu, before continuing into America, all the way to the Mississippi. The map was dated 1960.

"What am I looking at?" asked Sam.

"History," said Jack. "Real history."

They showed her pictures from the drawers of Hitler's desk, photographs of gas chambers in the Nevada desert. They showed her slides of Nazi soldiers posing with American prisoners of war—in one, an SS officer tortured a man who stood on a cardboard box, arms raised, wires attached to his fingertips, his head masked in a cone of black fabric.

Using a long pointer, Jack tapped the map at a dark circle in the center of Alaska. "This is HAARP. The forgetting signal originates here. It gets picked up and rebroadcast by hundreds of relay stations around the globe, most disguised inside the architecture of skyscrapers. We can't attack HAARP directly. It's fortified. Too secure for a nine-person team. As you know, we have to go for the relays."

He hesitated a moment, looking at Tony. It was a crazy plan. A terribly tricky plan. "Like Tony said, you can't take out just one relay," said Jack. "There's a redundancy built in so that if one fails, or even two, other relays are close enough to blanket that area with a weakened signal. We need to create a safe zone, a region completely outside the signal's range."

"But how?" asked Sam, looking at the map.

Jack circled an area on the eastern seaboard. New York to D.C. "We can make this entire zone safe from the signal if we take out these four relay stations. Two at the World Trade Center. And two in D.C., at the Pentagon and the Washington Monument."

Sam shook her head. "We're going to march down Seventh Avenue and blow up two of the world's largest skyscrapers?"

"No," said Tony. "We're going to crash planes into them."

Sam searched Tony's eyes to see if he was joking. "You're talking about murdering thousands of innocent Americans."

"No, we're not," said Jack. "Tony got more of those belts the Hounds use. The Germans left them behind."

"We get to the mainland," said Tony. "To Boston. We hijack four flights. Release the passengers. Force the pilots to take off, just like Cooper did back in '71. We send the pilots back on the belts. Then, right before impact, we use belts to come back ourselves."

"So you can all fly jumbo jets now?"

Jack nodded. "The Captain can teach us how. Not well enough to land or take off, but enough to steer. That's what's happening in the hangar today."

"And what about the people in the Twin Towers?" asked Sam. "Just collateral damage?"

"When we get back to the mainland, I'll talk to Jean. She can call in the threat when we're on our way. They'll evacuate the buildings before we crash the planes. No one has to die. We're just after the relays."

Sam scratched her chin distractedly. "When?"

"September eleventh," said Jack. "Early morning. We've got about a month to train."

"Do we have enough volunteers? Did you find nine?"

Jack nodded. "Two pilots for each plane: me and you, Nils and Tony, the Captain and Cole, and then Zaharie and D.B. They both stepped up."

"And the ninth?"

"Becky," said Tony, his voice gruff, assured.

"Becky?" said Sam. "She's *thirteen*."

"She doesn't have to do much," Jack said. "Her part's easy."

3   Inside the German hangar, Amelia Earhart's Lockheed Electra sat like the main attraction of the Smithsonian, reflecting the rays of sunshine slanting through the high windows. The volunteers had all gathered below it, behind makeshift consoles constructed from pieces of what was left of Malaysian Airlines Flight 370. The Captain leaned over Cole, who sat at a row of toggles and switches.

Cole put a hand on a lever and pushed forward.

"No!" shouted the Captain. "You need to pull the yoke above the horizon before you open the throttle. And you forgot about the transponder again."

Sam leaned against the wall behind Cole, watching Jack and Tony dick around with those things the Hounds called boomerang belts. Jack removed the buckle from his belt, turned it around in his hands, and pushed the red button on the back. Then he placed it in the air and walked away. The detached buckle hovered, defying gravity, three feet off the ground, spinning ever so slowly. A light pulsed inside it, radiating along its edge. As Jack walked away, that pulse flickered faster. And faster. Jack stopped halfway across the hangar, turned, and waited. He cringed, half shut his eyes.

"Ahhhhhh," he said. "I don't like this!"

And then suddenly he was on the other side of the room and the buckle clicked audibly into his belt again. Jack collapsed to his knees. "I'm okay!" he shouted. Then he puked.

It wasn't teleportation. Not really. It was all about perception, Tony had explained. The belt and buckle were always connected. By pushing the button, you only resolved the distance. Whatever. It looked like teleportation to Sam.

Tony pushed the button on the back of another buckle and then tossed it in the air over a thick mat. Sam watched him evaporate and then appear midair and bellyflop onto the mat.

"Woo-hoo!" he shouted.

"Show-off," the Captain mumbled beside her.

Sam smiled. Then she tilted her head toward Earhart's plane, where Zaharie was hammering at a patch of aluminum. "We're really leaving in that?" she asked.

"She only has to get us to Sea-Tac," the Captain said.

Through the open hangar doors, Sam could see an army of disposal bots clearing a new path through the park. The statue had been temporarily relocated to the city. The bots were repairing the runway, getting ready for the big day.

Sam sighed. "We're all going to die," she said. "You know that, right? That's probably how this ends."

T W O

IT'S A GOOD LIFE

The last night on Mu, they gathered in the indoor park of section three. All the castaways who lived near Tony were there, even some of the new Chinese who had begun to acclimate to life in Peshtigo in the seven weeks since the crash. Nine of them, engineers from a Beijing tech firm, were designing a more efficient bookbinding machine for section eleven. Great canvas tents were set up by the pond, their sides rolled and tied so that the artificial breeze of the hidden AC units could find its way through. They hung electric lanterns on poles. From a distance, it looked like a grand wedding.

It was actually a feast in honor of Jack and his crew. Pigs from the jungle and dodoes from the beach were roasted on spits over electric grills. Corn and squash and a vegetable called rune, a root that resembled a purple carrot, were brought out on platters. Young girls danced for the assembled crowd on a stage by the tunnels leading to the dome. Two men played a happy song on a washboard and a jug.

At eventide, two women in white gowns escorted the group to the head table: Jack, Sam, Tony, Cole, the Captain, Nils, Zaharie,

Becky, and her father, D. B. Cooper. A man named Frank Morris, an ex-con who'd escaped from one island prison only to find himself on this one, stepped forward to address the crowd. He was a solemn man with a weathered face and a fine thatch of yellow hair above his ears.

"There's a saying on Mu," he said, loud enough so that the children in the back could hear. "'You don't find Mu. Mu finds you.' If that's true, I'm sure as hell glad Mu found the men and women of Malaysian Airlines Flight 370." A round of applause interrupted his speech and he nodded until they quieted. "This city is a haven. The last truly free place on Earth. These people have pledged to preserve it and to restore the true history of our world before it is completely forgotten. What we have here, I believe, can still be taught to those we left behind. Imagine if the entire world could be as peaceful as Mu."

"Hear, hear!" a man called out.

"We send with them one of our most legendary citizens, Dan Cooper, who, I believe, returns at great peril, as there remain several outstanding warrants for his arrest."

The crowd laughed. D.B. lifted his hand in mock salute, smiling, gray himself now, far from the arrogant confidence man who'd pulled off one of history's most brazen heists.

Morris lifted his glass and the crowd did likewise, lifting arms to the skylights, one by one. "To Jack and his crew," he said. "Godspeed and good luck!"

"Here, here!" they shouted. "To Jack!" they shouted. "To Dr. Sanders! To Cooper!"

And finally they were fed. Ceramic dishes filled with meat and potatoes and veggies were passed around. When the platters were emptied, they were promptly filled again by a staff of eager young men in dark tunics. They drank from never-ending mugs of wine and beer.

"Dude, check it," said Nils, leaning his seat back to talk to Jack. He was holding a leg of roasted fowl. "Fuckin' dodo, man!" He bit into it and talked with a full mouth. "Tastes like chicken."

Sam squeezed Jack's hand under the table. Tomorrow they would fly home. And the morning after that, they would separate into pairs for the coordinated attack.

"I can't pilot with you," she said.

"What do you mean?"

"I mean you gotta pair with someone else."

"What are you talking about? Of course you're going with me."

"No, Jack," she said, and her tone caused him to set down his drink and look at her. "If something happens to you, I wouldn't be any use to anybody."

"Nothing's gonna go wrong."

"You can't say that. Don't promise me that."

"Well, what if something does?" said Jack. "I'd want to be with you."

"You mean if I died?" said Sam. "You'd want to die with me?"

"I'm not saying die. Nobody's saying that. If you got hurt or something. I'd want to be there."

"I'm talking about dying. It's a real possibility."

"Jesus, Sam . . ."

"Did none of you think about this?" And right away she knew they hadn't. Not one of them. "Jesus. Why can't you think ahead? Why can't you imagine repercussions?"

"Shh."

"I can't be with you that day," she said. "You have to switch with someone."

"Okay," he said. Though there was a very real part of him, instinctual, that desperately wanted to command her to obey him, that wanted to tell her to just shut the hell up and do what he said. Everything could be so smooth, so simple. There was such a thing as thinking too much. Sometimes you just had to take action even if you couldn't foresee the outcome, if only to make something happen.

"Okay?"

"I said okay," said Jack, a little too harshly. "I'll fly with Tony. You can copilot on Nils's flight. Now would you just shut up and

kiss me?" He pulled her to him and she smiled as she closed her eyes
and parted her lips.

Pushing away from his empty plate, D.B. pulled a pipe from the
inside pocket of his coat and packed it with dried green leaves he
kept in a pouch tied to a loop in his jeans.

"What's that? Mu tobacco?" asked Nils, dislodging a bit of dodo
gristle from his front teeth with a thumbnail.

"Nah, brother," said D.B. "It's Peshtigo *gungi*." He struck a match,
brought it to the green, and inhaled deeply. He held it like a champ
and exhaled a cloud of brown. Then he passed it to the Viking.

Nils took the pipe and inhaled. His body immediately warmed,
a welcome rush of fire throughout his chest. It tasted like the earth
after an August rain. In the dimness around him, the edges slaked
off the world, rounding away every sharp corner there ever was. It
was a world waiting to be touched.

"Good shit," he said, passing it back.

"Before Mu was given to the Seven Tribes, it was occupied by
the Nazis," said D.B. "And before the Nazis, Mu belonged to the
Mayans. I knew the Voice, Constance, when she was young and she
told me some of their stories. She said there were people here even
before the Mayans. A race of people called the Mestie-Belles."

Cole leaned toward them, listening intently. Under the table,
Becky held his hand. He let her.

"During the time of the Mestie-Belles," D.B. continued, "Mu
was invaded by a fierce warrior-king from a faraway land who came
to the island on a great wooden ship, a square of lumber fifty miles
wide. He brought a whole city with him. They called this warrior-
king Tsar Niev. He challenged the Mesties and won control of Mu.
But even ruling an entire continent did not make Niev content. He
was jealous of the powers the Mesties possessed. He wanted to see
sound like they could, to taste color, to hear the music of the sunset.
So Niev commanded the Mesties to teach him their tricks. But they
could no more teach him what the color blue feels like than a bird
could have taught him how to fly. Niev became furious. If he could
not possess this knowledge, then no one could. And so he forbade

the Mesties to speak of these powers. And he burned the great library at the center of Peshtigo, where the stories of the Mesties' culture were stored. In less than a century, the Mestie-Belles forgot themselves, what they were. And soon they died out altogether and their magic abandoned this world." D.B. looked at them, one by one, in turn. "We have one last chance to keep that from happening again."

Nils sighed. "I'd like another hit now," he said. "If you don't mind."

Dessert was served—fruit from the jungles in heavy cream. Everyone ate their fill and more. When they finished, a rotund man with a gray pompadour and thick white sideburns took a seat in front of the great table and strummed old tunes on a battered guitar. His voice was low and full of bass, a black man's voice in a white man's body. His hips jiggled atop his perch and he remembered how he used to dance.

And there was dancing. Jack and Sam. Cole and Becky. The Captain, too. It was a fine send-off.

_____

THREE

THE CHANGING OF THE GUARD

1 By the time the nine of them squeezed into the back of Earhart's Electra, the morning sun had risen from the sea. The cabin was cramped and had no seats, stuffy and hot like breath inside. From where he sat, Jack watched the Captain climb down into the pilot's seat from the hinged door in the cockpit ceiling.

The Captain checked the various gauges all around him. He looked out the window at both wings, then began to fiddle with the dial that regulated the engine's mix of oxygen and fuel. They'd found a bladder of gasoline in the ground just west of the runway and siphoned enough to fill the tanks.

"If you're the praying type . . . ," he began. But he didn't finish. He pushed a white button and the propellers began to twist. At first there was a grating sound, like the scraping of a muffler against an undercarriage, and then whatever was sticking gave out and the aircraft hummed loudly around them, shifting back and forth, a racehorse behind the gate.

The Captain found a pair of aviator glasses tucked into a binder resting on the jump seat and slipped them on. He peered out the windshield. The robots had finished their job and the runway continued through the park now. That section wasn't paved, but the gravel was tightly packed.

The Captain opened the throttle and the aircraft lunged forward, picking up speed. Through the porthole, Jack looked out at the city of Peshtigo three miles to the west. It gave no commentary on their departure, but its silence was judgment enough. As they accelerated, the plane jostled side to side. Jack's ass bounced against the cabin floor. Nils's big frame squished Cole against the wall. D.B. and Becky tried to pull him free.

The Captain shouted something, but Jack couldn't make it out. He looked down the length of the plane, out the windshield. He could see the end of the runway now, a wall of bong trees, their tops chopped off.

"Hey!" Jack shouted. "There isn't enough room! Let's try again!"

But the Captain didn't slow. He adjusted a dial and pushed the throttle as far as it could go.

"Hey! Goddamn it! Stop!"

The Captain grabbed the wheel and pulled hard. The plane pitched up and everyone tumbled over one another to the back of the cabin, where the compartment narrowed into a cone. There was a bump and then a violent shudder as the wheels touched down again, tilting to the right. The Captain cursed and pulled back hard again. The trees loomed. They were up. Higher. A gnarled tree reached out with white claws, but it was too late; they were in the sky, in the blue, and Mu was shrinking beneath them, that incongruous capital city and its treasury of forgotten stories marking their retreat like a giant eye.

2 It was Monday morning, September 10, and Paige was late for school. Jean brushed her hair out, teasing out the nappy parts that had formed in the night, a bobby pin in her teeth. "Hold still, dear," she said.

Paige stuck her tongue out at the mirror's reflection of her mother.

The bus had come five minutes ago. The whine and hiss as it stopped at the end of their drive had awakened her. This was getting to be habit. Jean was finding it difficult to adjust to her new routine—though she had never been happier.

Jean ran Nostalgia now. Had since late June. It was hard work. Not just the refab of the dressers and curios, but the day-to-day inventory and Internet sales. That first month had been killer, but she felt as though she was getting the hang of it. If September went as well as August, she might get the store back in the black. Anyway, it was nice to have a job again. It felt good to honor Sam's memory.

Paige was tying her shoes when the phone rang. Jean almost ignored it. But it was a little too early for a telemarketer. She picked up the receiver on the third ring.

"Hello?" she said.

"Jean," said Jack. "It's so good to hear your voice."

3   It was late when Sam returned to the motel in Cambridge, Massachusetts, with a twelve-passenger van she'd snagged from a shady rental company outside Logan, her last task for the day. They'd gotten into Boston at five o'clock, on a commuter plane from Seattle they'd hopped after ditching the Electra in a hangar at a muni airport outside Ariel. Jean and Paige would be arriving at the motel soon. It was all coming together. *Too easy*, she thought, and shivered. She was only being paranoid.

In their room, Sam showered with Jack. He washed her hair. He kissed her wet shoulders. After a bit, he sat on the bed, wrapped in his towel. He rang the front desk for a wake-up call and flipped through channels until he found CNN. The screen was locked on a shot of women and children holding candles in a park in Newtown.

Sam came to him, dripping wet, and pushed him down against the mattress. Her hands found his towel and tugged it off. Her thin fingers slid across his thighs and his body reacted. It was a refined lust, their lovemaking, varying between favorite positions and ending in caresses and laughter. When she finally came, she held him tightly.

"You okay?" he asked, after.

"Of course not." Sam curled an arm behind her head. She looked up, chewing on her bottom lip. "I'm afraid I might fuck it all up."

"What? You? You're probably the best fake pilot on our team," he said, forcing a laugh.

"I thought about just shutting the fuck up, because I thought if I said something, it might undo all this. But I'm going to tell you anyway, because you need to know in case something bad happens tomorrow. So you have to promise right now that no matter what, you're going to do what we came here to do."

"Sam, there's honestly nothing you could say that could change my mind."

"I'm pregnant."

4   "Hey," said Tony when Jack stepped out of his motel room. Tony was sitting on the stoop, a twelve-pack of Miller Lite between his legs. He handed one to his old friend. Something had changed, Tony thought. Jack suddenly looked five years older.

"Thanks," said Jack. He sat on the concrete beside Tony and twisted off the cap, chucked it into the parking lot. "What are you doing?"

"Organizing," said Tony. He pulled his suitcase around and unzipped the top. Inside were sixteen boomerang belts, each without its buckle—they'd left the buckles back on Mu. There was one for each of their crew and the hijacked pilots. He had spent the last hour writing names on each with a wax pencil. "So what's eating you? She throw you out or something?"

"Nah, just needed some air."

"Spill it."

"Not tonight."

Tony let it drop and looked over to Nils, who leaned against the brick wall under a sodium arc light, talking to his wife on the pay phone. "Poor bastard," said Tony. "I wonder how you explain disappearing the way he did."

"You should know."

"Touché." He stood, stretched his back. "Hey, man, watch these, will ya? I need a smoke. I saw some Swisher Sweets at the gas station. You want one?"

Jack shook his head.

"Cheer up, Jack. We're saving the world tomorrow." He walked away then, leaving Jack alone. A few minutes later, Cole came out of his room and shuffled over.

"What's the first thing you're going to do tomorrow, after we're done?" the boy asked.

"I haven't thought about it," said Jack. "I might just find a place to take a good, long nap. What about you?"

"I'm going to ask Constance for a copy of that book."

"What book?"

"The one my dad got rid of. The one with the funny name. I'm going to make a million copies and give one to everybody I meet for the rest of my life."

"Tell me the story," said Jack.

Cole did. And as he finished, Jean pulled into the lot. Paige waved excitedly from the backseat. They were a long way from Franklin Mills, but they were finally home again.

5   "Wake up, old man."

It was Jack, standing above the Captain's bed in the unforgiving light of the stale motel room. There was gray in his son's hair now, but still, whenever he heard his voice, he pictured the child first, the five-year-old who used to sit on his lap watching *Lancelot Link, Secret Chimp*. He could remember how his hair had smelled: like the sunlight and the grass and the wind and the rain.

With effort, the Captain sat up and glanced at the clock. Five minutes till four. They should leave soon—some of them had connecting flights.

"It's oh-dark-hundred," he grumbled. "What the hell are you so chipper about? Goddamn, I hate morning people."

"Dad," said Jack. "Cole figured something out. I think we can all talk to each other up there."

The Captain found his clothes: a Hawaiian shirt and khakis. "Well? Stop chewing cud and tell me."

"You said we shouldn't use the radio to communicate with each other. But Cole, he got to thinking last night. What if we all just called into the same place?"

"I'm not following, brainiac."

"A conference call. We can use disposable cell phones to call into a designated line. Cole already put it together. And he bought four phones to spread around."

"Not bad," he said. "And the other stuff?"

"What other stuff?"

"The box cutters?"

Jack tensed and looked away. "He got those, too."

The Captain waited until Jack met his gaze. "You understand what's at stake, don't you?"

"Of course. But nobody has to die."

"We can plan all we want and something could still go wrong. The more complicated the plan, the easier it is for something to fuck it up. And this is a damned complicated plan we have here."

"I can't kill anybody," said Jack.

"You might have to. And if things go wrong . . ."

"Nothing will."

"If something happens, you owe it to the rest of us to keep going. If we don't finish it today, you may have to try again."

Jack didn't say anything. He sat on the bed and watched his father gather his things. "Dad?" he asked after a while.

"Huh?"

"After everything you saw in Vietnam, why did you have kids?"

The Captain laughed. "You and Jean helped me forget Vietnam," he said. "You were the only way I could put it behind me."

6   Becky's job was relatively easy, but she was still scared. You could tell. She stood in the middle of Jean's motel room, jumping up and down on her toes a little, watching Cole nervously. Her father was there, too. And Jack. Jack helped her with the belt, making sure both belts were secured tightly around her hips. Only one of the belts was missing a buckle.

"How many pounds can it carry?" asked D.B.

"Nils is three-eighty," said Jack. "It worked on him."

"But will it still work so far away?"

"Of course it will."

But of course nobody knew, not for sure. That's what Becky's whole job was about. She was the guinea pig, even though they didn't say so. There were eight pilots, all too important to risk. But her? They could risk her.

"Let me go," D.B. said.

"No," the Captain barked. "Stop it. It's too late to change the plan."

"It's okay," Becky said, nodding her head. "I'm ready."

Jack pushed the button where the missing buckle was. Then he removed the remaining buckle on her second belt. He passed it to her father.

"Back in a sec," Becky said.

One . . . two . . . three . . .

Suddenly she was falling. Down. Up. Slantways. Falling everywhere at once and inside herself. It was dark and cold wherever she was, but Becky had the distinct impression that she wasn't alone, that there were things in the dark here, in the void of distance, the in-between. The Everywhen. Mindless old monsters floating in the ether . . .

And then she was back in the hangar in Mu. It was very dark there, still the middle of the night. Though she wasn't keen on fall-

ing back into that void, Becky did as instructed and unclasped the
buckle from the belt and left it revolving in midair with the other
ones. Then she pushed the button on her second belt. Already, her
head was buzzing the way it sometimes did when she spun around
and around on the beach too fast. How many times was a person
supposed to use these things? Could it hurt her if she did this more
than once a day?

In a minute she was back in the motel room, the return belt snapping into the buckle her father had placed above the bed. She landed
softly atop the mattress and sighed with relief. D.B. went to her and
stroked her hair.

"You okay, darling?" he asked.

"You bet," she said.

They brought Paige in then. Becky held her close and Jack tied
the belt that would take them both to Mu tightly around them. Jean
kissed her daughter.

"I'll see you soon," she said.

"Mom!" said Paige, but they were already falling and falling and
Becky held the girl still and shushed her so that the things in the
void couldn't hear, and soon they were back on Mu, where they
could do nothing but wait for the others to return.

7   The lights of Boston Logan were grim beacons on the horizon,
will-o'-the-wisps by the water. They abandoned the van at long term
parking and took the shuttle to the arrivals entrance for American
Airlines. There they separated for a few minutes as D.B., Sam, Nils,
Jack, and Tony walked to the United Airlines kiosk.

Tony knew as soon as he saw the security guard that his carry-on
was going to be searched. He tried to lower his heart rate. He
thought of his father and a trip they had taken to a carnival when he
was very little. "Sir, step over here, please," said the guard, motioning to a cubicle beyond the metal detector.

Jack pretended not to notice as he put his new phone into a dog-
gie dish.

"May I have permission to search your luggage?"

"Sure," said Tony.

The guard unzipped his suitcase. Secured to the inside lining were sixteen boomerang belts and four box cutters. "What's this?" she asked.

"I'm a contractor," he said. "The belts are presents for my crew."

She touched a belt, fingering the place where the buckle snapped into the front. "Oh, these are nice," she said. Then she zipped the suitcase closed and passed it back to Tony. "Have a safe trip."

Five minutes later they met in the food court and had a light breakfast. The mood was oddly upbeat, teammates before a big game. There were no tears shed. Tears came later.

8   "We gotta do something about Newtown," the man said to Scopes over the phone. "I can't get the Maestro on the phone. Why isn't he answering his phone?"

Scopes sighed. He was back in his office at Area 51, recoding the algorithm as best he could. It was slow going.

"The Maestro is dead," said Scopes. "But I can patch it up. Just give me a couple days."

"While you're dicking around, our stock is tanking. It had to be a Halliburton guy, didn't it? Fuckin' contractor shooting up kids because of all that PTSD he brought back from Iraq. It's all the news cares about. That it's Halliburton. Oil futures all skittish now. What we need is a story about some nut kid went crazy. That's what you need to write into their memories. Make the debate about gun control. That'll get the right fired up again, make the NRA stronger, fill out their rosters for the year. Do that. Can you do that?"

"Sure," said Scopes. These guys. They had a way of finding the evil before he could even walk them over to it. "Anything else?"

"Yeah. Finish the Deepwater story while you're at it."

Scopes hung up. Not a moment later, his cell phone rang. He looked at the screen. It was Nikko, a lieutenant Hound back east.

"What is it?" he asked.

"Tony Sanders's passport just popped up at Boston Logan," the Hound said. "Thought you should know."

He clicked on the television he kept in the corner and found CNN. It was happening. Just like he'd been told.

9 D.B. and Zaharie handed their tickets to the attendant and walked to the waiting 767 jumbo jet at precisely 7:26 a.m. They placed their bags in the overhead bins and sat in seats 2A and 2B, in first class. The air inside was cold and stale and made D.B.'s nose run. He wiped it on the sleeve of his shirt and looked out his window into the lightening morning. The last time he'd hijacked a plane, it was a morning just like this.

"Empty plane," Zaharie whispered as a flight attendant closed and locked the door.

D.B. peered down the aisles. About half the seats were vacant.

At 7:59, American Airlines Flight 11 pushed away from the gate and rolled toward runway 4R.

"It's time," Zaharie said.

D.B. nodded and pulled the box cutter from his pocket.

"On three. One, two . . ."

10 "Mimosa?" the flight attendant asked, leaning over Tony.

"Yes, please," he said, taking a flute from her tray.

Jack shook his head. "I don't think we should be drinking," he whispered when she left. They had barely made it to Gate A17 after their connecting flight landed at Newark International twenty minutes late. They needed to focus.

"This is a hopeless fucking plan, man," said Tony. "We're going to end up in Guantánamo by the end of the day. Have a drink."

The attendant appeared again, crossing the cabin to secure the door.

"Where's everyone else?" asked Jack.

Tony followed his gaze and looked down the aisle. He estimated the 757 had about 180 seats, but he counted only forty passengers.

"It's weird, right?" said Jack.

"I read an article once," Tony said. "Some statistician looked at a bunch of plane crashes, found out how many people were on them compared to planes that didn't crash. Turns out, full airplanes crash less often. It's like people feel an accident coming and for one reason or another find an excuse to skip the flight."

Their seats rocked a bit as United Airlines Flight 93 pulled away from the gate. Tony reached under his seat and pulled out a box cutter.

"I don't want one," said Jack.

"Suit yourself," said Tony. He downed the rest of his drink and wiped his mouth. "Let's roll."

11   The Captain and Cole jogged toward Gate D26 at Washington Dulles International as the attendant announced final boarding.

"Wait!" yelled Cole.

The attendant took their tickets. "Just made it," she said.

They were the last two passengers on American Airlines Flight 77 that morning. The stewardess closed the door behind them as they entered.

"Creepy," said Cole, pointing at the empty seats. Less than half of them were filled. He sat in 12A and the Captain slid into 12B after him.

"Ready for this?" the Captain asked as the plane pulled away from the gate with a rough jerk.

Cole nodded, but his stomach was a tight knot and he felt light-headed, as if he wasn't getting enough oxygen.

"Stay with me."

12   Sam and Nils were seated in the second row of the first-class compartment on United Airlines Flight 175, which was also mostly empty that morning. When the airplane pulled away from Gate 19 at Logan International at 8:00 a.m., Sam's mind was on the baby inside her womb. Was it a girl? She hoped it was.

"Samantha," said Nils. "We gotta do this right now."

She nodded and gripped the box cutter tightly.

Then Nils jumped out of his seat and ran toward the cockpit door.

13 "Listen to me, damn it," Jean yelled into the pay phone. "There are bombs in the World Trade Center. Both towers. And the Pentagon. Set to explode in a half hour. You have to evacuate everyone. Get them out of there, now!"

"Calm down, ma'am," said the voice on the other end, which she mistook for a woman's.

But Jean was not calm. She could see the Twin Towers ten blocks down Church Street and nobody was running out. This was her third call to the police. The buildings were filling with people on their way to work. Her job was supposed to be the easiest part of the plan. And nothing was happening.

"I'll calm down when you get those people out of there."

"Ma'am, I assure you the World Trade Center is in no danger today," the voice said, calm, self-assured.

"Listen to me. If you don't get everyone out of there in thirty minutes . . ."

"Jean."

Jean froze. This wasn't the police. "Who is this?"

"Jean, I commend your altruism," said Scopes. "But you can go home now. Go home and get ready to forget this terrible day. We know what Jack is up to. Steps have been taken to prevent the attack. You needn't worry. Nothing will bring these buildings down today. Now, please, go home and leave the rest to us."

The phone clicked as the call disconnected. Jean looked around. Was she being watched? It didn't matter. They could lock her up in prison, an asylum if they wished, but she was going to get those people out of the towers.

She hailed a taxi. "World Trade Center," she said. "Fast as you can."

14   "Stop the plane," the Captain said, his voice a calm tenor. He held the box cutter to the pilot's neck, a gaunt man with white hair. There was a drop of scarlet at its tip where it had punctured the man's skin. "Call for air stairs. Get the passengers off. Now."

Cole held another knife to the back of the first officer's neck. He willed himself not to faint.

"What are you doing?" the pilot asked.

"I'm hijacking your goddamn plane and I will put this thing in your heart if you don't do exactly as I say."

The man coughed. He eyed his first officer. Then he pushed a button on his armrest and spoke clearly to the tower. "Ground control, this is American Airlines Flight 77 requesting assistance on runway thirty. We have a situation in the cockpit. We have been hijacked." He looked at the Captain, afraid he had said something wrong, but the Captain only nodded for him to continue. "Request air stairs be brought to our position."

"Flight 77," said a male voice through a burst of static. "This is Dulles ground control. Please repeat."

"We've been hijacked," said the pilot. "There are two men in the cockpit with knives. They want stairs, pronto. I think they want to let the passengers out."

"Ground control to Flight 77, come again?"

"Tell them we have a bomb," said the Captain. "And if they don't get that staircase out here in two minutes, I'm going to set it off."

The pilot relayed the information, less calmly this time.

"Roger that, Flight 77. We have stairs en route."

"Ten-four, Dulles."

"Do they have any demands?" asked the controller.

"Tell him to shut up until we get everyone off the plane," the Captain barked.

"Uh, Dulles. Radio silence, please."

A minute later an odd-looking truck pulled away from the concourse and drove toward them. Slanted over its roof and down the back was a set of stairs. Cole noticed other planes were frozen on the runways across the tarmac. Soon there would be sirens. They needed to be gone before that happened.

"Tell your attendants to get everyone off. Right now," said the Captain.

The pilot gave the order. Beyond the cockpit door that Cole had barricaded with a fire extinguisher, they heard the airtight seal open and a clamor of activity as the passengers disembarked. When there was no more noise, the Captain nodded at the boy.

Cole opened the cockpit door. The plane was empty.

"Door's still open!" he shouted to the Captain.

"Close it!"

"I don't know how."

"There's instructions!"

Cole found a graphic decal on the wall beside the door. It was pretty simple, really. He closed it, turned the red latch until it locked, and the seal gave a short hiss. He ran back to the cockpit and took his place behind the first officer.

"Get us up," said the Captain.

The pilot and his first officer began checking the instrumentation around them. Then the pilot pushed the throttle forward and the plane started down the runway, engines whining.

"Dulles tower, this is Flight 77. We've been ordered to take off. Please clear the air."

"Negative, Flight 77," the controller responded. "Stand down."

"Do it," said the Captain.

"We are going to take off, Dulles."

"Negative, Flight 77. Stand down. We have FBI five minutes out. They are ready to listen to demands."

The pilot pivoted the plane on the runway until it was pointed down the length of it. "These men have no more demands, Dulles. My apologies. Somebody call my wife."

"Go," said the Captain. "Take us to twelve thousand feet."

15   "Don't you have more than one set of air stairs?" Nils asked, his voice betraying his anxiety.

From the cockpit of Flight 175, they watched the last few passengers unload from Flight 11, D.B. and Zaharie's plane, which was parked a hundred yards in front of their own.

The air stairs pulled away and they watched Flight 11 roll onto the runway and lift into the air. But instead of driving toward them, the air stairs turned back toward the concourse.

"What the hell?" said Nils.

"Call them back," Sam shouted to the pilot.

The pilot pushed a button and spoke loudly into his mic. "Newark ground control, this is Flight 175. We need those stairs."

But nobody answered.

"Goddamn it!" said Nils. "What the fuck is going on?"

As if to answer him, twelve police cars turned onto the runway from behind a low concrete terminal, lights flashing angrily.

"Motherfucker!" yelled Sam.

"It's over," said the pilot. "Don't do anything stupid."

16   At 8:15, United Airlines Flight 93 leveled out at twelve thousand feet over western Pennsylvania. Tony opened the backpack and removed two boomerang belts with "pilot" written in wax pencil on the leather.

"Punch in the autopilot and then climb out of your chairs," he instructed.

The pilots climbed out of their seats. The cockpit was now crammed with their four bodies and Tony hurriedly strapped the belts around the men's waists before they could take advantage of the close quarters.

"Belts?"

"It's too hard to explain," said Tony. He pushed the buttons where the buckles should be. When the pilots vanished, Tony and

Jack were pulled into the void they left behind, thumping together like characters from a silent comedy.

Jack picked himself up and went to the console between the seats. The transponder was right where his father had said it would be, a little black box with four knobs. He turned a dial until it clicked off, then he climbed into the first officer's chair and slipped his headphones on. Tony climbed into the pilot's seat.

Tony pulled a cell phone from his pocket, dialed a number, and hit the button for speaker. Then he used a piece of electrical tape to secure it to the dash. While he did that, Jack found Reagan National Airport on the computer's autopilot feed and programmed it to turn the jet toward D.C.

"Anybody there?" came a male voice from the phone's speaker.

"Who's this?" asked Tony.

"It's D.B. Tony? Is that you?"

"Yes, we're here. Everything okay on your end?"

"On ours, yes, but it looked like Nils and Sam were having some trouble back there."

"Who's this?" asked a gruff voice, just keying in. "Who's there?"

"Dad? It's Jack. I'm here with Tony. D.B. and Zaharie are fine. How 'bout you and Cole?"

"We're hanging on," said the Captain. "Where's Samantha? She here yet?"

"Not yet."

"Guys, we're turning back for New York," said D.B. "We're ten minutes out."

"Sam," said Jack. "Sam, you there?"

Only silence. Jack looked out the window. The sky was vivid blue, full of puffy white clouds. "Oberlin Center to United Airlines Flight 93," said a voice in his ear. "Come in, 93. We've lost your signal."

"Dad," said Jack. "You turn your transponder off?"

"Yep."

"Shit," said D.B. "Thanks for the reminder."

"Oberlin Center. Come in, Flight 93. Oberlin Center to Flight 111. You have visual on Flight 93?" asked the air traffic controller from the open channel coming through their headsets.

"Negative, Oberlin Center," said another pilot's voice.

"Where the hell did they go?"

"Sam?" said Jack, again. "You there?"

Tony looked to Jack. Sam and Nils should be at twelve thousand by now. If they were still on the ground, they were fucked.

They sat in silence, watching the world below. When seen from this distance, it was impossible to tell what side anybody was on.

"Hey! Hey, uh, hello?"

"Nils?" yelled Jack, sitting up.

"We're here," said Nils, out of breath. "We're level at twelve thousand."

"What took you so long?"

"Jack," said Sam. "Jack, we have a big fucking problem."

"What?"

"We couldn't get rid of the passengers. They're still on board."

Jack stared at the console, unable to speak. Tony pulled out the smartphone he'd secretly purchased from the gas station in Cambridge when he'd gone looking for Swisher Sweets. He entered a command on an app he'd downloaded last night.

"Jack?" said Sam. "Did you hear me? I still have sixty people on board."

"It's all right, Sam," said Tony. He looked at Jack, his first real friend. What he'd done with Sam had broken Jack's heart. And he'd wanted it to break. As much as he'd loved Jack, he'd wanted to break his heart, because Jack had always had everything he ever wanted. It had always been easy for him. Having Sam on top of everything else was too much. But that betrayal was nothing compared to what he had to do now. "Nobody has to die today," he said. "I want you all to listen to me for a minute. Just listen. I have something to say. I decided to go along with this stupid fucking plan, thinking if we could pull it off, fine. But I kept a contingency open because I knew it was too complicated to work. I made a deal with that Hound, Scopes. He'll let us go back to Mu and keep the island a secret from the world, until the end, but we have to turn around and land the planes first. We can't take out a single relay. It's over. I'm sorry."

"You son of a bitch," said the Captain. "You little fucking brat."

"I made up my mind last night," said Tony. "I decided that if anyone might really be killed, I'd call it off. I've just keyed in a command to disable your belts. They won't work. If you crash your planes into those buildings, you'll die, too."

Jack stared at him, eyes wide. He didn't say anything. Maybe he couldn't. He just sat and stared. And time ticked onward.

"Why?" the Captain asked.

"This world can't be saved," said Tony. "And why should we fight to wake them up when they just want to forget? I'm just giving them what they want."

There was silence, and then they heard Nils's voice. "If the belts don't work, you've killed us anyway. We don't know how to land."

"These jets can land on autopilot," said Tony. "Ask the Captain. The control towers will walk you through it."

Somewhere, hundreds of miles away, Sam sighed loudly. "I hate you, Tony," she said. "I hate you and no signal is strong enough to make me forget that. I will feel it so deeply forever."

"What do you want to do, boss?" asked D.B. Everyone knew the question was directed at the Captain.

After a moment the Captain answered, and when he did his voice was full of emotion. "The way I see it, nothing has changed. Tony is still the little shit that he is. And we still have a job to do."

"What do you mean?" asked Nils.

"Jack," said the Captain. "You remember that story you hated in Sunday school? The one the priest told you when you were six years old? You were so mad, you yelled at Father Donohue. Told him it was a stupid story."

Jack nodded. "The kid on the bridge."

"Yes."

"It was an allegory," Jack explained to the others. "But I didn't know it then. I just thought it was a sad story. Father Donohue said there was this guy who worked on a bridge. One of those bridges on the Cuyahoga that opens up in the middle to let the big ships through. The guy took his three-year-old son to work with him one day. Somehow the kid got away from his dad, ends up on the bridge when this big ship comes up the channel. The ship is full of people and it can't stop because it's going too fast. The man, the father, sees his son out there on the bridge and realizes he must make a choice: open the bridge and let his son fall to his death or keep the bridge closed, which would save his kid but kill all the people on the ship. He sacrifices the boy to save all those other lives."

Nobody said anything for the space of many seconds. He thought he heard Sam sniffling.

"Oh, hell," said D.B.

"Count me in," said Cole.

"But what about the people on Sam's plane?" asked Tony. He could hear the fear in his own voice and was ashamed of it. This was something he hadn't planned on. They could not do this. Not when they were all so close to a better ending.

"We're waking up the world today," said the Captain. "If the world knew that true freedom only cost sixty souls, people would line up to volunteer. That's the difference between true heroes and you, Tony. Some people are willing to sacrifice themselves."

"They'll call you terrorists," said Tony.

"They'll call us patriots."

"Okay," said Sam. "We'll do it. I can do it."

"You're all being stupid!" Tony screamed into the mic. "You're going to die. You're going to die for a world that wants to forget. Don't you know they voted to forget? They willingly gave up their freedom."

"The difference is," said the Captain, "now they don't have that choice."

"Well, you need all four planes for it to work. And this plane is not going to crash."

"Jack?" asked Sam.

"I've got this," he said, a resolute and humorless grin stretching across his face.

"I will put this thing in the ground before I let you crash it into the Washington Monument," said Tony.

"No you won't," said Jack. "Because you're not ready to die."

Tony laughed. "*My* belt still works, asshole. I'll turn the plane upside down and transport out of here and be back on Mu before it crashes."

"Tony, Tony, Tony," said Jack. "You think I could ever forget what you did to me? I know better than to trust you. When you showed me the belts, I wondered to myself, why would he label them if they all do the same thing? I tried to think what you might be up to. I never expected this. But as a precaution, I switched the names on the belts."

"Good boy," said the Captain.

"So who the fuck has my belt?"

"Who do you think?"

"Jack, no!" said Sam. "I don't want it. Don't. Jesus. I don't want to be the only one left to remember all this."

"You know why you have to live," said Jack.

"He's right," said the Captain. "Somebody should survive. Somebody should know what happened here."

"Goddamn it, Jack!" she yelled. "Goddamn it!"

"No," said Tony. He was pushing at the button where his buckle should be. It glowed red for an instant, then faded away "No!"

"I hate to interrupt, gentlemen," said Zaharie. "But I can see the two towers." They all heard the scream of a plane's engine over the phone as Zaharie nosed down.

"Don't!" screamed Tony.

"Goddamn," said D.B. "New York was always so beautif—"

Their transmission cut off, followed by a burst of static, then nothing.

"I'm proud of all of you," the Captain said. "So damn proud."

And then Tony was on Jack and they rolled to the floor behind the controls, at each other's throats.

17 "There are bombs in both towers," Jean told the security guard at the front desk. "You have to evacuate. Right now, man."

"Calm down," said the guard, standing up.

"Don't tell me to calm down, damn it. Get everyone out."

"I'm not going to do that. I've already been briefed about your hoax. If you'll just wait here, help is on the way."

Cursing the guard, Jean ran toward a red fire alarm set into the granite wall by the bank of elevators.

"Don't!" a woman shouted at her.

Jean turned. The woman had curly brown hair and was dressed like some special agent with the FBI, although Jean suspected she really worked for a forgotten branch of the NSA.

"What are you doing, Ms. Felter?" she asked.

"Two planes are about to crash into the towers. We have to get everyone out."

"I want you to calm down and come with me. Let's sort this out together."

An elevator opened and a dozen businessmen walked out between the agent and Jean. She disappeared behind them, into the empty car. She pushed a button and then thumbed Close Door. The doors shut tight and carried her up.

To reach the top, Jean had to transfer elevators twice. It took her seven minutes to reach the 110th floor. There she found herself in an area full of glass cubicles crammed with electronic equipment. Technicians walked about, pushing buttons and speaking into headsets.

"Get out!" she shouted. "Everyone out! Hey! Listen to me! There's a bomb in the building! You need to evacuate right the fuck now!"

People stared, waiting for the punch line of the joke. The older men looked for Allen Funt. The younger ones expected Ashton Kutcher.

"I'm serious! Everyone outside! Go! Go! Go!"

"Is this for real?" asked a young woman with a headset.

"This building is about to come down. You need to get out! Everyone out!"

The woman threw her headset and ran for the elevators. Four men ran after her. That opened the floodgates and soon everyone in the office was running.

"No!" Jean shouted as a woman was about to get into the elevator she was holding. "Use the stairs! If the bomb goes off, the elevators won't work. Down the stairs. Tell everyone you see!"

Jean stepped back inside and keyed the button for the next floor. Floors 108 and 109 were filled with more electronic equipment. Floor 107 was a bustle of activity, though, a wide expanse of restaurants.

"Get out!" she screamed. "This building is going down! Everyone evacuate! Right now! Let's go! Down the stairs!"

By the time she reached the ninety-ninth floor, word had traveled and people were running out of the offices of some company called Marsh USA. They were lining up at her elevator, pushing against each other.

"The stairs!" she shouted. "You need to take the stairs!"

When the doors opened on ninety-four, a crowd of insurance brokers pushed inside like a wave, forcing Jean out. "No, damn it! You have to take the stairs!" But the people inside only stared back, eyes wide with fright, as if they had just remembered they were part of a chaotic world and their bank accounts meant nothing. They looked like children, a box full of children squished together, frightened by a storm.

The doors closed, so Jean ran through the offices shouting at those who remained. She stooped to speak to a man who had crawled under his desk.

"We have to leave," she said, reaching out to him. He took her hand and stood. His eyes moved past her, to the windows, and he screamed.

Jean turned. The jumbo jet bore down on them, growing in size exponentially. She could see into the cockpit, could see the pilots sitting at the controls.

There was a deafening sound of crumbling metal and glass and a great pressure upon her chest. And then there was silence and the only sensation was the feeling of weightlessness. No pain. No worries. No notion of which way her body was going or if she were still attached to it. And then Jean knew no more.

18 Jack grabbed Tony's face, digging a finger into his good eye. Tony pulled away, landing a kick against Jack's sternum, sending him falling against a panel of controls. Jack launched himself off the wall and brought his shoulder down, plowing it into Tony's chest, knocking the wind from his lungs. Tony pulled Jack's hair as they fell, wrapped his arms around Jack's back, bringing him down, and they were a pile upon the floor, a folded mass of arms and legs and sweaty torsos hitting and kicking and grabbing.

"I . . . fucking . . . loved you," said Jack, landing punches between words.

"You're ruining it!" Tony screamed at him. "Nobody wants to remember."

"What do you get out of this?" Jack asked, grabbing at Tony again, scratching at his face, squeezing his cheeks together in his hand. His eyepatch caught in Jack's grip and fell away, revealing the torn, twisted, and scarred tissue beneath.

"Peace," he said. "I get peace."

19 "Here we go," the Captain said, twisting the yoke to the right and pushing down while he nudged the throttle forward. "Help me."

Cole pushed, too, and soon they were picking up speed. He was crying. He couldn't help it. His chest heaved in great sighs for all the experiences he would never have. But he found he did not hate the universe. He felt an overwhelming sense of grace, for having loved so many people in a short time.

Suburban homes rushed to meet them. Cole could not yet see any capital landmarks. The Captain seemed to know where they were going, though. Their target was low and only the Captain could hit it at this speed.

"It'll be too quick to notice," the Captain said. "You won't feel a thing."

20 "Stay calm," Sam said into her microphone. She was speaking to the sixty passengers and crew in the cabin beyond the locked door. "We have some bombs. They are meeting our demands so we are returning to the airport. Please remain in your seats."

"Why'd you tell them that?" asked Nils.

"Let them have a little hope."

"There!" Nils pointed out the windshield as the New Jersey foothills fell away, revealing the island of Manhattan. Black smoke boiled up from the North Tower, darkening the city.

"They did it," said Sam.

"Help me," said Nils.

Sam took the yoke and pulled the plane to the right and nosed her down, gently, just like the Captain had taught them. Then Nils pushed the throttle forward. The airplane picked up speed in a hurry and soon the landscape became a green and gold blur. The engines protested, whining loudly. Someone pounded on the cockpit door.

"Go," said Nils. "Go now."

She pushed the belt's button, picturing the baby inside her, hoping it was a girl and not a boy.

"Jack!" she cried.

"I'm here!" he shouted.

"I love you. I love you. I love . . ."

And then she was being pulled as if by an invisible hand, out of the airplane, out of the sky, out of the world, through that dark void, back to the hangar on Mu.

21 "How you doing, Jack?" the Captain asked, nosing down, increasing their pitch and speed as they approached D.C.

Through the cell phone's speaker came the sound of a fist smacking its target. "I've got it under control."

"Good boy," he said. He looked at Cole and nodded. The kid put his weight into the throttle, kicking it up a notch. The engines were angry banshees. "I probably never told you this, but I was scared as shit the day you were born."

Jack didn't answer. The sounds of his struggle came clearly through the phone.

"I was so worried that something might go wrong. That something might be wrong with you. The world is so hard, you know? I didn't want you to have some extra handicap or something to make it harder. Never been so scared in all my life. But then the doctor pulled you out and you were this big, fat baby, this healthy baby lying on the cart. And you started crying. Crying so loud you hurt my ears. But you were so big I knew you were fine. That you would be fine. And I've never had to worry again. You were a good kid. A good goddamn kid and I never told you that enough. I was only hard because the world is hard."

Over a patch of trees, the Pentagon appeared.

"This is it!" said Cole.

The Captain adjusted the yoke slightly and nosed it down so that they were pointed at the center of a long gray wall.

"God is great," the Captain whispered.

In the second before impact, the Captain was filled with such a sense of calm, of rightness, that he couldn't help but smile. The plane was traveling so fast he did not perceive the exact moment when the cockpit crumpled and the velocity and the physics of it all turned his mortal body into particles that merged with the wreckage and the building until he was no more.

22 Jack, bloodied, a tooth broken, nose busted, picked himself off the floor and came for Tony. But Tony was done fighting. He pulled the box cutter from his pocket and stuck it into Jack's side. Jack cried out and fell against the console. The plane tilted wildly and seven indicator buttons flashed bright red. Alarms went off. The engines protested. The plane banked. Jack fell to the floor, the knife tumbling away.

Tony went to the controls and stabilized the airplane. Then he stood over Jack, watching him, shaking his head. "All I ever wanted was a little peace."

"It wouldn't be real," said Jack. "It would be meaningless. And it wouldn't be earned."

"Earned," said Tony. "What do you know about it? You always had happiness."

"No, Tony. You took that from me, remember?"

Alarms sounded again and the aircraft shook violently. Tony pulled back on the yoke, but it tore free from his hands. He tried the throttle, but it wouldn't budge. "Fuck me," he said. "I think you broke it." Tony looked out the cockpit window. They were somewhere over Cleveland, heading east, the plane moving swiftly along, angled low on the horizon.

"We did it," said Jack. "We did what you set out to do when you left Franklin Mills. Help me finish it. It's not too late. We turn this bird around and head for D.C. The Washington Monument is the last piece. If it falls, millions of people will remember everything they've forgotten. Don't you want that? Isn't that what you wanted?"

"Nobody out there cares. So why should I?"

"You could have made a perfect life with Sam."

Another alarm sounded. A low *whoop, whoop, whoop*. The lights in the cockpit went off. The console buttons blinked. Jack smelled burning plastic.

"How?" Tony asked him.

"You could have had kids, you stupid idiot. Didn't you ever think about that? You could have made a family with her. You could have given those kids what you never had. And you could have seen the world through their eyes. That's what it's about. Making the world just a little better for the next generation. Make their story a little better than your own. Eventually we'll get it right."

"You don't know, Jack. You don't fucking know."

"Sam's pregnant," said Jack. "You're right. I don't know. But I want to."

"You're lying. You're fucking lying!"

"You know me well enough to know when I'm lying. Am I lying?"

The alarms went silent and the aircraft sputtered. Then the two engines on the port side failed and suddenly the plane was rolling. Jack fell onto the ceiling, hard, his cheek smashing against a panel of lights.

Tony picked himself up again.

"You'd kill yourself knowing you had a child in this world?"

"I'd sacrifice myself if I knew it meant freedom for my children," said Jack. "Yes."

"I was so happy," said Tony. "Why was that taken away when I was still a kid?"

"I don't know, man. I don't know. But you had us. And that's more than some people ever get."

"Goddamn. Goddamn it, Jack." Tony reached into his bag and came out with a shiny buckle. He tossed it near the door to the cabin, where it hung in the air and rotated slowly. The red light began to blink at once, speeding up, merging into a steady light.

"What are you doing?" mumbled Jack. He was beginning to lose consciousness.

Tony picked up the box cutter and pointed it at a space about a foot above the buckle. When Scopes appeared a second later, Tony drove the knife into the flesh of its neck and across its throat, opening a wide gash. The Hound tried to talk, tried to reach out for Tony with his paws, but only managed to grab Tony's watch. The time-piece ripped from Tony's wrist as the Hound fell to the ground, dead.

An explosion rocked the aircraft. There would be no fixing it. Jack felt his body rise, weightless, off the floor as they fell, with the aircraft, back to earth.

Tony pushed off a wall, sending his body floating after the Hound's body. He rammed into it and held tightly, spinning against it in the air. He undid the Hound's second belt, the one it kept for a return journey, and brought it over to Jack.

Tony wrapped it around his old friend as they twisted around each other like dancers. "I don't know where this takes you. Probably the Underground. But the Underground is better than dead, right?"

"Can you come with me?"

"Not this time."

Once he had it around Jack's waist, Tony pushed away.

"Be a good dad," he said, grinning.

Through the cockpit window, Jack saw the ground rushing to meet them, a patch of hillside in the country, a gravel pit in the distance. Just before the aircraft collided with the earth, Jack's body was pulled from the plane.

FOUR

PEOPLE ARE ALIKE ALL OVER

"Huh," said the Maestro. He pushed back from Clementine's monitor and rubbed his chin.

Jack and his team had done well. He had expected them to take down one relay. They'd gotten three. That was real progress.

The Maestro sat at the controls and considered the basic irony of war: What is it that each side fights for? Peace. They fight to end fighting. Like drinking to get sober.

What came next was the part the Maestro enjoyed the most. Rewriting Scopes's memory to make the Hound believe he'd killed him had been easy. A little song. What came next was a symphony.

The Maestro wrote the final forgetting in three acts.

The first act he wrote that afternoon, moving his hands across the dials and sensors in a whir of motion. He told a story of fundamentalists from the Middle East hijacking planes and targeting the centers of American capitalism and military might on 9/11. He borrowed characters and motifs from the real world and built upon them, for that is what the best storytellers do. There is nothing new under the sun after all, and too much invention makes a story feel untrue. The Maestro borrowed the names of the hijackers and victims from the cruise ship tragedy and inserted them into this new narrative. And the world forgot again.

After the debris from the towers was cleared away, the Maestro wrote the second act. In this one, the attacks of September 11 were rewritten to have happened in 2001. It needed to be deeper in the past in order for people to parse any meaning from it.

For the third act, the Maestro wiped the minds of the Hounds and the twelve Collectors.

The signal around New York was weaker now. In fact, there was a four-block section in lower Manhattan that was completely clear of the signal coming out of HAARP. As it happened, those blocks around Union Square were the headquarters of the great publishing companies. Outside the broadcast range, the editors there were free to consider stories that challenged the accepted history. Soon there would be novels that hinted at the truth, as strange as it was. There would be books that allowed people to question reality, just a little at a time. Peeks at the world beyond the cave. Those stories were the gradient they could follow into the light. A fire had started. And it was about to catch.

And what of Jack?

The Maestro directed the algorithm to exclude Jack's mind as he had done for Cole so many years before. Let Jack remember.

And then there was nothing left for the Maestro to do.

He considered traveling to Mu as well. The Maestro watched the monitors that showed various parts of the island when he was feeling blue. Sometimes, at night, Sam nursed her baby girl by the eastern shore and looked out toward Alaska, waiting. Sometimes Paige waited with her.

But there was more work to be done, the Maestro came to realize. He was immortal, or near enough, and so he was best suited for this new quest. It would take too many years to count, he expected.

Humanity had lost the point of their story. But it was out there, somewhere, in the narratives of forgotten civilizations, in the half-remembered tales of ancient tribes, the mistranslated fables of dead languages. The Maestro would search the world, slowly. Secretly. He would search out this lost theme, the answer to the question: Why are we here? It was out there somewhere. We had only forgotten.

A PROLOGUE

Kimberly Quick was waiting under the portico in front of Haven when Earl Mason arrived in his brown sedan. He parked in the visitor's space and then went to meet the young director.

"Ms. Quick," he said, shaking her hand.

"Hello, Earl," she said. "And call me Kim." She led the coroner into a common room with tall windows. Her heels clacked on the polished linoleum. He followed her through a set of double doors and into her office. "Sit, please." She pointed to a chair facing a television.

"You came to see Jack Felter," she said. "And I've got no problem with that. But I want you to understand a little more about his peculiar psychosis before I bring you to him." She pushed a button on the TV and a recording began to play. On-screen, Jack looked haggard and worn, but his words were earnest and full of energy.

The version of Kim on the television leaned forward over her notes.

"Tell me again why you won't drink the water we give you."

"Because it's poison. I keep telling you. The government puts poison in it that makes us forget."

"Makes us forget what?"

"That we lost a hundred years, that 9/11 wasn't about the Middle East. I won't drink the water. And I can't tell you more until you start boiling your own water."

On-screen, Kim shook her head. "Mr. Felter, you are suffering from a delusion."

"That's what you tried to tell Cole, too."

"As I've told you before, I do not know this person."

"You do! You just forgot."

"There is no record of him."

"The signal makes it so you can't see the records," said Jack.

"The government could not perpetuate a conspiracy of that magnitude. They just couldn't."

"Fine." He sat back in his seat. "How long do I have to stay? Can I leave? Can I please leave?"

"You have to stay until you are no longer a danger to yourself and others."

"I'm not a danger . . ."

"You tried to hijack an Alaskan crab boat. At gunpoint."

"I was trying to get back to Mu."

"Mu doesn't exist. It's a story you made up when you suffered a mental breakdown after your friend Tony died on 9/11."

"No."

"How does it end for you? How does the story ever end for you, Jack? Can you tell me that?"

"I have to do what Cole was going to do," he said. "I think that's all that's left to be done. See, the forgettings aren't happening anymore. There's no more new forgettings. They've stopped. Now we just need to fight the HAARP signal. And Cole had an idea about how to do that. We need to remind ourselves why it's important to remember in the first place. We have to get that book back into the world."

"The cookbook?"

"It's not a cookbook."

"It sounds like a cookbook. Like it's the temperature you bake a pizza or something."

"*Fahrenheit 451*," said Jack. "That's the temperature at which books begin to burn. That's what happened in the story. They burned all their books and realized too late that taking away our stories, our histories, strips all the meaning from life."

"And if you don't bring the book back into the world?"

"We'll go on killing each other until we finally succeed. That book is just a beginning. A spark. If you ever see a copy, you'll know I did what I said I'd do. If you ever see a copy of that book, you'll know I won."

"Well," she said. "I'll keep my eye out for it."

Kim shut off the TV and turned to Mason. "His paranoia is complete," she said. "But his specific compulsion is the need to bring those around him under the influence of this delusion. He manipulates. He grooms. He pushes you until you begin to question reality, until you begin to wonder if maybe you really should boil your water. He's really quite clever."

"I understand," he said.

"You still want to meet him?"

"Yes, please. I just need to clear something up."

Ten minutes later, Kim escorted Jack from the dormitory. He was dressed in soft hospital sweats. He was secured to a wheelchair by thick leather bindings. She left them alone by the windows that overlooked the pond.

"Hello," said Jack.

"Mr. Felter, my name's Earl Mason. I'm the coroner out in Somerset County, in Pennsylvania? That's where Flight 93 crashed on 9/11."

Jack's eyes widened. "What brings you here, Mr. Mason?"

He dug into his pockets and brought out the silver watch. Etched into the back was *RIP, Tony Sanders. 1978–2012.* Jack smiled.

"Where did you find this?"

"In a field." Mason didn't mention the strange ape hand tattooed with a swastika. He couldn't bring himself to say something so crazy just yet. "Tony was a friend of yours?"

"My best friend."

Mason nodded. "You know, of course, that Tony was on Flight 93 that day. He was one of the passengers who fought back against the terrorists."

"Yes."

"But that happened in 2001."

"Did it?"

"I was hoping you could explain the engraving."

Jack ran his thumb along the words, feeling the defects in the metal. "Do you know what a gradient is?" he asked.

"Like an incline in the road?" asked the coroner.

"Sort of. Sort of like that. If you have the time, I can explain what you found. I can tell you a story. But you have to play along a little."

Mason leaned forward. "I'd be very interested in an explanation. I haven't slept well since I found this thing."

"So humoring me a little wouldn't be too much to ask?"

"Of course not."

"I need you to start boiling your water, Mason. Will you do that for me?"

"Yes," he said, with little hesitation.

"Then come back tomorrow and we'll talk. In the meantime you should do a little research."

"Research? On what?"

"Fluoride," said Jack. "Come back tomorrow, and we'll share some stories."